The Mother

Alex Kane is a writer from Glasgow, specialising in gangland crime and psychological thrillers. When not writing, Alex can be found relaxing at home reading, or drinking tea and/or gin (sometimes all of the above).

Also by Alex Kane

THE
Mother

Alex Kane

hera

First published in the United Kingdom in 2022 by

Hera Books
Unit 9 (Canelo), 5th Floor
Cargo Works, 1–2 Hatfields
London, SE1 9PG
United Kingdom

A CIP catalogue record for this book is available from the British Library.

Print ISBN 978 1 80436 033 0
Ebook ISBN 978 1 80436 075 0

This book is a work of fiction. Names, characters, businesses, organizations, places and events are either the product of the author's imagination or are used fictitiously. Any resemblance to actual persons, living or dead, events or locales is entirely coincidental.

Cover design by Chapman & Wilder

Look for more great books at www.herabooks.com

Printed and bound in Great Britain by Clays Ltd, Elcograf S.p.A.

MIX
Paper from
responsible sources
FSC® C018072
www.fsc.org

This book is dedicated to my husband and daughter.

'Never to Suffer Would Never to Have Been Blessed.'

Edgar Allan Poe

Prologue

Reaching her husband at the altar where she was about to renew her wedding vows, Angie Bryson's smile faded quickly as the sound of shattering glass sent everyone cowering to the floor. She watched as her family crawled under chairs, taking cover from the glass as bullets were pumped into the hotel conservatory from outside. The sound of her daughter Ashley's screams filled the air, along with her husband, eldest son and brothers-in-law shouting at them all to take cover. The quick-fire popping sound of bullets being fired almost synced in time with her thumping heart.

Grabbing her youngest close to her, Angie held on to him as securely as she could and attempted to roll on top of him. Her eyes shut tight against the potential massacre of her family. If she survived, she imagined opening them when the ordeal was over and seeing her beautiful white dress saturated in her family's blood. She couldn't help but think the worst would happen as gunshots continued, the sound piercing her ears.

'Mum?' Ashley's voice penetrated through the echo of bullets leaving the barrel of a gun somewhere outside. Angie opened her eyes and saw nothing but fear in her daughter. Reaching out a hand, she gripped Ashley tightly and attempted a reassuring smile before mouthing, 'We're going to be okay.'

Dale's voice was close to Angie's ear, yet she could barely hear what he said. Something about it being over soon. Over, how? Dead? All of them? Or would their assailant leave just one of them alive? Because that was her worst nightmare. Her entire family, dead. All except her.

And just like that, the shooting stopped. And everything fell silent.

—

A figure dressed in black skulked away from the hotel, head down and gun inside the large front pocket of his hoodie. They'd missed intentionally. The idea wasn't to kill, but to warn. The Bryson family might once have been the high and mighty of the city, but now they would pay for all the chaos and grief that followed their actions.

Climbing up the hill into the woodlands, they heard the sound of voices coming from the hotel behind them. The Brysons were outside, looking for their attacker. Not that they'd find them. Not now, anyway.

If the Bryson family thought that the shooting was a one off, then they could think again. Each and every one of them would be targeted as many times as necessary, until it was time to remove them all. Glasgow would see a new crime boss. And the city would watch as the old ones died.

Then/2013

The cell door slammed shut and James MacTavish began banging on it with his fists. 'This is fucking bullshit! I'm fucking innocent!'

'They all say that, pal,' the screw on the other side of the door shouted as he locked MacTavish in. 'Enjoy your stay.'

James continually banged on the steel door, screaming and claiming his innocence of the crime for which he'd been convicted. Double murder. It had been a ridiculous trial – the evidence stacked against him even though he was innocent. He'd been nowhere near that bloody disused track; he'd only witnessed the police pull the car from the reservoir, yet forensics were able to match gun residue to his jacket. The only way that could have happened was if someone had taken the gun and used it themselves. But there had been no other prints on the gun. Only MacTavish's.

'I've been *fucking* set up,' he shouted again, although this time his voice wasn't so loud. It was hopeless. He knew that. It hadn't taken the jury long at all. He'd worked for the Frasers over the years, and the jury had been informed that he hadn't been happy with how they were treating him. That had obviously been motive enough in their eyes. He'd had no chance.

His fists and arms began to ache and he pulled away from the door. Turning, he surveyed his cell and stared at the bunk bed in the corner.

'Fucking hell,' he hissed as he sat down on the bottom bunk. 'Fucking murder. I might be some things, but I'm not that.'

The cell was cold, dull. He'd never been in prison before. Always managed to keep himself out of the limelight. He knew who'd set him up – someone much bigger than the Frasers could have ever aspired to be. It was blatantly obvious; he just couldn't get his head around how. And he wasn't going to say it in court. Doing so would be like signing his own death certificate. Now, he was fucked. In prison for a minimum of twenty-five years. He'd be in his sixties before he was even eligible for parole for something he didn't do.

The cell door clicked open and James looked up to see a man enter. The screw behind him shut the door loudly and the man glanced down at him.

'You look rough, mate,' the man said.

'Cheers,' MacTavish replied.

'You're that lad who murdered the Fraser brothers, aren't you?'

MacTavish shook his head. 'It wasn't me.'

'Ha, aye. Heard that one before.' The man laughed, before moving across the small cell and pulling a chair out from under a table in the opposite corner. He lit a cigarette and offered one to MacTavish, who shook his head in response.

'I'm not lying. Do I look like the type who could murder two gang bosses?'

His new cellmate looked him up and down and sniggered. 'They do say it's the ones you least expect who can do the most damage. Look, mate, innocent or guilty, yer in here for the foreseeable. So my advice would be, shut up. If you want to survive in here, you'll need to just get on with it. Nae offence but I can't be arsed listening to you or anyone else whining. Got it?'

MacTavish stared at him in shock but said nothing. Instead, he remained silent. This was day one of a long sentence. On some level, his new cellmate was right. If he wanted to survive in this shithole, he was going to have to keep his head down. For the next twenty-odd years. It didn't matter that he knew who killed the Frasers. He'd have been as well to do it himself, since he was now locked up. No one would ever believe him.

Part One

Then/2013

Chapter One

Cara Fraser watched as her husband, Kyle, raised his arms in celebration as he won his third FIFA game in a row against the boys. Ryan and Sean shook their heads and threw cushions at him, complaining that he was a cheat and they were never playing with him again.

'Och, come on, boys, don't be sore losers,' he laughed. 'You'll be as good as your old man one day.'

'Shut up,' Ryan said, but Cara could see a hint of a smile on his elder son's face. 'One day, we're going to beat you over and over and we'll laugh in your face for hours on end.'

Kyle laughed loudly and sat down on the sofa between Ryan and Sean. He pulled Sean into a headlock and ruffled his head. Cara used to complain about their play fighting all the time when they were younger, worried that it might lead to them getting hurt. But then she realised that they all gave as good as each other, and seeing her boys bond with their dad just made her love them and Kyle even more.

'No one will ever beat me, I'm the king of FIFA.'

'You're quite sure of yourself,' Cara remarked.

Sean pulled out from Kyle's grip and bounced off the sofa. 'You might be the king of FIFA, but we're the champs at wrestling and you know we'll kick your arse in any challenge.'

'Oi, young man,' Cara said, 'language!'

Sean's face fell and his eyes widened, but Kyle was still laughing. 'You could've said worse,' he whispered.

Cara rolled her eyes. She was outnumbered with this lot. But secretly, she loved it.

'He's right. We would annihilate you in a match,' Ryan said, standing next to Sean. 'And I'm the master at the deed leg and the kidney.'

Cara got to her feet and decided that she'd be best leaving them to it. Kyle could deal with the dead legs and kidney shots while she was busy preparing dinner. Nothing special, just macaroni cheese with smoked sausage and garlic bread. The boys' favourites, and Kyle's. As she busied herself in the kitchen, she listened to Ryan and Sean laying into their dad, and Kyle shouting that he surrendered.

When she'd fallen pregnant with Ryan, Cara had been worried about how they'd cope as parents. Their income was low, but Kyle had made sure that he provided enough money to give Cara and Ryan a good life. Not a luxurious, or particularly glamorous one, but happy. Dealing in drugs wasn't exactly how Cara had expected him to do it, but it was all Kyle could manage and if she was honest with herself back then, it was more than enough to pay the bills and keep a roof over their heads. So, she'd turned a blind eye to it, hoping that one day, it would pass and that Kyle would move on to something more honest. But then Sean came along just two years later. That meant double the food, clothes and toys, which in turn meant the need for more income. So, Kyle had continued his venture in dealing. And he was making more than enough. Cara had got used to it, and in a way, the less she knew, the better.

More laughter erupted from the living room and then Kyle was at her back. His arms slipped around her waist as she whisked together a roux for the cheese sauce, and she felt his lips kiss her cheek.

'They finally let you go, then?' She smiled.

'Aye,' Kyle laughed. 'I swear, Ryan is becoming more and more like me by the day. He's ruthless.'

Cara smiled. She loved Kyle more than ever. And she loved her boys. But the one thing she was nervous about was Ryan and Sean leading the same life as their dad. Going into a life of crime wasn't what she'd imagined for them.

'They're both handsome, like you,' she said, pushing the thoughts out of her head.

'Nah, they get their good looks from their mum,' he said. He drew some plates out of the cupboard and placed them on the countertop just behind her in their narrow, basic council-owned kitchen. 'Ian might stop by for dinner, that okay?'

Cara nodded. 'Like most nights you mean. I don't know why he doesn't just rent our sofa off us? He's never in his own flat.'

She turned to see that there were five dinner plates already out. The boys would be happy to see their uncle.

'Because you won't let him bring his ladies of the night back here,' Kyle laughed. She glanced at him and saw his brow raised in humour. She couldn't help but smile at the joke. Ian wasn't the type to pay for it. He just seemed to have an endless supply of women who were charmed by him.

'Tell the boys to be at the table in ten. This won't take long.'

Kyle kissed Cara on the cheek again, before slipping out of the kitchen. Quickly, more hilarity erupted from the living room and Cara was so thankful that her family were as happy as they were, even if she was constantly worrying every time Kyle went out the door.

Later, Cara served the boys dinner at the small foldaway dining table in the living room. They were sitting patiently, like little dogs waiting to be served at their bowls. They thanked her, and as she sat down, she smiled at Kyle. This was the quietest part of the day, when the boys were eating.

Ian appeared, and he too joined the table. Cara watched as Kyle gave Ian a nod. She knew what it meant. They would be working later that night. Something that she dreaded each and every time. She would try again to talk him round. To make him see that a life on the straight and narrow would be better for them all round. But he would tell her the same thing he always did. His career in the crime world was all for her and the boys, so they could lead a better life. But Cara wasn't looking for luxury and wealth. The happiness they shared in their tiny, two-bedroom council flat on the scheme was her wealth.

Chapter Two

Angie Bryson stood by the coffee machine and waited for her morning dose to be ready. It was the only thing that could get her going. With a daughter who wouldn't utter two words to anyone for most of the day, and a hormonal teenage son, Angie would have preferred a gin or a wine to get her through the mornings; of course she wouldn't be able to drive afterwards, so settling for coffee was the best and only option.

'You two better be ready to leave on time this morning, I've got a busy day ahead of me,' Angie said, staring at both her kids sitting at the kitchen table. Ashley swirled a spoon around in her untouched muesli and Conor was looking at the sports pages on the back of the *Daily Record*. Neither of them answered her. Typical for a school morning.

'Earth to children. Did the aliens possess your bodies and leave your souls in bed upstairs?' Angie said just as the coffee machine ended its process.

Ashley looked up at Angie, blinked and gave a sarcastic smile, but still remained silent. Angie shook her head, retrieved her coffee and left the kitchen. Carrying the mug upstairs to the home office that was hardly ever used because neither she nor Dale could ever get any peace to work in the evenings due to loud music and even louder games consoles, Angie opened the door to see Dale sitting behind the desk.

'Great minds,' she said.

'Eh?' Dale looked up at her, confused.

'Is everyone else on another planet today?' She shook her head. 'I was going to come in here to do some work this morning. You know, check that wages had gone through and all that?'

'No need, already done. I wanted to get the little jobs out the way so I could get to the casino early to make sure everything is in place for the weekend. And then I need to go to the construction site to be with Paul and Bob. They're meeting with the new builders later this afternoon.'

Angie pursed her lips and shrugged. 'Looks like I can take the day off then?'

'No. You can deal with making sure the orders get out to the dealers today. I'd do it, but I've got too much on,' Dale replied. He switched off the computer and got to his feet. 'You can get the kids to school, can't you?'

Angie nodded. 'God, you really are on another planet today. You say that as if you do the school run on the regular,' she laughed.

'Thanks, babe. You're a star. I'll catch up with you all at dinner tonight.'

He slid out from behind the computer desk and leaned in to kiss her. She smiled and followed him downstairs to the hallway, where he picked up his briefcase and keys, before opening the front door.

'See you two later,' he called into the kitchen without looking to see if they were even in there. 'And try to smile today, Ashley.'

Angie closed the door behind him and stood there for a moment. She loved Dale; loved the lifestyle they led because of how hard they'd worked over the years to reach this point. But there were times when she wished that he was around more, that they could spend more time together. Not that Ashley or Conor would want to. They were always in their bedrooms or out with friends. She supposed that's what teenagers and almost-teenagers did these days.

Angie could barely remember what it was like when it was just the two of them, before she had fallen pregnant with

Conor. Just Angie and Dale. Almost immediately after they got together, they had their business heads on. Dale was already a rising figure in the Glasgow underworld, and Angie saw an opportunity to better her life. Coming from a family who'd just scraped by, she'd always wanted a life where money wasn't an issue. Being with Dale would provide that. He'd said that having a stunning and powerful woman on his arm was exactly what he needed. Angie had soon earned the respect of Dale's colleagues and family, and very quickly became a well-respected, familiar face of the business. As much as she fronted the Bryson businesses and remained a very intricate cog in the workings, Angie felt like that was all she was good for. Even her kids weren't interested in her these days.

Taking a deep breath, Angie straightened her shoulders and scolded herself for the self-pitying thoughts in her head. That was not who she was. She was Angie Bryson. Businesswoman, wife and mother – and as much as it often annoyed her, that was very much the order in which those titles came.

Angie headed back into the kitchen and immediately noticed that Ashley and Conor were in the same positions she'd left them in.

'Right, it's almost half eight. You've both got five minutes to get your arses in that car or you can walk to school.'

Conor got to his feet and headed upstairs. Ashley sighed like a stroppy teenager even though she was three years off becoming one, and pushed back her seat from the table.

'What's wrong with you this morning?' Angie remarked. 'You look like someone told you you'd won the lottery but they'd set fire to your ticket.'

Ashley shook her head and shrugged. 'Nothing's wrong. I just don't want to go to school, that's all.'

'Why not?'

'Well, Dad never went to school, did he? And look at him now. A mansion, a million cars and even more in the bank.'

Angie laughed. 'Not quite a million cars, Ashley. And your dad was just lucky. Not everyone who evades education comes off well in the end. Hence why we pay for you to go to the best school in the country.'

Ashley tutted loudly and placed her muesli bowl next to the sink. Angie looked at her watch and then said, 'And now you've got three minutes to get your arse in the car. If you don't want to go at all, I'd presume walking there isn't an option for you?'

Ashley drew Angie a dirty look and stomped out of the kitchen and up the stairs.

'Jesus, if this is what she's like now, what the hell is she going to be like when she's peak teenager?' Angie asked herself aloud.

As if an alarm had gone off, Angie was met at the front door by Conor and Ashley exactly three minutes later. Both looked like zombies who needed feeding. Angie couldn't help but laugh.

'Look at the state of you two, you'd think you were going to your own funerals.'

As they climbed into the car, Angie set the house alarm and checked the angle of the security camera above the front door. All exterior cameras were linked to her phone, so she could check in on the house whenever she wasn't there. Happy with everything, Angie climbed into the car and started the engine.

'So, what's the plan for today?' Angie asked them as she pulled out of the driveway and down the private road.

'It's usually the teacher's job to make the plan,' Ashley answered. Angie took a steadying breath and held in her frustration at how cheeky her daughter was becoming.

'I have football today. That's all I really care about,' Conor replied.

Angie nodded in acknowledgement.

'Do you think Dad will actually sit down with us and discuss the family holiday I suggested two weeks ago? Or is work more important?' Ashley chipped in.

It came out of nowhere, and Angie was so stumped she didn't know how to answer. In truth, Ashley was right, there probably wouldn't come a time where Dale would sit down with them to plan the holiday that had always been on the cards but never actually booked.

'I mean, it's not as if we don't have the money to go,' Ashley continued.

'Right, young lady. That's enough lip from you. Remember who you're talking to and about.'

Conor said nothing, and Ashley turned to face the window with a glum expression.

Whatever side of the bed Ashley had woken up on, it wasn't the right one, Angie thought.

A little over ten minutes later, they reached the school gates and without saying goodbye, Ashley got out of the car and headed for the prep school entrance. She was in prep six now, but her attitude was like that of someone in senior six.

Conor followed her, and headed for the senior entrance at the other side of the building. He didn't say bye, but gave a half-hearted wave before closing the door.

Angie was left in the car on her own, feeling alienated from her children. It was highly frustrating that they didn't seem to understand how much effort and time Angie and Dale put in to give them the life they had. Ungrateful little swines, she thought.

Turning up the radio, Angie pulled out of the space and headed back to the house, a great big mansion that would be empty for the rest of the day. As she sat in the office, she would set up and assign the drug orders to the dealers, which was the grittier side of the Bryson business which she was in charge of most of the time. Secretly she enjoyed it, it helped her feel the power she possessed. All of the dealers treated her with the same respect as they did Dale – with much more respect than her own kids did. But she knew why. They didn't appreciate how much Dale and Angie had to work to keep their lifestyle afloat. They would one day, when they were older and working for the family business themselves. If Angie had had the lifestyle she was giving her kids now, she'd have at least smiled at her parents once in a while.

Chapter Three

Angie Bryson sat behind the desk in the casino and swivelled side to side as Dale poured a whisky from the decanter.

'And he said he'd be here at one?' Dale asked.

'Yes, and it's only five to. Would you relax? He'll be here.'

Angie could see how pent-up her husband was. Not that she could blame him. Hearing the rumours about the Frasers would be enough to send any boss over the edge.

A gentle tap at the door made Dale spin around and Angie got up from her seat. 'I'll answer it. If he sees you at the door in this state, he'll do a runner.'

She watched as Dale moved across the floor to the desk and sat down in the seat she'd just occupied. Angie opened the door to one of the security lads and smiled.

'There's a James MacTavish here to see you, Angie?'

She nodded. 'That's right. Send him in.'

As the security guard moved away from the door and down the short corridor, Angie could hear the distant ringing of puggy machines and cheers from punters as they won their bets.

'This better work, Angie,' Dale said.

'It will work, Dale. Have I ever been wrong when it comes to our businesses?'

He shook his head and took a long drink from his glass. As she watched him, she thought back to when they'd first met. Dale was just starting out in his line of business, and had made no secret of the fact that he wanted to climb to the top in the criminal underworld in Glasgow. Most women would have cut and run, especially at the age of seventeen. But not Angie. She'd loved how powerful hearing those words had made her feel. Dale had made it clear he wanted her involved from the outset. Unlike her previous relationship before Dale, where the guy had purely wanted her on his arm or on the back burner. He'd been a control freak, and she'd spotted the signs immediately. Her ex had moved on relatively quickly, and had flaunted his new love interest around the city, ensuring that Angie knew he'd got over her fast. Angie had been thankful for that, and even more thankful that she was no longer with him. Still, as a woman, she'd hoped his new love interest was strong enough to slap him down if he'd started his shit; but as far as she was concerned, Angie was done with that part of her life and had shifted her focus to the new man in her life.

Dale had been the opposite, detailing just how instrumental she would be in his future. And now, more than two decades later, they were the most powerful family in Glasgow and she'd been the brains behind it all. Associates' wives and girlfriends could only dream of what it would be like to live the life of Angie Bryson; to have the respect of the city the way she did. Not that Angie was one for shouting her mouth off about her successes. People only had to take one look at her to know what she'd built. Dale and his brothers were the face and muscle, but Angie was the brains of the businesses.

She heard footsteps approaching and stood back from the open door, waiting to welcome their guest. He appeared in front of her just seconds later, and she greeted him with her warmest smile.

'Mr MacTavish, come in. Take a seat.'

Allowing him to enter the office, Angie watched as MacTavish's expression fell when he clocked Dale behind the desk.

'Don't look so worried, James,' she said. 'We don't bite.'

MacTavish gave a slight smile and sat down on the seat opposite Dale. Angie could see that he was nervous, and she understood why. Being called into the office of Dale Bryson,

Glasgow's biggest gang boss, had to be scary when you didn't know why you were there.

'Why have you asked to see me?' His voice wobbled slightly.

Dale took another gulp of whisky and glanced up at Angie. 'One for James, here.'

Smiling to herself, Angie went to the drink stand and poured a whisky before placing it in front of James. He acknowledged her with a nod and knocked it back in one gulp. Brains and beauty didn't mean she was opposed to doing things for her husband when asked.

'You're a distributor for Kyle and Ian Fraser, yes?'

James nodded and Angie sat down on the seat next to Dale behind the desk so they were both facing him.

'Yeah,' he replied, placing the glass down on the coaster in front of him.

'Did you know that the Fraser brothers are employed by me?'

MacTavish's eyes darted between Angie and Dale before he shook his head. 'No, I didn't know that. They never told me.'

Sounds about right, Angie thought. Why would they tell him? They would want people to think they were the top players in this game. Not that they had anything on Dale, Paul and Bob Bryson. They were more street players, cardboard cut-out gangsters who wanted to be more than they ever would be. They weren't real businessmen like the Brysons. They didn't own casinos, nightclubs and construction companies. They didn't own their own security firms and supply the entire city's nightlife with men to guard the doors. They didn't supply the demand for drugs across Glasgow. And they didn't have Angie behind it all.

'No, they wouldn't, would they? Because if they did, it would mean admitting that they're just employees like you are. And why would you work for someone who is at the same level as you?'

Angie could see that James didn't know if he was supposed to answer or not. He simply shrugged and said, 'I just need money to pay my rent.'

Dale nodded and shifted in his seat. 'And how much are they paying you, James? I mean, give me an estimate.'

Angie was enjoying watching the conversation unfold. James MacTavish was going to land his 'bosses' right in it without even realising it. Then Dale would be able to lure him in.

'What do you mean?'

'Well, they have you doing distributions, don't they? Delivering drugs to the regulars. Craigton Heights, Bellpark, those sorts of areas. So, what? You do maybe sixty to eighty deliveries a week?'

MacTavish nodded. 'Aye, that sounds about right.'

'And you get paid?' Dale allowed the last word to linger on his tongue.

'I usually get about a hundred a week.'

Angie stopped her mouth from falling open and giving away her shock. That was far less than Dale was paying Kyle and Ian to do the same job, which it turned out they weren't doing at all. They were undercutting MacTavish to do it for them.

Dale let out a long breath and gave a tight-lipped smile. 'Any complaints from the punters?'

MacTavish hesitated for a moment and Angie leaned forward. 'You don't have to worry about Kyle and Ian Fraser finding out about this. Even though you've been told you work for them, you actually work for us. So, telling us anything of value will work in your favour, James.'

MacTavish took a breath in and said, 'Well, actually, yes. I've had punters throw deliveries back at me and refuse to pay.'

'And why is that?' Dale inquired.

'They said the products aren't worth the money. They're not getting the right or the same hits as before. And one guy told me that his coke smelled like washing powder and slammed the door in my face.'

'And what did you do about that?'

'I demanded the money. A little aggression goes far. Anyway, they eventually paid me, thankfully, otherwise I probably wouldn't be sitting here in one piece. Or at all, actually.'

'And how much are we talking? You know, how much are the Frasers charging for – I don't know – say, a gram?'

'Sixty quid.'

Dale's eyes fell to Angie; he didn't look it, but she could tell he was livid, as was she. Not with MacTavish, but with the Frasers. They were taking the absolute piss out of Dale and the rest of them because they'd been given the go-ahead to run things on their own patches. Now they were cutting the drugs with household substances, selling them at a higher rate and keeping the profits for themselves.

'That's twenty-quid profit per punter, and that's assuming each one only buys a gram,' Dale said through gritted teeth. He looked up at MacTavish and Angie hoped he would keep his cool. 'So, let's say you're doing sixty deliveries per week, at a gram per punter...' Dale trailed off for a moment and then said, 'that's twelve hundred quid a week profit; minimum.'

MacTavish nodded. 'If my maths serves me right, which it never has done, to be honest. I'll take that as gospel.'

Angie noticed Dale pick up the glass of whisky and his knuckles were strained. He was about to blow. She needed to defuse things.

'James, thank you for being so honest with us. Now, you said that you're being paid a hundred pounds a week? Is that even covering your rent? Food?'

MacTavish shook his head. 'Barely. I'm on benefits too, but they're just as shite as the money Kyle and Ian are paying me.'

'So, you're bringing in, what? Six hundred a month?'

'If that,' MacTavish replied. 'Look, I don't want to be in the middle of this. You're not going to tell them I've grassed them up, are you? My life won't be worth living.'

Dale shot a glance up at MacTavish from his whisky glass and raised a brow. 'You're not the one in the wrong here, James. It's those little cunts, thinking they can cut our product and sell it on for more than street value and keeping the money for themselves.' He knocked back the remainder of the whisky and slammed the glass down on the desk.

MacTavish jumped slightly and Angie swiped the glass away from Dale, but instead of pouring him another, she left it on the drink station. He needed a clear head if he was going to figure out what to do next. As much as Dale liked a drink to help calm him, Angie wouldn't allow him too much.

'James, I want you to start working directly for us. Not through the Frasers,' Dale said. 'You won't be distributing for me. You'll be my eyes and ears. You'll report back to me any suspicious activity with the distribution. Do you understand what I'm asking you to do?'

Angie observed the anguish in MacTavish's expression. He didn't want to get involved, that was obvious. But he had no choice now. He would have to do what Dale told him, even though this had all come from Angie.

'You'll be provided with a phone, you'll use it only to contact me, or be contacted by me. You will tell me how much they're selling, how much for and what they pay you each week. Once I've got enough evidence, I'll be able to deal with them.'

MacTavish frowned. 'Isn't what I've told you enough evidence already?'

Dale shook his head. 'No, I want so much that they can't deny it. I want photos of the packages; I want voice recordings of what the punters are saying to you when you go to collect the money. Fuck it, I want voice recordings of all your conversations with the Frasers too. As much as you can get. This is big, MacTavish. I appreciate this is a lot for you to take on. But if you do this for the Brysons, you'll be rewarded in a big way. I'm talking life-changing; enough money you won't know what to do with it. But I need concrete proof. You got that?'

For a moment, Angie felt sorry for James MacTavish. At thirty-five; the same age as Dale, he was just a street lad and their lives were very different. Opposites, in fact. The Frasers were taking the piss out of both MacTavish and the Brysons. How they thought they'd get away with it was baffling to Angie. But here they were, faced with the situation they were in.

'I said, have you got that, MacTavish?'

'Aye, got it.'

'Good. I'll arrange a phone for you. You don't use it for anything other than answering or making calls to me. But I don't want you using it for the photos or recordings. I'll have a separate device set up for that.'

MacTavish gave a long blink as Dale stood up and opened the safe under the desk. He handed MacTavish a pile of notes and said, 'This is an upfront payment. Call it a deposit for your services. If you can get me information in the next two days, I'll double it.'

MacTavish looked down at the money in his hand and his eyes widened. 'There's five hundred quid here.'

Angie nodded. 'That's how serious we are about this, James. It's important you co-operate for this to work for all of us.'

Kyle and Ian Fraser needed to be brought down for this. The Brysons couldn't be seen to be doormats. If the other distributors found out that this had happened, the respect for the family, for her, would be compromised. That would be bad for business.

'Oh, and another thing,' Dale said. MacTavish looked at him as Dale produced a handgun from the safe, half wrapped in a cloth. 'You might need this.'

Angie saw a look of fear cross MacTavish's face. 'Erm, I'm not really into that kind of thing.'

'You don't have to be into it to have it in your possession,' Angie replied.

'It's not up for debate, MacTavish. You might need this one day if the Frasers get wind of what you're doing. Here,' Dale said, handing it to him. 'It's loaded. Six bullets. If you have to, make sure you use them wisely.'

MacTavish hesitated before reaching out his hand and taking the gun from Dale. 'I won't use it.'

'That's your call. But take it anyway with you and store it at your flat. If you're going to keep it anywhere, tape it to the back of your bath panel, or underside of the kitchen sink,' Dale replied.

'You probably won't ever have to use it, James. It's just a precaution. That's all,' Angie said.

She could tell by the look on his face that he wasn't happy about it. But he didn't have a choice. The Brysons were in charge of this situation, and he *would* do as instructed.

Chapter Four

Stepping onto the street, James looked up at the casino building and tried to process what had just happened. When he'd gone inside, his pockets were empty and now he had five hundred quid and a job to do. A dangerous job; one that required him to possess a bloody gun. He was at the mercy of both the Frasers and the Brysons. How the hell had he managed to get himself in the middle of a bloody gang war?

Walking along Ingram Street in Glasgow's city centre, James headed towards Queen Street to get the bus back to Craigton Heights. In fact, if he had five hundred quid, he could get a taxi and it would barely make a dent in the cash. Getting the bus would give him time to think about how he was going to do this without getting himself killed, all the while being paranoid about having a gun stashed down the back of the waistband of his jeans.

'Fuck sake,' he whispered to himself as he pulled his hood over his head when the rain started. As he passed by the homeless guy leaning his back against the Glasgow City Council bin, he thanked his lucky stars that he wasn't in that position. He wasn't a drug user himself. He'd seen what that had done to many of the people living in his scheme, being the person who delivered their poison. He often felt guilty about contributing to that shit, but he had no other option. James hadn't been clever enough at school to even take his exams. He hadn't managed to hold down any jobs, even the ones he didn't need qualifications for, like stacking shelves or scrubbing pub bogs. Dealing for the higher order was all he was able to do. It was cash in hand and guaranteed income. Shit income, but income nonetheless.

Turning onto Queen Street, James crossed the road and took shelter at the bus stop. His bus was due in five minutes, so he wouldn't have long to wait. He pulled a nipped cigarette and his lighter from his pocket and lit the remainder of his smoke; it helped kill the time while waiting on the bus. Dale had made him hang around for a further half an hour while he sent out one of his boys to buy a pay-as-you-go mobile, a cheap camera and a voice recorder. They were all in his jacket pocket, and he'd been told to guard them with his life.

Just as he took his first draw, the bus rounded the corner and stopped in front of him. Extinguishing the cigarette on the pavement, he slid it back into his pocket, paid his fare and sat down at the back of the bus.

Dale and Angie Bryson had promised that the Frasers wouldn't know about the job MacTavish would be doing. But would he be able to keep the fear of being caught off his face? Would they just know?

James told himself he had to be careful. He had to make sure that he behaved as normal around them, even if he had a voice recorder in his pocket. He couldn't ask suspicious questions. He couldn't do anything that would make the Frasers think he wasn't being loyal. It wasn't worth his life, but the idea that he would be rewarded with life-changing money – Dale Bryson's words – was enough to make him want to do it. MacTavish's life was a pile of shit. He had nothing to call his own of any value. In doing this, his life could change for the better and then maybe, just maybe, he could get out of the game.

Surely the benefits of double-crossing the Frasers outweighed the risk? Of course they would, so long as he didn't get caught. If Kyle and Ian knew what he was doing, he'd end up at the bottom of a canal somewhere. That was no way to end your life. James knew that he was stuck between two crime bosses and he would be no match for them. If he didn't give the Brysons what they asked for, he'd be as good to tell the Frasers of his betrayal.

'Fuck,' he hissed. He felt eyes on him from one of the other passengers sitting opposite. He gave them a soft smile and turned to face out of the window. The rain ran sideways along the glass as the wind picked up, but it didn't stop Craigton Heights from coming into view, looming over him like a bad dream. But it wasn't a bad dream. Craigton Heights was James's life. It was where he grew up, and where he would die. There was no escape from that place. Once you were in it never let you go. The high-rise flats were like dark, overbearing security guards who kept a close eye to make sure you always returned.

Getting up from his seat, James pressed the bell, alerting the driver to stop. He thanked him, then stepped off and onto the pavement. The smell of weed hit him in an instant and when he looked up, he saw the window in the bottom-floor flat was wide open. They were either growing, or smoking in there. Growing seemed less likely. Everyone around the scheme knew that this was Fraser territory. Or Brysons', as James knew it to be now.

'Oi, MacTavish?' a voice called. A face appeared at the open window and the person waved him over. James really wasn't in the mood, but he stepped up off the pavement and crossed the grass towards the window.

'Aye, what is it?'

'Any dope on you?'

James shook his head. 'You know you need to put an order in. I don't just carry it about with me on the off chance you might see me in the street.'

The young girl frowned and ran a hand through her greasy ponytail. 'Don't be a cheeky bastard, I was only asking.'

Breathe, James told himself before answering. 'The only cheeky bastard around here is you, Stella. You think I'm going to give you more dope when you still haven't paid me for your last stash? It'll no' be me that comes looking for it if you don't pay up in the next few days. It'll be the boss man, and you really don't want that, Stella.'

'Fuck off,' she cackled, taking a long draw on a cigarette. The sound of kids laughing filtered out of the window, along with the smoke from her cigarette. 'Shut it in there, ma heed's banging!'

James had turned his back on Stella and begun to move away when she shouted him back. 'Please, mate. I need it.'

'Smells like you don't, Stella. You've either got some left, or you're growing your own. So, which is it?'

'It's ma last bit, honestly.'

James shook his head and kept walking. 'When I have your money, you'll get your dope and whatever else you want. But from now on, you'll pay up front.'

'Fuck you, MacTavish!' Stella hissed back before slamming the window shut.

He ignored her and kept walking along the edge of the tenements towards the cul-de-sac of derelict-looking flats. Craigton Heights often fell into darkness near the middle of the month. Most folk couldn't pay their electricity bills, and most were living on the emergency funds in the meters until their money came through. There was always enough money for drink and drugs, right enough.

James reached the entrance to his own flat and as he pushed the door open, he felt a presence behind him. Turning, he was faced with a smiling Kyle Fraser.

'Handled nicely, MacTavish. If I had a medal, I'd give you one.'

Kyle smiled widely as he chewed loudly on some gum. Suddenly, the memory of the gun at his back sparked a fear in him he hadn't felt before. What if Kyle saw it sticking out from his clothes? What if he asked where he got it from, and why he had it in the first place? He had to stay calm, keep his expression stress-free and behave normally. So James gave a tight-lipped smile in response and said, 'She's a chancer. The only way to deal with them is to tell them they'll get fuck all unless they pay.'

Kyle nodded and followed James into the building. The lift was out of order, as always, so James started to climb the stairs to the third floor where his flat was located. He never wished to live higher than that. Third floor was close enough to the ground that if there was a fire, he'd still have a chance of surviving if he jumped.

'You're right. But sometimes you need to be a little tougher on them, you know what I mean?' Kyle said as James pulled out his key and opened his front door. He stepped inside and Kyle was right at his back. All James could think of was that Kyle was going to see the gun. Thankfully, he didn't.

'Aye, well, like I said, she won't be getting fuck all off me until she's paid.'

'Correct, MacTavish. Because if she doesn't pay, I'll take it out of your wages. And you know what – since I'm feeling like I'm in a good mood, I'll tell you this. If she doesn't pay you in a few days like you said, then you get to be the one who dishes out the punishment. How's that sound?'

James turned and stared at Kyle. He went to remove his jacket, then remembered that if he did, he'd be exposing the gun. 'What do you mean?'

'Anything, really. Whatever you see fit. A broken jaw, leg, I'm not fussed. Maybe you could threaten one of those scruffy kids of hers. It's really your call.'

The horror of that last suggestion crept up on James and he suddenly felt sick. 'Nah, man, no way. I'm not involving no kids. That's sick.'

Kyle laughed menacingly and folded his arms across his chest. They stood staring at each other in silence and James waited for what was to come next. Kyle could be so unpredictable, and it set James on edge every time he was in his company. Ian was a little easier to be around, but that was why Kyle was the enforcer of the two.

'I'll make sure she pays,' James replied after a long silence. He didn't know how, but he would. Just not the way Kyle had suggested. He wasn't that kind of man.

'Good. Make sure you do, and all will be dandy.'

James opened the boiler cupboard door and took out an envelope.

'Here, this week's takings, minus Stella's.' James handed the envelope to Kyle and prayed to God he'd counted it all correctly. He hadn't missed anyone out, other than Stella. So the money should've all been in there.

'Nice one,' Kyle replied, snatching it from James. 'I'll be back later with everyone's orders. Make sure you're in.'

James nodded. Now was his chance to start the ball rolling. 'If It's easier, I could come to you? Pick them up?'

Kyle eyed him for a moment, his brow furrowing in the centre and crinkling the skin on his forehead. 'Aye, actually that's not a bad idea. Saves me coming back out. Got the weans to deal with tonight, you know how it is?'

James nodded and relief flooded his chest. He watched as Kyle left before closing the door behind him. Turning the key in the lock and making sure that it was secure, James exhaled slowly before removing his jacket. He pulled out the devices from his pocket: the phone, the camera and the voice recorder – and felt sick. This was the craziest, or stupidest thing he'd ever agreed to do in his life.

He opened the boiler cupboard door and hung the jacket up, while placing the devices on the shelf to the left. Shutting the door quietly, James moved through to the bathroom. He stood before the bath as he reached around his back and carefully removed the gun from the waistband of his jeans. Staring down at the weapon in his hand, he couldn't help but admire it slightly. As much as he was terrified about possibly having to use the thing, he felt powerful as the cold steel rested against the palm of his hand.

James knelt down, tugged at the corner of the bath panel and pulled it off, revealing the pipework underneath. He didn't have tape, like Dale had suggested. Instead, he reached in as far back as he could and placed the gun on the floor underneath the bath. It would have to do. No one else knew it was there, other than the Brysons and James himself.

Replacing the panel, James got to his feet and dusted down his jeans. This job that he was doing for the Brysons, he couldn't afford to fuck it up. His life depended on getting it right on both sides.

Chapter Five

As Angie stepped through the front door of her new and luxuri-ously decorated home, that same feeling washed over her that she'd felt on the day she'd crossed the threshold for the first time. It was everything she could have ever dreamed of when she and Dale had first met. They'd always talked about building their own home on the outskirts of Glasgow where they'd be able to purchase a bigger piece of land, and with the casino bringing in the big bucks, they'd managed to do it. The kids loved the house too, and it had been a good distraction for Ashley after what had happened. Seeing your dad in a gunfight wasn't something any ten-year-old should have to witness. A swimming pool, a gym and a jacuzzi, as well as a games room for her to spend time in with her friends, was all the diversion Angie had hoped for.

'Mum?' Conor called out from the games room at the opposite end of the house. 'That you?'

'And Dad,' Dale called back. He glanced at Angie and smiled. 'Nice to know I'm thought of.'

Angie laughed in response. 'Och, come on, you know I'm his favourite.'

'Aye, because you give him whatever he wants when he asks for it. I'm telling you, that boy is going to become a spoilt brat if you're not careful.'

Angie shook her head. She knew Dale was joking, but she worried that if he said it often enough, Conor might live up to that expectation. Not that he had bratty tendencies, but parents have such an influence on their kids, and Angie wanted them to grow into good people – even if they did have a gangster for a dad.

Paul Bryson appeared from the games room and closed the door behind him with a solemn expression etched on his face, and Angie started to worry.

'A'right, bro,' Dale said, dropping his keys onto the table and shaking off his jacket. 'What's up?'

Paul took a deep breath and glanced at Angie before replying. 'It's Ashley.'

'What's happened? Where is she?' Angie took a step forward.

'She's upstairs, in her room. Don't worry, she's fine. Well, physically she's fine. But she's been crying all afternoon. She's tried to hide it from me but I caught her coming out of the bathroom and, well, it was obvious. Her eyes were puffy, her nose was bright red.'

Angie closed her eyes. She'd thought Ashley had been doing okay. The distractions had been working.

'Has she said why she's upset?' Dale asked. Angie shot him a look as she headed for the winding staircase in the hallway.

'Oh, come on, Dale. You know damn well what this is about. That fucking prick, Reilly.'

Dale winced at the sound of Angie's tone and inhaled loudly.

'Keep your voices down,' Paul said, glancing over his shoulder at the games room where Conor was playing on the Xbox.

'He should have been taken care of properly. If he had been,' she glared at both Paul and Dale, 'then Ashley wouldn't have been subjected to the horrors of seeing her dad attacked in the street by a fucking psycho.'

'Angie, come on. It was a sensitive situation,' Paul said.

Angie shook her head. 'Aye, and look what "sensitive" did. I couldn't give a shit about the guy – he subjected my daughter to the most appalling scenes because he got the sack from the casino. Do *you* think that's acceptable? If the three of you had done away with him like I'd told you to, then this wouldn't be happening right now.'

Paul and Dale fell silent, and Angie waited for a response. There couldn't be one. They knew she was right. Reilly was off-the-scale nuts, he loved the power of standing at the doors of the casino and making the punters' lives a misery before letting them in. The night he took it too far and beat a guy to within an inch of his life, throwing the casino's reputation into jeopardy, was the moment Angie had told Dale, Paul and Bob what she thought they should do to handle it. Bumping him off was the only way to show people that they wouldn't be allowed to behave that way while representing the Brysons.

'But you felt sorry for him, was that it? Because he'd been a loyal doorman for years? Because he had a kid to provide for? Was he thinking of our kid when he tried to kill you, Dale? Was he?'

'Fucking hell, Angie,' Dale said under his breath. 'It's not like any of us wanted this to happen.'

'No, least of all Ashley, eh? Oh, don't worry, I'll go up and check on our daughter. You stay down here and wallow in the guilt.'

Angie stormed her way up the stairs and headed along the hallway to Ashley's room, slowing her pace as she reached the closed bedroom door. Leaning in towards it, she rested her head gently on the wood and listened. There was no sound coming from the other side, no sniffing or whimpering. Maybe she'd stopped. Maybe she was all cried out.

'Ashley?' Angie called gently, tapping on the door. 'It's Mum. Can I come in?'

Ashley didn't respond, and for a moment Angie wondered if she was in her room at all. Maybe she'd gone to another part of the house to take her mind off things.

'I'm opening the door now, Ashley.'

Pulling the handle down, Angie pushed the door gently and when she looked inside, Ashley was fast asleep on her bed, facing the other way. Her shoulders rose and fell with each breath, and Angie decided she didn't want to disturb her daughter. But she also had to find out if what she'd been upset about was the Reilly situation. She couldn't exactly ignore it. What kind of a mother would she be if she did that?

'Ashley?'

Inching closer to the bed, Angie made sure she stepped lightly. Sudden sound and movement seemed to trigger her daughter into a panic attack. Was it any wonder after what she'd witnessed?

'I'm sleeping,' Ashley said quietly. 'And I'm fine.'

'Are you, though?'

Silence followed the question. Angie reached the edge of the bed and lowered herself onto it. Placing a hand on Ashley's back, she felt like the worst parent in the world. How could she have let this happen? How could Dale have let this happen? She'd told him what to do. Get rid. That's what the Brysons did with anyone who crossed them. Reilly was a thief and a smartarse who thought he'd got away with it. And for a while he had. Doing drugs on the job, a combination of steroids and cocaine while working the door at the casino had sent his brain into overdrive. Paranoia and aggression had driven people away, except for one guy who'd chosen to stand up to him and paid the price. It made the company look bad.

'Leave me alone, Mum.'

'Not until you tell me what's wrong. Uncle Paul said you've been upset most of the day.'

Ashley sat up quickly and turned to face Angie, her hair frizzy and damp at one side from where her tears had landed.

'Oh, now you care?'

So shocked by the outburst, Angie didn't respond.

'You've not said one word to me since that man almost killed my dad on the street. It's been months, Mum, months. And what did you do? You moved us here. Gave me a swimming pool and a place where my friends could come and hang out, as if that would make things better. I think you've asked me once if I'm okay.'

Angie drew back from her daughter. But Ashley was right, Angie should have done more after what had happened. And the fact that her nine-year-old daughter had had to point that out to her was embarrassing. There wasn't a lot she could say to defend herself at that moment. She was ashamed that Ashley felt let down and alone in the situation. No nine-year-old child should feel that way about their parent.

'Ashley, sweetheart, if you were struggling with what happened, you should have spoken to me about it.' As soon as the words were out of her mouth she regretted it. She sounded like she was blaming her daughter.

Ashley's face contorted. 'I'm nine. I'm not an adult, but I'm not stupid either. *You* should have checked on me more.'

Angie exhaled slowly and tried to pull Ashley in for a hug but she resisted.

'No, Mum. It's too late. I need to forget about what happened but I can't get it out of my head.'

'We'll get you the help you need, Ashley. No matter what it takes, you can count on me now. I'm sorry if you think I've failed you. I thought what I was doing was the best thing for you and your brother. I really did.'

How was she having this conversation with her nine-year-old daughter? How had this happened? She was speaking the way an adult would address the fact that she'd been through a traumatic experience.

'Make his face go away, Mum. All I can see when I close my eyes is his face.'

Ashley began to sob and buried her face into the pillow. She gripped it tight and Angie wondered if she wanted to scream.

Angie lay down beside her daughter, wrapped an arm around her and pulled her in tight. She said nothing. Instead, she allowed her daughter to sob, to let the anguish of what had happened out.

–

Ashley was sound asleep and looked peaceful as she lay on the bed. She'd cried herself to sleep and Angie stayed with her. But now, as she crept out of the room as quietly as she could, she headed downstairs to speak to Dale. Their daughter needed help. Help they couldn't give her.

'How is she?' Dale asked, standing at the bottom of the stairs holding a coffee mug in his hand.

'Exhausted. Traumatised. Terrified.' The words came in a whisper. If she'd said them any louder, she'd have cracked.

'Fuck!' Dale hissed. 'Our poor girl.'

Angie nodded and stepped off the staircase onto the hard floor in the hallway. She needed something stronger than coffee. Much stronger. Heading to the kitchen, she heard the faint sounds of *Grand Theft Auto* coming from the games room and didn't have the energy to tell Conor to turn it off. He'd had more than enough screen time for the day, but all she wanted was a glass of wine.

Reaching the fridge, Angie pulled out the half bottle of Pinot Grigio Blush and poured herself a large glass. Leaning against the kitchen counter, she watched as Dale sat down at the table and stared into his coffee mug.

'We need to act, to get her help. I think she should see a childhood counsellor. They'll be able to help her through this. I don't have the first clue how to fix this.'

Dale glanced up at her and she could see the anguish on his face. He blamed himself, the way she blamed herself for not doing anything about it when she had the chance. It was obvious. But they couldn't wallow in self-pity.

'Do you think she'll ever get over what happened?' Dale asked.

'Eventually she will.'

Dale nodded but remained silent.

Angie lifted the glass to her lips and closed her eyes.

The wine burned the back of her throat as it went down, and she opened her eyes to find tears streaming down her face.

'We'll get her a counsellor. I'll call first thing tomorrow,' she said, clearing her throat.

Angie thought about the versions of herself. The businesswoman, the mum, the wife. She had the businesswoman and wife bit down to a fine art, that she was sure about. Being a mum was hard, and in this particular circumstance, even harder. She'd failed her daughter.

Chapter Six

As James MacTavish stood at the front door of Kyle Fraser's flat, he worried that his face had 'guilty' written all over it. Would Kyle be able to see through him; be able to tell that he was recording him? The thought of getting caught sent a fear through his veins he'd never felt before.

'Come in,' Kyle said after he'd opened the door.

James stepped into the flat and the smell of a homecooked meal hit him immediately. He hadn't had one of those in years. It was all microwave or oven-ready food, dry and bland. It was all he could afford.

'Hi,' Cara said, stepping out of the kitchen and smiling at him. 'You must be James?'

James nodded and held out his hand. Cara smiled, shook his hand and then said, 'Thanks for coming to Kyle. It means he can keep an eye on them. I'm heading out tonight. A girls' night out.'

James nodded, not sure what to say in response. He really didn't care what Cara was doing. All he wanted was to record as much information as possible on the recorder in his pocket and get away from the flat as quickly as possible.

'MacTavish, in here,' Kyle said, gesturing for James to follow him into one of the rooms. Glancing at Cara, he smiled before going into one of the back rooms of the flat.

The place was nothing like his own. It was certainly bigger. A council flat, yes, but Kyle had clearly had it renovated to a high spec. He'd made it look like an old-style tenement, with high ceilings, solid oak doors and fancy lights above him. The reception hallway was long; longer than James's, with more doors than his own leading to separate rooms. And if James had had time, he was certain he could stand in the middle of the hallway with arms stretched out either side of him, and there would be at least a four-foot gap between his fingers and the wall on both sides. Unlike in his own flat where he could touch the walls on either side of the hallway by barely bending his arms. Even having a council flat looked luxurious in comparison to James's.

He couldn't help admiring the place, but it also angered him. When he thought about the amount of money that Kyle was paying him compared to how much he should've been getting, his blood boiled.

Kyle closed the door behind them and James took in his surroundings. The room resembled a bedroom with an office desk in the corner. Kyle walked over to the desk and opened the bottom drawer, before producing a bag.

'All this week's orders are inside. Each one labelled with an address as usual.'

James nodded and hoped the recorder hadn't randomly switched off in his pocket.

'Prices are on them too. Don't hand them over until you get paid, I don't want another bitch like Stella thinking they're getting away without handing over the cash.'

'Okay,' James replied. He knew he needed to ask questions to get Kyle talking, but he didn't know what to ask, or how to ask them without Kyle becoming suspicious.

'I've upped the price on a few of the orders,' Kyle said. 'So if people start complaining, tell them to come to me about it.'

James nodded. 'Why have they gone up?'

Kyle eyed him and then smiled. 'Because I said so, that's why. Cost of living goes up, food, bills etcetera, so I put the price of my product up. Do you have a problem with that?'

'No,' James said, thankful that he hadn't had to push too hard to get that out of Kyle. 'Should I say that to the punters?'

Kyle smirked. 'Aye. And if they don't like it, fuck them.'

James took the bag from Kyle and felt the handle almost slip from his grip. His palms were clammy and his heart was hammering in his chest. But from what he could gather, Kyle hadn't noticed.

After what seemed like a long silence, Kyle gave James the once over and said, 'What you still doing here? You've got deliveries to make.'

Blinking and turning to the door, James reached for the handle and opened it. As he walked down the hall towards the front entrance, a door to his left opened suddenly and two young boys came rushing out, screaming at each other about something James couldn't fathom. As they brushed past him, they knocked the bag from his hand and it fell with a dull thud to the hardwood floor.

'Oi, Ryan! Be careful, eh?' Kyle shouted as James bent to retrieve the bag. 'Don't be such a wee shit when there's folk in the house.'

James glanced at the young lad and gave him an apologetic smile, to which he responded with, 'Sorry, mister,' before running after his brother down the hall.

'Sorry about that,' Cara said, sticking her head out of the kitchen. 'They get a bit hyper when they know it's coming up for dinnertime.'

'It's fine. James here was just leaving,' Kyle said, reaching around him to open the front door. Cara disappeared back into the kitchen and James stepped out into the communal close.

'Kyle?'

'What?' Kyle asked. James could tell he wanted rid of him quickly.

'If you've put your prices up, will I get a rise? You know, for each delivery, will I get more?'

Frowning, Kyle lowered his eyes before setting them straight on James. Then out of nowhere, he started to laugh. 'Ha, aye right. Good one, MacTavish.'

Before James could respond, the door was closed in his face and he was left standing on his own with a bag of drugs hanging by his side.

As he moved down the stairs to the exit, he shook his head. 'Hope you got all that, Mr Bryson,' he whispered as he stepped outside and onto the street.

Chapter Seven

Getting out of the taxi, Angie Bryson looked up at the bar on Byres Road and smiled. She'd had many a good night there over the years. But since having the kids, and becoming a main player in the family businesses, Angie had taken a step back from her wilder days. She missed it only to a certain extent. But as she looked up at the old converted church building, her wilder side was slowly creeping back in.

'Come on, Angie,' Maxine called as she joined the queue with the rest of the girls. Angie hadn't been on a night out in such a long time. In fact, she hadn't seen the girls since forever, so being invited out for Maxine's thirtieth had been a perfect excuse to finally allow herself some down time, away from the family, the businesses and the kids.

She wobbled a little as she negotiated the stairs in her heels. It wasn't as though she never wore heels, but mostly she wore block heels for work at the casino. A stiletto was a very different entity, especially when pre-night-out drinks were involved.

'Alright, ladies, what's the occasion?' the bouncer asked.

'It's my twenty-first birthday,' Maxine cackled, along with Siobhan and Elaine.

'Fuck off, twenty-one,' Elaine shouted. 'You're thirty like the rest of us. And twenty-one-year-olds don't bring handbags out that could be used to go away for a weekend to Tenerife.'

Angie burst out laughing and recalled the last pub they'd been in before getting in the taxi. Elaine had literally climbed into Maxine's bag and posed for a picture. They'd all been so rowdy that the bouncers had told them to keep it down.

'Shut up, Elaine,' Maxine laughed. 'There's nothing wrong with my bag. And I didn't hear you complaining when you asked me to keep your perfume in it because that pissy thing you call a bag is too small.'

The bouncer laughed with them and then his eyes fell on Angie. He nodded and said, 'Dale at home with the kids tonight, then?'

'I've got to have my freedom sometimes, Liam.'

He stepped aside and allowed them to head downstairs to the club. The girls all handed in their jackets and held out their wrists to be stamped, before heading straight for the bar.

Elaine bought a round of shots for the four of them, and Angie sighed inwardly. She really didn't want a hangover the next day. Being a mum in your thirties with two kids wasn't exactly easy when you felt like you wanted to die.

'Not for me,' she shouted, holding her hand up.

'Lightweight!' Siobhan shouted, thrusting the shot glass into her hand. 'Get it down you. Maxine is the last of us to turn thirty, we have to have at least one!'

Angie rolled her eyes and quickly knocked it back at the same time as the girls, before they made their way to the dancefloor. 'Summertime Sadness' by Lana Del Ray blared out of the speakers. Angie closed her eyes as she danced. She hadn't realised how much she needed to feel free until that very moment.

She allowed herself to be consumed by the music, feeling the bass in her chest as she danced and laughed with the girls. The shot hadn't gone straight to her head like she'd thought it would but she could feel the effects of the previous drinks working on her.

Slipping off the dancefloor, she headed for the bathroom and shut herself in the cubicle. She pulled a small stash of coke out of her bag, poured some onto the back of her hand and sniffed it up quickly, rubbing the remnants onto her gums. Taking a tissue from the shelf behind her, she quickly rubbed it along the edge of her nostril and disposed of it down the toilet.

Perfect, she thought. Her head was clearer now. And she'd be able to last the night, so long as her shoes didn't kill her first.

Closing her bag, she flushed the toilet and headed out to the sink area. The bathrooms were empty, aside from the woman at the sinks with the baskets of toiletries. She was on her phone, and didn't even look up at Angie as she stood, reapplying her lip gloss.

A figure appeared next to her as she was washing her hands, and when she looked up at the mirror, Cara Fraser was staring back at her.

'Angie,' Cara said in acknowledgement. There was a certain arrogance to her tone, and even the toilet attendant noticed it.

'Don't speak to me, Cara. In fact, don't even look at me.'

Cara turned away from the mirror to face Angie and her brow crinkled. 'Excuse me? What the fuck's your problem?'

Angie took a breath. She couldn't say anything. She needed to let MacTavish do his job. If she spoke up now, they wouldn't get the information they needed.

'Nothing,' Angie said through gritted teeth.

'Nah,' Cara put her hand on her hip, 'if you've got something to say, fucking say it.'

The toilet attendant stood up. 'Take it outside, ladies.'

Angie smiled at the woman and then took another breath. If she had to take Cara outside, she would. But again, she couldn't say what she wanted to say. It would blow MacTavish's cover before he even got started.

'I don't have anything to say. But just remember who your boss is, Cara.'

'I don't have a boss, and even if I did, it certainly wouldn't be you.'

'But Dale is Kyle's boss, isn't he? So, the Brysons pay your wages. Well, I assume Kyle pays you an allowance, since you don't work for yourself?'

The look on Cara's face made Angie smile. She'd hit a sore spot. It was obvious that Cara didn't have a job. Anytime Angie

43

saw her, she was either with her kids, or on a shopping spree. She was a kept woman; but how was she doing it? She was always commenting that she didn't have a lot of money. When Dale had enough to take the Frasers out, he would. And they would have no comeback. Dale and Angie would make sure that every single dealer and punter in Glasgow knew to stay the hell away from the Frasers. Glasgow was Bryson territory, and the Frasers were taking the utter piss out of them.

'Who exactly do you think you are, Angie? Just because you're married to Dale Bryson doesn't give you the right to speak to everyone you meet like they're something you've just wiped off the bottom of your shoe.'

Angie laughed. 'Like I said, the Brysons are your boss. We employ you. If you don't like it, then maybe you and your family should find another way of bringing in the cash? Don't push me, Cara. I hold all the cards and you know it.'

Lifting her bag from the sink area, Angie moved past Cara and headed for the door, but before she could reach for the handle, she felt a tug on the strap of her bag. Spinning round, Cara was in her face, their noses almost touching.

'I'll knock you out if you speak to me like that again,' Cara said through gritted teeth.

'Girls, I said, outside. I'll call in security if I have to,' the toilet attendant said, trying to squeeze herself between them.

Angie smiled and stepped back. 'No need for that.'

Cara smirked back at her just as Angie swiped the back of her hand across Cara's face. Her red hair splayed out as she was knocked from her feet and sent stumbling backwards.

'Right, that's it.' The toilet attendant left the bathrooms, and Angie leaned in and gripped Cara by the upper arm.

Cara steadied herself and glared at Angie.

'Let that be a warning to you, Cara. And the rest of you Frasers. Fuck us over, and you're done.'

Angie left the bathroom and snuck back onto the dancefloor, where the rest of the girls were seemingly oblivious to the fact that she'd even left. She watched as the security guy followed the toilet attendant to the bathroom, but she knew that even if she was approached, nothing was going to happen.

The Brysons owned every security company in the city; supplied every bar and club. They all knew Angie. She couldn't be touched because she was their boss.

'Another shot?' Siobhan shouted. She didn't wait for an answer, she was already headed for the bar. And as Angie followed her, out of the corner of her eye, she watched as Cara Fraser was escorted from the nightclub.

The security guard glanced over at her and nodded. It paid to be the wife of a crime boss.

Chapter Eight

'I'll fucking kill her,' Cara Fraser bellowed as the bouncer let go of her when they were outside. 'This is a fucking disgrace. You're throwing me out but not her?'

The broad-shouldered man folded his arms across his chest and raised a brow. 'Do yourself a favour, hen, go home and sleep it off. You're not getting back in here tonight, and don't think you're standing out here waiting for her to come out either.'

Cara glared at him. 'Are you *fucking* kidding me?' she screeched.

'No, I'm not kidding. Now, are you going to piss off or do I need to phone the polis?'

Cara laughed sarcastically. 'Aye, go on. Phone them. At least they'll do something. Or maybe I'll phone my husband, get him down here to sort you out.'

The bouncer smiled and shook his head. 'I highly doubt that, love.'

'Oh really? You've not heard of Kyle Fraser, then? Shame, least then you'd know what you were in for when you see him coming towards you.'

The bouncer's smile turned to laughter; loud, brash laughter that made Cara even more furious.

'Oh, I've heard of him alright. He's got the same fucking boss as me,' he said before pausing, as if waiting for the words to sink in. 'Aye, that's right. Dale Bryson is my boss, and Kyle's. Different areas of work, mind. So, I don't know if your man will come for me tonight, will he? And before you ask, aye, I

46

do class Mrs Bryson as my boss too. So, there's your reason for standing out here in the street, shouting like a fucking lunatic.'

Cara took a step back and gritted her teeth. 'Fuck you!'

'Aye, go on, you ginger nutter, off you pop back to big, bad Kyle.' He laughed again. 'Fucking idiot's the height of shite, what did you think he was going to do to me? Stand on a ladder to knock me out?'

A crowd of people waiting in line to get in started to laugh along with him, and for the first time since being kicked out of the club, Cara Fraser wanted the ground to open up and swallow her. But then she stopped for a moment and reminded herself of who she was, and more importantly, who her husband was. Kyle Fraser might work for Dale Bryson, but he was no idiot.

She glanced down at her phone screen and realised that the girls she'd been on the night out with hadn't tried to contact her. They hadn't even noticed she was gone. And there was no way of getting back inside. She was going to have to call it a night.

Turning her back on the club and the bouncer, Cara started walking along Great Western Road, away from the city centre end of Glasgow and further into the West End. It would be easier to get a taxi the further away from the nightlife she was. She was annoyed with herself that she hadn't clicked that Dale Bryson's security firms worked for the majority of Glasgow's nightlife establishments. And now that she'd been thrown out of one, word would spread that Kyle Fraser's missus had caused a scene.

Shit, she thought. With what was going on with Kyle and Ian trying to make a name for themselves, this wouldn't go down well with Kyle.

As she reached the pedestrian crossing outside One Devonshire Gardens, Cara realised she'd been walking for fifteen minutes and not one taxi had passed with its vacant light on. The only other option would be to jump on the bus back to the flat. Massaging her temples, she realised that her hangover was starting to kick in.

Pulling out her phone again, she called Kyle. He picked up after one ring.

'What's up?' he answered. 'You never phone when you're out with the girls.'

'Yeah,' she sighed. 'Something kicked off.'

'What do you mean?'

'I ran into Angie Bryson and she started on me. Can you come and pick me up?'

Kyle fell silent on the other end of the phone, and she couldn't work out if he was trying to contain his frustration, or if the line had gone dead. She pulled the phone away from her ear and looked at the screen. He was still on the line.

'Kyle?'

'What do you mean, she started on you? Why?'

Sighing, Cara replied, 'Can you come and get me and I'll tell you then? I'm walking towards Anniesland and I can't get a taxi. And I'm on my own.'

'I'll get Ian to come and sit with the boys. Give me fifteen minutes. Where are you?'

'Outside One Devonshire Gardens,' she replied.

'Right, go inside and I'll come in and get you. For fuck sake, Cara.'

Before Cara could respond, Kyle had already hung up. Why was he pissed off with her? She hadn't done anything wrong.

Sliding the phone back into her bag, Cara turned to face the hotel and walked along the pathway, away from the main road. The hotel bar still looked open, so she climbed the seven steps and pulled open the heavyset door before stepping inside. The hotel bar was quiet, which suited her. She went to the bar and ordered a large vodka and Coke before taking a seat at the bay window to wait on Kyle.

She hated that Angie had the power to have her thrown out of the nightclub. Who did she think she was? She was no better than Cara. Both married to gangsters. They both had kids. The only real difference was that the Brysons had more money than the Frasers. Much more, to be precise. But that was all going to change. Kyle and Ian were sick of working for pennies. They were going to start their own empire, and there would be nothing Dale Bryson could do about it. The city was big enough for them both to run it.

Sipping on her vodka, Cara wished she'd ordered a coffee instead. The hangover had properly kicked in now, and that dry weary feeling of dread was creeping in that always came after a night on the sauce with the girls.

Almost half an hour had passed before Kyle arrived, and when he sat down opposite her, he didn't look best pleased.

'What's up with you?' Cara asked, finishing her vodka even though she hadn't wanted it.

'I could ask you the same question, Cara. Getting into a fight with Angie Bryson, are you fucking insane?' he hissed.

'I didn't get into a fight with her. She was off her face on coke, and she just started on me.'

Kyle shook his head but didn't say anything. Cara watched as he sat back on the large leather armchair and glanced out of the window. His eyes darted back and forth, as if he were tracking the cars on the main road. He was thinking about something, and the fact that he was being silent made Cara feel uneasy.

'Is something wrong, Kyle?'

He turned sharply and said, 'What exactly did Angie say to you?'

Frowning, Cara narrowed her eyes. 'What does it matter what she said? That wasn't the issue. I could have dealt with her easily if she hadn't sent the bouncers on me and had me thrown out on the street like some fucking tramp. It was humiliating, Kyle. And I want to know what you're going to do about it.'

Kyle's eyes widened, and a smile raised the corner of his mouth, but she could tell it wasn't in humour. 'Are you serious? You want me to deal with Angie Bryson, like she's a no one?

Cara, she's married to the most dangerous gangster in Glasgow, who just happens to be my boss. The boss I am trying to fucking fleece out of cash so Ian and I can start up our own shit and give you and the boys the life you deserve. And you want me to fucking deal with it?' His voice was low, so low that she had to lean forward so she could hear him. He obviously hadn't wanted anyone to hear him. Not that there was anyone else around. Even the barmaid had left the small snug-like bar to collect glasses from elsewhere.

Cara wanted to lift her glass and throw it at him. But as much as his response annoyed her, he was right. He couldn't just go wading in there with Dale and demand an apology. Dale would laugh in his face and sack him on the spot. Where would that leave them?

'Look, I'm sorry. I didn't mean to put pressure on you. I'm just so angry at her. She thinks she's above everyone else and I'm not having it.'

'Well, you'll just have to, because she *is* above everyone else. And if you start a war with her, you're starting a war between both families and I can't afford to fuck this up for us. If the Brysons think we're against them in any way, my plan for greater things for us goes out the fucking window. So, from now on, you keep away from Angie Bryson, you stay away from the clubs that are run by Bryson Security and you do what I say. Got it?'

Cara slumped back in her seat. She'd been humiliated three times that evening. Once by Angie, the second by the bouncer and now by her own husband.

'Fuck sake, Kyle,' she hissed, pushing the chair away from the table and getting to her feet. Grabbing her bag, she stormed out of the snug and onto the street, ignoring the barmaid as she called goodbye after her. Kyle followed her out to the car and she stood by the passenger door, arms folded across her chest, impatiently waiting for him to unlock the door.

'Don't "fuck sake" me,' Kyle said, climbing into the driver's seat as she pulled the door open and let herself inside. 'I'm trying to make our lives better, Cara. And you almost fuck it up? I'm going to have to do some damage control here, Cara. You do realise that, don't you?'

'I didn't think you would do this,' she replied quietly. 'Make me feel like shit about what happened when it wasn't my fault.'

He sighed. 'Look, I didn't mean to make you feel like shit. That's the last thing I intended. But you have to understand where I'm coming from here. It's important that you do what I say in this situation. Ian and I need to have control here, and you getting into a fight with the boss's missus in one of their own clubs isn't going to do us any favours. We need to be our own bosses, Cara. And I can't make that happen if our plan ends up ruined because you two clashed egos on a night out.'

She felt his eyes on her. Kyle had the taste for life as a gang boss now. He wasn't going to let that slip from between his teeth for anyone. That would be his undoing.

Chapter Nine

Back in his flat now, James had finished his deliveries for that evening – and his investigations. He'd been quite surprised at how much people were willing to bitch and complain about their suppliers because the prices had gone up and the product wasn't as good as it once was. James hadn't really known what to say, other than he wasn't in production, only delivery, but he'd pass on the complaints. That in itself made him laugh, because what the hell were they expecting would happen? That they'd get a written letter of apology and a month's free product?

Withdrawing the camera, voice recorder and phone out of his pocket, he set them down on the coffee table in the centre of the living room and slumped down on the sofa. It had been a long night, mentally. He'd had to be at the top of his game, making sure that people didn't know he was recording their conversations. And prior to them even opening the door to him, he'd had to take photos of the street, the buildings and the door numbers of who he was delivering to. It was what Dale had requested, along with trying to get as much recorded information from Kyle and Ian as possible.

As much as James was used to working on his own through the night, it had been stressful for him. He was working for several men, all set against each other, and he was the one stuck in the middle. Most likely, he'd be the one who'd end up coming off worse out of all of them.

'All this just so I can afford to live. Fuck's sake,' he hissed, running a hand through his hair. Sitting forward, he picked up the camera and went through the images he'd managed to capture, all from Craigton Heights. He wouldn't be delivering to other schemes until later in the week. He'd even managed to get some images of punters from a distance. The more he gave to Dale, the quicker he'd be able to get out of this predicament.

He reached for the voice recorder this time and pressed the play button to listen to some of what he'd managed to get.

'*Seventy-five quid up front,*' James heard himself say. He hated the sound of his own voice.

'*Are you fucking kidding? That's the price gone up again. That's twice this month, MacTavish,*' the male voice replied. It was a guy simply named Glass. It was a nickname the locals had given him when he'd been fitted with a glass eye after losing his own in a fight a few years previously. James didn't know the details, and he didn't want to know. The guy was dodgy, but not as dodgy as Kyle and Ian, and certainly not on any level with the Brysons.

'*I don't make the prices, Glass. The Frasers do, you know that,*' James replied.

'*Aye, well it's fucking bollocks. I'm getting less and less for my money here. And the weed is nowhere near as strong as it used to be. Or the coke. The hit's shite.*'

James had stood in front of him in the communal close, the package still in his hand, and waited for Glass to stop ranting.

'*Do you want this or not? I can take it back, but you know what would happen if I did. They'd be the next ones at your door. And they're not as pleasant as I am, are they? I'm sure you wouldn't want to be fitted for a second glass eye, would you?*'

Glass had hesitated, his eyes darting between James's face and the package in his hands. James knew he'd pay up. That was what they all did in the end. It didn't actually matter that they were being made to pay more for less. In the end, they were all addicted to the stuff, so they'd part with their money anyway.

'*Fucking rip-off merchants,*' Glass had said, shoving the cash into James's other hand and grabbing the package from him. '*This is my last, I don't want anything else from them. I'll find another supplier.*'

James had simply nodded and turned away from the door. As he made his way downstairs, he'd slid his hand into his pocket, felt around for the stop button and pressed it.

That was the way most of the conversations had gone that evening. It was exhausting, hearing the same moans and groans over and over. No one seemed to threaten him, though, which he'd been surprised at.

James had a call scheduled with Dale tomorrow at Dale's request to provide him with evidence he'd gathered on the deliveries. He hoped that what he'd gathered on this first night would be enough for him to walk away. But deep down, he knew it wouldn't be.

Chapter Ten

Waking up to a hangover wasn't on her list of things to do today, but Angie didn't have much choice, given that she'd spent the night taking shots and dabbling in a few lines with the girls.

'Morning,' Dale said, and she sensed humour in his tone, like he was enjoying the fact that she'd rolled into bed at six in the morning, incoherent, and would now be regretting her actions.

'Don't,' she replied, but not before peeling her tongue from the roof of her mouth.

'Don't what? Say good morning?'

Angie's eyelids were stuck together with twenty-four-hour-old mascara that felt like glue. Forcing them open and despising the sand-like sensation, she blinked a few times to adjust to the morning light.

'You know what I mean. Don't revel in my misery.'

'Oh, but I can't help it. You always revel in mine,' he laughed. Staring up at the ceiling, she felt the bed shift and suddenly, Dale was standing by her side looking down at her.

'Yeah, well, that's because you don't know your limits and always end up on a two- or three-day bender,' she replied, licking her lips to get some form of moisture on them.

'Ah, but you see, last night you crammed a three-day bender into just a few hours. I like to pace myself.' He smiled down at her. 'Coffee?'

Forcing herself up the bed, she slid into the sitting position and rested her head against the plush velvet headboard and nodded, instantly regretting the movement and feeling the headache intensify.

Dale leaned down and kissed her on the top of the head before disappearing from the room and heading to the kitchen. The noise of the coffee machine was a welcome sound. She needed something to clear her head.

Reaching for her phone on the bedside table, she glanced at the screen and saw a notification pending. Opening it, there was one message from a number not stored in her contacts.

> Angie, it's Kyle. Can we arrange to meet? I want to talk to you about last night.

Her stomach flipped then, as she searched her memories from the night before. What exactly happened last night? It didn't take long to remember, even though the images were hazy.

Her run-in with Cara at The Ailsa Craig Bar. She'd had her thrown out after smacking her across the face for being a cheeky bitch. Sighing, she glanced down at the words on her screen again and wondered why Kyle would want to speak to her about it. It was likely he wanted to make sure things wouldn't get out of hand. But Kyle would have his own worries to contend with when he realised that Dale was on to him.

The scent of fresh coffee wafted up the stairs as she heard Dale approaching. Entering the room, he handed her the mug and perched himself on the edge of the bed.

'So, anything exciting happen last night?' he asked.

She took a sip from the mug, welcoming the heat and the flavour as it wet her mouth. 'Yeah, actually,' she replied. 'I ran into Cara Fraser. And when I say ran into her, I mean we had an actual run-in.'

Dale's ears pricked up like a dog listening for the treat cupboard to open. 'Oh aye?'

'Yeah. I mean, it was me who started it, but I was just so angry that she even approached me. So I told her to remember who I was, and that Kyle would do well to remember too.'

Dale replied, 'Awe, Angie, you didn't tell her we're on to Kyle and Ian, did you?'

'No, of course I didn't. To be honest, she was acting as though she doesn't know about their little scam. But she's just putting on a front. Anyway, I ended up slapping her and got her thrown out.'

Dale sighed and shook his head, but there was a hint of a smirk forming at the corners of his mouth.

'What? She bloody deserved it. Stupid cow forgot who she was talking to and where she was. I mean, having the audacity to come up to me and get cocky when she knows what her husband is up to. It's fucking brazen, I'll give her that.'

Taking another sip from the mug, she felt the caffeine start to work its magic, even though the headache was worsening.

'So, what happened after she got thrown out?' Dale asked.

'I don't know. I didn't follow her to find out. But I have just received a message from Mr Fraser himself, asking if I can meet him to discuss what happened?'

Dale's humorous expression fell and a shadow passed over his face. 'He actually messaged you? That family are brazen, right enough.'

'I know,' Angie replied. 'Should I meet him? See what he has to say?'

'Well, he obviously went to you because he thinks you're the easier target, which we both know is far from the truth,' he said with a smile. 'So, if you feel comfortable enough, then yeah. See what he has to say for himself. And see if you can trip him up without realising it. But I'll come too, sit close by in case he tries anything.'

Angie glanced at Dale, her brow furrowed. 'You think I can't handle a little swine like Fraser on my own? He's a nobody, Dale. I'll take care of it.'

Dale shook his head. 'No, actually. I've changed my mind. You're not going. It could be a trap.'

It was Angie's turn to laugh now. 'What kind of trap?'

'The kind that he wouldn't set for a man. I don't mean that in disrespect, love. No, you're not going. Simple. And you can text him back and tell him that.'

Angie's head was too sore to argue, so she simply took another mouthful of coffee and nodded in agreement. 'Fine, any excuse to stay in bed a bit longer.'

Dale kissed her on the head again and smiled. 'Right, I have to get to the office. I'm expecting a call from MacTavish today for an update, so when he gets in touch, I'll let you know what he's got for us.'

Angie listened as Dale went downstairs, before she heard the front door open and close, followed by the sound of his car disappearing down the driveway.

She opened up the message on her phone again and began typing her reply. Once she'd composed the message, she read it back to herself and, happy with her response, Angie pressed send.

Chapter Eleven

Cara popped two paracetamol tablets into her mouth at the same time and swallowed them down with a large mouthful of ice-cold water. She'd been suppressing her gag reflex all morning and swallowing tablets to help her feel better almost made her feel worse.

Thoughts of the run-in with Angie Bryson swirled around in her head, and now as she stood in the cold light of day, Kyle's words haunted her too. As much as Angie Bryson was a first-class, stuck-up bitch, she was Kyle's boss's wife. And what Kyle had said last night sat heavily on her shoulders. Today, he'd have to go out and try to make good with the Brysons. And on top of that, keep under wraps what he and Ian were trying to do.

'I'm heading out,' Kyle called in from the hallway. Cara turned and made her way out to meet him at the door before he left.

'Where are you going?' She was already nibbling at the side of her thumbnail, a thing she did when she was anxious.

'Where do you think I'm going? I'm going to fix the mess you created last night,' he replied while putting on his jacket. He didn't even bother to look at her.

'I didn't *create* anything, Kyle. Miss High-and-Fucking-Mighty started all this,' she said through gritted teeth. 'But that's not the point. The point is, I should be the one to go and apologise for what happened, even though I don't think I have anything to apologise for. But if it means keeping the relationship between you and Dale on the straight and narrow, then I'll do it.'

That was when he lifted his eyes to look at her. A frown line appeared between his brows, and she could tell that he thought what she'd said was stupid.

'You've done enough, Cara. I'll go and speak to her, and Dale if I fucking have to. You do realise that the Brysons are our ticket to a better life, don't you?'

Nodding, Cara said, 'Of course I do.'

'Then you let me handle it. And do me a favour, stay away from pubs and clubs that are manned by Bryson Security, eh?'

'So all pubs and clubs, then? If you haven't noticed, they man them all.'

'Aye, *all* pubs and clubs,' he said, sliding his mobile into his pocket and taking his keys off the hook next to the door. He gave her a softer look, then, and moved closer to her. 'Look, I'm not angry at you. I know you didn't start things last night. But you have to understand, I need to stop this getting out of control. Dale Bryson might pull the plug on me and Ian working for him. And if he does, I've got no product.'

Cara sighed and wrapped her arms around him. 'I know that. But you're going to be manufacturing your own shit before long – why can't you just do that now and step away from them sooner?'

Kyle kissed her on the nose and smiled. 'Starting up any business means start-up costs, Cara. I need a place to grow the weed, including all the equipment that comes with that, hydroponics and heat lamps and all that. I can't magic that shit out of thin air, can I? And once that's all up and running, and we're earning enough off it all, we're going to get going on the harder side of things. You know, supply the demand for the party drugs. And we'll undercut the Brysons so much, that it'll put them out of business and we'll be fucking loaded by this time next year. Mark my words.'

Cara smiled, although the whole plan made her nervous.

'Look, I'll sort this shit out and then when I come back why don't we take the boys round to Ian's for pizza?'

She nodded but didn't say anything.

Kyle left and Cara decided to go and tell the boys to get ready for their dad coming back. Turning, she jumped when she saw Ryan standing directly behind her.

'Oh my God, you scared me,' she laughed, feeling a pressure on her temples; the paracetamol hadn't kicked in yet.

'Mum, where's Dad going?' Ryan asked.

'He's just gone out to see someone about work, he'll be back later and then we're all going round to Uncle Ian's for pizza.' She smiled at him.

She could see that his thirteen-year-old mind was processing her words. After a few seconds, he said, 'Who are the Brysons?'

Cara's stomach flipped. 'Just the people your dad works for.'

He nodded slowly. 'And Dad is going to put them out of business?'

Shit, she thought. He'd been listening. 'What makes you say that?'

'Well, that's what he said.'

Drawing her lips into a tight line, Cara didn't quite know how to deal with this. Ryan was only young; he wouldn't understand what he'd just heard, and if he did, what would he think of it?

'I think what your dad meant was that he wants to go into business by himself. So he's learning the tricks of his trade with the people he's working with now, so that he can apply his knowledge to his own business ideas.'

Ryan frowned, smiled and then laughed. 'Mum, I'm thirteen. I'm not stupid. Dad said he's going to put the Brysons out of business. He *said* that we'd be loaded by this time next year.'

Cara sighed. There was no way around this. Ryan was right, he wasn't stupid. He was a very switched-on young lad, and as much as it pained her to think that he understood everything he'd just heard, she was proud that he would one day grow up to be a smart man.

'First of all, you shouldn't be listening in on adult conversations, do you hear me?'

He nodded, but she knew he wasn't taking her seriously.

'And second of all, keep this conversation between us, okay? Don't tell your dad what you heard, and don't tell Sean. He's only two years younger than you, but that's a lot at your age. Let's just keep this between us, okay?'

He nodded, but the smile remained. 'We're going to be minted, aren't we?'

Cara shook her head and placed a hand on her son's shoulder. 'Ryan, enough. Go back into your room and play that Xbox. Do what kids your age do.'

Ryan turned and went into his room, closing the door behind him.

Cara stood, staring into the space in which her elder son was standing just seconds earlier, and all she could think of was her boys' futures. She hoped that with the money that Kyle would earn in his line of work there would be enough to allow the boys to lead themselves a legit life, with real jobs that didn't leave them looking over their shoulders all the time.

Chapter Twelve

Bob and Paul Bryson sat opposite Dale on the other side of the desk, and Bob spun on his seat like an overactive child. Dale ignored him, focused on the clock and waited for MacTavish's call. Dale had warned him: not a second later than eleven o'clock, or he'd go looking for him.

'You think he's going to bail, don't you?' Paul said, eyeing him across the desk.

'If he knows what's good for him, he'll deliver. I'm not worried about that. Even if he doesn't, I'll deal with the Frasers.'

Paul frowned. 'You mean, *we'll* deal with them.'

'Aye, we,' Bob interjected. He stopped spinning and sat forward, placing both hands on the desk. 'I've been thinking about when that time comes. Maybe we bury them in the foundations of one of the buildings? You know, deep, deep down where they'd never be found? Or in the walls?'

Dale took a deep breath and shook his head. 'Has anyone ever told you that you've got a screw loose?'

Bob smirked and cracked the knuckles in each hand before sitting back and pulling his leg up to rest on the opposite knee. 'Och, Dale. We've all got a couple screws loose. That's why we're in this business. The personality and attitude fit the game.'

Paul laughed and just then, Dale's phone rang loudly on the desk. He glanced up at the clock. Bang on the button. Lifting the phone, he answered it and pressed the button for loudspeaker.

'MacTavish?'

'Boss,' he started. 'I have some things you might want to see.'

'Good. Make your way to the casino now.'

Dale hung up and glanced at Bob and Paul.

'Interesting,' Paul said. 'You think he's got enough?'

'Anything will be enough. But I want plenty so the wee shits can't talk their way out of it. Bob, you're meeting with the Frasers this week, are you not?'

'Aye,' he nodded. 'They put in an order and I'm due to get it to them by Friday.'

Dale nodded in response. 'Right. Well, let's see what MacTavish's got for us and then we can decide what the next course of action is.'

Dale watched a shadow pass over his brother's face. Bob always had that sinister look about him when something that could cause trouble was going on. He was always planning to kill someone. Shame he couldn't have been around when Reilly had attacked him outside the casino instead of Ashley. Maybe then she wouldn't be suffering the way she was from the trauma of what happened.

—

An hour or so later, Dale opened the office door to MacTavish. He was standing in the corridor, his face pale with beads of sweat forming on his forehead.

'Come in,' Dale said, stepping to the side and allowing MacTavish space to enter.

As MacTavish stepped inside, Bob spun around on his seat and gave him a smile. Dale shook his head while closing the door. His younger brother always liked to play the role of the intimidator. It seemed to give him a kick.

'Have a seat,' Dale said, gesturing towards a seat. Paul had vacated it and was now standing by the whisky table in the corner.

MacTavish sat down and placed the camera and voice recorder on the desk before sitting back and clasping his hands together on his knee. Dale noted how his left knee trembled. A sign of nerves.

'Hope you've brought what we need,' Bob said.

MacTavish nodded. 'You might want more. But everything I have so far is on there. A brief conversation with Kyle, conversations with the punters about the higher prices and the fact that the product is shite compared to what it used to be. Addresses, names, everything.'

Bob frowned. 'What do you mean, the product is shite compared to what it used to be?'

MacTavish shrugged. 'I don't know. I didn't ask. I just did what I was told.'

Dale puffed out his cheeks and exhaled loudly. 'Right, let's have a look.'

MacTavish slid the devices across the table towards Dale and sat back. He looked nervous, as if he was waiting for someone to tell him he'd fucked up, which he hadn't. The Frasers were the ones who'd fucked up.

Dale lifted the camera to begin with and went through the images on the screen. Everything that MacTavish had said was on there, was staring Dale right in the face: images of punters, none of whom he recognised. It wasn't his job to run the deliveries, do the door-to-doors. That was why he'd hired Kyle and Ian. Other images of the streets, buildings, money collections and the packages themselves were all there.

'Good work, MacTavish,' Dale said, placing the camera on the desk and picking up the voice recorder. He pressed play and listened for several minutes. The first conversation interested him. He listened as Kyle spouted his shit. He kept his eye on Bob as he knew this would rile him. Dale wasn't wrong. As Bob listened, his eyes grew darker and he cracked his knuckles over and over. MacTavish shifted in his seat, giving the impression that the sound was making him uncomfortable.

The recording clicked on to several others involving punters, just like MacTavish had said. The men inside the room were silent for several minutes as they listened, and when the recording stopped, Paul sat a measure of whisky in front of MacTavish and said, 'Here, you've earned this.'

Dale looked up at Paul. 'Aye, he has. But I want more.'

Paul frowned. 'What do you mean, you want more? How much more can he give us? I say we deal with them tonight.'

'I'll second that,' Bob said, getting to his feet and making his way across the office floor and pouring himself a drink.

'I want a confession, of sorts,' Dale replied. 'Obviously, he's not going to come right out to MacTavish and say that he's trying to fuck us over. But I want him to pretty much back himself into a corner. Can you get that on record, James?'

MacTavish stared blankly down at the whisky glass, lifted it, poured the amber liquid down his throat, then said, 'I can't promise anything. But I'll do my best.'

'Aye,' Bob said while lifting a glass of whisky to his lips. 'You better. It's bad enough we're paying those thieving little fuckers for nothing. We won't make that mistake twice.'

Dale shook his head and gave MacTavish a reassuring smile. 'On you go.'

MacTavish got up, retrieved the devices from the desk and left the office. Bob drank greedily from the glass and Dale shot Paul a concerning glance. One wrong move from MacTavish and Bob would put an end to him. When Bob got an idea in his head, there was no changing his mind.

Chapter Thirteen

Getting out of the car at the bottom of Queen Margaret Drive, Angie crossed Great Western Road and headed for The Ailsa Craig Bar. As she approached, she thought about the previous night and her run-in with Cara, and how Kyle seemed desperate to put things right. It seemed necessary for them to meet in an establishment where she would be surrounded by people employed by Bryson Security.

Approaching the steps to the ground-floor bar, the bouncer smiled at her and stepped aside. She didn't recognise this one, but they all knew who she was and she liked it that way. All employees should know their boss, new or not.

'Mrs Bryson?' A low-toned voice came from her left, and as she turned, she was faced by a small man, sporting glasses and a grey suit. He was front-of-house, by the looks of it; he was stood behind a counter with a set of menus and an open diary on top of it. Another employee she didn't recognise.

'Yes,' she said, smiling, then removing her leather jacket and hanging it over her arm.

'There's a Mr Fraser waiting to see you. He's in booth twelve,' the man replied, his eyes wandering up the bar towards the area where Kyle was waiting for her.

Angie thanked the man and headed for booth twelve. A booth where she'd sat with Kyle Fraser before. A long time ago.

As she reached the table, Kyle looked up at her before getting to his feet. He stood, silent for a few seconds before smiling at her. 'Angie. Good to see you.'

Angie narrowed her eyes before sitting down. She slid into the far end of the booth and sat her jacket and bag beside her. Kyle sat opposite; his eyes firmly fixed on hers.

'How long has it been since we last sat here?' Kyle said. There was a suggestive tone to his words, and Angie chose to ignore it.

'Why did you want to see me?'

A smile raised the corner of Kyle's mouth and she remembered that smile from when she knew him before. He was as much a smarmy bastard now as he was then.

'I wanted to apologise on behalf of my wife,' he said. 'I understand there was a bit of a spat last night in here.'

Angie shook her head and raised her eyes to the waitress as she was passing by. 'Fresh orange and lemonade, please. Large, lots of ice.'

The waitress nodded and disappeared behind the bar to make Angie's drink. She watched her go, not wishing to make eye contact with Kyle for any longer than was necessary.

'You feeling rough too?' Kyle smiled.

'Just get to it, Kyle. I don't have all day.'

His expression turned serious. 'I remember a time, back in the day, when you weren't so...' he paused, as if looking for the right word to use, 'severe.'

'Severe?' Angie pulled her lips into a tight line. 'I wouldn't have to be if your wife remembered her place.'

'Yeah,' he sighed. 'Again, sorry about that. I don't know what got into her.'

The waitress returned and placed a pint glass in front of Angie. 'On the house, Mrs Bryson.'

Angie thanked her and turned back to Kyle. He regarded the waitress. He'd noticed that people were acknowledging her as the boss. Not that the Brysons owned the place, but they did own the security firm and supplied the place with bouncers; they worked closely with the owners of all the establishments they supplied security for.

So many words were running through her head at this point. She wanted to ask Kyle what the hell he thought he was playing at, trying to screw the family over. But she couldn't. Kyle Fraser had a way of talking himself out of any situation. He had a certain charm about him, and if she was a stupid little girl now, she could see herself falling for it. Thankfully, Angie was a lot smarter than Kyle gave her credit for. The fact that he'd invited her to meet him alone showed just how stupid he thought she was. Or how intimidated he actually felt about Dale.

'Look, I don't want what happened between you and my wife to get in the way of our business agreement, Angie.'

'Business agreement?' Angie laughed. 'You say it like it's a big thing, Kyle. You deal on our behalf. You deliver our product. That's all it is. It's not as if you're contracted to us. Although we do expect you to be loyal when you work for us,' she said, staring into his eyes. It was a warning, one that she hoped he'd pick up on. If Kyle was careful, things could get resolved. But she knew that wasn't ever going to happen. Kyle Fraser was an opportunist, always had been.

'You know what I mean. I don't want to part from you and Dale on bad terms.'

She kept her expression neutral, not wishing for him to suspect that she knew exactly what he and Ian were up to.

'If you follow our instructions to the dot, then that won't happen.'

Kyle nodded, lifted his beer bottle and took a large mouthful from it. He swallowed hard and Angie noticed how his Adam's apple quivered in his throat.

'So, we're okay, then?' he queried.

Angie leaned back and rested her shoulders against the high-backed seat. 'Yes,' she said. 'But make sure that wife of yours keeps her trap shut, or we'll be forced to pull the plug on your involvement with us. I don't take kindly to someone disrespecting me like that, Kyle. That goes for you too. Understood?'

Kyle nodded swiftly before taking another drink. 'So,' he said, 'how have you been? Married life treating you well?'

'Kyle, don't do that.'

'Do what?' he said, looking around innocently.

'Make small talk with your boss. If we're done here?' Angie rose from her seat.

Kyle tilted his head. 'You like to keep your chats short and sweet, don't you?'

Angie sighed and gripped the frozen pint glass in her hand before taking a drink. 'Short, yes. There's nothing sweet about this. I mean it, Kyle. One step out of line and you and your brother are out. You think I'm here alone? Dale's close by,' she lied. 'And he knows exactly what you're like.'

'And what's that?'

'Opportunistic, misogynistic, to name but two.'

Kyle raised a brow, but a smile remained on his face. He was getting under her skin, and he knew it.

Glancing down at her bag and jacket, Angie lifted them and slid out from the booth. Kyle got to his feet but she didn't wait for him to start moving. Turning her back on him, she moved towards the exit.

–

After she stepped onto the street, she stood at the pedestrian crossing and pressed the button.

'Maybe we could go for a catch-up drink?' Kyle said. He was so close to her; too close. She felt his breath on her ear and an all too familiar feeling washed over her.

'Kyle, if you knew what was good for you, you'd piss off right now.'

'Och, come on. Lighten up, Angie.'

'You know what, it's Mrs Bryson from now on. Have some respect for your employer,' she replied. In her head, she wanted to end that sentence with, *you utter piece of shit*. But instead, she chose not to. He wanted to break her, that's what he did.

70

Focusing on the street in front of her, she saw the green man on the pedestrian crossing flash, and Angie began crossing the road. The sound of the wind at her back distorted her senses and she couldn't tell if he was still behind her. She chose not to turn around to check, she didn't want to see his face, it would only send her into a rage. Getting into a fight with Cara Fraser was one thing, but if she allowed Kyle to push her over the edge, and she lashed out, Dale wouldn't be happy. Especially since he'd told her not to meet him in the first place.

Reaching the car, Angie pulled her keys out of her bag, unlocked the door and climbed inside. Glancing up, she saw that Kyle was still standing at the pedestrian crossing. He hadn't followed her. He'd stayed back at a distance but he could still see her. She shouldn't have gone to see him. She should have listened to Dale.

Starting the car, Angie pulled out of the parking space and turned the car around before heading back up Queen Margaret Drive.

'You're a bastard, Kyle Fraser,' Angie hissed. 'I fucking hate you.'

Chapter Fourteen

Angie parked up outside the back entrance to the casino and breathed a sigh of relief. The further she'd driven away from Kyle Fraser, the more she realised she should have listened to Dale and not gone to meet him. Kyle would have kept her in his company for as long as he could, tried to sweeten her up so that she wouldn't suspect him of trying to fuck her family over. It was stupid of him to think of her as such a fool.

Her thoughts were interrupted by the sound of her phone ringing. Taking it out of her bag, she saw Dale's name flash up and she answered it immediately.

'Hi, I've just pulled up outside. I'll be in in two minutes,' she said. Should she tell him she went to meet Kyle? Would he be angry? Even if he wasn't angry, she decided not to tell him. It was best that way.

Moments later, she was walking along the corridor towards the office when she met Bob coming towards her.

'Hi,' she said, noting his frustrated expression.

'I tell you something, Angie, I can't wait to get my hands around that Kyle Fraser's fucking neck. I'll squeeze the life out of him before the fucking year is out.'

He stopped in front of her and began cracking his knuckles. She considered what he had said, and wondered if it wasn't a bad thing that Bob was so angry. Maybe his anger towards Kyle would work in her favour.

'What's happened?' she asked.

'MacTavish let us listen to some of the recordings. Fucking bastards, honestly. I'd have them thrown off the top of this building right now if Dale would let me,' he replied through gritted teeth. 'Look, I need to go. I'll catch up with you later.'

Angie waved him off and watched him disappear through the double doors leading down to the main area of the casino, before turning and heading towards the office. Opening the door, she stepped inside just as Dale was coming out.

'I'm just off to speak with one of the bouncers. I'll be back in a minute,' he said, kissing her on the cheek before heading out in the same direction as Bob.

'Hey,' Paul said, holding up his glass. 'Drink?'

'Do I look like I need one?'

Angie took off her leather jacket and hung it on the back of the door, before sitting down on one of the chairs at the desk.

'Actually, you do look a bit stressed. What's up?'

Sighing, she shook her head. 'You really don't want to know.'

'Fair enough. You sure you don't want to talk about it?'

'No, I'm fine.'

Paul hesitated, and then said, 'Look, I know there's history there. I don't know why you would put yourself in a situation where you're alone with him after... well, you know what. You don't want him to find out, do you?'

Hearing Paul referring to Angie's past like that sent a chill through her she hadn't felt in a long time. So much time had passed where it wasn't mentioned, because only two people knew about it. And that was the way she wanted it to stay.

Angie frowned. 'Of course I fucking don't. And the fact that you could even ask me that shows how little you know me.'

Paul shook his head. 'I'm sorry. But if Kyle has something he could sink his teeth into – especially about you – then you know he'll never give up.'

Angie felt her face grow hot with anger, because she knew Paul was right. But before she could do or say anything else, a sound in the hall set her on alert. It was close, like shuffling feet on a hard floor. Paul turned sharply and strode towards the door, before pulling it open. And there, standing in front of Paul, staring past him at Angie, was Ian Fraser.

Chapter Fifteen

'What the fuck are you doing here?' Paul said, his fingers gripped around the door handle. Angie could see his knuckles turn white and something in her stomach flipped.

Shit, shit, shit. Ian had overheard their conversation. How could he not?

'I'm here to pick up the orders,' he said, eyeing Angie. 'You know, I could be wrong here, but I could've sworn you two were talking about my brother. What exactly is it that you don't want him to find out about?'

The door at the end of the corridor was thrown open, and loud footsteps echoed outside the office. Ian turned to his right, and immediately shut his mouth.

'What you doing here?' Dale's voice pierced the air. Angie breathed.

'Kyle's busy, I said I'd come for the orders.'

Dale appeared next to Kyle and pushed past him into the office. He looked annoyed. 'Well, next time, you tell Kyle to inform me beforehand. And don't bother your arse to invite yourself up here. You wait down in the casino as agreed and I'll come down to get you.'

Angie glanced at her husband and then back at Ian, whose eyes were once again fixed on her. Whatever he thought, he would tell Kyle. That was the bit between the teeth that Paul was talking about – even though he had no clue, he would stop at nothing to find out. She knew the Frasers would stop at nothing to get one over on them.

74

'Fair dos, boss,' Ian said, holding his hands up in mock defeat. Angie regarded Ian. He was a large man, looked a lot like someone who relied on steroids to achieve his build. Sounded a bit like it too. He was the muscle behind the Frasers, and Kyle was the brains. Not that he had many.

Ian turned his attention to Paul as Dale busied himself getting the orders for Ian ready. He said nothing, merely stared through Paul, a knowing look that sent a shiver down Angie's spine. Whatever he thought, he knew that Angie and Paul were hiding something that involved Kyle.

'Right,' Dale said, slamming the safe door shut and shoving the bag into Ian's hand. 'Do one, eh? I have a meeting in five minutes.'

Ian frowned at Dale, but didn't respond. Based on his size, Angie had expected him to at least draw them all a dirty look. But he didn't. He simply nodded, turned and headed back down the corridor. Angie's heart thudded in her chest and she tried to control her breathing.

'Are you okay, Dale?' Paul said, closing the office door.

'I've just had to convince Bob not to go after Kyle and Ian Fraser. He's fucking livid with what's going on and was about to explode. It's a good thing they didn't bump into each other here or I think Bob genuinely might have killed him on the spot.'

Angie nodded. 'Yeah, he was a bit het up when I met him in the corridor.'

'He'll calm down,' Dale said. 'I've warned him. Going after them too quickly isn't an option. I want enough on them so that I can watch them try to squirm their way out of this.'

Angie stole a glance at Paul, before lifting her bag and getting to her feet. 'Look, I'm going to go. Leave you to get on with things. I've got some stuff to be getting on with myself.'

Dale looked at her, his expression softening. 'Aye, no bother.'

She kissed him and said goodbye to Paul before heading out of the office. She expected Paul to follow, but he didn't.

Instead, he stayed behind with his brother. Angie imagined Paul's conscience getting the better of him, and telling Dale everything. The thought made her move quicker along the corridor and out into the main casino, before pushing through the back door and out to the alley where she'd parked the car. She sucked in large mouthfuls of air and tried to push down the panic that was quickly rising from her stomach to her throat.

Get a grip, she told herself. She couldn't panic. She had to focus.

'Interesting little chat I interrupted up there.'

Spinning around, she stumbled back when she saw how close Ian Fraser was to her. Angie hadn't even heard him approach. Maybe he'd been there already, waiting for her to come out.

'Yeah, well, Dale's a busy man. He doesn't like it when people just randomly appear,' she attempted to lie.

'You know that's not what I'm talking about,' Ian replied.

Breathe, she told herself. 'So, what are you talking about, Ian?'

He lowered his head slightly, and began pacing back and forth, tapping the phone he held in his left hand lightly against his chin.

'You're hiding something from us, something to do with Kyle. What is it?'

'And what exactly do you think we'd be hiding?'

He stopped pacing and glared at her hard. 'No, don't do that. I heard you and Paul talking. I heard what you said. I heard it loud and clear.'

'And what you didn't hear loud and clear was the fact that we're on to you, Ian.' *Shit!* She hadn't meant for that to come out, but she couldn't show him that her words were a mistake; that they'd slipped out in anger. She had to keep going. 'We know what you and Kyle are trying to achieve. And it's not going to work, you hear me?'

Ian stepped forward, almost as though he was squaring up to her. It wouldn't surprise Angie if that, in fact, was what he intended.

'And what are you going to do about it? Because from where I'm standing, Angie, you're in no position to be threatening me, are you? I mean, I could go back up to your husband's office right now, and tell him exactly what I heard.'

Angie nodded and narrowed her eyes. 'You're going to tell Dale that we know what you and Kyle are doing? That you're trying to fuck over the Brysons? Because that's what we were talking about. Fucking hell,' she said. 'You really should lay off those steroids, Ian. They're making you paranoid.'

He said nothing, simply glared back at her. She'd stumped him and she was glad of it. But did he believe her? The paranoia comment could well be true. He could chomp down on this as much as Kyle would have, and not let go.

Ian blinked, and stepped back again. He raised his hand, and pointed a bony finger at her. 'This isn't over, Angie. Not by a long shot. I'm going to tell Kyle about this. And he's going to want to know if what I heard runs deeper than you say.'

Angie stood stock still and watched as Ian turned his back to her and walked towards the main road. She held her breath as he moved further and further away from her, and didn't let it out until he was out of sight.

'Shit,' she hissed. 'Fuck!'

She took her phone out of her bag, located Paul's number and sent him a text.

We have a problem.

Angie got into the car and gripped the steering wheel with both hands.

Her phone sounded in her bag and she took it out. A reply from Paul, which simply read, *I'll sort it.*

Paul was the only one who could sort it. If he involved Bob, it was inevitable that Ian would use what he thought he knew to get out of a violent face-off with them. He'd throw Angie under the bus. And why wouldn't he? If he thought he had something over her, he'd certainly use it.

Staring down at the message, she drew a blank as to what to reply. She simply said thanks to her brother-in-law, knowing that her thanks to him was for lying for her.

Chapter Sixteen

Ian opened the door and the boys ran into his flat, excited and hyper about having pizza while playing on the Xbox. It was all they seemed to want to do these days, she thought.

'I don't think they'd even notice if we weren't here,' Kyle laughed as they went inside.

'Never mind notice, I don't think they'd care. So long as they had pizza and a working games console, they'd be fine,' Ian replied.

Cara smiled and took off her jacket. She hung it over her arm and followed the boys into the living room. She sat down on the sofa and stared blankly at the television screen as the boys loaded up some game that involved zombies. She was physically present, but far away in her mind, worrying about the plan that Kyle and Ian had to take down the Brysons. If she was honest with herself, she had zero faith that they were capable of doing it. Not that she would ever voice that to either of them. It would cause ructions. But what if they did do it; or at least attempted to, and got caught? Where would that leave her and the boys? Because the Brysons would make sure to deal with Kyle and Ian's betrayal.

'Mum?' Ryan's voice bellowed in a sarcastic tone.

She blinked and realised he'd called on her several times before she'd responded.

'Can we get a Domino's Pizza?'

Plastering on her happiest expression, she nodded. 'I'll go through and tell your dad and uncle that's what you want. Pepperoni, I take it?'

Sean nodded frantically. 'And stuffed crust.'

Cara got up from the sofa and headed back out to the hallway. Kyle and Ian were in the kitchen, she could hear them chatting. But the door was closed. Not just closed, but shut tight. They were obviously talking about something they didn't want anyone else to hear. Taking a silent step nearer to the door, she held her breath and listened to the hushed whispers coming from inside.

'Maybe you heard wrong. What could they be hiding?' she heard Kyle say.

'I know what I heard, Kyle. I might be the younger brother but I'm not fucking stupid, or deaf. I'm telling you, they said they didn't want you to find out,' Ian replied.

'Find out what? Did they say anything else?'

'No, they didn't. They were speaking in code. It was as if they knew I was there. Then when I walked in, they stopped talking. The look on their faces when they realised I'd heard something was priceless.'

Cara frowned and stepped closer again, but as she did something caught in her throat and caused a coughing fit. As she coughed and spluttered, she stepped back from the door so that it didn't look as though she'd been listening in on their conversation. The kitchen door was pulled open and Ian was standing in front of her.

'You alright?' he asked, giving her a quizzical look. The kind that asked either, *what are you choking on?* or *were you listening in?*

'Yeah,' she said, clearing her throat, and scolding herself for choking on her own saliva. 'I'm fine. I was just coming to tell you that the boys want Domino's Pizza tonight.'

Kyle squeezed past Ian and stood in front of Cara, staring at her intensely. 'Are you sure you're okay?'

His expression was serious, with a line forming between his brows. He wasn't really asking her if she was okay, he was asking if she'd overheard their conversation. Not that she'd heard anything that could be explained – it sounded as though Ian didn't even know what he'd heard.

'I'm fine,' she said, putting on a gentle yet humourless laugh. 'So, Domino's?'

Kyle nodded. 'Aye, but I won't get it delivered. MacTavish can bring it here. Then we can give him that order you picked up earlier,' he said, turning to Ian.

Something in Cara's head clicked. If Ian had picked up an order, it would have been from the Brysons, which meant that was who they were talking about.

'They want a stuffed crust pepperoni,' Cara said.

Kyle nodded and smiled. 'Right, I'll get onto MacTavish now, then, get him to make the order and bring it here.'

She watched Kyle take out his mobile and disappear into the kitchen again as he called MacTavish. Ian went to move through to where the boys were sitting but Cara threw a hand out and grabbed his wrist. 'Wait,' she said. 'While he's on the phone, I want to ask you something.'

Ian glanced down at Cara's fingers wrapped around his wrist and she instinctively let go. 'Sorry,' she said, keeping her voice low. 'It's just, I heard you both whispering. Is there something else going on that I should know about, other than what you're already doing?'

Ian frowned and eyed Kyle, who was still on the phone. He turned back to her and said, 'What are you on about?'

'I heard you tell Kyle that you'd heard something. Were you talking about the Brysons?'

Ian shrugged, but she could tell that her query was making him nervous as he shuffled from one foot to the next.

'Cara,' he said, leaning in. 'Leave the business stuff to us, okay?'

The condescending tone left her stunned. The way he'd said it was almost as though he didn't think she was capable of handling being involved in their criminal world. If that was the case, she would've left a long time ago. She wasn't particularly opposed to their line of work, just the dangers that came with their plan to screw over the Brysons.

'MacTavish is on his way,' he said, leaning in and kissing Cara's cheek before pushing past her and into the living room to be with the boys.

Ian gave her a smile she didn't like. Another way of patronising her. A look that told her he thought little Cara should be kept in the dark. Then he turned his back on her and went into the room after Kyle.

Chapter Seventeen

James held on to the pizza box with his right hand, and used his left to grip the bannister as he climbed the communal stairs inside the close where Ian Fraser lived. The Frasers had pulled another fast one, getting James to run personal errands alongside picking up the delivery orders.

'Just delivering pizza before picking up the order,' James said quietly, knowing that the voice recorder in his jacket pocket would pick him up. 'Bet I don't get paid extra for this either.'

He reached Ian's front door, rang the bell and waited. The smell of the pizza was making his mouth water. It wasn't as though he could afford a bloody Domino's based on the wage the Frasers were paying him.

Cara Fraser opened the door and stood aside to let him in. 'Hi,' she said, taking the pizza from him. 'They'll be out in a minute.'

James closed the door behind him and stood in the hall. He watched as Cara disappeared through the door to the kitchen and shouted at her sons, telling them that their pizza had arrived. A few seconds later, the boys appeared in the hall and the youngest went straight into the kitchen, but the oldest, Ryan, stopped and stared at James.

'A'right, wee man,' James said.

'Do you work for my dad?' he asked.

James frowned, finding it a bit odd that a young boy would ask such a question out of the blue.

'Erm, aye. Why do you ask?' James replied.

'Are you one of the Brysons?'

James's stomach flipped then, and he wondered how he knew that name.

'No, I'm not one of the Brysons.'

'Are you one of the people who is going to help my dad put the Brysons out of business?'

The shock of the question rendered him silent. This young lad had obviously heard a conversation he wasn't supposed to have heard.

'My dad said we're going to be minted because he'll put the Brysons out of business. You work for my dad, so you *must* know about it?'

James cleared his throat and shook his head. 'No, sorry. I don't know what you're talking about, wee man.'

Ryan tutted loudly and went into the kitchen, leaving his questions ringing in James's ears. Jesus, he thought. The Frasers had just been grassed in by their boy, and his recorder had heard everything.

'MacTavish,' Kyle said, emerging from a room at the other side of the hallway with a bag in his hand. 'My boys got their pizza?'

James nodded, swallowing hard and realising his throat had completely dried up.

'Good,' Kyle said, handing the bag to James. 'Here, all orders in there. You can hand the cash in to us tomorrow. We're having a family night in, so don't come back and disturb us, eh? I'll pay you then.'

James nodded, and as he was about to turn to leave, Ryan emerged from the kitchen with a plate full of pizza in his hand. He didn't look again at James. It was as though he'd forgotten he was there.

'Your boy asked me a strange question while I was waiting for you,' James said.

'Oh aye?' Kyle frowned.

'Aye, he asked me if I was one of the Brysons.' James could tell the question had unnerved him.

'And then when I told him no, he asked if I was helping you to put the Brysons out of business.'

Kyle paused, and then after a few seconds he started to laugh. 'Kids, eh? They've got some imagination.'

James noted the dark shadow that passed over Kyle's eyes. It was a warning. Keep your mouth shut.

'Aye, they do that,' James replied.

Just as James was about to leave, Kyle took a step forward, breaking the personal space barrier between them. Glaring deep into James's eyes, Kyle said, 'You heard nothing, MacTavish. Do you hear me? You forget the Bryson name. It never left my son's mouth. And if anything comes back from this, I'll know who it came from. Do you understand me?'

James nodded rapidly. 'Aye, loud and clear.'

'Good. Now fuck off, get on with your job. And like I said, I'll see you tomorrow.'

James turned and left the flat with the bag in his hand. He remained silent until he was out the main door and across the road.

'If that's not a confession, then I don't know what is.'

Making sure he was out of sight of Ian's flat, he pulled the recorder out of his pocket and hit the stop button. He returned it to the confines of his jacket and took out his phone – the one Dale Bryson had given to him – and called the only number saved on it. It rang just once, before Dale answered.

'MacTavish?'

'Aye, it's me. I've got something that you're going to want to hear,' James said, gripping the bag in his other hand. 'I've got deliveries to do first, though. Just picked the bag up from Kyle. Should I meet you after I've finished?'

He listened as Dale exhaled loudly on the other end of the line, and then said, 'No. Don't do the deliveries. I want to hear what you've got now. I'll send someone to pick you up. Go to the bus terminus at the bottom of the estate and wait behind the disused bothy.'

'Now?' James asked, glancing around him to make sure no one was listening.

'Yes, MacTavish. Now.'

Dale ended the call abruptly and James headed for the obsolete bus bothy at the bottom of Craigton Heights, hoping that it would be Paul Bryson who would collect him, but knowing his luck it would be Bob Bryson who turned up. James wasn't keen on any of the Bryson men, least of all Bob. He was an angry guy, always looking for the littlest excuse to knock someone out. It was as if he was on dodge steroids – his stocky build and angry temperament aroused that suspicion in James.

After a short walk, he reached the bus bothy and stood inside the bus shelter, waiting for whoever was coming to collect him.

He thought about how things would change for him if the task he was doing for the Brysons went to plan. If it did, Dale had promised to make it worth James's time. He wouldn't have to do this anymore, this soul-destroying job of going around the doors in Craigton Heights: taking abuse from the punters because they couldn't or wouldn't pay, because the product was shit compared to how it used to be, didn't hit the same way, and because they were getting less for their money.

James wasn't stupid. He knew exactly what the Frasers were planning. He just hadn't heard them say it out loud, because why would they tell James anything? As far as they were concerned, James hadn't known the Brysons existed until the son brought them up. Which was probably why Kyle had warned James to keep his mouth shut.

A few more minutes passed before a car pulled up in front of the bus shelter. The tinted passenger side window opened, revealing exactly the person James had been dreading.

'You getting in, or are you just going to stand there, gawping at me like an ape?' Bob said.

James moved towards the Audi and climbed in. The car was hot and stank of cigarette smoke. There was an open can of Red Bull in the cup holder and the stench from that also lingered.

'Thanks for picking me up,' James said.

Bob laughed brashly which turned to a hardened smoker-like cough. 'Like you had a choice.'

James refrained from rolling his eyes. He pulled his seatbelt around him and glared up at the top of the high flats which peered across the rest of the estate. The top windows were dark. No one lived in those flats. No one wanted them. They were mainly used as drug dens, and even then, James wasn't sure if they were always occupied in that manner.

'Right,' Bob said, turning the car around. 'Off to see my big brother. I hear you've got some news for him?'

'Aye.' James nodded, feeling for the recorder in his pocket, terrified that he'd lose it.

'Let's hear it, then?' Bob said, keeping his eyes on the road while lifting the can of Red Bull and taking a large mouthful. James watched him from the corner of his eye. The energy drink could explain the glint in Bob's eye. He seemed wired. That, on top of a possible steroid stimulant, it was no wonder he was the way he was.

James pulled the recorder from his pocket and pressed play. He wasn't going to go against anything Bob said.

They both listened to the recording, and when Ryan's voice came through the speaker, and the Bryson name was heard, Bob's expression changed. James expected him to get angry, to grip the steering wheel with white-hot knuckles and put his foot down. But he didn't. Instead, he smiled, nodded and said, 'Good one, MacTavish. That's what I'm talking about. Concrete proof. Ha, imagine being grassed up by your own son. Dale's going to fucking love this.'

James's heart thumped in his chest, a mixture of fear and relief. Fear of being in the car with Bob, who James viewed as an absolute lunatic, but relief that he wasn't angry. An angry Bob Bryson would be enough to scare the grim reaper.

'I'm buying you a large whisky when we get to the casino. You deserve it.' Bob laughed loudly before breaking into a cough again as he gripped James's shoulder and shook him a little in his seat.

'I just want to get this over with,' he replied.

'Aye,' Bob said. 'I'm sure that's what Kyle and Ian fucking Fraser will be saying when we get our hands on them.'

A thought struck James in that moment. If the Brysons were planning on killing the Frasers, then they'd drag James in on it. That was inevitable. They weren't going to let him walk away from this without some kind of insurance. They were gangsters; dangerous bastards. Much more dangerous than the Frasers. Dale and Paul might be the quieter brothers of the family, but James was sure that they all had Bob's mentality. How else would they have got to the top?

A second thought struck him, one that hadn't really crossed his mind before. What if James was caught in the crossfire? What if the Brysons thought that James knew too much, and they did away with him too? They would do whatever they had to to protect themselves, and that meant silencing anyone who could speak out against them. Including James. Should he cut his losses and run, get away before he got in too deep?

Taking a breath, James closed his eyes, and cursed himself for ever getting involved with any of them.

Chapter Eighteen

The five Frasers sat in Ian's living room, while the boys gorged themselves on pizza. They hadn't taken their eyes off the screen, and Cara found it quite fascinating how they could still play the game while eating at the same time.

Kyle and Ian sat back on the sofa, already on their fourth or fifth beer. She could see where this was headed. They'd end up going to the pub. That was a given.

'Let's go out,' Ian said, almost immediately after the thought had entered her mind. 'I think we've got some celebrating to do.'

Kyle turned to Ian. 'That's a bit premature, is it not?'

'Kyle, the punters are massively complaining about the weed and the price. I'd say we've got a week or two before we can start the second stage of the plan and show the punters that we can up our game.'

Cara narrowed her eyes as she listened, then realised that her husband and brother-in-law weren't doing a thing to keep their voices down in front of Ryan and Sean. She gestured for them to follow her out to the hallway. They did, and she closed the door behind them.

'I'd rather you didn't speak so openly in front of the boys, Ian.'

'Why? They'll be in on this in a few years anyway,' Kyle said.

'They're still just kids, Kyle. I'd rather they stayed that way for now,' she said, trying not to show her anger.

Silence hung heavily between them for a moment, before Ian broke through the awkwardness and said, 'So, as I was saying…' He trailed off and led both Cara and Kyle through to the front door and out into the communal space. He moved across the landing to the flat opposite and unlocked the door with a key he produced from his jeans pocket, and allowed Kyle and Cara to enter first. Kyle walked into the flat, a confidence in his stride that told Cara he knew what he was walking into.

'Why do you have a key to the flat across from you?' Cara asked Ian.

'Just call it our office. Welcome, Cara, to the place that is going to make us fucking minted,' Ian said, raising his arms out to the side demonstratively.

Cara took in her surroundings as Ian closed the door, and wondered how the hell she hadn't smelled it before now. Ian must have figured out a way of keeping the smell from travelling throughout the entire flat – or the entire building for that matter.

'It stinks to high heaven in here,' Cara said, almost choking on the sweet scent.

'It smells like money, and lots of it,' Ian said, rubbing his hands together.

Cara's eyes darted between Ian and Kyle. Kyle was smiling widely as he moved towards one of the closed doors, and when he opened it, the smell intensified. Unblinking, she stared into the room, and took a moment to process what she was looking at. As she did, Kyle moved along the hall and opened another door. And then a third, and a fourth.

In each room, the windows couldn't be seen. The entire space was taken up with what Cara could only describe as an insulated tent. Lamps, fans and wires hung above them, and at least forty plants took up the space in the centre of the tent.

'You're using this place as a cannabis farm?' Cara asked.

'We are indeed. These babies only take between sixty to ninety days to grow. These are all at a different growth stage, which means we can harvest them as we go. In doing it this way, it's a quick turnaround for us,' Ian said, as if Cara had asked. 'And

I'll tell you this, the Brysons are none the wiser. You see, these plants are of the finest quality. But here,' he added, pointing to one corner of the room, '*these* plants aren't what you'd call a good smoke. They're shit quality. We purposefully harvest these ones too early.'

'What's the point in that?' Cara asked.

Ian smiled. 'Well, it means that the punters don't get as good a hit as what they pay for. You see, we've been swapping the orders the Brysons have been supplying for our own earlier-harvested plants. We've been upping the price for a shittier product and making sure that the punters are well and truly pissed off. Our plan is to eventually offer them a better product. By doing that, we're cutting the Brysons off at the source. We'll tell them we want out of the game, that we want to go straight. And then we offer up a better product, a better price to the everyday user, and we up our profit.'

Cara felt her jaw drop slightly. 'Are you two off your nut?'

'What?' Kyle said. 'You knew this is what we were doing.'

'I didn't know you had a full-on fucking Mexican drug cartel on the go. Jesus Christ, Kyle. What if the police find this? What if the Brysons find it? You said yourself that Angie is above everyone. Why the hell would you do something so stupid?'

Kyle shook his head and tutted loudly. 'Nice to see you have faith in us, Cara. This is our future, our boys' future. I don't want to be working for the man, I want to be the man. Cannabis is the most popular illegal drug in the UK. Over two million people use it. We want a cut of that, and eventually we'll be able to sell to dealers who will make our money for us. Then we can move onto new business ventures.'

Cara shook her head in disbelief. 'Like what, exactly?'

'Security, taxi firms, nightclubs. The opportunities are endless in this city.'

Cara narrowed her eyes and laughed humourlessly. 'You mean you two want to be just like the Brysons. Give me fucking strength.'

Kyle shot her a look of utter disgust. 'Oi, watch your mouth.'

'Kyle,' she said. 'With all due respect, you're *not* Dale Bryson. You never will be. You two have signed your own death warrants doing this, you know that? And to think you lost the plot at me last night for having a to-do with Angie. Fucking hell, pot, kettle, black. You do remember what happened to that security lad that used to work for them, don't you? Reilly? The rumours are still going around that they murdered him and his body is still missing. Do you want that to happen to you?'

The three of them stood in silence, Kyle and Ian looking a little like disciplined children, but only for a few seconds.

'Och, Reilly was just livid he got the sack,' Ian interjected. 'You don't go after a man like Dale Bryson with a knife in broad daylight and live to tell the tale. We're not fucking stupid like he was. Cara, you don't have anything to worry about. This is all under control. Trust me. In a year, you'll look back on this and wonder what you were worrying about.'

Cara sighed and shook her head. 'I doubt that.'

Turning to leave the flat to check on the boys, Cara stopped when she saw Ryan standing in front of her in the hallway. He was wide-eyed at what he was seeing, and had the same look on his face as Kyle did when they first walked in.

'Wow! What are all these plants?' he asked.

Cara bit her top lip and shot Kyle a look of disgust. 'Never mind,' she said, placing a hand on Ryan's shoulder and turning him to face the door. 'You should be with Sean.'

'Wait, Cara,' Kyle said, rushing around and blocking the door. He glanced down at Ryan and smiled. 'He should know what lies ahead of him.'

'He's just a child, Kyle.'

But it was too late, Ryan was already under his dad's spell, moving away from under her grip and into the room she'd just been standing in. She stood in reluctant silence as Kyle showed their older, more impressionable son what he was looking at, explaining how this was what was going to set them up for life and that one day, it would all be Ryan and Sean's.

'What is all this, Dad?' Ryan asked, seemingly amazed by what surrounded him.

Cara watched a look of pure joy cross Kyle's face as he started to explain. There was nothing she could do or say to stop it from happening.

Kyle wrapped an arm around Ryan's shoulders and walked him further into the flat. 'This, my boy, is your future. One day, this will all be yours, and most likely on a bigger scale. You're going to be part of a family business that will see us make enough money to set us up comfortably for the rest of our lives. When me and your uncle are gone, you and Sean will inherit all of this, and you'll keep it going.'

Cara saw the look on her son's face. He'd been captivated by it all – by his dad's words. It wouldn't matter if Cara explained the dangers to him now, it was too late.

'Really, Dad? This is all ours?' Ryan asked. 'But what is it?'

'Cannabis, Ryan. People pay big money for it.'

'Why?'

'Lots of reasons. But that doesn't matter. All we want to know is that people *are* buying it and that we're making a profit.'

Ryan had barely blinked the entire time, and Cara felt desperate. She wanted to go and check on Sean, but she didn't want to leave Ryan inside a cannabis factory with his dad and uncle. Not that what she wanted would make a blind bit of difference now. What she wanted was out the window. All she could do now was go along with things, and hope that they came out the other end unscathed.

She stood with her back to the front door and watched as son and father bonded over the drug factory Kyle and Ian had created, and she felt utterly helpless and clueless. It was one thing for Kyle to want to make money by doing a bit of dealing, but it was something else entirely involving the kids. She loved Kyle more than anything, but this plan was going to put them all in danger, and there was nothing she'd be able to do to get them out of it.

She'd imagined something different for her life and for her children. Falling for a bad boy wasn't something her parents had approved of, coming from a more middle-class background. When she'd married Kyle, her parents were so strongly against it that they disowned her. They'd never met the boys and in fact she had no idea where her parents lived now. Staring into the flat, she realised this was the kind of thing they'd have wanted Cara to avoid.

'I'm going to check on Sean,' she said. Turning, she opened the door and stepped onto the landing, before closing the door behind her quietly. She exhaled slowly, and wondered how long it would be before someone would report the smell; how long it would be before the police, or the Brysons came knocking.

Chapter Nineteen

Conor and Ashley were sitting opposite each other in the games room, staring mindlessly at the screen as Conor played FIFA. Ashley seemed like she was away in her own world, very distant from the present. A bit like how Angie was feeling right now. All sorts of nightmarish scenarios swirled around in her head. Ian *would* have told Kyle by now that Angie and Paul had a secret they didn't want Kyle to know about. What was to stop Kyle pursuing the matter? His nose might get the better of him? Or worse, Ian might want to push it.

As much as it weighed on her mind, Angie couldn't think of that right now. She had a daughter to help, a son to look after.

'What do you two fancy doing tonight?' Angie asked, trying desperately to take her mind away from things.

Conor shrugged and without taking his eyes off the screen said, 'This. And maybe a takeaway?'

'Ashley?' Angie pressed, noticing that her daughter hadn't reacted. She'd barely moved the entire time they'd been sitting in front of her.

'I don't mind,' Ashley replied softly. But Angie's attention was pulled from her daughter toward her phone. A message had pinged through, and as Angie stared down at the screen, she froze. It wasn't from Paul. It was from Kyle.

I hear there's something you don't want me to know. Any ideas what that could be?

For a second, she couldn't breathe. Couldn't think. A surge of adrenaline coursed through her and it felt like all the blood in her body had rushed to her head.

She picked up the phone with a quivering hand and thought about how to reply. Should she reply at all? Or should she just send the message on to Paul?

Her thumbs hovered over the screen, and then she simply typed,

Nothing we didn't discuss at the pub.

Almost immediately, her phone started to ring, and when it vibrated, she almost dropped it. Ashley looked up from her blank stare at the television and she frowned.

'I'm so clumsy,' Angie said, attempting a laugh as she leaned forward to retrieve the phone from the floor. She saw the name on the screen. Kyle Fraser. She ended the call and put her phone on silent. Just like she thought, he was going to pursue this, even though to him it could be nothing.

'Mum, can I ask you something?' Ashley said. Angie gripped the phone in her hand and took a breath.

'Of course you can, sweetheart. What's up?'

Ashley blinked, and then sat forward. 'Do you think Reilly was scared that day? Do you think he knew he was going to die?'

Shit, Angie thought. Here she was, sitting on the sofa, worrying about herself, and the whole time her daughter was wondering about someone else's pain.

Angie got up from the sofa and moved across the room. Sitting down next to Ashley, she took her daughter's hand gently in her own and gave it a reassuring squeeze. 'He died very quickly, sweetheart. I doubt he felt a thing, or knew anything about it.'

Conor paused his game and put the controller to the side. 'Don't think about it, Ashley. The guy was trying to hurt Dad.'

He put a hand on his sister's shoulder and for a second, Angie felt tears begin to threaten.

Yeah, she thought. Worst fucking mum in the world.

'I'm going to go and see what takeaway menus we have. You can choose what you want and I'll get it ordered.'

She squeezed Ashley's hand again before letting go and getting to her feet, then left the games room and pulled the door closed behind her, letting out a breath and swallowing hard. She couldn't cry in front of the kids.

Angie moved through to the kitchen, opened the drawer under the microwave and pulled out a handful of takeaway menus. Her phone vibrated silently in her hand and she swore under her breath.

'Kyle, just fuck off,' she hissed, hitting the end call button. Her voice cracked on the last word, and tears pooled.

Slamming the phone down on the kitchen counter, Angie placed both hands flat on the cold surface and tried to compose herself. A few deep breaths, then she would contact Paul. As she breathed in and out, her phone vibrated again but this time, only once. A message on the screen told her she had a voicemail and her stomach leaped.

She didn't want to listen to the message. His voice – the words he had to say – could only spell disaster for her and her family. The one who would come away worst from this was going to be Conor. She absolutely couldn't allow that to happen.

Picking up the phone, she placed it to her ear and listened to the short message.

'Angie – sorry, Mrs Bryson,' he said, although she detected sarcasm in his tone. 'I'm curious to know what it is that Ian thinks he heard. I'd like to meet to discuss things.'

The line went dead and Angie shook her head. He would be loving this, tormenting her. He could leave this alone, considering Ian pretty much heard nothing. But this was a way Kyle could try to get close to Angie. And she had to remind herself that she was his boss and that Dale would put a bullet in him if he thought Kyle was harassing her.

Breathe, she told herself. He has nothing on you.

Chapter Twenty

Leaving the boys with Kyle and Ian's mum wasn't something that Cara ever found easy. Moira was old school, the type for whom kids should be seen and not heard. Ryan and Sean had never liked her much, but they didn't have much choice. She was their only grandparent. Kyle and Ian's dad had abandoned Moira when they were barely toddlers, leaving her to look after them on her own. Cara often wondered if that was the reason she was so bitter towards them, and her grandsons. She possibly resented them, blamed them for the reason she was alone. When she'd tried to voice her concerns to Kyle about Moira – and the fact that she was always telling the boys to be quiet, leave her in peace, stop moaning or she'd give them something to moan about – he would brush it off. He'd tell her that there was nothing wrong, and that he and Ian had turned out fine having her as a mother, so the boys being with her for a few hours wouldn't do any harm.

They entered the local pub, The Bellpark Arms, and as rarely as Cara visited the place, she wasn't surprised to see how busy it was. It was a Saturday night after all. The Bellpark Tavern was just about the only pub in the entire Glasgow area that didn't have its security supplied by the Brysons, hence why Kyle and Ian drank there.

They took a seat at the back wall which allowed them to be able to see the entire pub. Franz Ferdinand's 'Take Me Out' was blasting from the speakers and Cara could already see Kyle and Ian were up for a long night. One that would consist of copious amounts of alcohol and most likely, the odd line here and there.

'Right, I'll get the first round in. What's your poison?' Ian asked, getting to his feet, reaching into his pocket and producing his wallet.

'I'll have a whisky,' Kyle replied.

'White wine for me,' Cara said, trying to paint a smile on her face. She watched as Ian made his way to the bar. He walked with an attitude, like he owned the place. Knowing Ian, she wondered if that would one day be his plan. He and Kyle were so sure that they were going to get away with fucking the Brysons over. Maybe they would – however, it was unlikely.

A few moments later, Ian returned to the table with a tray of drinks, plus six shot glasses filled with tequila. She didn't have to ask to know, she could smell it.

'Right,' Ian said, placing the tray down on the table carefully and smiling at Cara and Kyle. 'Take one.'

Kyle didn't hesitate. He picked up a shot glass before holding it up. Cara reluctantly chose one, although she had no intention of drinking it. The last time she drank tequila, she was in bed for three days afterwards.

'Here's the fucking Frasers!' Ian shouted over the live band playing on the stage at the opposite side from where they were sitting. 'And fuck anyone who tries to get in our way.'

Kyle laughed and raised his own glass. 'Aye, too fucking right, bro.'

Cara watched as they knocked the tequila back greedily. She tried to smile, but it wasn't working. She couldn't bring herself to do it. They were drawing attention to their table. There would be at least one person in this place who knew the Brysons. Ian and Kyle's rowdy toast would get back to them, and they'd start asking questions.

'Straighten your face, Cara, eh?' Kyle whispered into her ear. 'We fucking deserve to celebrate what's coming.'

Cara shot him a look and faked a smile. 'How's that for you? Straight enough?'

Kyle drew his eyes away from her and picked up a second shot glass before knocking it back. He shivered and laughed loudly, as did Ian. They shook hands and gave each other one of those triumphant hugs, the kind men give each other when they've achieved something. Not that they'd achieved anything yet.

'Look,' Cara said, 'I just think that we should be keeping as low a profile as possible right now. You've not even made the transition from working for them to working for yourselves and you're already toasting the occasion. And you're not exactly being quiet about it, Kyle.'

Ian laughed and picked up his pint glass. 'Och, calm down, Cara. We're almost there.'

'Aye,' Kyle said. 'Just relax. It's all fine.'

'I just think we should be exercising as much caution as possible,' Cara replied. 'It's important for our future, for the boys' futures.'

'No, what's important for our boys' futures is security. We need to go our own way, Cara. And we're doing it now. Fucking hell, if you had it your way, we'd be living in a fucking bunker underground. What are you so scared of?'

She glared at him, unable to hide her anger. Picking up her wine glass, she took a large mouthful and swallowed hard. 'If I'm not wrong, you were the one who thought you had to go and apologise to the Brysons on my behalf. Now you're the one acting as if they're nobodies.'

Kyle shook his head and picked up his own pint. She knew this conversation wasn't heading anywhere other than an argument. Just as Kyle opened his mouth in retaliation, Cara's phone rang in her pocket. Sliding it out and into her hand, she saw it was Moira calling. Usually, she'd be cursing the woman. They'd only been out half an hour and already she was phoning to complain about the boys. But in that moment, Cara welcomed the call. She needed to get out of the pub, away from Kyle and Ian. If they were going to draw attention to themselves, then she didn't want to be a part of it. If she wasn't there, and something happened, then at least she wasn't involved.

Cara answered the call and placed a finger in her opposite ear. 'Moira? Everything okay?'

She could barely hear her mother-in-law on the other end, so Cara got up from her seat and pushed her way through the pub and out to the street.

'Sorry, Moira. What did you say?'

'I *said*, these boys are absolute hooligans. I've had enough. You'll need to come back here, they're out of control.'

As much as Cara was glad to be getting out of sitting with Kyle and Ian while they got drunk and said too much, she couldn't help but roll her eyes.

'What do you mean, they're out of control?'

'They're refusing to go to bed. Telling me that they get to stay up late on a Saturday, refusing to go and brush their teeth. Honestly, Cara, you'd think they were feral.'

Shaking her head, Cara looked at her watch. It was only eight thirty. No wonder they were refusing to go to bed.

'It's still early, Moira.'

'No. No it's not. It's well past their bedtimes. In my day, Kyle and Ian were in bed by seven o'clock. And what's all this computer game stuff. Zombies and violence. It's shocking to see them exposed to it.'

'Right, Moira. I get it. I'll come home.'

Cara hung up before she said something she'd later regret, and realised that Moira was the reason Kyle and Ian were the way they were. She'd wrapped them in bubble wrap as kids, never let them do anything, or take risks. It seemed that they were the feral ones, based on their plans.

She headed into the pub and straight for Kyle and Ian, who were drinking Cara's shots. 'I'm heading back. The boys won't settle for your mum and she's doing her nut at me. I'll see you when you get home?'

Kyle raised a brow and then shook his head. 'Honestly, it's a wonder we were even born. Aye, fine, I'll see you later.'

Cara lifted her wine glass and drank back the remainder before heading out for a taxi. As she headed home, she thought about how the night might unfold at the pub. If Kyle and Ian kept drinking, they'd only get louder. And they'd lose their inhibitions. They weren't stupid by any means, but they were also overly confident, and that, mixed with alcohol and possibly drugs, worried Cara.

Chapter Twenty-One

He couldn't help but pace the floor as he waited for Bob to bring MacTavish to the casino. This was it, the moment he'd been waiting for. He was going to make sure the Fraser brothers knew who they'd crossed. Dale had an idea of how to make them beg for mercy and forgiveness. Hanging them off the top of a building whilst holding a gun to their heads satisfied his imagination. Or maybe something a little less conspicuous? Poisoning, or perhaps a traffic accident?

Just as he pictured how he'd end them, Bob entered the office with MacTavish at his back. MacTavish was carrying a bag and had a worried expression on his face. Bob was wired, Dale could tell just by looking at him. High on coke, or speed most likely. Not the way Dale liked him to conduct his business, but all the same, he got MacTavish to the office and that was all that mattered.

'Bro, you're going to fucking love this, I tell you,' Bob said, smacking MacTavish on the shoulder and shunting him towards the desk. 'Go on, show him what you showed me.'

MacTavish cleared his throat and placed the recorder on the table. Dale glanced down at it and then up at Bob in suspicion. 'You've heard this already?'

Bob nodded emphatically. 'Oh, I've heard it alright.'

Dale lifted the device and pressed play. As he listened, he couldn't believe what he was hearing. Kyle Fraser's son had landed his dad right in the middle of a huge pile of shit and hadn't even realised it.

'Fucking hell,' Dale said as the recording ended. He glanced at MacTavish and nodded. 'That's it. You did your job. You can go now.'

MacTavish's brow furrowed. 'That's it?'

'Aye, that's it. You've done your bit. Don't worry, you'll get paid like I said.'

MacTavish nodded slowly, then lifted the bag. 'What do I do about this?'

Dale looked at it and shrugged. 'What is it?'

'Your orders. Do I still deliver them?'

Dale was quiet for a moment as MacTavish held the bag in the air. Meanwhile, Bob had sat down on the opposite side of the desk to Dale and was smiling menacingly. He had in his head what he wanted to do to the Frasers, and was likely going over it again and again.

'Can I see that for a minute?' Dale asked, holding out his hand.

MacTavish handed him the bag and sat down on the seat next to Bob. Dale opened it and pulled out the envelopes – the ones he'd handed to Kyle earlier that day. There was something off about them. The seal was loose, as if it had been tampered with. Not ripped, but maybe steamed open and then resealed.

'Are you seeing what I'm seeing?' Dale said to Bob.

'What?' Bob said, getting to his feet and taking a closer look.

'This package has been opened.'

Dale looked inside the bag at the other packages and pulled them out one at a time. They were all the same. Going back to the first package, Dale ripped the envelope open and pulled out the contents before dropping them on the table.

'Dirty bastards,' Bob hissed.

'What's wrong?' MacTavish asked.

Dale shook his head and gritted his teeth. 'These aren't the buds we harvested. I don't know how or where, but it looks like the Frasers have fucked us even more than we realised. They're growing their own supplies – shit ones at that. And they're swapping our product for their own and hiking the price.'

Dale watched as MacTavish leaned down to take a closer look. He picked up the buds in his hands and sniffed them, then said, 'That's why the punters are complaining.'

'I'll fucking kill them,' Bob said, punching his fist into the desk. 'Dale, we need to deal with this right now.'

Dale held his hand up and shook his head. 'Just wait, Bob. We can't rush in.'

'Are you kidding? These bastards have been screwing us for fuck knows how long. And you want to wait?'

MacTavish placed the buds back down on the table and eyed Dale. 'What do I do?'

'Nothing. You do nothing. You leave this bag with us, you go home and you cut all contact with the Frasers. Do you understand?'

MacTavish and Bob both gave Dale a look of horror.

'I can't just cut ties with them. They know where I live. When I don't turn up with the takings tomorrow, they'll come looking for me.'

'You've got that gun I gave you?'

MacTavish nodded slowly, and Dale saw the look of realisation cross his face.

'Nah, you're not letting MacTavish do the honours. I want to see the life leave their bastard eyes, Dale,' Bob hissed.

'And you'll get them,' Dale said, feeling a sense of calm wash over him. He glanced at MacTavish again. 'Go home. Now. I'll call you on that mobile if you need to know what's going on. Otherwise, keep your head down and keep your mouth shut. Got it?'

MacTavish nodded, his expression telling Dale he was reluctant to go along with this. But Dale wasn't giving him a choice.

MacTavish left the office and Bob followed him to the door, closing it behind him.

'Right, get Paul on the phone. He needs to hear this,' Dale said, staring down at the buds on the table and the bag sitting next to it. 'We need to come up with a plan that will put the Frasers in the ground and keep our names out of it.'

Chapter Twenty-Two

Cara Fraser opened her eyes to the sound of someone knocking on the door. Having gone back to Ian's flat the night before to relieve Moira of her babysitting duties, Cara had decided to take the boys home. She had fallen asleep on the couch around two in the morning, after having tried several times to get in contact with Kyle to see if he had keys to get in. She hadn't got hold of him, or Ian for that matter.

The knocking continued for a brief second and then changed to a gentle tapping. She sat up and checked the time on her phone. It was seven in the morning. Shaking her head, Cara got to her feet and made her way through to the hallway quickly so that the sound wouldn't wake the boys.

'Drunken bloody idiots,' Cara whispered as she unlocked the front door and opened it, fully expecting Kyle and Ian to be propping each other up in a drunken mess having staggered out of a nightclub or a house party. But when she saw the police standing there, she frowned.

'Can I help?' Cara asked as her heart began to bang hard in her chest.

'Are you Cara Fraser?'

Her eyes darted between the two officers. One short, one tall. Both male. Neither had their hats on.

'What's this about?' she asked, folding her arms across her body defensively.

'May we come in?' the short officer asked, taking a step forward.

Cara instinctively stepped back and allowed the officers to enter. Narrowing her eyes, she frowned. 'He's got himself arrested, hasn't he? For God's sake, he can't even go to the pub for a bloody drink without getting himself into trouble.'

The taller officer glanced down at his colleague and then back at Cara. 'My name is PC Bolton and this is my colleague, PC James. I'm afraid we have some bad news. Is there somewhere we can sit down?'

Cara's throat constricted, but instead of saying anything, she closed the front door quietly, and made her way through to the living room. The officers stood in the middle of the room as she shut the door, desperate not to wake the boys. She feared the worst, and didn't want them to hear what was inevitably about to come out of the mouths of the officers.

Turning to face them, she felt her face begin to tighten as her eyes pooled with tears.

'Please, take a seat, Mrs Fraser,' one of them said. Cara couldn't remember who was who.

'He's dead, isn't he?' Her voice cracked. 'My husband. He's dead?'

'I'm so sorry, Mrs Fraser.'

The words echoed around her, before a white noise took over as she fell to the floor. The pooling tears disappeared, and were replaced with a ball of emotion in her throat that she couldn't get out. She wanted to scream, but something stopped her. The boys, asleep in their beds.

'What happened?' she asked, glancing up at them.

'We're not certain, but we can tell you that a car registered to a Mr Ian Fraser was found in the reservoir. Two men were inside. I'm so sorry.'

Cara gasped loudly, and this time the tears came. They cascaded down her cheeks and she sobbed. One of the officers crouched down and placed a hand on her shoulder. The sound of the livingroom door opening made her turn, and Ryan was standing there, staring down at her.

She could tell by the look on his face that he knew what had happened. He'd heard the officer's words.

Stretching out her hand to her elder son, she watched his little face lose its colour and his eyes glaze over.

'Is Dad gone?'

His soft little voice struck her, and another wave of emotion washed over her. She couldn't speak; simply nodded as Ryan rushed to her and into her arms. They both sobbed silently.

Part Two

Now/2021

Chapter Twenty-Three

Ryan sat on the opposite sofa from his mum. She drank back the last of her coffee and watched him through narrowed eyes, then gave a smile. 'You're quiet. Everything okay?'

'Just thinking about the last time we lived here, how different things were,' he sighed.

Cara inhaled loudly and set her cup on the coffee table. 'I know. It is strange being back. But you know, we come from Glasgow. Born and raised, why shouldn't we feel like we want to come home. I for one am not going to let anyone make me feel like I don't belong here.'

Ryan nodded. His mum was right. Glasgow was in his blood, in his bones. Just like it had been with his dad and uncle.

They'd only been back in Glasgow a month, but for Ryan Fraser, it felt like they'd never left. He, his mum and brother had chosen to move back to the city together, having lived in Aberdeen for eight years. Cara had moved them away after his dad and uncle had been murdered.

'You miss him, don't you?' she asked, her voice barely audible.

'Every single day,' Ryan replied, trying not to allow the emotion to creep up on him. 'It's easier for Sean, he was sheltered a lot from what happened.'

'That's thanks to you. You looked after us, Ryan. You looked after me. And you were only thirteen when I moved us all away. You shouldn't have had to deal with that and I'm sorry I put you through it.'

'It wasn't your fault, Mum. You didn't kill them. It was…' he let his words trail off. He couldn't bear to say the name out loud, it would send him into a rage, one that he had to control. 'We had every right to come home. There's more for us here.'

Cara nodded and smiled.

Once they'd decided to come back to Glasgow, Ryan had made sure to secure a job for himself and Sean, working as doormen in a local snooker hall. The pay wasn't awful, but it certainly wasn't brilliant either. The good thing about being back in Glasgow was that he felt closer to his dad, Kyle, not to mention getting to know his home city again – although it did bring back some bad memories. There was one in particular that sat heavily on his chest and in his gut; one that caused a level of guilt he didn't think was possible. Ryan pushed the thought from his mind. He couldn't deal with it right now.

'How's the job going?' Cara asked, relaxing her shoulders and sitting back on the sofa.

'Not too bad, it's money and an insight into what goes on in the city these days,' he replied. 'What about you?'

Cara chortled. 'It's a cleaning job, Ryan. It is what it is. Nothing like the life I used to have when we lived here before.'

Ryan often wondered what her life was like back when he and Sean were still kids. She was the wife of a gangster; a man who was determined to go places without being told how or where. She'd have lived a very different existence. Not that she ever really talked about it – it still must've been too difficult, or perhaps not a topic she wanted to divulge to her sons.

'But you're settled in?' Ryan pushed.

'You don't have to worry about me, Ryan. There is nothing that will turn me to the bottle again. You won't have to take responsibility for me ever again. I promise, I'm fine.'

'I can't help but worry about you. You're the only parent I have left.'

Cara gave a gentle smile, and Ryan knew her words were genuine. Bringing his mum back to Glasgow was always a risk, but it was something that his dad would have wanted.

Having been the lead in their move back home, Ryan had chosen to rent himself and Sean a flat to share, and he'd sorted one for Cara too. They weren't too far away from her. It was the first time that he'd really left her side for any length of time since his dad had been killed. He trusted that she would be okay, he'd seen real progress in her sobriety.

Being back in the city, Ryan had done his research. The place looked the same; smelled the same. It seemed the Bryson family still owned most of the city too, with more and more businesses turning up in their name: construction, taxi, security companies. The snooker hall was about the only place they didn't provide security for, which was why Ryan had gone for the job. He didn't want the Brysons hearing the Fraser name and becoming suspicious that there was a link back to his dad and uncle. It was too risky.

'Look, I'm going to go home. I've still got some unpacking to do and I fancy an early night,' Cara said.

Before Ryan could answer, Sean appeared in the living room. 'You're going already?' he asked.

'Yeah, but I'll see you both tomorrow?'

Sean nodded and gave his mum a hug as she stood up.

'Bye, boys, see you soon,' she said, kissing Sean on the forehead. She didn't do the same with Ryan. Instead, she gave him a smile before Sean saw her to the door.

Ryan felt guilty about having lied to his brother for all these years. He'd kept the truth about what really happened to their dad from him, but for good reason. But today would be the day that he would come clean. Now that Sean was a man, Ryan could tell him the truth about what happened.

–

Ryan Fraser clicked on every link as he scrolled down the search results. Eight years on, he'd thought the anger and grief would have eased, but it had only increased the older he became and the more he understood. There were pros and cons to living in a world where technology was readily accessible. It meant that every detail you wanted was there if you knew where to find it – however, that wasn't always a good thing. It meant that if you didn't want to know certain things, they were rammed down your throat anyway.

'Want a beer?' Sean asked. Without waiting for his older brother to respond, he sat the bottle of Peroni down next to Ryan as he stared at the screen, before taking a seat next to him and glancing over the text and images on the screen himself.

'This is all stuff we already know, Ryan. Why are you bothering to torture yourself with it?' Sean asked, slurping loudly from his bottle.

Ryan sighed and shook his head before turning to face Sean. 'We were kids back then, Sean. More so you than me. You were protected a lot more than I was from what happened. And you were more naïve because you were still blissfully ignorant. I heard Mum sobbing every night. I managed to stop you hearing that. I saw her crack open the voddy and tank half a bottle every single night, while you were upstairs on the PlayStation. I got rid of the evidence so you didn't have to see the empty bottles or smell the vomit.'

Sean held the bottle to his lips but his eyes were fixed on Ryan. 'Why the fuck did you never tell me this?'

'Because I was protecting you from it all. That's what big brothers do.'

Sean stood up from the seat and crossed the bedroom. 'So what's changed? Why are you bringing all this up now, eight years later?'

Ryan kept his eyes on the screen, wishing that things didn't have to be this way. But he'd always promised himself that when he was old enough, he'd take revenge for what happened to his dad and uncle.

'We grew up without our dad. Do you really understand what happened to him and Uncle Ian, Sean? Because if you don't, then I'm going to have to explain it to you.'

'Of course I fucking know what happened to them. They were murdered.'

Ryan nodded. 'Aye, but do you really know what happened? Or have you shut yourself off to it? I didn't have that luxury as a kid. I had to look after Mum in the aftermath because there was no one else to do it.'

Sean stood still, staring at his brother. A pang of guilt hit Ryan; he really had kept his younger brother in the dark about everything. Sean had no real clue what had gone on.

'It's time you knew what really happened, Sean. You've been kept in the dark long enough.'

'I'm not in the dark. I know what happened. They were murdered and the scum that was on trial was found guilty and sent away.'

Ryan nodded. 'That's what the media and the courts say. But you don't know the ins and outs, Sean. And I'm going to put you in the know, so that when I'm finished, you'll be where I am right now.'

Sean frowned. 'What are you on about, I'll be where you are right now?'

'You'll be ready to do what the courts didn't. You'll help us to get our own form of justice.'

Sean smirked, as if he wasn't taking Ryan seriously. 'Revenge? Fuck off, Ryan. This isn't some American mafia movie. It's real life. How are we meant to get revenge if the fucker's already in prison?'

Silence hung between them as Ryan allowed Sean to process the conversation. Eight years ago, they'd lost two of the most important people in their lives, suddenly and brutally. And because of that, Ryan had lost a part of himself, and his childhood from having to care for their mother and keep Sean from hearing horrific details no eleven-year-old should be exposed to.

'The person who killed our dad and uncle isn't in prison, Sean. The guy was set up.'

Sean glared at Ryan and started to laugh. 'Are you hearing yourself? This is beyond nuts, Ryan. How could you even come up with something like that?'

Ryan kept his face dead straight, staring at his naïve younger brother and actually wished that he was making all of this up. But he wasn't. It was all true.

'Because I went to see James MacTavish in prison.'

Sean's light expression turned sour. 'When the fuck did you do that?'

'Couple of months ago. Something was niggling in the back of my head. I needed to understand why he did it, what made him want to put a bullet in both their heads and then release the handbrake so their car rolled into that reservoir.'

'And he fed you a bullshit line that he was innocent? Of course he fucking did, Ryan. That's what guilty people in prison do. If there is any way they can get out of there, then they'll do or say anything.'

Ryan was shaking his head. 'No, you couldn't be further from the truth.'

'And neither could you. Fucking hell, Ryan. What are you trying to do to me here? Our dad is dead. The guy who did it is in prison where he fucking well belongs. Leave it alone. Or you're going to end up dragging me and Mum down with you. Do you really want her to go through everything again?'

Ryan sighed. This was exactly how he'd reacted at first after hearing MacTavish's story from across that visitor's table.

'Ask her.'

'Ask who what?' Sean replied, almost venomously.

'Ask Mum about it. She knows about this too. And she believes him.'

Sean got to his feet and started to pace the room, his eyes wide and darting from one side to the other. He was shaking his head. 'Nah, this isn't happening. Are you trying to tell me that you've been sitting on this for a month and you haven't said a fucking word to me? Either of you?'

'That's why I'm telling you now.'

Picking up an empty beer bottle, Sean threw it with force across the room and it smashed against the wall, showering the carpet in shards of glass.

'Calm down, bro,' Ryan said.

'I want to speak to him. MacTavish. I want to speak to him now!'

Chapter Twenty-Four

There was a loud shrill ringing in her ears as she cradled Jack, her youngest son. Angie could barely hear anything. She locked eyes with her daughter, Ashley, who sobbed in silence.

'It's okay,' Angie mouthed. 'It's stopped.'

The gunshots had fallen away, and everyone remained on the floor. Just as she was about to turn to Dale to see if he was okay, her blood ran cold when he cried out:

'Fuck, no! Bob!'

She turned her head, straining her neck and not daring to get up in case the shooter opened fire upon seeing her. What she saw was something she would never be able to unsee.

'Bob! Talk to me!' Dale shouted as he crawled across to Bob, who was already in Paul's arms.

'Oh my God,' Ashley gasped.

Angie watched as the Bryson men, including her eldest, Conor, went to Bob to check him over. He'd been hit in the chest, not once but twice. Blood soaked his wedding suit, and his face had lost all of its colour. Angie knew just by looking at him that he wasn't going to make it, his shallow breathing alongside the blood loss told her he was on the way out, but she couldn't bring herself to believe it.

The way she cradled Jack, he couldn't see what was going on. She needed to get him out of the conservatory, away from the horrors that no child should ever have to see.

'Ashley, I need you to take Jack out of here. Now. Can you do that?' Angie said, her words clear and firm. The sound of sirens in the background told Angie that the police were already on their way. Someone from the hotel reception would have called them. Firearms would be en route, along with some officers that were likely on the Bryson payroll.

Ashley's eyes were fixed on the men, and a look of sheer terror crossed her face.

'Ashley, look at me! I need you to focus. You need to get your brother out of here. I need you to take him up to the room. He doesn't need to see this, and neither do you.'

Ashley blinked, and her eyes fell on Angie. 'Mum…' her voice trailed off. Angie knew what her daughter was thinking. Back to when she was just a kid herself and she'd witnessed her dad's attack.

'It's okay. You're both going to be safe if you take Jack upstairs.'

The sirens grew closer, louder. Jack began to sob and clung tighter to Angie.

'Bob, wake up!' she heard Paul say. 'Dale, apply pressure. We need to stop the bleeding.'

Although Jack couldn't see what was going on, she knew he'd understand what was happening. He was a bright kid, and old enough to comprehend his uncle's words.

Ashley reached across and pulled her brother into her arms. He didn't resist, and as he moved into his sister's embrace, Angie noticed that he had his eyes closed – but not just as if he was asleep. He had them shut tight, keeping out the scenes around him. She was glad.

The police were in the building, she could hear their boots on the floor, hear their voices calling out. Almost immediately, they were in the conservatory, and Angie felt a sense of relief. If the shooter was out there, they'd have seen them arrive and will have done a runner.

'He's dead, Dad,' Conor's voice pierced the air.

Angie turned, and forced herself to look down at her brother-in-law. Conor was right. Bob's eyes stared up at the glass ceiling, wide and still. The light had gone out of them.

Paul fell silent. But Dale's voice erupted from his throat, letting out a sound that Angie had never heard before.

Today was meant to be a day of celebration as Angie and Dale renewed their vows after twenty years of marriage. Now, her husband cradled his dead brother; his *murdered* brother. She went to him, knelt down in her white dress and put her arms around him as he sobbed. His loud, angry sounds vibrated through her chest and she felt every shred of pain he did.

Glancing at Conor, she reached out and grasped his hand, which was soaked in his uncle's blood. Glancing down, she noticed her dress was spattered too.

Angie, Dale, Paul and Conor sat with Bob, and all the while, all Angie could think about was who it was that had killed him.

'I'll make sure the city streets are soaked in the blood of the bastard who did this to you, Bob,' Dale said, his voice low and deep. 'I will burn down every fucking house to find the bastard. I promise.'

Chapter Twenty-Five

Ashley Bryson sat on the edge of the bath in the hotel room and tried her best to take deep breaths but no matter how much she counted, she just couldn't feel the oxygen going into her lungs.

'Ashley,' Jack called from the lounge, 'is Uncle Bob going to be okay?'

The question caused further panic which led to a rush of nausea. She threw herself across the room to the toilet just in time. Even with loud retches, she could still hear the gunshots ringing in her ears, along with the question from her brother. He was only seven; a year younger than she was when she witnessed that psycho Reilly attacking her dad. History seemed to be repeating itself.

'He'll be fine, buddy. Dad and Uncle Paul are with him. And the paramedics will help him too.'

Jack didn't answer. If he was anything like she had been at that age, he would know she was lying to try to keep him calm.

'Fuck,' she hissed as she closed the toilet seat and pulled herself onto it. She'd been doing so well. The therapy had been working and she'd been coping with everyday life. Going out, being in crowded places no longer seemed to affect her. But now, after what had just happened, she knew that she would end up back at the beginning.

She heard a rap at the hotel room door and got to her feet quickly. Moving out of the bathroom, across the plush carpet, she peered through the spy hole and felt relief when she saw her mum. Angie entered the room and Jack ran to her. She held him close, and for a split second, a pang of jealousy hit

Ashley. She didn't remember her mother hugging her like that after the Reilly incident.

She caught a glimpse of herself in the mirror. Her eye make-up was running and there were black smears under both her eyes from her mascara. Ashley quickly wiped them away and took a breath.

'Jack, are you okay?' Angie said, holding him at arm's length and checking him over.

'I'm okay,' he replied. 'Is Uncle Bob going to hospital?'

Angie pulled her lips into a tight smile, and Ashley felt her throat constrict.

'Yeah, he's going to hospital.' Angie cleared her throat, got to her feet and moved across the room before switching on the television. 'Look, the football is on. Why don't you watch that while Mummy talks to Ashley?'

Jack perched himself on the edge of the bed and did what he was told. Exactly as Ashley had done that day eight years previously. Staring into a TV screen and hearing the external noise fight against the sounds repeating in her head had been overwhelming. The same might happen to Jack.

Ashley eyed her mother, who gestured for her to follow her to the bathroom. Once inside, Angie shut the door.

'Are you okay?' Angie asked, placing her hands on each of Ashley's shoulders.

'Do I look okay?' Ashley gasped. 'What the fuck *was* that down there?'

Angie shook her head and gave a sigh. 'An ambush. Whoever it was got what they wanted. Your Uncle Bob is dead, Ashley.'

Ashley turned, glared at her mum. Her expression was stony, like she didn't care. That was just the way she was in situations where there was high stress and emotion. Ashley had learned that a long time ago. The news about Bob took a few seconds to kick in before Ashley started to cry. She kept her sobs silent so she didn't startle Jack. Ashley was never close with Bob, but he was still family. And dying the way he did – well, no one deserved that, did they?

'Who would want to kill us?' Ashley asked, finally able to compose herself.

Angie hesitated and Ashley stared at her, waiting for an explanation. There was no way that her mum wouldn't know. How could she not? She was married to the biggest gang boss in the city.

'I don't know, Ashley. I *really* don't.'

Ashley frowned. 'How are you so calm? Someone just put the windows of a hotel in to shoot our family, killed Uncle Bob, and you're acting as though they accidently bumped into your car or something.'

'I'm trying to keep a level head for your dad. You should try to stay calm, Ashley.'

'No!' Ashley said, slamming her hand down on the bathroom sink. 'I won't *fucking* stay calm.'

Angie moved towards her, tried to wrap her arms around her but Ashley moved away. 'Don't touch me. Everything this family touches ends up fucked.'

She saw the shock creep on to her mum's face. 'Ashley, don't speak to me like that. It's not like you're the only one who's scarred by what happened down there.'

'Yeah, but aside from Jack, I'm probably the only one who wasn't part of the reason why the psycho with a gun decided to take a fucking pop at us and kill Bob in the process.' She took a steadying breath, the first she'd managed since hearing the first shot. 'I can't do this. I can't be around this family. It's ruining my life. My head is fucked because of you lot.'

Ashley slid out of the space between her mum and the sink and headed out to the main room. Opening her suitcase that sat on the floor next to the window, she started to pack up her belongings. Jack didn't seem to notice, and if he did, he paid no attention.

'What are you doing?' Angie whispered.

'I told you, I can't be around this family. It's toxic and not good for me. If I'm honest, I've been thinking about moving away for a long time. This is the perfect excuse.'

Before her mum could answer, the door opened and Ashley's brother Conor walked in. Ashley glanced up at him but continued to pack her case.

'Aye, probably a good idea to get away from here. Uncle Paul has said we can go to the new apartment complex and stay there for a few days. They're finished now, so they're properly kitted out for us.'

Ashley sneered and shook her head. 'Like a little family fucking holiday, eh, Conor?'

Conor frowned. 'What you talking about?'

'She's leaving us, apparently,' Angie said. 'Ashley, it's not safe for you to be on your own right now. And you're only seventeen.'

'I'm eighteen soon enough. And it's less safe for me to be a Bryson. I've made up my mind and you can't stop me.'

Ashley finished filling her case and did one last sweep of the room before lifting her car keys and pulling her case into an upright position. She noted that her brother was standing in front of the closed door, and she could tell that she wasn't going to get out of the room without a fight.

'Mum's right, Ashley. You can't be alone. It's not safe.'

'Get out of the way, Conor.'

'No.'

'Get out of the way or I swear I'll fucking scream. This place is crawling with police, am I right? One scream and they'll come running.'

Conor's eyes darted towards his mum, and Angie sighed loudly.

'Ashley, please think about this.'

'I've already thought about it. Get out of my way.'

Conor hesitated, and then slowly stepped to the side.

'Ashley, where are you going?' Jack asked suddenly from across the room.

Turning to face her little brother, she plastered on her biggest smile and went to him. 'I'm just going away for a little bit, wee man. I'll be back soon.' She kissed him on the forehead and held in her tears before moving back to the door.

Ashley pulled the door open and headed down the hallway.

'Jack, wait there. I'll be back in a minute,' she heard her mum say before she and Conor followed her.

'Where are you going?' Angie asked.

'The less you know, the better. If you don't know where I am then what's the likelihood of anyone else knowing?'

Dragging her case down the stairs to the reception, she handed the key card for her room to the receptionist. 'Checking out of the Buchanan Suite.'

She saw her dad, sitting in the foyer, with Paul by his side. He had lost all the colour in his face and his hands and clothes were covered in blood.

Ashley went to him and crouched down in front of him. 'Dad, I'm so sorry about Uncle Bob.'

Dale stared at her and gave a gentle smile. She didn't bother to look behind her at the conservatory. With the ambulance and armed police present, she wondered if it would be a hassle to get out of the hotel. But she had to try.

'Dale,' Angie's voice came from above her, 'she's trying to leave.'

Dale looked up at Angie and then back at Ashley. 'What do you mean, leave? Where are you going?'

Ashley sighed and her chest swelled with guilt. 'I can't stay here, with this family. There's been too much violence, too many horrors to deal with. I have to go, to keep myself safe.'

Dale sighed and said nothing. It was as if he didn't have the energy to argue with her. Paul didn't say anything either.

Everyone was in shock. Ashley kissed her dad, headed out of the foyer towards her Range Rover Velar and packed her case into the boot.

'Don't do this, Ashley, please,' Angie said, and she could hear the emotion cracking in her voice. 'I need all my kids with me right now to know you're safe.'

Ashley noticed that the police hadn't locked the place down yet, so now was her last chance to get away.

'No, you need to find out who did this.'

She climbed into the driver's seat and locked the doors before Conor or her mum had a chance to jump in the car with her, started the engine and pulled out of the car park.

Ashley didn't bother looking in the mirror in case she saw Jack. It was hard leaving her little brother behind; he was so innocent in all of this. But staying just for him was a risk to her. She didn't want to have anything to do with them. Not anymore. The gang-related crimes they'd all been pulled into because of the type of business her dad and uncles were involved in had happened once too often. If that was the life they wanted to lead, that was fine. But there was no way that Ashley wanted that for herself. Bob had been murdered because of it.

She would make her own life, choose her own path. Even if that meant getting a job cleaning pub toilets just to get herself by, then she would do that. They could have their car back, they could keep their monthly allowances and designer clothes. All Ashley wanted was to be safe, and almost getting shot at her parents' vow renewal wasn't her idea of safe.

Pulling up her boyfriend's number on the Bluetooth screen, she hit call.

'Hi, it's me. Can I come over?'

Chapter Twenty-Six

'You're telling me you don't think we should follow her?' Angie screamed in his face. 'Fucking hell, Dale. Your daughter has just driven off after someone just murdered your brother, and you don't think we should go after her?'

Dale massaged his temples a little too vigorously and shook his head. 'Angie, you need to chill the fuck out. There's a lot going on here and I need a minute to figure out what the fuck to do next. You screaming at me isn't helping me do that.'

Dale Bryson had only just finished speaking with the officers who'd shown up almost immediately after the attack, and were now away looking at CCTV. Bob's body was still in the conservatory, and the room was being dusted down for evidence. The police had instructed everyone else to change out of their clothes and hand them over as evidence. They were all dressed in casual clothes, or dressing gowns. A far cry from the glamour of just a few hours ago.

'You need to get out there and start looking for our daughter because she's out there on her own, Dale. Alone, after someone just tried to kill all of us.' Angie's voice was lower now, but still had an edge to it.

Dale sighed. 'Paul and Conor will go,' he said. 'Won't you, boys?'

''Course we will, Angie. Don't worry. We'll find her,' Paul replied with a gentle smile.

Dale watched as Angie's shoulders relaxed and he felt a little wash of relief come over him. Thank God she was starting to calm down. Angie could be destructive when she got going and he didn't need her screaming at him while he tried to process what had just happened.

'We'll go as soon as the armed officers let us out,' Conor said in a soft tone, placing a hand on his mum's shoulder.

'Keep an eye out for her car, let us know if you find her. But don't do the macho uncle-and-brother thing and drag her back kicking and screaming. Just talk to her, tell her she'd be safer with all of us around her,' Dale said, wondering himself if in fact that was true. Maybe his daughter was right. Maybe she would be safer if she was away from the family. The Brysons had stepped on a lot of toes to climb their way to the top over the years. Maybe someone out there had decided they'd had enough? They'd snapped and taken a shot, not caring if they hit one or all of the Bryson family.

'*Just…*' Angie stopped and took a breath. 'Just find her. Please. I need to go back upstairs and check on Jack.' She turned and headed towards the stairs which led to the honeymoon suite.

'Any idea who this might have been?' Dale said, running a hand through his hair.

Paul sniggered. 'Are you serious? Could have been anyone we've ever done business with, good or bad. There's a long list to get through. It's fucking impossible, unless that CCTV shows up anything.'

'Highly doubt that,' Dale replied. 'Whoever did this had it planned. They knew where we were going to be, all of us in the same place. Our chances of finding out who did this are slim, unless they fuck up on their next hit. Because they'll come back, Paul. You know they will. Knowing that they've taken out Bob will spur them on to try again for the rest of us.'

Paul eyed him. They both knew that if the Brysons were going to survive, they would have to find the person who killed Bob, and quickly.

Chapter Twenty-Seven

Cara Fraser sat on her husband's bench in the cemetery and looked out at the view in front of her. She could see for miles from where she was sitting, and it brought her peace to know that she could stay there for as long as she wanted and ponder life. And she had a lot to ponder, especially after what she'd just done.

This was all because of gang rivalry, she thought. Kyle had been dead for eight years and she could remember telling him and her brother-in-law Ian not to go ahead with their plan to fuck the Brysons over. But, as always, Kyle knew best and told her so, and said to let them get on with things. Maybe if she hadn't, maybe if she'd put her foot down, then they'd both still be alive right now. She had that same thought every day since.

The sun beat down on her and she liked the feeling of warmth on her face. Most of the time, Cara felt cold and bitter. She thought back to when she took the boys away from Glasgow and up to Aberdeen, away from their home, their school and friends – all because of Glasgow gang territory and how much it meant to Kyle.

Sean had been quiet for months after the killings, he seemed to retreat into himself and didn't speak much about his dad. Ryan was the opposite. He asked questions constantly, the same questions every single day. What happened to Dad and Uncle Ian? Did the Brysons kill them? How did they die? Would they ever go back to Glasgow? It seemed her boys had become exposed to the horrors of what Kyle had been up to more so after he'd died than when he was alive.

Cara had tried to avoid the questions but it was impossible – along with the media coverage, which Ryan had access to. The internet, newspapers; it was the biggest story to come out of Glasgow that she'd ever known. That was when she'd started drinking. At first, she'd tried to wait until the boys had gone to bed, but Ryan was a lot smarter than Cara ever gave him credit for. He'd read the stories, seen the hype on the internet. He knew what was being said, whether the papers got things right or whether they filled in the gaps themselves.

Ryan sat down one night and told her that he knew his dad had been murdered. But that wasn't the worst part. He'd gone on to tell her that it was his fault. He remembered telling a man that his dad was going to take down the Brysons and that his family were going to be minted. That same man was convicted of Kyle and Ian's murders. The pain of his words would have hit harder, had she not been numbed by the alcohol. They'd agreed not to tell Sean, not until he became an adult. Cara felt sick at the prospect of her son blaming himself. That feeling never went away, not even when she was drinking.

It had taken almost six years to get sober, and the last two years had been spent in Aberdeen with her boys who were now adults. She felt stronger than she'd ever felt, and just a few months ago, Ryan had sat her down and suggested it was time to go home to Glasgow. He was older, wiser and now that he understood more about what happened, he wondered if the wrong person had been convicted. Cara had agreed with him, but what could they do? They had no power and no proof to change things.

But of course it was the Brysons who'd killed Kyle and Ian. Why would MacTavish have done it? He was just a street player, a guy who did what he was told for money. Unless he'd been paid off by the Brysons? Cara knew that was a long shot.

Now, as she brought her thoughts back to the present, she glanced down into the large handbag next to her on the bench. The balaclava stared back at her and she resisted the urge to smile. As much as she loved the idea of the Brysons having no clue as to who would have shot at them on the most special day for their family, she wanted the satisfaction of walking up to them and telling them it was her before finishing them off.

'But that would be too easy, Mum,' Ryan had said to her when she'd voiced her desire to her son. 'They need to pay for what they did to our family. And they will pay. But with Dad and Uncle Ian gone, it's left to me to sort this. And you don't have to worry about a thing. I'll make sure they all pay the ultimate price. Just you sit back and enjoy.'

She zipped the bag closed and sat back before taking a few deep breaths. Today was just the beginning of it all. The Brysons had no idea what was coming to them.

Chapter Twenty-Eight

Ashley sat by the window of the coffee shop where Jamie had arranged to meet her. She'd driven straight there from the wedding venue without stopping, all the while feeling both incredibly sad that she had to abandon her family and furious that she'd been put in such danger because of them.

'Can I get you anything else, love?' the waitress asked, giving the untouched coffee mug a judgemental glance.

'No, thank you. I'm fine for now.'

She glanced down at her hands and saw that they were trembling. Was it any wonder? She'd just witnessed her uncle's murder. That hadn't actually sunk in yet.

Just as the waitress left the table, Jamie entered the coffee shop with a concerned expression on his face.

'Are you okay?' he asked. 'You sounded really shaken up on the phone.'

Ashley stood up and went to him. She gripped him tightly and wondered how she was supposed to tell him what had happened. It wasn't your typical family celebration. How would he even understand what her family was like?

'I'm okay, I think,' she responded, letting go of Jamie and sitting back down at the table. Jamie sat next to her and looked into her eyes.

'You've been crying. What's happened?'

She took a breath to steady herself, and then decided that she was going to tell him everything. What would be the point in holding back?

'Well, you know that my mum and dad's vow renewal was today.' Ashley swallowed. 'Oh Jesus Christ, Jamie. Someone attacked us. They shot at us through the glass and...' her voice trailed off and she composed herself. 'My Uncle Bob got hit. He's dead.'

Jamie frowned, sat back on his chair and took her hand in his. It felt reassuring; safe.

'I've never felt so terrified in my entire life.'

'Are you hurt?' Jamie asked, sitting forward and inspecting her face, her hands.

Ashley shook her head. 'No, I'm fine. But I had to get away from there.'

Jamie exhaled loudly and ran a hand over the back of his head. 'So what? You bolted?'

'Yeah. I didn't want to be around my family. I mean, who the hell just randomly targets a family wedding? No one. It was planned. Whoever did this knew who we were, knew we were there.'

Jamie frowned. 'So, you think this was *planned*? Why would someone want to kill your family?'

'To be honest, I don't know *how* to say this. My family, they're wealthy. *Really* wealthy. But it's not all legit, and they've made enemies along the way. More than I care to imagine. The hard thing about what happened today is that my dad won't know for sure who it was that came after us, so he won't be able to stop them from coming after us again. Which is why I left. I'm safer away from them.'

Jamie's eyes were wider than normal as he listened to Ashley, and for a moment she thought he was going to get up from his seat and leave without saying a word. Not that she would blame him. They'd only been seeing each other for a month, maybe a little more. But he was the only person in the world she felt safe around right now.

'You're sure you're safer without your dad around? I mean, he *could* protect you?'

'He wasn't able to protect us today, and my uncle is dead,' Ashley said. 'The further I am from them, the better. As much as it hurt to do that to my mum, especially today of all days, I need to start putting myself first.'

Jamie gave her hand a squeeze and instantly she felt reassured, like he was validating her decision.

'Can I stay with you at your flat? Just until I get myself sorted. If I'm going to do this, I don't want to be living off their money. I'll get a job and save for my own place.'

Jamie sighed. 'You can stay with me for as long as you need, Ashley. You'll be safe with me. I promise. I just have to make a quick call and then we can go. Okay?'

Ashley forced a smile as Jamie got up and went outside. She could see him through the window as he spoke on the phone, and kept her eyes on him the whole time. The call was quick and he was back at the table with her.

'Who were you phoning?'

'Just work. I told them I had a family emergency and I wouldn't be in. You need someone to be with you today.'

Ashley felt a lump grow quickly in her throat. 'Thank you.'

'Are you sure you don't want to be with them? I mean, they'll be stressed and grieving enough as it is without you going on the missing list.' His tone was gentle.

Ashley shook her head. 'No. I can't go back there. What if the person who killed Bob comes back and I get hit next? I don't want to die, Jamie.'

Her voice cracked and she let out a sob she'd been holding in since that first gunshot. Jamie wrapped his arm around her and held her tightly against him.

'It's okay. You don't have to go anywhere. And you're not going to die. Like I said, you're safe with me.'

Chapter Twenty-Nine

He stared at the two young lads across the table from him and an uneasiness settled in his chest and stomach. The one he'd met before, Ryan, seemed calm. But the other had a face on him that told MacTavish one wrong move could cost him his life.

'How's things?' Ryan asked, as he sat back casually on his seat, his eyes never leaving MacTavish's.

'As well as can be expected in a place like this,' he replied. 'What can I do you both for?'

'My brother, Sean, here. He wants to talk to you about what happened.' Ryan gestured towards Sean.

MacTavish's eyes fell on the other lad, and he sighed inwardly. Having to go over everything again was a pain in his arse that he didn't need, but by the look on Sean's face, it was clear he didn't have much choice.

'No detail left out.' Sean leaned forward and lowered his tone. 'And every word you say better be the fucking truth, or I won't hesitate to pull you over that table and break your fucking neck.'

MacTavish frowned and gave Ryan a questioning glance. 'Is this guy serious? There's screws everywhere.'

'I'd do time for the fucker who took my old man away from me when I was just a boy. Now, start talking,' Sean replied, leaning closer to the point where MacTavish could feel his breath.

James MacTavish could see that was the truth, and it was clear that Sean had been kept in the dark about what had really happened.

'I didn't kill him, or your uncle.'

'Then who did?'

It was a question MacTavish had been asking himself every day since being sent away in 2013. In fact, before that day. Ever since he'd discovered the car in the reservoir, and had found out that the bodies inside were the Fraser brothers.

'I don't know. And that's the truth.'

'Fucking liar,' Sean spat.

'I'm not lying, I don't know who killed them. But I do have my theories on who could be responsible. I have since the day I was sent to prison. It's the only real explanation I have for any of us. And if I'm right about it, and I can somehow get evidence, I can get out of this shit hole and on with my life. But they're not the kind of people who leave themselves open. They're big time, have been running this city for a very long time. I wouldn't be surprised if the screws in this place are in their pockets and the polis are on their payroll.'

Sean glanced at his brother, who was nodding at him. 'Just listen to what he has to say, Sean. And stop being such a fucking hot head or we're going to end up getting thrown out of here and you won't get to hear MacTavish's side of things.'

In some small way, MacTavish felt sorry for Sean Fraser. He was the youngest of the family, had just been a boy when his dad was murdered. MacTavish knew how it felt to grow up without a dad, even though his own had died from liver disease. Not quite the same set of circumstances, but the absence was very much the same.

'Whose side are you on here, Ryan?' Sean hissed at his brother.

Ryan laughed. 'You're more like him than you think. Shut up and listen.'

Sean gritted his teeth and turned back to MacTavish.

'I think the Bryson family are responsible for your dad and uncle's murders.' He exhaled slowly, remembering the look on Cara and Ryan Fraser's faces when he'd told them the same thing. 'I used to be employed by Kyle and Ian, but the rent was rising quickly and I needed more cash. So I took on another job on the side.'

Ryan smirked at MacTavish from across the table and raised a brow, but MacTavish tried to ignore it.

'What kind of job?' Sean pressed.

'Similar to the one I had with your old man. But it was under the Brysons.'

Sean blinked a few times before sitting back in his chair. 'Were you on a death wish?'

MacTavish shook his head. 'I didn't exactly have a choice. It wasn't like I applied for the job. I was pulled into it.'

MacTavish thought back to that day and still kicked himself about it. He wished he'd known what was going to happen. He'd have run if he'd been given half the chance.

'What happened?' Sean asked, almost as if he was genuinely intrigued, like he'd forgotten why he was sitting across from MacTavish and listening to his story.

'Your old man and his brother were trying to screw over the Brysons. Sabotaging orders, hiking up prices on Bryson product. I was instructed to find out information, gather evidence and report back so that the Brysons could deal with it.'

Sean's eyes widened and a slight smile rose in the corners of his mouth. 'Are you seriously telling me that you were spying on my dad and reporting back to his boss?'

MacTavish nodded. 'Don't you see why it makes sense? I had no reason to kill your dad or Ian. But the Brysons did and to get away with it they fucking framed me for it. I've no idea how, but they did.'

Sean looked at Ryan and MacTavish saw the realisation creep in.

'You think this is the truth?' Sean asked his brother.

'Yeah. And the fact that I told MacTavish here that our old man was going to take the Brysons out is proof enough for me. I was just a boy, didn't know what was going on. Not really.'

Sean gave MacTavish a hard stare through narrowed and angry eyes. 'And you reported back that information?'

MacTavish shook his head. 'I wish I hadn't. If I could go back and change things, I would do it in a heartbeat. I just want out of here. I didn't kill anyone.'

Sean launched himself forward and slammed his hands on the desk. 'As good as. You threw them under the fucking bus. I swear, if you do get out of here, you won't live to see the light of day for more than twenty-four hours, cos I'll break your fucking neck.'

Ryan pulled on his brother's arm, but Sean shook him off.

He pushed his chair back, and the sound of the legs scraping against the floor echoed around the room. The other visitors and prisoners in the visiting hall looked up, and two prison guards took a few steps towards the table. James held his hand up and nodded, indicating that things were okay. They hesitated, and everyone else fell silent before they continued with their conversations.

'I need air,' he said, turning and heading for the exit. The prison officers retreated back to their spots.

MacTavish and Ryan watched him go and when Ryan turned back, his expression was neutral. 'Why didn't you tell someone about this sooner? The polis – or you could have got in contact with my mum?'

MacTavish nodded. 'Are you kidding? I didn't know where you all were. And I did just say that the polis are probably on the Bryson payroll. Every other fucker in power seems to be. And even if they weren't, they wouldn't have listened to me. As far as the justice system is concerned, this was an open-and-shut case.' MacTavish took a steadying breath. 'When you came to see me the first time, just after you came back to Glasgow, I knew that telling you this was a risk. But I had to try to clear my name. I knew you might have lost your shit and tried to kill me.'

'Doesn't mean to say I still won't.' Ryan Fraser's parting words were followed by the sound of his chair, scraping more loudly on the floor as he pushed it back and rose to his feet. He gave MacTavish one last stony-eyed stare, before turning his back on him and following his brother out of the visiting hall.

MacTavish's heart thrummed hard in his chest, because he knew that Ryan Fraser wasn't kidding. Knowing that MacTavish had betrayed his dad and uncle, which led to their murder, would be reason enough to want him dead. What was worse? Spending what should be the best years of his life in prison for a crime he didn't commit? Or getting out and being killed for betrayal?

Chapter Thirty

A week had passed since the shooting; since Bob had been murdered. The worst part about that was that Angie hadn't seen or heard from her daughter in that time, and it was worrying her sick where she might be or what might have happened to her. How was she to know that her daughter wasn't dead if she hadn't heard from her?

'She's just a teenager, Dale,' she said as she sat back on the chair in their office at Diamond Casino. 'I should have been stricter with her that day and told her she couldn't go. Fuck, I should have made the police stop her. They *should* have stopped her.'

Dale had thrown himself into work since Bob had died and had barely spoken. She was worried about him, but not as much as she worried about Ashley. She needed him to take charge, to find their daughter and the person who was responsible for her disappearing.

'Dale, are you listening to me? I need you to get out there and find her,' she said with a firmer tone.

Angie frowned as she stared at her silent husband. 'It's as if you don't care, Dale. Are you not at all worried that something could have happened to our daughter? Or have you forgotten our entire family was the target of some mad gunman last weekend?'

Just as the last syllable left her lips, Dale stood and swiped his arm over the desk, sending documents and folders hurtling across the office. Angie flinched, and she too got to her feet as Dale moved across the floor towards the drink station.

He poured a large whisky and downed it in one go, before launching the glass across the room. It shattered against the red marbled wall and showered the floor in shards.

'Are you fucking serious, Angie? Are you sure *you* remember what happened last weekend? Just now you failed to mention that my brother was shot dead. He *literally* bled to death all over me, and you're standing there, giving me fucking grief!'

For the first time in their marriage, Angie felt shaken by his outburst. She took a breath and steadied herself. 'Of course I haven't forgotten. I was there, I saw the whole thing. But Dale, you have to realise that as brutal as this sounds, Bob is dead. We can't save him now. But we can save our daughter if we can get her back.'

Dale picked up another glass and poured another large measure. This time, he sipped at it.

'I'm not trying to take away what happened to Bob. He was your brother, my brother-in-law. But you need to understand where I'm coming from. Ashley isn't like us, she's young, and out there on her own.'

Before Angie could stop them, tears pooled in her eyes and began to pour down her face.

'Angie,' Dale said, 'we will find her and bring her home. You think I haven't been torn up inside, worried about her? I have, on top of my fury-fuelled grief for Bob. This city is going to be torn apart until I find out who did this.'

Angie hesitated. Of course, she believed her husband that something was being done about what happened, but the real question was, would that bring Ashley home? More violence would surely keep her away longer?

'Good,' Angie replied. 'I'll happily nail their heads to the wall to know that our daughter and the rest of our family are safe.'

She saw a sadness in his eyes then, and she went to him, taking him in her arms. He didn't cry. Hadn't shed a tear since the shooting. And even now as she held him, his eyes were almost black. His grief was most definitely fuelled by rage.

He kissed her briefly on the cheek, then sat down at his desk. 'I need to phone Paul; he's arranging the funeral and I want to go with him to the funeral directors. We're allowed to see the body if we want to.'

He lifted the landline phone and soon started talking in hushed tones to Paul on the other end. Angie's phoned pinged in her bag and as she opened up the notification, her blood ran cold. Staring down at the words, Angie tried to process what she was reading. Was this a joke?

One down, six to go…

She tried to scroll down the screen to find a contact number, but there wasn't one. The sender was anonymous. And whoever it was, clearly wanted to remain that way.

Holding the phone up to Dale, she showed him the message and his already dark eyes grew darker.

Whoever was responsible for sending that message had just signed their own death warrant. Dale and Paul would kill anyone who got in their way of finding out who sent that message. Unless Angie got to them first. Threatening her children was one line she wouldn't allow to be crossed.

Chapter Thirty-One

The family funeral car pulled into the cemetery, with the hearse in front. Angie kept her eyes on the road ahead, all the while keeping Dale's hand in her grip. Paul and Conor sat behind. The silence was deafening. As the cars headed up the hill towards the top of the cemetery, the hearse took a left turn towards the parlour where the service would be held ahead of the burial.

'Oh my God,' Conor said under his breath. Angie gasped with him at the amount of people standing outside the parlour.

'Yeah, word gets around when a high-flying gangster is shot,' Dale remarked. Angie heard venom in his voice, but she knew it wasn't directed at the people gathered to pay their respect. It was more directed at the tabloid press who were scattered around the grounds with their cameras. They'd been all over the Bryson family since Bob had been killed. It was like Christmas to them.

'Don't rise to it, Dale,' Paul said. 'And don't look at their shitty cameras. That's what they'll want.'

Angie knew Paul was right. They were like leeches, trying to suck out as much as they could from a grieving family. They'd be loving the fact that Ashley wasn't present.

The car stopped and the driver got out before opening the door to Angie. As she stepped onto the concrete, the silence from the throngs of mourners hit her. Hundreds of people lined the pavements, with their heads bowed as the rest of the family got out of the car. She took in the scene. Armed police officers lined the perimeter of the cemetery. It was something that they'd been informed of before the day had arrived. The funeral of a high-profile murder case of a gangland boss in Glasgow didn't exactly scream 'safe place to be'. With their presence alongside the press, the air around her felt tense.

Angie looked at Dale and gave him a reassuring gaze, before he, along with Paul and Conor, went to the hearse. They were helping to carry the coffin in, with three of the men from the funeral director's.

As they moved away from her, Angie entered the seated area on her own. She should have had her daughter by her side, but there was still no word from Ashley. They had no idea where she was or who she was with. It was unlikely she'd be lurking in the back somewhere. If she was staying away because she feared for her safety, then there was no way Ashley would turn up to her uncle's funeral. Even Angie knew the funeral was a high-risk place for the Brysons to be – with no one knowing who took Bob out, the killer could be hiding in plain sight.

Angie took her seat at the front as the rest of the mourners poured in through the doors. Press wouldn't be granted access, but what she did notice were two armed officers at either side of the back row of seats. She barely recognised anyone, they were most likely old friends or business associates from years gone by. It was the old business associates she had the issue with. It could be one of them.

She placed her handbag on her lap, and felt the weight of the gun inside. If someone was going to take a shot at her or her family today, then Angie would fight back. She hadn't told Dale that she was carrying it. He would have only discouraged her.

As the music started, it caught her off guard. 'Everlong' by Foo Fighters. It was the song Bob had always sung; it was his favourite. He'd even sung it at Angie and Dale's first wedding. Emotion caught in her throat and she swallowed hard as Bob's coffin was brought in, with Dale and Paul carrying it from the front. Seeing Dale trying to hold himself together was heart-breaking.

Dale, Paul and Conor took their seats next to Angie, and to her surprise, Dale took her hand in his and squeezed it tightly. She was surprised, thinking that he'd keep his emotion hidden from everyone.

Taking a deep breath, Angie focused on the coffin, and listened as the music faded out, and the humanist celebrant began his eulogy.

–

Gathered at the graveside, looking down at Bob's coffin after it had been lowered into the ground, Angie felt a sadness creep over her that she hadn't expected. It had finally hit her that Bob was dead. He wasn't coming back. And that was going to change Dale. He was going to be angry, full of rage that wouldn't go away until he'd avenged his brother's murder.

The humanist spoke as he stood at the top of the graveside, but Angie wasn't listening. She peered out at the crowd through her sunglasses, trying to take in every face; trying to work out from their expressions and features if they had it in them to blow someone away at a wedding. Taking out a top gangster took some courage, but turning up to his funeral was even ballsier.

Every blade of grass was covered by men in suits and glamorous-looking women on their arms. Some women stood alone, and Angie wondered if they'd ever been romantically involved with Bob. He'd obviously had some kind of effect on these people, whether it was good or bad.

Armed police lined the rows of mourners, and the odd camera flash caught Angie's attention as the press got their shots for the tabloids. They'd all be hankering for the best scoop on Bob Bryson's funeral.

Her mind switched quickly to her daughter, and she instantly began looking for her even though she knew that Ashley wouldn't be there. The killer would be, however, that was something Angie was sure about. They'd be watching her and her family, planning out their next hit. The thought made her stomach flip.

Chapter Thirty-Two

Hiding in plain sight gave her a thrill she'd never felt before. It hadn't taken much to disguise herself. A wig, a hat and sunglasses did the trick. Not that anyone would expect to see her there. As far as the Brysons were concerned, Cara Fraser was a widow, far away from Glasgow and never coming back. But she was very much present in the city that the Brysons claimed as their own.

She watched Angie Bryson, knowing full well that behind her sunglasses she was scanning the crowds of people for the potential killer. It gave Cara great pleasure in knowing they were utterly clueless as to who had killed their brother.

She watched the pain on Dale Bryson's face as Bob Bryson was lowered into the ground, and remembered the day she cremated her own husband. Thoughts of that day still plagued her, not because of her loss, but because of the loss to her boys. Seeing their little faces that day as the curtains closed was something she would never forget. Now she was able to stand there and watch that same deserved pain. Hatred for the Brysons ran through her veins as she planned to cause them nothing but pain and terror for what they'd done to her family.

Cara eyed the armed police as they patrolled the perimeter of the cemetery. They were quiet, eyes open and surveying every single mourner, including her. Not that they'd recognise her.

As the graveside service came to an end, the crowds began to move, giving their condolences as they passed by. Dale's expression didn't change, he remained neutral the entire time. Angie was the least restrained in her display of emotions.

It was time to move, Cara thought, before the gaps in the crowds exposed her. As much as she was disguised, she didn't want to risk someone sensing a familiarity about her.

This was the first funeral of many for the Brysons.

Chapter Thirty-Three

Ashley scrolled through endless job adverts on the S1 Jobs website, while sitting on the sofa in Jamie's flat. He'd left earlier that morning to go to work, and as he'd said every morning since she'd moved in with him, she should make herself at home. It was nothing compared to the family home she was used to. It was smaller; much smaller. In fact, Ashley guessed that Jamie's flat could fit inside her parents' house at least six times. She did, however, like the simplicity of the place. It was much cosier, and she liked the fact that everything in it belonged to Jamie. He didn't rely on his parents like she did. That was something she aspired to.

As much as she liked it, she didn't feel like she was at home. She didn't have a home anymore, not one that she felt like she belonged in, at least. That was the whole reason why she was scrolling through the job adverts on every single website she could find. Having left school at sixteen, she'd lived off Daddy's money since and it was a huge regret of hers now. Ashley knew she should have gone to college or got a job as an apprentice something. Hindsight was a wonderful thing when she was up to her eyes in stress. She'd loved her life as a daddy's girl – well, she'd loved the glamorous side to it. Getting driving lessons as soon as she turned seventeen and passing her test as quickly as she could, Dale had taken her out to the car showroom of her choice and allowed her to pick whatever she wanted. She remembered him saying that there was no budget, and she didn't have to worry about paying for insurance or tax. It would all be taken care of. Ashley knew she was spoiled and for the most part, she was fine with that. But if she wanted to make it in the world on her own, she would have to start from the bottom and make her way up.

Opening up her email account, she saw yet another rejection from one of the applications she'd sent in a few days earlier. She'd thought it wasn't a job that required a lot from her: answering phones and redirecting calls in an office in the city centre. But from the email it seemed her assumption was wrong.

'This is bullshit,' she hissed, slamming the laptop shut and placing it on the carpet next to the sofa. She was trapped between sticking to her morals, or going home to her parents with her tail between her legs. If she did that, they'd never take her seriously with anything else in her life.

She opened up the laptop again and hovered over the keys. She didn't want to do it, but she felt like she had an obligation to at least know how things had gone at her uncle's funeral yesterday. Not that she'd ever liked Bob. He was too hot-headed for her, and a madman for his cocaine and alcohol. She couldn't remember the last time she saw him sober. He used cocaine on a daily basis the way people made themselves a coffee.

Typing his name into the Google search bar, Ashley saw the results fill the page immediately. She scanned over the headline articles and shook her head.

NOTORIOUS GANGLAND FIGURE
FUNERAL GOES AHEAD AMID FEARS
OF A SECOND HIT
Glasgow Gangland Funeral Takes Place with
Armed Police Presence

Hundreds of mourners gathered for Bob Bryson's funeral at Old Dalnottar Crematorium and Cemetery on the outskirts of Glasgow today.

Brothers from the notorious Bryson clan, Dale Bryson, 43, and Paul Bryson, 40, alongside nephew, Conor Bryson, 20, and sister-in-law and

wife to Dale Bryson, Angie Bryson, 39, stood
proud at the graveside.

Bob Bryson died aged 41, just last weekend at
a family wedding, where he was shot dead at the
Buchanan Arms Hotel in Drymen.

Ashley glared at the screen, and seeing her family gathered with
people she'd never seen before made her feel a little alien to it
all. A small picture of Bob at the top of the screen, with various
press images of the funeral around it, made Ashley close the
laptop again. She took a breath and tried to push the images
out of her head. The last time she'd seen Bob, he was bleeding
to death. Seeing his smiling face on the screen brought it all
back.

Picking up her phone, she rang Jamie. He answered after
two rings.

'Hi, what's up?' he asked.

'Nothing,' she lied. 'Just wondered what you're up to?'

'Bored, I take it?' he laughed, and it slightly irritated her.

'It's not like I'm sitting here watching daytime telly all day,
Jamie. I'm applying for everything and anything and I just keep
getting knockback after knockback. I'm sick of it.'

Jamie fell silent on the other end of the phone, and she knew
snapping at him wasn't helpful.

'Sorry, I don't mean to moan at you. I'm just so frustrated.'

'I get it. And I don't think you're moaning. Look, why don't
you come out and help me today? I know the funeral took place
yesterday, so this might take your mind off everything.'

Ashley smiled. 'You mean, in the van?'

'Why not? It'll get you out of the flat for a bit and then you
can get a feel for what I do. Maybe if you like it, you could get
a job doing something similar?'

Her smile widened. 'I'd love to. But won't you get into
bother for having your girlfriend distracting you?'

'Nah, I'm my own boss, sort of. I get to choose my own
hours. Why don't I come and pick you up?'

Ashley was already on her feet, heading to the bedroom to get changed. She was so grateful for Jamie, considering they'd only been together a month, and he was treating her as if they'd been together for years. And she loved him as if they'd been together for years.

She'd first met Jamie in a local café, where he'd knocked into her by accident, causing her to spill hot coffee all over him. Smiling at the memory, Ashley recalled how many times she'd apologised. He'd insisted that he was fine, and she didn't have to worry. He'd ended up buying her lunch and they'd sat down at the table by the window and chatted for two hours. Immediately, Ashley was taken in by him. He was charming, handsome, and his voice enchanting. And he was older than her by three years, which was a big attraction. Never in a million years would she have thought that a month later she would be living with him because she was too scared to be around her family.

Ashley knew her family were gangsters, and her brother was falling into that category very quickly. Like father, like son, she thought to herself. Well, she certainly didn't want to be like mother, like daughter. Being a gangster's moll wasn't something she aspired to. As much as the lifestyle suited her, the way the money was earned did not. Not that she knew the true ins and outs of the business that was conducted. All she really knew was that they owned a casino, a construction company and various security firms that leased out bouncers to nightclubs all over the city. That was as far as it went for her. Ashley might not be eighteen yet, but she wasn't stupid. It was highly likely that there were drugs involved. Something she wasn't interested in at all. That, and the fact that death was also a part of their world. Reilly being one of the dead. She shivered at the thought.

Turning her attentions away from her thoughts and back to the task in hand, Ashley continued to get ready to go and meet Jamie.

Climbing into the van, Ashley pulled on her seatbelt and Jamie leaned over and kissed her. 'Welcome to your horse and carriage, Cinderella.'

'If my fairy godmother is around, fancy asking her to send a job my way?' she joked, trying to push the horrors that were her life out of her head.

'Are you okay?' he asked.

Ashley sighed. 'Not really. Bob's funeral is the hot topic of the tabloids. I mean, whose funeral is attended by actual armed police *and* tabloid journalists? I'm so glad I didn't go.'

She felt his eyes on her, and saw doubt in them.

'You think you won't regret not going? I mean, he was your uncle.'

Ashley shook her head. 'I was never keen on him, Jamie. I know that's horrible for me to say when he's just been murdered, but just because he's dead doesn't mean that I'm suddenly going to change my mind about him. He was a gangster, like my dad and the rest of them. But he was wild; always on drugs and behaving as if he was still an angry teenage boy off his face while hanging about the schemes. Unpredictable, that's how even my dad described him. It wasn't pleasant at the way he died, and I'm not saying I'm glad he's dead. But...' she trailed off. 'Och, I don't know what I mean. All I'm saying is, I don't regret not going to the funeral and I certainly don't regret not being with my family. I've felt safer this past week with you than I have my entire life in the family home.'

Jamie was silent, his eyes slightly wider than usual. It was as though he was shocked at her revelation. Of course he would be. His girlfriend of a month had just aired her family's dirty laundry – and they weren't just *any* family. A gangster family. It was like something from a TV show.

'Well, if you feel safe, then I'm happy and that's all I care about,' he said, leaning in and kissing her. Then he started the engine and looked at his phone. Ashley noticed a list of addresses and assumed these were the places Jamie had to deliver to.

'So, what kind of deliveries do you do?' she asked.

'All sorts really. Anything from Amazon, eBay... those types of places.'

Ashley nodded. Sounded simple enough. Something that she could do herself, since she had a driving licence. How hard could it be to deliver parcels every day? Google Maps would keep her right, all she'd have to do was make sure she gave the correct packages to the correct recipients.

Jamie pulled out of the street and onto the main road, heading for the next address on his list. He reached over and rubbed Ashley's knee and gave her a smile. 'See, this is better than being cooped up, driving yourself mad all day, isn't it?'

'The same jobs kept coming up, over and over. It was like a never-ending loop of secretaries, receptionists, apprentice this and that. It got to the point I was starting to see jobs I'd already been knocked back for.'

'Well, this pays well and you've got your freedom with it. Driving around all day, meeting new people and never staying in the same place,' Jamie said, removing his hand to change gear.

The van turned right into a scheme Ashley had never heard of before. Craigton Heights. And it was just that: full of high-rise buildings that looked dull and tired. At the end of the road, there was a cul-de-sac of tenements, and Jamie stopped the van in the middle.

'Two seconds,' he said, getting out of the van. She heard him open the doors at the back, and then just a few seconds later, he slammed them shut. Passing by the window, she watched as Jamie crossed the road. He was carrying an A4-sized soft package as he headed into one of the tenements.

Ashley took in her surroundings, and began to pick out small points she'd failed to notice as Jamie had pulled into the street. The graffiti on the side of the building to her right, in neon pink spray-paint read, 'Denny Hayburn is a grass!'

Ashley frowned, wondering one, who this person was, and two, what he'd said that constituted him being a grass? Just above the words was a boarded-up window, with another to the right, from which a young lad was hanging out. A baseball cap was balanced on his head as he smoked a cigarette. He clocked her, and smiled a toothless smile at her. Pulling her eyes away from him, she turned to the other side of the cul-de-sac and glanced over the windows. Most of them were boarded up, but the place still looked lived in, to a certain degree.

'Jesus,' Ashley whispered. This place was a far cry from where she'd grown up.

Jamie reappeared from the flat and approached the van. He glanced over at the flat where the toothless lad was hanging out the window when his name was called and waved up at the guy.

'You know him?' Ashley asked as he climbed into the driver's seat and shut the door.

'A regular I deliver to,' Jamie responded, starting the van and driving out of the scheme.

'Well, whatever he orders next, he might want to ask for new teeth,' Ashley smirked.

Jamie shot her a look of shock before a smile raised the corners of his mouth. 'Ashley, that's horrible.'

'So is his mouth,' she laughed back. 'What the hell is this place like?'

'Yeah, it's a bit rough, I'll admit.'

'I don't like the idea of you delivering stuff to this place on your own. It's like something out of *Silent Hill*.' Ashley mock shivered and glanced in the wing mirror, back at the place.

'It's not *that* bad,' Jamie scoffed. 'You never struck me as the gamer type.'

'I'm not. My older brother used to play it when we were younger and it scared the shit out of me.'

Jamie stopped the van at the edge of Craigton Heights and killed the engine. 'Got a couple packages to deliver in this high rise. Do you want to come with me?'

Ashley frowned. 'No, I'll wait here if that's okay.'

'Fine by me. Might be about twenty minutes. The lift in this place doesn't work,' Jamie said as he got out of the van again.

She listened as he rummaged around in the back of the van, and then watched him go into the high rise. He was carrying a large box, with a few smaller packages on top.

Ashley had already decided that this job wasn't for her. She didn't like the idea of being on her own and delivering stuff to the people of Craigton Heights. She hated that part of herself that was so judgemental, but she didn't feel safe.

Now that she thought of it, there weren't many places she felt safe. In fact, whoever had attacked her family at the wedding could be from a place just like Craigton Heights. And they could have eyes on her right now.

Glancing down at the door, she noticed the lock button. She pressed it quickly, and sat back, keeping her eye on the entrance to the high rise for Jamie to reappear. Looking up, she counted the floors. Twenty. The only good thing about being up that high would be the view, and even that made Ashley shiver.

As she waited for Jamie, Ashley's thoughts turned to her family. This was the longest she'd gone without speaking to her mum, and she was missing her little brother, Jack, like crazy. But if she contacted them, it would make staying away even harder because they would somehow convince her to go home. Her mum had a way of making Ashley think she was overreacting, or in the wrong. Not this time. Ashley needed to be strong.

Perhaps she could check in, just to say she was okay. A quick call, giving the basic information to set their minds at ease, wouldn't do any harm to anyone. As much as she'd never liked her uncle, she still felt sad for her dad.

She pulled out her phone, dialled her mum's number and listened as it rang, her heart thumping in her chest the entire time.

'Ashley? Oh my God, are you okay?' The despair in her mum's voice caught in Ashley's throat.

'I'm just calling to tell you I'm okay.'

'You're coming home?'

Ashley sighed. 'No, I'm not. I just didn't want you thinking the worst had happened. I'm alive, and I'm safe. That's all you need to know. Tell Jack I miss him, and I'll see him one day soon.'

Before her mum could respond, Ashley ended the call and swallowed hard. She didn't want to cry, but it was an inevitable response.

Her phone started to ring in her hand and it was her mum trying to call her back. Ashley immediately switched the phone off and shoved it back into her pocket, turned her head to the flat Jamie had entered and watched with intent for his return.

Chapter Thirty-Four

Angie Bryson stood at the school gate, avoiding the clique of school mums as they twittered on about PTA meetings, sports day and the baking competition due to be held the following week. Angie had always sworn she'd never involve herself in that group. Those women were a bunch of fakes whose smiles shone artificial teeth and lip fillers. Of course, Angie had the money for that kind of thing, but it was never something she'd wanted to do to herself. Why would she? It was expensive and painful. And she liked herself the way she looked, as did Dale. Not that she needed anyone's approval.

'Excuse me, Angie?'

The voice of one of the mums brought her back from her thoughts and she glanced up at her. On closer inspection, the woman didn't just have fake teeth and lips. Her breasts were unrealistically huge, and sat perfectly as though they'd been propped up on a shelf the night before.

'Yes?' Angie feigned a smile – something that entire group were used to doing themselves. Angie recognised the woman. Her name was Penny, and little Jack often played with her son, Teddy.

'Are you okay?'

Angie frowned, knowing that her private business would be the talk of the clique. 'Why wouldn't I be?'

'It's just, well, we all heard about that awful business at your wedding last week. It's just terrible. And then the funeral. It must have been so hard. Are you *sure* you're okay?'

Angie took a breath and nodded. 'Thanks for your concern, Penny. But I'm fine.' Her tone was short and Penny clearly heard it.

'Sorry, it's just that Teddy told me about it. He said Jack was crying in the playground when the boys were role playing. Goodies and Baddies, as Teddy put it.' Another fake smile, wider this time, spread across Penny's face. Angie couldn't help but want to slap it right off her. 'Don't you think he's come back to school a little too early?'

The audacity of the woman hit Angie so hard that it nearly rendered her speechless. *Nearly* being the operative word.

'And what business is that of yours? I mean, I could ask you the same about your plastic surgery. Don't you think it's a little early to be having lip and cheek fillers? Don't you think it's a little vain to be having a breast enlargement at your age?'

Penny drew back in shock, and that fake smile disappeared quickly. 'What business is my body and my appearance of *yours*?'

'It's not my business. Same as it's none of your business when I send my son back to school after a private family matter,' Angie replied. She made sure to keep her expression straight, and nor did she blink. She held Penny's eye, hoping that the stupid bitch would walk away before Angie lost control and knocked her flying.

'That was really unfair, Angie. I was only asking if you were okay,' Penny replied, her voice low.

'No you weren't. You were being nosy because of what you saw in the papers yesterday. So do yourself a favour, Penny. Fuck off, eh?'

Penny's eyes widened before she stood back and turned away from Angie. Heading back to her group of friends, Angie couldn't help but feel a little pleased with herself that she'd put that woman in her place. They could gossip all they wanted, so long as Angie didn't have to hear it.

Angie wasn't so much angry that Penny had approached her, women like her she could handle. She was more frustrated with

Ashley. That quick phone call had somehow made things worse. Yes, she was happy that her daughter was alive and well. But she was still choosing to stay away when there was someone out there trying to pop them off.

The school bell rang and the playground was flooded with screaming children. Angie picked out Jack immediately. He was running towards her, his school bag hanging off his shoulders and she noticed yet another hole in his school trousers.

'Hi, Mum,' he said through laboured breaths. 'Look what I got today.'

Angie smiled at her son as he pulled a packet of jelly babies from his school jacket pocket and held them up.

'Lovely,' she said as they began walking to the car parked at the end of the street. They passed Penny and the other mums, who kept their eyes off Angie. 'Did the teacher give those to you for being her top pupil?'

Opening the car door, Angie watched as Jack climbed up and settled into the seat in the back. 'No, a man gave them to me at playtime.'

For a second, Angie thought she'd misheard her son. But as the words slowly sank in, so did the ice-cold chill.

'What man?'

'I don't know. He handed them to me through the fence up at the football pitch,' Jack said as he pulled the jelly babies packet open and popped one into his mouth.

'What did he say, Jack?'

'Hmm,' he deliberated while chewing loudly. 'He said sorry.'

'For what? Sorry for what?'

'For what happened at yours and Daddy's wedding. He said sorry that Uncle Bob died.'

A wave of nausea washed over Angie as she watched her son innocently eating his sweets. He had no idea the danger he'd been in.

'What did this man look like, Jack?'

Jack shrugged. 'Can't remember. Can I go to Teddy's to play football tomorrow after school?'

Angie strapped her son into the car and closed the door. She needed a moment. Needed to breathe. Turning her back on the car, she leaned against it and stared out at the sea of parents and cars in front of her. It could have been one of them. It could have been innocent. But why would one of the parents turn up at playtime and suspiciously hand sweets to a child through the perimeter of the school? Why not wait until pick up and do it when his mum was with him?

Angie's heart hammered in her chest, because she knew full well that it wasn't innocent. This man was the person who'd attacked them – who'd killed Bob. He had to be. He knew which school Jack went to. He probably knew everything about them; he certainly knew where they were getting married and when.

Tears threatened, but she had to keep it together in front of Jack. He'd seen enough terror, fear and emotion from his mother in the last week, he didn't need to see more.

Taking a few steadying breaths, Angie opened the driver's side door and climbed into the car before fastening her seatbelt.

'Mum?'

'Yes, Jack?' Angie attempted a light-hearted tone and failed.

'The man said that next time, he'd bring a bigger bag of sweets. I hope he does because the wee packets don't last very long.'

Glancing at Jack in the mirror, the nausea came on stronger than ever. This was an indirect threat through the most vulnerable member of the Bryson family.

'Jack,' Angie spun on her seat, 'look at me.'

Jack looked up at his mum with the most innocent light in his eye, waiting for her to speak while still clutching the empty bag of jelly babies.

'If that man comes back, you need to stay away from him. You don't accept sweets from strangers, darling. Remember? And if that man ever comes back to the school, you need to tell a teacher *right* away. Do you understand?'

Jack frowned and then nodded slowly. 'Okay, Mummy.'

'Good boy.'

Angie switched on the engine and gripped the steering wheel tightly until her knuckles turned white. Whoever this was had crossed a line. Killing Bob was one thing, but to target her youngest son was something else entirely. If Dale caught him, the bastard would never walk again. But if *Angie* caught him, she'd kill him.

Chapter Thirty-Five

Ryan stepped into the flat just as Sean was coming out of the back room with a huge smile on his face. Ryan knew that smile, it meant Sean had done something he probably shouldn't have.

'What?' Sean asked, tilting his head to the side a little.

'You've got that mischievous look on your face. What have you done?'

Shrugging his shoulders, Sean closed the door behind him and headed into the kitchen. Ryan followed him and watched as Sean pulled a beer from the fridge.

'Want one?'

'No, I want you to answer my question.'

Sean laughed as he opened the bottle and took a drink. 'Nothing really. I just injected a bit more fear into the Brysons.'

Ryan frowned. 'What do you mean?'

'Paid their kid's school a visit.'

Ryan felt a rush of dread move through him. 'What the fuck do you mean, you paid his school a visit?'

'Calm down. I just spoke to the little guy, gave him a bag of sweets. That's all.' Sean laughed and took another gulp from the beer bottle.

'Are you fucking serious, Sean? What the hell are you doing messing around at a kid's school? That's a line you *never* cross.'

Sean's expression turned from light to frustrated in an instant. 'You make it sound like I'm some kind of fucking pervert.'

'And when word gets out that some weird guy was giving sweets to kids at a primary school, that's exactly what people are going to think. Fucking hell, have you lost your mind?'

Sean fell silent and slammed the bottle down on the kitchen counter. 'No, I haven't. Those bastards need to pay for what they did to our family, Ryan. They left us without a dad, and you're standing there giving me shit.'

Ryan began pacing the kitchen floor. 'There are ways to go about things, Sean. And involving young kids isn't one of them.'

'Ah, so it was okay for Mum to try to kill the entire family with the boy there – even shoot one of them dead, but I can't go to visit him at the school? Double fucking standards, mate.'

Between his mum and brother, Ryan couldn't work out which one of them was the harder to deal with.

'Look, if we're going to find out for certain why the Brysons killed our dad and Uncle Ian, then we need to do it quietly. We can't go doing stupid shit like this and expect to keep our anonymity. And by the way, I'll speak to Mum about the fucking shooting. That wasn't how I wanted things to go. First of all, we need proof and killing them before we know anything isn't going to get us that.'

Sean's jaw clenched and Ryan sighed. 'Look, I know this is hitting you the hardest because you've only just found out, but if you allow me to do things my way, I promise that you can be the one to snuff out the bastard that killed them.'

'I don't need your permission to do anything, Ryan.'

'No, you don't. But you will respect me. I'm head of this family, Sean. And if our old man was still here, we'd be expected to fall in step behind him. So do me a favour, wait till I give the fucking signals before you do anything else, eh?'

Ryan watched as the tension fell out of Sean's shoulders and he sighed in silent relief.

'By the way, I don't need to find out why they killed them. I just need to know that each and every one of them will get what's coming to them,' Sean said.

'I know that's how you feel, Sean. I get it,' Ryan replied, before deciding to change the subject quickly while he had the chance. 'How's the grow coming along?'

'Fine,' Sean replied.

'Equipment all good? There're no lamps need replacing?'

Sean smirked. 'Look, I know what I'm doing. Equipment is all fine. The tents are fine, the lamps are fine and the temperature is perfect. And we've got enough there to fulfil any orders that come in for the next couple weeks.'

Ryan nodded happily. 'Glad to hear it.' But he couldn't help but worry about Sean. Ryan had created a monster by letting him know what had truly happened to their dad. And that monster was the most dangerous out of them all.

Chapter Thirty-Six

Angie watched as Jack ran from the car into the house, dropping his school bag at the front door and letting his jacket fall from his back next to it. By the time she reached the hallway, closing the door behind her, Jack was already in the games room and playing on his new PlayStation 5. She didn't even have the energy to fight with him about doing his homework first. Instead, she headed for the kitchen and sat down at the island. Head in her hands and heart hammering inside her, Angie began to process the full dangers that her son had faced at school that day. She couldn't fathom why anyone would want to involve a child in their quest to destroy a family. It took a certain type of person to want to do that.

She had to tell Dale what had happened. Their attacker had cranked things up by involving Jack. Going to his school was scarier than the shooter at the wedding. Angie would happily stand in front of that gun if it meant protecting Jack.

Angie called Dale.

'Hey, what's up?' he answered.

'Someone turned up at Jack's school and gave him sweets.'

There was a pause, before Dale responded. 'What do you mean?'

'It was him, Dale. The guy who killed Bob and tried to take the rest of us out. I'm sure of it.'

'How do you know?'

Angie swallowed the hard lump in her throat. 'He told Jack he was sorry about what happened at the wedding, and sorry about his Uncle Bob getting shot. He was standing on the other side of the fence and handed him a pack of fucking jelly babies. Dale, you need to do something about this. We're all in danger, especially Jack because he's the most vulnerable.'

She heard him take a heavy breath. 'I'll deal with it. I'm going to the school, right now.'

Before Angie could say anything else, Dale ended the call.

—

Dale Bryson stood at the school reception and tapped his index finger on the glass loud enough to startle the receptionist.

'Can I help you?' she asked, an annoyance to her voice.

'I need to speak to the head,' Dale replied, ignoring her shitty tone.

'Do you have an appointment?'

'No, I don't have an appointment. But this is urgent and it needs her attention immediately.'

The receptionist pushed her chair back from her desk and got to her feet before settling her focus on Dale.

'I'm afraid I can't let you through without an appointment, sir.'

Dale exhaled loudly and banged his fist on the surface of the counter. The receptionist jumped and took a step back.

'There's been a security breach at your school involving my seven-year-old son and I want to speak to the head about it, *now*!'

Her expression changed then, and she began to nod. 'Okay, first of all, if you could just stay calm, please. I understand your frustrations, but—'

Dale held up his hand and shook his hand. 'No, you *really* fucking don't. This is a matter of life or death. If you could just get the head out here, it'll save us both a lot of time.'

He could see that she was gritting her teeth behind closed lips, but she gave another nod and said, 'Take a seat,' before she disappeared into the rear of the large reception area.

Dale stood back and relaxed his shoulders a little. He sat down on the seats in the waiting area and stared out into the hallway of the school. Displays of pupils' work were all over the walls and in the far corner a woman in overalls mopped the stairs leading up to the second floor.

A few moments later, the reception door opened and a woman appeared, smiling sympathetically at Dale.

'Mr—?' she lingered on the greeting.

'Bryson. I'm Jack Bryson's dad.'

'Ah, Mr Bryson. Please, come through to my office where we can chat.'

Dale got to his feet and followed the woman. He'd never dealt with the school before, only when he and Angie had enrolled Jack in the pre-school. She'd gone on and on about how private education would be the best thing for Jack, and when Dale had agreed to it, Angie had gone ahead and booked an appointment with the head of the early years department. Dale hadn't set foot in the place since. Angie took care of that side of things. But now that there had been a security issue, Dale knew he had to take the reins.

The woman opened the door to her office and gestured for Dale to go in first. He stepped inside and glanced at the name on the door. Ms Phillips. Dale made a mental note and took a seat at her desk as she closed the door behind her.

'Firstly, I'd like to offer my condolences to you and your family. What happened was truly awful and I can't assure you enough that we will do everything we can to support your family and Jack through this difficult time.' She smiled, and then continued. 'So, Mr Bryson, what can I do for you? My colleague out there said there was a security breach? How so?'

Dale sat forward and explained to her what had happened, trying to keep himself calm through the revelation. The more he spoke about it, the more he thought about what could have happened, and the angrier he felt.

'You're saying a man handed Jack a pack of sweets through the fence at the football pitches?'

'You say it like it's not a big deal, Ms Phillips.'

'I'm not suggesting anything of the sort. I just need to establish the facts.'

Dale nodded. If Angie was here, she'd be able to keep him calm. He needed to keep his cool or she could very well throw him out of the school before he got anywhere with the issue.

'Look, the facts are this, the man who gave my son sweets is the same man who murdered my brother and tried to have the rest of us killed. Jesus, I pay sixteen grand a year to send my son here, I expect you to take this seriously.'

Her expression fell then and Dale couldn't work out if it was the mention of murder or money.

'Mr Bryson, I can assure you that Jack's safety is our absolute priority. We will have a look at our CCTV cameras from today, see if we can identify the man Jack has mentioned. We can also send a copy of any suspicious footage to the police on your behalf.'

Dale nodded, satisfied to some degree that things were starting to move. 'I want my son kept safe here, Ms Phillips. I don't care if you have to have a teacher on his tail everywhere he goes every second of his school day until this person is caught. I pay you enough to facilitate that. I would also like to remind you that my family invested a lot in the regeneration of the original building of this school just two years ago because we wanted our son to come here. And we plan to continue investing where we see fit.'

Ms Phillips frowned. 'I wasn't aware of such an investment. I've only been at this school for six months, Mr Bryson.'

Dale nodded. That was obvious, considering she hadn't known who he was when she first addressed him.

'Well, now you do. So, if you don't mind, I'd like to take a look at this CCTV footage, then I would like to hear how you plan to up your security here at the school.'

Chapter Thirty-Seven

She closed the supply cupboard and locked it. Resting her forehead on the surface of the heavy-set wooden door, Cara Fraser breathed a sigh of relief. He hadn't seen her, thankfully. She wasn't sure he'd have recognised her at all, it had been eight years and she'd changed a lot since then. And he'd been too busy shouting his mouth off at the receptionist that he hadn't even looked in her direction.

As she'd mopped, Cara had listened to Dale Bryson screaming at the receptionist about a security breach, and something inside her chilled. At least the Brysons seemed to think that it was a male who'd shot and killed Bob at the hotel the previous weekend. It would keep her in the clear for a while.

Moving into the staff room, Cara picked up her bag and slung it over her shoulder. She needed to get out of the school before Dale saw her. It could blow everything up and she might not be responsible for her actions if they came face to face right now. And as much as the job had been a way of getting closer to the Brysons, Cara really needed the money. The money that Kyle had left her was fast running out and the boys weren't earning enough to keep her.

'Cara?' A voice from behind her startled her and she jumped. 'Oh God, sorry, I didn't mean to give you a fright.'

It was her supervisor and as Cara came face to face with her, the woman's face was etched with concern.

'Erm, you didn't. I was just miles away, that's all.'

'Are you okay? You don't look so good.'

'I'm fine,' Cara said. 'What's up?'

'I just wondered if you'd managed to do the inventory for the supply cupboard yet? The order's due tomorrow and I don't have it?'

Shit, Cara thought. She'd been so caught up in her own stuff that she'd forgotten to do it.

'Aw, Lissa. I'm so sorry, I forgot to do it. Can I do it tomorrow?'

Lissa shook her head. 'No, sorry. I need to have the order in by ten tomorrow morning or we won't have the cleaning supplies for next week.'

Cara sighed. That would mean another hour in this place at least, and she wouldn't be paid for it because it was her own fault she hadn't done it.

'Okay, I'll stay back and do it now. I'll leave it on the pinboard before I go. I'm so sorry.'

Lissa gave her a tight-lipped smile and left the staff room without saying anything.

Dropping her bag onto the sofa, Cara shook her head. How had her life come to this shit? A cleaning job in a private school, when just eight years previously she was married to a man who was bringing in a shit ton of money to the household and providing a life for her and the boys.

Cara headed out of the staff room and back to the supply cupboard. The smell of bleach and disinfectant was nauseating. She turned back and stared at the door. The rest of the cleaning team had gone home, including Lissa. The only others in the building would be teachers who'd stayed behind to do marking and they would be in their classes. And, of course, Ms Phillips and Dale Bryson.

She glanced out of the small window of the store cupboard onto the tennis courts and sighed. The Brysons were evil. How was it fair that her boys, Ryan and Sean, had had to grow up without their dad, while the Brysons got to carry on with their lives? Sending their youngest to a private school, with multiple sources of income and a happy life – it just wasn't right.

Killing Bob Bryson was the single best decision she'd made since Kyle had died. And she would continue on her quest to make sure that the rest of them ended up just like him.

Chapter Thirty-Eight

Sitting in front of the screen, Dale Bryson felt the rage build in his stomach. 'How can the fucking footage be *missing*?'

'Mr Bryson, I'm sorry you're going through a tough time right now, but this is a school. Could you please refrain from swearing.'

Dale shot Ms Phillips a look and then decided against answering her back. Being a head teacher – or in fact any kind of teacher – must mean that you couldn't vary the way you spoke to adults and pupils. It was like the switch was stuck on teacher mode all the time.

'I think we should contact the police about this matter. Maybe they'll be able to pull footage from cameras in the surrounding areas to determine who the person is that approached your son?'

Dale nodded. 'I'll do that,' he said, thinking about his connections with the local police. They'd listen to him far quicker than they'd listen to her because a lot of them were on his payroll.

'Mr Bryson, I can assure you that we will do *everything* we can to keep Jack safe. We can encourage him to stay inside at break times, we can ask that staff circle the perimeter of the school during break times to make sure that anyone who seems suspicious is dealt with quickly. But what I don't want is for us to fall into the trap where Jack feels unsafe *because* we're taking these measures.'

'He already feels unsafe after what happened last week.' Dale sighed, feeling deflated. 'I'd prefer proper security measures were put in place. I can look at placing my own guards around the grounds. Or maybe we should home school him until we've dealt with the culprit.'

'I understand your reasoning for that, Mr Bryson. But isolating Jack isn't in his best interests. I think the thing to do for Jack is to keep things as normal as possible. I'm not sure the education board would be too happy about external security coming onto school grounds, though.'

'I need to speak to my wife about all this,' he replied, ignoring her comment about his own security plans.

'Of course. I'll be here whenever you and your wife want to speak. Anytime, no appointment needed.'

Dale was grateful for the fact that Ms Phillips had finally dropped the teacher act and was now treating him like an adult. Maybe now she could see how serious he was.

'Thank you. I appreciate that your school's reputation is on the line here, Ms Phillips. We wouldn't want other parents finding out that their children are in danger because the school failed in its duty to keep good surveillance. If they thought a gunman had been near their children, I'm sure they'd whip their kids out in no time, which would mean a great financial loss to the school.'

Ms Phillips stared at Dale, her eyes wide and unblinking. He was sure she heard the words the way he'd intended them – as a warning.

'I'll try to locate the missing footage, Mr Bryson.'

He nodded and then left.

–

When he got home, Angie was serving Jack dinner and Dale noticed the innocence on his son's face. He'd have had no clue he was in danger when he was handed those sweets. How had no one seen what had happened?

'Daddy,' Jack said through a mouthful of spaghetti, 'you're home early.'

Dale couldn't help but laugh that his seven-year-old son already knew it wasn't normal for Dale to be home at dinner time.

'Just fancied some time with my best boy,' Dale replied, ruffling Jack's hair.

'Did you hear about the bad man who gave me the jelly babies?'

Dale stole a glance at Angie, who looked like she'd been crying.

'I heard.'

'He wasn't scary, Daddy. He was kind. But Mummy said that sometimes the kindest people in the world can be the scariest.'

He shot a look at Angie, but she'd turned her back to him and was staring out the window. What the hell was she playing at, saying something like that to a seven-year-old?

'Jack, most people who seem kind are just that. But because of what happened to Uncle Bob, and because a stranger came to your school today, we just have to be extra careful. Can you use your super senses to do that?'

Jack frowned. 'How?'

'Well, we just need you to be very careful at school. We need you to stay away from the fences around the school playgrounds, and make sure you tell a teacher if a person you don't know tries to talk to you, or give you sweets. Can you do that?'

Jack nodded while shovelling another forkful of spaghetti into his mouth.

'Good lad. I just need to talk to Mummy for a minute. You okay on your own for a bit?'

'Can I watch *Spider Man* on the iPad?'

Dale smiled and set the iPad up for Jack on the dining table before he and Angie left the room. He followed Angie into the lounge and closed the door.

'Are you okay?' Dale asked, but by the time the words had left his mouth, Angie had already broken down. He went to her and held her close, allowing her to sob silently into his chest.

She finally spoke. 'Why is this happening? And why target our son?'

'They're doing it because they know it's the best way to get to us. They'll be thinking that we're already vulnerable because they got Bob, and now they're going for the weaker spot in us that is Jack.'

Dale spoke to Angie about his meeting with the head at the school, but it was as if she wasn't listening. She was far away, somewhere else that Dale wouldn't reach.

'So, I was thinking that I'll deploy some of our own security to the school?' he suggested, then waited for a response. When it didn't come, he continued. 'Angie? What do you want to do?'

'I want to sit in on all his classes, I want to stand in the playground and watch his every move. I want to stab the bastard who did this in the heart.'

Dale exhaled. 'I do too. But that's not realistic. Like I said, I think we should deploy some of the security team to patrol the grounds around the school for the next few weeks. The CCTV from that part of the football pitch is missing from the recordings in the school. But if we have some of our own guys there, then perhaps if this guy comes back, we'll be able to deal with him ourselves.'

Angie nodded, wiping at her cheeks with the back of her hands. 'Yeah, good idea.'

'I did suggest this to the head, but she wasn't keen.'

'I don't give a shit if she wasn't keen. It isn't her son that's in danger,' Angie replied.

Dale hugged her tightly and was overwhelmed by her scent. She still had the same effect on him that she did when they'd first got together twenty-two years previously. He'd never thought he'd be one for marriage and babies, but as soon as he laid eyes on Angie, he knew all that was out the window.

'I'll keep him safe, Angie. I'll keep us all safe. I promise.'

'What about Ashley? She called me today, you know. Just to let me know she was okay. But she wouldn't tell me where she was. She could be in bloody Spain for all we know.'

Dale laughed. 'Well, we would know if she was in Spain. All her transactions are linked to our accounts, remember. All we have to do is check where she's lifted money from to see which area she's in. But I think we both know how that would go, she's her mother's daughter after all. And she doesn't want to be around us right now.'

Angie glanced at him. 'I know she doesn't, but that doesn't stop me worrying about her. God, my daughter is pretty much missing, and my youngest son was threatened at school. It's a wonder I haven't had a bloody heart attack.' She took a breath and continued. 'I've been checking Ashley's account. There's been no activity from her card in the last week apart from when she lifted cash just before the wedding. She took out a grand from various machines. God knows what for, but she's obviously not run out yet.'

'Well, we know she's safe, and the fact that she called you shows she cares that you worry about her.'

Angie blinked away her tears. 'Why is it that having children can be the most magical thing on the planet, yet the most crippling at the same time?'

'I know. Don't worry, Angie. Things will settle down. I'll get the security lads on the case. If I have to, I'll have people manning the house, the school and all of the businesses. I'll make sure we're all safe.'

She looked at him through narrowed eyes and frowned. 'You're very calm about all this. Why aren't you angry?'

'Trust me, Angie, I'm not angry. I'm on the fucking warpath. But I'm keeping a lid on it so that when I find this bastard, he gets all my rage. And I will find him. Mark my words.'

Dale knew it was time to start his quest to find out who killed his brother. He'd begin by paying a visit to some of his lower-end associates. The punters who'd been avoiding paying for product. If he got nowhere with them, he'd move on to the others; the higher-end dealers and so on, until he found out the truth. He'd take Paul and Conor along with him. It was time that Glasgow was reminded that the Brysons weren't to be fucked with.

Chapter Thirty-Nine

Chewing on her thumbnail was a habit that Ashley had when she was nervous or stressed. And as she sat on Jamie's couch, scrolling through the job adverts again, she chomped down so hard she drew blood.

'Shit,' she hissed, wincing at the sight. She got up to go and find a plaster, just as Jamie walked through the door.

'Hi,' he said, meeting her in the hallway. 'What happened?'

He glanced down at her thumb and Ashley shook her head. 'Nothing. I just bit down too hard.'

Ashley opened the cupboard in the kitchen, pulled out the plasters and put one on the wound.

'You've been quiet since I took you out this afternoon. You okay?'

'Not really. I just...' she hesitated. 'I don't want you to take this the way it's going to come out. But I don't think couriering is for me, Jamie. Craigton Heights gave me the fear. That lad with the missing teeth freaked me out. And the whole place just didn't feel safe.'

Jamie smiled and nodded. 'Yeah, it wasn't the best advertisement for the job, I'll admit. But just because the place looked like a shit hole doesn't mean the people are bad.'

Ashley tried to keep her face neutral, but his words didn't hit the way he probably intended them to.

'I'm not judging, Jamie. All I'm saying is the job isn't for me.'

She could tell by the look on his face that he was slightly irritated by her decision, and she didn't want things to escalate. He was letting her live with him rent free and they'd only been together for just over a month. Any other guy would have ghosted her by now.

'Look, why don't I try coming out with you again? Maybe it was just first-time nerves?'

Jamie seemed to warm to the idea quickly and he slid his arms around her waist before pulling her close. 'Sounds like a good idea. You could do some of the doors yourself, see how you get on? And I'll pay you for the ones you do?'

Ashley nodded. She really didn't want to do this, but she didn't have any other options in front of her.

'Okay.' Before she could say anything else, Jamie's lips were on hers and somehow, the conversation they'd just had melted away as if it hadn't happened.

Later, as Ashley lay in Jamie's arms in bed and he snored gently, his phone vibrated on and off consistently for a few minutes. He didn't hear it at first, and she considered leaning across and glancing at the screen to see if it was anything important. If it was, he'd want her to wake him, wouldn't he?

'Jamie,' she whispered, 'your phone's going.'

Jamie didn't respond. He was deep in a slumber. Propping herself up, she leaned across him gently and reached for the phone. Just as her fingers grazed the edge of the iPhone, Jamie's hand gripped her wrist and she let out a shocked yelp.

'Oh God, sorry. I didn't mean to startle you,' he said, letting go of her.

'Your phone's been going mad,' she said, falling back onto her side of the bed.

Jamie reached for the phone and lifted it at an angle so Ashley couldn't see the screen. She wondered if he'd done that on purpose. Maybe there was something on the phone he didn't want her to see.

Ashley rolled her eyes. That was a ridiculous thought. What exactly would he have to hide from her? They'd barely been away from each other for the last seven days.

'I've got to go,' Jamie said, jumping up and pulling on his clothes. Ashley lay back, hugging the duvet close to her chest and watched him get dressed.

'Where you going?'

'I need to go back out. A few more deliveries have come in and we're short on drivers.'

Ashley nodded. 'Maybe I could come along with you now?'

Jamie smiled down at her. 'No. I want you right here when I get back. Plus, it'll only be a few runs. It'll be better if you come out for a full shift.'

Ashley sighed inwardly, but was also secretly glad that she didn't have to get up. Jamie's bed was too comfortable to warrant getting out of it.

Jamie leaned down, kissed Ashley and then headed out, calling 'Bye!' before closing the door. She heard the key turn in the lock and listened as his footsteps fell further from the door. Smiling, Ashley couldn't help but think how lucky she was to have him.

Chapter Forty

'All entrances to the house are to be manned at all times, including the main gate. Make sure you communicate with each other when you do a perimeter run, and if there is anything suspicious, no matter how minute it may be, you flag it with each other and call me immediately. Do you understand?'

The six security men nodded in agreement and Dale shook each of their hands. He looked at Angie, waiting for her to indicate that she was happy with the arrangement. She nodded and thanked the men Dale had offered to pay triple time for the twelve-hour shift.

'Great. Right, you can take your spots outside now,' Dale said. The men left the house and Dale closed the door behind them.

'Do you have to go to this thing tonight? Can't you just stay with us?' Angie asked.

Jack's voice could be heard from the playroom at the other end of the hallway. He was blissfully unaware that his house was under surveillance. That was the way Dale and Angie agreed it should be. If anyone's life should be blissful and peaceful, it should be Jack's; he was just too little and innocent to get dragged into their mess.

'You know I have to go. It's our casino, Angie. We can't throw a charity event for the community and not be there.'

Angie sighed. 'I know. But isn't it enough for Paul and other employees to be there? I really want you, Conor and Jack here with me.'

Dale shook his head. He understood where his wife was coming from, but staying tucked up at home just wasn't an option for him right now.

'Angie, it's important that we're out there, that we're seen. If our attacker notices that we've gone into hiding, then they're getting exactly what they want from us. I want them to know that we won't be backed into a corner; that we're stronger now than ever; even more than we were before they took Bob from us. I have enough security here to keep you both safe tonight. The rest of us will be out there, doing what we do best. And then I'll be home with you and Jack. Honestly, we'll be back before you know it.'

Dale kissed Angie before slipping out to the car. As much as it would ease her concerns for him to stay, the Brysons had a job to do tonight. A job that Dale hadn't told Angie about because if he did, he knew she'd try to convince him not to go through with it.

The security men waved Dale off as the car moved down the private drive and then onto the main road, before heading into the city to the casino.

The charity event would go ahead as planned. But Dale, Paul and Conor wouldn't be there. They had a more pressing issue to tend to.

–

Dale parked up the car and got out before heading towards the van in which his brother and eldest son waited for him. When he climbed in, he imagined Bob sitting in the driver's seat, smiling at him. His tongue would be protruding slightly between his teeth, buzzing to get started and to go on a hunt to find the person who'd shot at them.

Paul was in the driver's seat now, silent, clearly thinking things over. Dale looked at him, wondered what was going through his head. He had always been the quietest of the three – the complete opposite of Bob, who would allow things to build up over time in his head until he had no space left. Then he'd explode and anyone who stood in his way would bear the brunt.

'You good over there, Paul?' Dale asked.

Paul fixed his eye on him and nodded. 'Aye, just thinking how Bob would react to all this. He'd probably be high on coke, ready to take on Mike Tyson if it meant finding the guy who shot him.'

Dale smirked. 'That's what I was just thinking.'

Conor's voice interrupted their shared moment regarding their brother.

'Dad, what exactly are we going to do tonight? I mean, we don't know for certain this is the guy. He doesn't seem the type.'

'They never do, Conor. But he owes us money. A big chunk of money at that. I've been a nice guy up until now. He's small fry. But if I was in his position – owing money to the likes of us – I'd do whatever I could to clear that debt without paying it. Taking us all out is the best way of doing that. You see where I'm coming from?'

Conor didn't respond.

'Trust me, Conor. I know what and who to look for with this. If I didn't, we wouldn't be doing it.'

–

The journey was made in silence, and around thirty minutes later, Dale noticed the signs. They were entering the shit hole that was Craigton Heights.

'This place fucking stinks,' Conor said.

'Aye, it hasn't changed at all, eh, Dale?' Paul said.

Conor leaned forward and gripped the back of Dale's seat. 'What do you mean it hasn't changed?'

'This fine estate, Conor, is where we all grew up,' Dale replied.

'Yep, got out as soon as we could. If you're not careful, the place will either turn you into a junkie, or it'll kill you,' Paul said in an almost whisper. 'But it's a good money maker. Well, it is when the punters pay their way.'

Paul drove to the end of the scheme and turned the van around before driving back down until he stopped about halfway between the cul-de-sac and the entrance to the building. He glanced up at the tenement which they were intending to visit and Dale unclipped his seatbelt.

'Right, lads, let's get this over with.'

Dale and the rest of them got out of the van and headed for the back entrance of the building. It was pitch black, and the sound of a mix of heavy metal and dance music could be heard up and down the scheme. The smell of weed was overwhelming, and Dale had to kick a used needle out of the way before using his sleeve to open the back door.

He stood aside and allowed Paul to enter first, followed by Conor and them himself. Dale followed them up the stairs, choosing to breathe through his mouth. The stench of piss was overwhelming.

After reaching the fourth floor, Paul stopped outside one of the flats and glanced at Dale. He nodded and Paul rattled the door with his fist.

They waited in silence, listened for signs of life inside. Only silence came, but the sound of music could still be heard in the distance from the other buildings.

'He's not here,' Conor said.

'Oh, he's here alright. He's just not answering the door because he knows it's us,' Paul whispered, rattling the door again, this time with more force. Dale listened as the sound of light footsteps padding across a floor could be heard.

'Smiler? You in there?' Dale called. 'I'm here for payment.'

A floorboard creaked from behind the door and before anyone could stop him, Paul had kicked the door in.

A figure flashed past them, into a room at the opposite end of the flat. The door slammed shut but Paul was already on it, kicking it in as hard as he could.

'Jesus, you don't do subtle,' Conor said, closing the main door to the flat.

'Wee bastards like Smiler don't understand subtle, and someone has to take on Bob's tactics now that he's not here.' Paul grimaced before the wood splintered under the force of his boot.

Dale stepped inside the room and the first thing he saw was a dirty mattress, with no form of bedding. A few ashtrays were strewn around the room and the stench was unholy: sweat mixed with weed.

'Smiler,' Dale said, baring his teeth at the young lad as he stood in the corner of the room, staring wildly at them. 'How's things?'

Paul appeared at Dale's side and was about to move around the mattress towards Smiler, but Dale held his hand up, indicating to his brother to wait.

Smiler didn't respond. He simply stared at them. All three of them. Dale could see the fear in his eyes. Good, he thought. If he's scared, he'll tell the truth, surely?

'Oi, he asked you a question,' Paul snarled.

'Erm, aye... what... why are you all here?' Smiler stammered.

Dale thought about how he should address the matter with this piece of scum. Brutal and violent was always the way to get people talking when they had something to hide. But that was usually Bob's role. He liked the violence and aggression.

Turning to Paul and Conor, Dale gestured for them to leave the room. 'Search this shit hole. If you find a gun, let me know.'

Smiler gasped. 'A gun? Why'd ye think you'd find a gun here?'

'Because we're looking for the little fucker who murdered Bob. And you've got motive to do that, haven't you, Smiler?' Conor chipped in.

Smiler frowned and a look of confusion washed over his face. 'Murder? Bob was murdered?'

'Oh, fuck off, you're trying to tell me you didn't know that? It was all over the news. Everyone's been talking about it,' Conor replied.

Smiler shook his head. 'I swear, I didn't know.'

'Aye, that's just what the guy who murdered him would say. Let's just hope we don't find the gun, then.'

Paul and Conor left the room to start searching, and Dale listened as they tore the place apart.

'I swear to you, Mr Bryson, I would never even dream of it.' Smiler pointed at himself as he frowned.

'You've owed us money for a number of weeks now, haven't you? And you've avoided us like the plague anytime we've arranged for the debt to be collected. Taking us out of the picture altogether makes that debt disappear, does it not? I'm pretty certain you meant to get us all, but you didn't. Unlucky for you.'

Smiler's eyes darted between Dale and the bedroom door, before he shrugged. 'I dunno what yer talking aboot.'

'Is that right?' Dale said, taking a step closer.

'Aye, that's right. And anyway, I've found a new dealer now. One who isn't so fucking expensive, and his gear's far better than the shit you punt.'

Dale laughed at the wee man's bravery. Or stupidity. He couldn't quite work out which of the two dwelled inside the smug little bastard.

'And who's your new dealer, then?' Dale asked. 'Or is that something you're telling us just so we'll go after them and forget about you?'

Smiler shook his head and sniggered. 'Am no' a liar, if that's wit yer saying.'

'But you did come after us last weekend?' Dale said. 'It makes perfect sense, eh?'

Smiler opened his mouth to speak when Paul shouted through from another room. 'You'll never guess what we found.'

Paul appeared in the doorway, Conor behind him. He was holding a gun in a gloved hand, and in the other were three bullets.

'Our names are carved into these,' Paul said. 'It was him. The wee bastard wanted us out the picture for the sake of a measly couple hundred quid.'

Dale glared at Smiler, who was shaking his head. 'Nah. No *fucking* way. I've never seen that thing before. Fucking hell, I wouldn't even know how to use it.'

Nodding, Dale moved closer to Smiler, who had backed himself into the corner of the room, between the mattress and the window.

'If it's not yours then why is it here? In your possession?' Conor asked. Dale stopped, face to face with Smiler. Now that he was closer, he could see the lad was trembling slightly. If he'd had teeth in that gaping mouth of his, they'd be rattling for sure.

'Someone must've planted it here,' Smiler replied.

'So, tell me. Who's been here? Narrow it down for me, Smiler. Oh, don't tell me, it must've been this new dealer of yours?'

Smiler's eyes darted wildly between Dale and the window, as if he was trying to come up with names. Names he'd likely pluck from thin air.

'Erm, I dunno. No one's been here in a few weeks.'

Nodding, Dale turned to look at Paul and Conor. It was obvious that Smiler was trying to buy some time and it wasn't working.

'Ah, see, this poses a problem for you, Smiler. Because we were shot at just seven days ago and our brother was fucking murdered. He bled to death on me, at *my* wedding. My kids had to witness that. Do you get how fucking traumatic that is? Do you?' Dale's voice was loud, even through gritted teeth. 'If you're saying that no one has been around here in weeks, then that means you had that gun in your possession eight days ago. If no one planted it here, because there hasn't been anyone here

190

in weeks, as you say, then the only person that could have used it, is you?'

Smiler shook his head furiously. 'Nah. I already told you it wasn't me, Dale. I wouldn't do shit like that to you or your family.'

Dale continued, ignoring Smiler's denial. 'And you must have replaced the bullets after you used them, right? Or was naming each bullet an idea that came to you after you killed Bob?'

Dale allowed silence to fill the room, allowed the fear in Smiler to grow. The more he feared Dale, and what might happen to him, the more he might give in and tell the truth.

'Tell me, how'd you find out which school my son goes to?'

Smiler's expression crumpled, and he glanced across at Paul and Conor. Settling back on Dale, he shook his head. 'What are you talking about?'

'You turned up at my kid's school today, gave him sweets. Told him that you were sorry about what happened at the wedding.'

'What *fucking* wedding? I dunno what you're on about, man.'

Dale closed his eyes. He'd had enough lies.

'He's fucking lying, Dale,' Paul said.

Without taking his eyes off Smiler, without blinking, Dale nodded. 'I know he is, Paul.'

–

The wind caught in the back of Dale's throat as he stood at the top of the high-rise flats. It hadn't seemed so strong down on the ground when they'd got out of the van, but up on the roof, it whipped around them like a mini tornado.

'I'll ask you one last fucking time, if the gun and the bullets aren't yours, then whose are they?' Dale snarled in Smiler's ear.

Smiler was facing away from them, hands bound behind his back and a pillowcase over his head, tied loosely around his neck.

'I dunno, I fucking swear it, man. I swear it's nothing to do with me.'

'Maybe he's telling the truth. He'd have caved by now if he was lying.' Conor's voice was carried on the wind.

Dale rolled his eyes. 'Come on, Conor. You know that's not the case. He has the gun, bullets with our names on them. You saw them yourself. This is the fucker who killed your uncle. Don't let him fool you.'

Conor didn't answer. Had he developed a conscience in the last few minutes?

'Conor, if you don't want to be a part of this, then you should leave. If you've not got the balls to help us get our own justice for what happened last Saturday, then you shouldn't be here at all,' Paul said.

Dale listened to his brother giving Conor his opinion, and had to agree. But he didn't say anything in response. Instead, he gripped Smiler tightly as they stood at the edge.

'Nah, please, Mr Bryson. It wasn't me. I didn't do it.' Smiler's voice cut off like the end of some old cassette tape, and Dale let go.

'So long, ya wee fucker,' Paul said before he turned his back and moved away from the edge of the building.

Dale watched as Smiler fell through the air towards the concrete at the bottom. A loud, yet dull thud echoed up from below. Dale expected to feel a weight lift, but it didn't happen. Bob was still dead, and nothing could change that.

'Job done. Back to the casino?' Paul said.

Dale exhaled loudly. 'Aye. Let's go.'

Dale caught his son's eye, and he realised that this was the first time that he'd ever been part of something like this. He'd only ever done security with the casino before now.

'You good?' he asked Conor.

'Aye,' he replied. But his eyes were still fixed on the edge of the building. He'd witnessed Dale throw a man to his death. 'Fine.'

'Try not to overthink it, Conor. It's all part of the world we live in. You don't achieve our status without picking off the ones who think they can get away with hurting your family. Call it an initiation into the darker side of what we do, Conor. And you can also call it retribution.' He patted Conor on the shoulder and turned him towards the door.

As they made their way down to the ground floor, Dale pulled out his phone and called Angie. She would be so relieved that this was over. Now Ashley would be able to come home, and Dale would be able to focus on the businesses again, along with grieving properly for his brother.

Chapter Forty-One

Angie hung up the phone and sighed with relief. Having just been told that the person who'd killed Bob – and tried to kill them all – was now dead was like the world's heaviest weight being lifted from her shoulders, and a smile spread across her face.

Now she didn't have to worry. Now, she could get back to normal, and not have to think about strange men turning up at Jack's school as a way of terrorising the family. She wouldn't have to worry about Ashley being out there on her own, with a madman with a gun on the loose, hunting them down.

Thinking of Ashley made Angie instantly pick the phone back up. She had to tell her daughter that if she wanted to come home, it would be safe to do so. But Angie wondered if Ashley would want to come home at all. Maybe she liked being away from the family, rather than it just being about her safety. Maybe having some distance was good for Ashley's mental health. She had struggled with that ever since she was little, after what had happened with Reilly.

'Jesus, no wonder she chose to leave us,' Angie whispered as she pulled Ashley's name up in her contacts.

The phone rang on the other end of the line, and to Angie's surprise, her daughter answered.

'Oh, I was expecting your voicemail.'

'Well, I'm here. So, what's up?' Ashley asked, her tone flat.

'I just wanted to let you know that it's over. Your dad just told me that they found the man who killed Bob. It's done. We're safe.'

There was a silence at the other end of the line. It seemed to last forever rather than a few seconds.

'So, you *can* come home now, Ashley.'

'No thanks. I'm fine where I am.'

Running her tongue across her teeth, Angie nodded. 'I thought you might say that.'

'Can you blame me?'

Angie didn't know how to respond to that. She didn't want to get into an argument with her daughter about this. It was a delicate subject, especially with everything that Ashley had done to try to heal herself. The guilt that Angie hadn't been the one to instigate the therapy years ago was still heavy on her chest.

'Are you okay?' Angie asked.

'It depends on what you mean by okay. If you're asking in terms of what happened last week, then no. If you're asking in general terms, then yes. I'm happy where I am and who I'm with. You don't have to ask me about it because I'm not going to tell you. Just because this guy's been dealt with doesn't mean there aren't more out there willing to take his place. I mean, let's face it, Mum, Dad isn't exactly a stranger when it comes to violence. I've already experienced that; I don't want to have to go through it again. And you should be making sure that the same thing doesn't happen to Jack.'

Angie bowed her head and closed her eyes. Her daughter was right. But it had already happened to Jack, just in a different way. The jelly-babies-through-the-fence had as much threat behind it as the shooting itself. In fact, it was worse. It was far more calculated, showing the Brysons that even the youngest members of the family were not safe. A threat that there was more to come. Well, not anymore, now that the bastard was dead.

'I have to go,' Ashley said. 'I'll see you around, Mum.'

The end of the line went dead and Angie let out a long and exasperated breath. Ashley might not be harmed, but the person who'd attacked them had separated the Bryson family. And that, to Angie, was a cause for grief anyway.

Chapter Forty-Two

Lying back on Jamie's couch, Ashley closed her eyes and used the breathing technique that her therapist had taught her. If she felt a panic or an anxiety attack coming on, then she was supposed to breathe through it. It didn't often stop the attack, but it would ease the blow when it hit.

Thinking of the day of the wedding and hearing those shots, seeing Bob lying there covered in blood, Ashley had been transported back to that day when she was just ten years old and had witnessed her dad getting into an argument with the guy she later learned was named Reilly. He'd pulled a knife on Dale and tried to stab him. It might have been eight years ago, but those memories had haunted her ever since. If she'd been old enough to get away from the family then, she may well have run.

'I'm back,' Jamie's voice filtered through from the hallway. The front door clicked loudly and Ashley sat up. The tightness in her chest loosened a little, although it was still present.

'Hey,' Ashley responded. 'Everything good?'

Jamie appeared in the lounge and smiled. 'It is now that I'm back.'

'What was up at work?'

Jamie shook his head and pursed his lips. 'Nothing, just a driver short. So, what's been happening?'

Should she tell him about the call from Mum? He might push her to go back home if he thought things were better again.

'I had a call from my mum.'

Sitting down next to her, Jamie rested his hand on Ashley's knee. 'Oh? What did she have to say for herself?'

'Apparently, they got the guy who attacked us at the wedding.'

Ashley saw a flicker in Jamie's eyes. 'What do you mean, *got* the guy? What happened?'

'She didn't say. All she said was that it's over and I can go back home because things are safe now.'

'And are you? Going back home, I mean?'

Ashley shook her head. 'I don't want to. It doesn't matter that the person's been *dealt with*, as she put it. The truth is, I'll never feel safe in their company. I haven't since...' Ashley let her words trail off. She hadn't spoken to anyone about what had happened when she was just eight years old, only her therapist, who she still visited on a regular basis for CBT therapy.

'Since what?'

Ashley shook her head. 'Nothing. Look, I think I'm going to have an early night. My head is bursting with everything that's happened over the last week and I think I just need to rest.'

Jamie nodded slowly. 'Okay, babe. If that's what you want.'

She kissed Jamie goodnight and headed for the bedroom, grabbing her phone on the way. She needed to make an appointment with her therapist. Things were getting on top of her again.

–

Sitting in the passenger seat of the van the next morning, Ashley took in the scenes in front of her as they approached Craigton Heights. The place was swarming with police and people head-to-toe in white forensics suits. Yellow police tape surrounded one of the high rise buildings and Ashley felt sick to her stomach at the sight. Something terrible had happened here, and she wasn't sure that they should be driving into the area at all.

'What the hell?' Jamie said as he pulled into the kerb.

'Something serious must've happened,' Ashley replied as Jamie unclipped his seatbelt.

'I have a package for that flat. There's no way I'll be allowed in there.'

'Could the recipient come out and meet you?'

Jamie shook his head. 'Nah, they won't be allowed out because of where they've sealed the place off. *Fuck!*'

Ashley jumped at his outburst. 'Okay, Jamie, calm down. It's not your fault.'

Jamie glanced at her. 'I know it's not.'

A woman hovered just on the pavement next to the van. She lit a cigarette and watched intently what was going on. Jamie rolled down the window and Ashley could instantly smell the smoke.

'Excuse me?'

The woman looked at Jamie and raised a brow. 'Aye?'

'What's going on?'

'Poor bastard was flung aff the top of that building. Well, I say flung. He could've jumped. But ye know wit it's like roon here. I doubt he did it willingly. Probably owed some drug dealer money or something.' She took a long draw on her cigarette and shook her head before glancing back over at the scene.

Ashley felt sick. What the hell would possess someone to do something like that? Then something in her head clicked.

Jamie rolled the window back up and opened the door. 'I'm just going to have a quick look, see if I can get in to drop this delivery. I'll be back in a sec.'

Closing the door, Jamie crossed the road and joined the gathering of people at the edge of the sealed-off area. Ashley watched him from inside the van and something inside her was screaming at her that she shouldn't be there. There was something, buried deep, that told her she should get far away from the scene. But she couldn't move. Fear rooted her to the seat and all she could do was watch Jamie.

He was talking to one of the people who'd gathered to see what was going on, but he was too far away for her to really get a grasp of what might be being said. She could swallow her fear, get out of the van and go and join him, couldn't she?

Just as she was about to unclip her seatbelt and force herself across the road, Jamie moved away from the place he'd been standing and walked deeper into the scheme until she couldn't see him anymore.

'I'm not getting out now,' she whispered, clicking her seatbelt back into place. She locked the doors of the van and pulled her phone out of her pocket. Tapping at her dad's number on the screen, she waited until he answered.

'Ashley?'

'Dad, I need to ask you something. And I want the truth.'

'Nice to hear from you,' he said with sarcasm.

'I'm being serious, Dad.'

Silence echoed from the other end of the line and Ashley felt a ball of anxiety form in her chest with the question she was about to ask.

'Go on, then.'

'A body has been found this morning. At the bottom of one of the high rises in Craigton Heights.'

She heard her dad clear his throat but he didn't say anything, so she continued. 'You wouldn't happen to know anything about that, would you? This isn't the guy, is it?'

'Ashley, the only thing I'm going to say right now is, you need to get the fuck away from Craigton Heights. It's no place for someone like you. And what the hell are you even doing there, anyway?'

Ashley closed her eyes but held the phone firmly to her ear. He hadn't answered the question. He'd avoided it completely.

'It doesn't matter why I'm here.' She glanced over at the ever-growing crowd. 'Just tell me, is the guy they've found anything to do with you? Mum told me that he'd been taken care of.'

'Ashley, you left for a reason, didn't you? You didn't feel safe around us, and that reason is the best explanation as to why I will not answer your question. The less you know, the better.

The guy who killed Bob is out of the picture, and that's all you need to know.'

Ashley exhaled loudly and shook her head. He didn't have to confirm it. She knew full well the answer.

'Murder, Dad? Seriously? You couldn't have... I don't know – forced a confession from him and had him arrested or something?'

'Ashley,' her dad lowered his voice, 'this guy turned up at your brother's school, spoke to him. A seven-year-old boy. Do you think I was willing to risk Jack's life by letting this guy live?'

Ashley felt her blood run cold. 'Jesus. What happened?'

'Luckily, nothing. He gave Jack some sweets, but the threat was very real. I'd do it again, no questions asked. Now, you get yourself out of Craigton Heights, right fucking now. I still don't understand why you're there.'

Ashley swallowed hard. 'My boyfriend's a courier driver for Amazon. I'm just here for the company.'

'Boyfriend?'

Shit, she hadn't told her parents about Jamie yet.

'Don't start. I'm almost eighteen and an adult.'

Her eyes remained fixed on the crowd, but just to the left of the throng of people, Ashley spotted Jamie walking back towards the van.

'I have to go, Dad.'

Before he could say anything else, Ashley ended the call and shoved her phone in her pocket before Jamie got back into the van.

'Where did you go?' she asked him.

'To check if any of the entrances were open. The place is crawling with polis and folk in white suits. There's no way I'm getting in there today.'

Ashley detected his annoyance but couldn't understand why he'd be so frustrated. It wasn't his fault he couldn't complete his deliveries for that particular building.

'Did you find out any more about what happened over there?'

'Aye. It seems the old woman was right. Someone threw him off.'

'Jesus. Who is he?'

Jamie hesitated. 'I don't know. Look, let's get away from here. I've got other deliveries to do, and there's no way the polis are going to let me in today. I'll come back once all this shit is gone.'

Ashley clipped her seatbelt back into place and watched Jamie with curiosity. Something about what had happened over at the high rise had really bothered him. It couldn't just be because he couldn't deliver a parcel. It had to be more than that.

'Are you okay?'

'I'm fine,' he said but it was more of a snap. 'I just don't like my schedule being messed up, that's all.'

He started the engine and turned the van around before exiting the scheme. If Jamie was hiding something, he wasn't the only one. Ashley was going to keep the conversation with her dad a secret. It would be too hard to share it with Jamie. He wouldn't understand what her family did for a living. No one outside of the criminal world did.

Chapter Forty-Three

Cara Fraser looked at herself in the mirror as she put on her eye make-up. Back in the day, Kyle was always saying how much better she looked with make-up on. 'You look stunning when you're done up, doll.' He'd always say it with a gentle manner, but when Cara thought about it now, she realised just what a cheeky bastard her husband could be. Most of the time he didn't even notice when she didn't have any on. As much as she'd hated his little comments like that, she still missed him. He hadn't deserved to die the way he had. And now, knowing that the wrong person had been put away for her husband and brother-in-law's murders, she felt more rage with every passing day.

Happy with how her lashes looked, Cara put her mascara back in the make-up bag and sprayed herself with her favourite perfume, Paco Rabanne's Lady Million. Kyle had bought it for her as a birthday gift when it had first come out and the scent reminded her of him so much that whenever she ran out, she'd immediately replace it.

Exhaling loudly at the thought of Kyle and all that he'd missed with his boys over the last eight years, Cara stood up straight and headed for the front door. For many, Sundays were a day of rest, but for Cara they were a day of shopping. Not like when Kyle was around and he promised that the money would start properly coming in; those days would consist of designer shoe and bag purchases via a credit card. Now, she had to settle for the high street since Kyle's life insurance money was fast running out and all she could do was rely on her own income.

He'd taken out various policies on himself – due to his line of work, she'd imagined. Not that he'd ever said that to her.

Because Moira had died from a heart attack just weeks after the death of her sons, Ian's policy automatically fell to the boys. That was all that was left of the Fraser brothers. Money. And after eight years of living off it, Cara had almost spent all of it. The last big spend was deposits on rent on the flat for the boys and her own.

Ryan and Sean had already made up their minds about what their lives in Glasgow would consist of: the same as their dad. At first, Cara wasn't happy about it, but they'd agreed it was the best way to take vengeance for their family. She was proud of her boys, even if she knew that they were putting themselves in danger by going after the Brysons.

Just as she was about to open the front door and leave, Cara's mobile rang in her bag. She looked down at the withheld number, puzzled. Could be a call centre. But something told her it wasn't.

'Hello?' she answered, ensuring that her tone indicated she wasn't in the mood for a cold call.

'Cara? It's James.'

Cara sighed. She wondered briefly how he had got her number, realised that one of the boys must have passed it on. What the hell did he want now?

'I thought you should know something.' She heard his voice crack with emotion and something told her she should sit down for what was about to be said. Moving through to the living room, she lowered herself onto the sofa and listened.

'My nephew was murdered on Friday night.'

Frowning, Cara shook her head. 'Why would I want to know that?'

'Because he was working for Ryan and Sean.'

Swallowing the hard lump in her throat, Cara pursed her lips. 'And you think that because he worked for them, they would know what happened to him? Or are you insinuating that they had something to do with it?'

James fell silent, and Cara hoped that he was thinking carefully about his reply.

'Could you have them come to see me? I just want to ask them if they know what happened? Maybe they could help find out who did this? He was the only family I had left, Cara.'

A pang of guilt hit her then, but she certainly wasn't going to voice it to James MacTavish. She still wasn't a hundred per cent sure she could trust him. In fact, Cara had struggled to trust anyone after Kyle was killed.

'I'll speak to them.'

Abruptly ending the call, Cara got up and headed out of the house. She'd speak with Ryan and Sean herself on the way to the high street. They'd be livid that one of their employees had been taken off their hands. And she'd be able to tell just by looking at their faces if they had been responsible for this.

With everything else going on with the Brysons, she really hoped not.

—

She rang the bell to Sean's flat and waited to be buzzed in. As she climbed the stairs, she couldn't smell anything suspicious, and was thankful that the boys were taking precautions against their neighbours suspecting they were growing their own drugs.

Sean opened the door just as Cara reached the landing and she stepped inside.

'Morning,' Sean said. She could tell he was irritated.

'What's up with your face?' she asked, closing the door behind her and following him into the living room.

'Just got some shitty news yesterday from Ryan. One of the lads who was punting for us turned up dead.'

Cara stopped in the middle of the room and stared at him. 'And did this person happen to be the nephew of James MacTavish?'

Sean's expression changed quickly from irritated to shock. 'How did you know that?'

'Because I had MacTavish on the phone this morning, asking if you and Ryan would go to see him. He wants to know if you had a clue who might have done it?'

Sean's shoulders relaxed and he slumped down on the sofa. The sound of the front door opening alerted Cara to the hallway. She peered through the livingroom door and saw Ryan entering.

'You must be psychic, I was just about to phone you,' she said.

'Why?' Ryan asked, passing by her and sitting down on the other side of the sofa from Sean.

'Because I heard about what happened to the guy who was working for you.'

Ryan gritted his teeth. 'Aye, Smiler. Some bastard threw him off the roof of one of the high rises. Fucking brutal. So now we're down a dealer. It's hard to get a dealer for that shit hole. No one wants to go near the fucking place.'

Cara felt sick. There was a familiarity to that scenario. Something about it didn't sit right with her. 'He was thrown off the roof?'

'According to the locals,' Ryan said. 'I'm fucking livid, this is going to set us back a couple grands' worth of deals.'

'We could just do the drops ourselves, Ryan. It's not as if we don't know the place. And with what's just happened to Smiler, I'd doubt anyone would want to fuck with us. If folk think he's been flung off that roof for owing money, like the rumours suggest, they'll pay us up front.'

Cara could hear the boys discussing it. But she wasn't processing what they were saying. Not really. She was too busy trying to think back to when Kyle was alive. He'd told her something years ago, about a guy being murdered under similar circumstances.

'Mum, what's wrong?' Ryan asked.

Glancing down at her elder son, she shook her head. 'It's nothing. It's just, well... something about this doesn't feel right.'

'Aye, I bet Smiler was thinking the same when he was standing up on that roof,' Sean remarked.

'No, I don't mean that. I mean…' she paused. 'Your dad told me a story once. Well, it wasn't a story, it sounded more like a nightmare. He told me that he knew a guy who was a dealer once. Back when they were younger. A lot younger, before you two were born. He said that the guy always threatened to throw people off the top of buildings if they didn't pay up what they owed.'

Sean shrugged. 'Sounds like a legit threat from a dealer.'

'But not long after that, it actually happened. It was on the news. A junkie was found at the bottom of a building – actually, he'd been thrown off and then stuffed inside a wheelie bin. He was identified by the locals as one of the junkies who was always causing trouble.'

Ryan sat forward on the sofa and Cara could feel his eyes burning into her. 'You think it's the same person?'

She took a breath and sat down on the armchair next to the door. 'When it happened, your dad was acting weird and when I asked him what was wrong, he told me that he was actually working with the guys who did it. Your dad wasn't an angel, but something in particular about that night stayed with Kyle.'

Ryan stood up and moved closer to Cara before crouching down in front of her. 'You said "guys"?'

She nodded. 'I found out later who your dad was working for. He was working for Dale Bryson and his brothers.'

Ryan stole a glance at Sean. They got it.

'This was them. Smiler was thrown to his death by the Brysons,' Sean hissed. 'But why would they do that? What would the Brysons have against Smiler?'

Cara sat back and shook her head. 'Maybe he was working for both of them?'

'Nothing's impossible,' Ryan replied. 'I'll speak to MacTavish. See what he can tell us.'

Cara sighed and nodded in appreciation. Her sons were her world now. But what had happened to Kyle and Ian had halted her life, and theirs. All she could think about now wasn't merely justice, but revenge.

'Speaking of the Brysons, Dale turned up at school on Friday,' Cara said. She noticed an exchange between Ryan and Sean and raised a brow. 'Was shouting the odds about a security issue with his boy? Any of you two know anything about that?'

Ryan said nothing, but she could see a smirk form on Sean's face.

'Do you think I was born yesterday? I know what you did, Sean. I fucking saw you. And if I saw you, someone else might have too. Are you stupid?'

Ryan held his hands up in defeat. 'I fucking told you, Sean. This wasn't part of our plan.'

'And what I did is *worse* than you killing Bob Bryson?'

Cara gritted her teeth. 'That was planned! You put both me *and* your brother at risk because you didn't even bother to cover your fucking face, Sean! You should've spoken to us about it first.'

Sean fell silent and Ryan shook his head.

'The school is of the highest standard, they have the most sophisticated security cameras all over the place. Did you think about that?'

Sean rolled his eyes like a child and Cara wanted to slap him. How could he be so bloody stupid?

'Luckily for you, I acted quickly. I got rid of the footage. But that put *me* at risk. If Dale Bryson got wind that I was working at the school, he'd put two and two together and we know that the Brysons are fucking ruthless, Sean. If I hadn't seen you, I have no doubt that we'd all be dead right now.'

Sean dropped his shoulders and the attitude. 'I didn't think of it like that, I was just so angry and wanted to scare them even more than you already had.'

'No, you didn't think, did you?' Cara got to her feet and placed a hand on Ryan's shoulders. 'If you two have a plan, you run it by me first. Got it? You might be the men of the family now, but if your decisions affect me, I want to know about it first. And no arguments. If you're going to act like a hothead, Sean, and be unpredictable, then you're going to have to take a back seat on this one.'

Ryan took his mum's hand and gave it a reassuring squeeze. He was a good lad, Ryan; level-headed. Sean was a little more of a hothead. Kyle had been a mix of both.

'Don't worry, Mum. Nothing like that will happen again, *will it*, Sean?'

Sean kept his head low. 'No.'

Good, she thought. Cara hadn't got herself sober for nothing. She wasn't going to let anything stand in the way of her taking from the Brysons what they took from her. But she needed proof first. And that was what Ryan and Sean were supposed to be gathering for her.

'Good, now get on with it. And report back to me with anything new, including what MacTavish says when you go to see him.'

Chapter Forty-Four

As Ryan approached MacTavish in the visiting hall, he wondered what was going through the prisoner's head. If it was absolutely the Brysons who'd thrown his nephew off that roof, then he'd want revenge like anyone else. But how would he get that, being stuck in prison?

'Thanks for responding to the urgent visit notice and coming back to see me,' MacTavish said as Ryan sat down opposite him. 'Your brother not able to come?'

Ryan shook his head. 'I thought it best I come on my own. My brother has things to sort out and it only needs one of us to hear what you have to say.'

MacTavish nodded and took a sip of water. Ryan had to admit it to himself, the man looked like someone had shat in his breakfast that morning. It was no wonder, given that the guy's only surviving family member had been murdered just a few nights before.

'You heard about Smiler?'

'Aye,' Ryan said. 'What did you want to ask me, James?'

MacTavish sat back on the seat and ran his hands through his overgrown hair. 'Any idea who could have done this?'

Ryan glared at MacTavish through narrowed eyes. 'You think I'm your personal secretary or something?'

'No. It's just that, well, I know he was working for you and Sean. He told me the last time he came here to see me.'

'Did he now? Well, he had no right to disclose that inform-ation.'

MacTavish frowned. 'Why does that matter, now that he's dead? Not just dead. Fucking skull smashed in from the impact of hitting the ground.' He fell silent and Ryan didn't say anything. 'Anyway, the reason I'm asking you if you know anything is that you know that estate. You know the people who live there, work there. I thought you might have heard something, that's all.'

Ryan felt a pang of guilt for MacTavish. 'Nah, sorry. I don't know anything. But can I ask you something?'

MacTavish's ears pricked up like an old dog being fed scraps from a stranger.

'Did Smiler ever mention anything about working for someone else at the same time? Or owing someone else money?'

MacTavish smirked. 'Smiler always owed out money. He was a fly wee bastard. Always trying to cheat his way through life. I warned him not to do that to you and Sean, though.'

Ryan thought about what MacTavish said. *Smiler always owed out money.*

'Do you think the Brysons could be behind it? I mean, they're the main dealers in the city?'

MacTavish stared at Ryan, unblinking. 'I mean, they knew who he was. Knew he was my nephew. They could've done him in purely for that reason.'

Ryan wasn't convinced. Why, after all this time would they do that now?

'I'll see what I can find out,' Ryan said, getting to his feet.

MacTavish got out of his seat too, and reached over, gripping a handful of Ryan's jacket. 'That's it?'

Ryan looked down at MacTavish's hand and then up at his face. 'Let go of me, James. We're in a prison, but I won't hesitate to fucking deck you.'

'Oi!' a prison officer shouted as he began approaching. MacTavish let go and flexed his fingers.

'Sorry. I'm just angry this happened and I can't do anything about it.'

Ryan looked up at the prison officer and gave him a nod. The man stopped in his tracks, hesitated and then moved back to his spot.

'I said I'd look into it,' Ryan said, turning his back on MacTavish and moving towards the exit.

He needed to get close to the Brysons if he was going to find out for sure. But then, he was already doing that, based on MacTavish's claims of innocence. In all honesty, Ryan couldn't give a shit that Smiler was dead, other than the fact that he'd lost a dealer. All he cared about was making sure that he got justice for his dad and uncle. Because if MacTavish was telling the truth about the Brysons being the ones that killed Kyle and Ian, Ryan Fraser was willing to do time in prison himself.

–

Stepping into the flat, Ryan kicked off his shoes and headed into the living room. Sean was packing up orders and a few empty beer cans sat on the coffee table in the centre of the room.

'How'd it go?' Sean asked.

'MacTavish thinks it could have been the Bryson mob that done Smiler in.'

Sean glanced up at him while sealing one of the packages of cannabis then exhaled slowly. 'I did wonder. What do you think?'

'It's highly likely if he owed them money. Or maybe Mum was right. Maybe Smiler was working for them too, just like his fucking uncle was.'

'So, what we going to do about this, then? We can't just sit on it. Those bastards have got away with shit for too long, Ryan. I'm getting fucking sick of it.'

Ryan sat down on the sofa and ran his hand over the back of his head. 'We keep doing what we're doing.'

Chapter Forty-Five

Standing by the side of the football field, Angie Bryson watched as Jack missed the ball and it hit the back of the net. She saw the obvious disappointment on his little face and felt sorry for him. But he bounced back quickly and was back in the game.

'Mrs Bryson?'

Angie turned to see the head teacher standing next to her. She looked nervous. So she bloody well should be, Angie thought. It was her job to make sure the overall running of the school was at its highest standard, and that included the security and wellbeing of the pupils –

most importantly, Jack's.

'Hi,' Angie said, ensuring she was short enough with her to maintain the tension.

'I assume you're aware of my meeting with Mr Bryson on Friday afternoon?'

Gritting her teeth, Angie wanted to reply with a sarcastic comment. Instead, she said, 'Yes. And I can only apologise if he was angry. But this is a very important matter to us, given what happened to our family.'

Ms Phillips nodded slowly. 'Yes, it must have been a terrifying incident, and I'm so sorry for your loss. I can confirm, however, that Jack seems to be doing very well here since what happened. It doesn't seem to be affecting his learning, or his ability to integrate into his social groups.'

'He's a resilient kid. Just a shame that his safety was compromised. I mean, this is a private school with the highest standard when it comes to teaching. Aside from the fees the parents pay, I'm sure I don't have to remind you of the Bryson family's investments in this school? And I hear the CCTV footage from that part of the school was missing?'

Ms Phillips readjusted her stance and Angie could see she was squirming. She cleared her throat before responding. 'Yes, for some reason it didn't record at all that day. I'm unsure as to why, but we have our technical team looking into it.'

Angie nodded slowly. 'Be sure to keep me up to date with that. And let me assure you, Ms Phillips, if anything like this ever happens again – to Jack or any other child – Bryson funding will be pulled immediately. Is that clear?'

Turning her back to the head of the school before allowing her to respond, Angie continued to watch Jack out on the field. As much as she didn't want to have to follow through on her threat, she would do what it took to keep Jack safe. She had done for the last seven years; in fact, from the moment she'd found out she was pregnant with him. She wouldn't falter now, not for any establishment.

Thinking about the fact that Dale had taken care of the culprit who'd caused such a mess for their family in the last week, Angie was relieved. As she took her phone out to snap some pictures of Jack in action to send to Dale, she noticed a notification on the screen. It was from a withheld number, and Angie froze when she read it.

> The look on little Jack's face when he didn't save the ball. Maybe next time.

Looking up, she glanced over at the faces of the other people standing at the edge of the field. It could be any one of them, goading her.

The final whistle sounded and Angie put a jog on to get out to Jack on the field. He was celebrating with his friends and jumping up and down screaming that they'd won the match.

His little face beamed up at her. 'Mum, we won!' But she couldn't force a smile back.

'We need to go home, right now,' she said, taking his hand and dragging him away from the field.

'But why?'

Think. Think. She drew a blank. What was she supposed to say? That the bad man with the sweets was coming after him again? But Dale said he'd taken care of him. So who the hell had this text come from?

'Mum? Stop pulling me.'

Angie stopped and realised that the other parents were staring at her as if she had two heads. She took a calming breath and smiled down at her youngest son. 'Daddy wants us home for a special surprise.'

His face lit up again and she felt guilty for lying to him. But she had to get him away from the school as quickly as possible. The person who'd sent her that message was watching them right now.

'A McDonald's?' he screeched.

'How did you guess?'

Lifting Jack, she half ran, half walked out of the school gates and to the car, bundling him in as quickly as she could. Closing the door, she lifted the phone and called Dale. His answering machine kicked in and she hung up before trying Paul, who picked up on the first ring.

'Paul, are you with Dale?'

'Nah, I'm at the site signing off a few things. What's up?'

'I've had a text. The guy you all took care of? It wasn't him. The real one just sent me an anonymous message. He was here, at the school, watching Jack. He knew Jack had missed a goal and… Jesus, Paul. What the hell are we going to do?'

The silence on the other end of the phone was deafening as Angie climbed into the driver's seat.

'Paul? Are you there?'

'Aye. Fuck!' he breathed. 'I'll get hold of Dale and meet you back at yours.'

'No,' she said, starting the engine and fastening her seatbelt. 'It's probably safer if we come to you at the site.'

She hung up and headed for the construction site on the other side of the city. She kept her eye on the rear-view mirror, checking to see if anyone seemed to be following her. She couldn't pick out anything suspicious, but that didn't mean they weren't there.

'Mum, I thought we were going home for a McDonalds?' Jack asked.

'We will, honey. We just need to go and see Uncle Paul first. He's at the construction site. You like diggers, don't you?'

She glanced at him in the mirror. He nodded, but she could see concern etched on his little face. He was thinking about what he'd heard. Had he heard more than she'd realised? Did he know that they weren't safe?

'Well, there will be lots of diggers and big machines there. Uncle Paul might even let you sit in one.'

Jack seemed to consider this, and then said, 'Will I be safe from the bad man in the digger? It'll be too big for him to get me if I'm in there, won't it?'

Shit, Angie thought. He'd heard what she'd said on the phone before she'd got back in the car.

'You're safe with me, Jack. I won't let anyone hurt you or anyone else in our family. Do you understand that?'

Jack was quiet, but he nodded before turning his attention to the window. It was all Angie could do to stop the tears from spilling over. She couldn't let her little boy see her fear.

–

The security guard at the gates gave Angie a nod and let her through without question. Paul must have warned him she was coming. Passing the huge sign which read 'Bryson Constructions', Angie took in the completed luxury apartment complex to her left and saw that further ahead lay a second site which was still undergoing work.

Parking up the car, Angie pulled out her phone and dialled Paul's number. He answered straight away and told her he'd be out to get her in a moment. Jack had been quiet the duration of the journey across the city. Anger built inside her that someone was doing this to their family, doing this to her son – and they couldn't work out who it was.

She reread the message over and over, trying to take something from it. But how could she? There was no number, no defining features within it. Even if there were, she didn't know what she was looking for.

A gentle tap on the window startled her and she looked up, to be greeted by Paul smiling at Jack in the back seat. Shoving her phone back in her pocket, she got out and stood stock still in front of her brother-in-law.

'Are you okay? Is Jack okay?'

'Hmm,' she nodded. 'We're fine, for now. What the hell, Paul? This is getting out of hand. I thought you'd sorted this?'

Paul blinked, keeping his eyes closed for a second longer than normal. 'We did.'

'Obviously not. My son has just been threatened again. This person is still out there.'

'I don't get it,' Paul said. 'We found the gun and bullets with our names on them. It had to be him.'

'Well, clearly, it wasn't. And where the *hell* is my husband? Why isn't he answering his phone?'

Paul placed a hand on Angie's shoulder and gave it a gentle squeeze. 'He'll be in a meeting at the casino or something. Once he sees the messages on his phone, he'll be with us immediately. Try not to worry. Now, what have you told Jack?'

Angie was about to answer when Jack climbed out of the car. 'Uncle Paul, can I sit in one of the diggers? Mum said I could.'

Paul knelt down in front of his nephew and smiled. ''Course you can. I've got some very important workers waiting for you. They'll even show you how to drive one.'

Jack glanced up at Angie as if waiting for permission to go. She nodded and Paul took his hand before leading him towards one of the machines just feet away. She would still be able to see him from where she was standing, and from the Portakabin office.

Angie watched as Paul lifted Jack into the machine, and the worker who was sitting in the driving seat gave Jack his hard hat. Instantly, she saw the distraction on Jack's face and was relieved that he wasn't thinking about the strange man anymore.

Paul was by her side again, and they stood watching Jack as he learned about the machine.

'You don't think this has anything to do with what happened with us, do you?'

'No,' Paul snapped. 'No one knows about that *apart* from us. And that's the way it's going to stay, Angie. If that gets out, it'll rip this family apart, you know that, don't you? Especially Dale. It'll kill him.'

She felt a heaviness in her chest at how sharp Paul's words had sounded. Angie knew that if the truth got out it would be a disaster for them. Not just for Dale, but for Paul too.

'I know, but don't you think that this is connected? I mean, it's possible, isn't it?'

Suddenly, Paul took hold of Angie's wrist, gripping it a little tighter than necessary. 'I said no. It's not connected. The only way it could be is if one of us spilled our guts about what happened and I certainly haven't.'

Shrugging him off, she gave Paul a narrow glare and said, 'Of course I haven't fucking said anything. But it's been eating me up ever since. You think I just brushed that shit under the carpet and forgot about it?'

Angie hadn't been able to say out loud what had gone on back then, even now, after all these years. And the fact that Paul was the only one who knew killed her every day. She didn't want that for him, although she was grateful for his loyalty.

Paul looked up at the dark clouds and exhaled. 'Shit, I'm sorry. I know you haven't said anything. Of course, you wouldn't. There's too much at stake.'

'Paul, I'm thankful that you have my back. But if you ever lay a finger on me again, I'll rip your fucking scrotum out. Got it?'

Paul stared at her, before a smile crept onto his face. 'Understood.'

'Right, I'm away to sit in the office until Dale gets here. I'll keep trying his mobile. I'll try the casino too. Can you keep an eye on Jack while you're out here?'

'Of course.'

'Has anyone contacted Conor?'

'I did. Conor's not seen or heard from Dale either.'

'For fuck's sake,' Angie hissed, locking the car before heading towards the Portakabin office. What the hell was Dale playing at? How had he not seen the messages? Surely he'd be checking his phone constantly after what had gone on in the last week?

Stepping inside the cabin, Angie pulled her phone out and decided to send a text to Dale, telling him to get his arse in gear and phone her. She wasn't worried about him. Yet. She was just angry. Angry about everything. Angry about Dale and the rest of them getting it wrong. Angry about Ashley still being distant, about Jack being the centre of the threats when he was just a little boy. But mostly, she was angry with herself. All of this could have stemmed from what she and Paul had done – from their secret. What if someone knew? What if that someone had decided to fuck with their family?

Chapter Forty-Six

Dale smoked the last of the cigarette before throwing it out of the window. Sitting in his car, staring up at the high-rise buildings in Craigton Heights from the lookout point at Hill View car park, he wondered how he'd got it so wrong. Listening to Paul's voicemail had shocked him. He'd really, truly believed that they'd got the right person. Finding the gun and the named bullets was enough for him to come to that conclusion.

'I *knew* it wasn't him,' Conor said, throwing his own cigarette out the window. 'Something was missing from the whole scenario.'

'Aye, leave it, eh? I don't need your fucking digs about this.'

'I'm not digging. What I'm saying is we should have gathered more proof before you went storming in there. I told *you* not to do it, but you told *me* to shut my mouth or wait in the car.'

Dale shot his elder son a look and frowned. 'Since when did you have a guilty conscience?'

'I don't, if we have the right person. But that lad had no clue what we were on about, Dad. And you threw him off a fucking building. That's the kind of shit Bob used to do. Act now, think later. That's not you.'

Dale leaned back into the seat and shook his head. 'Aye, I said I know. I couldn't give a fuck for Smiler. He was someone else's headache as much as ours. I've done that entire fucking scheme a favour getting rid of him.'

From the corner of his eye, Dale saw Conor shaking his head.

'We're back at square one, Dad. And Jack is the one being threatened here. So what the fuck are we doing here, sitting in a fucking car park? We should be with Mum. We need to get Ashley back. We need to all be together so that we can figure this out and find the real culprit.'

Dale was pleased to hear Conor making some sense instead of blasting him for making a mistake. Conor was right, they needed to get the family back together and quickly.

'We need to go and get your mum and brother,' Dale said, leaning forward and starting the car.

'Why don't you do that, and I'll go and find Ashley?' Conor suggested.

'And how will you do that, if you don't know where she is?'

Conor shifted in his seat and looked out of the window.

'What is it?' Dale asked, suspicious of what Conor might say next. Although, he could guess.

'I put a tracker on her phone.'

Dale stared at his son in shock. 'When the fuck did you do that?'

'Months ago, when she first told me she wanted to leave home. She hates what we do, Dad. And no matter what you and Mum think, she's still utterly traumatised by what happened with Reilly. It's scarred her for life. I thought she was doing okay. Well, not okay, but better than she had been. The therapist seemed to be working for her. When Bob died, I knew it would send her back. She's got PTSD, or at least some form of it.'

'Jesus,' Dale sighed, gripping the steering wheel with both hands. 'My poor girl.'

'So, when she told me that she wanted to leave home, I put a tracker on her phone. I know I shouldn't have, and if she ever found out she'd disown me too. I haven't used it. Not at all – I wanted to respect her wishes, even though it took me all my strength not to go and find her right away. But I will now. Because this is far from over, Dad. And I don't think that Ashley is safe out there on her own.'

Dale frowned. 'She's not on her own. She's staying with that boyfriend of hers, isn't she?'

'Boyfriend? She never mentioned anything to me about having a boyfriend,' Conor said, sounding disappointed that he'd been in the dark. 'Have you met him before?'

'No, I've only just found out myself. But she's a smart girl. She wouldn't pick a dodgy bastard, coming from a family like ours.'

'Does anyone *really* know anyone? Look, I know I'm not going to be able to drag her back home. If I did, she'd put up a huge fight. But if I can locate her, go and speak to her and tell her what's actually going on, then at least I know who she's with, where she is and we can keep an eye on her. And maybe I can look into the boyfriend – you know, get a feel for who he is. He is living with my sister, so I have a right to get big brother-y,' Conor smiled. 'In all seriousness, though, if the guy who killed Bob knows what school Jack goes to, then it's likely he'll know where Ashley is. And he'll probably know every detail about all of us.'

'You're a good lad, Conor,' Dale said as he put the car into gear and pulled out of Hill View car park. Craigton Heights fell from his sights and a heaviness bore down on his chest. Dale had taken his eye off the ball with Ashley. In fact, he'd taken his eye off the ball with the whole family. But at least Conor hadn't seemed to be affected by that. Maybe that was one thing he'd done right. Conor's family loyalty shone out of him.

'Open that glove box,' Dale said as he pulled onto the A82. 'Take that with you.'

Conor did as instructed, and looked inside at the gun. 'I won't need it.'

'I don't care if you don't *think* you'll need it. Take it with you. It's better to have it. What if you bump into this fucker? Do you really want to be unarmed when you're faced with him?'

Conor hesitated just for a moment, before taking the gun out of the glove box. 'Is it loaded?'

'Just did it this morning,' Dale replied.

Conor nodded and leaned forward, slipping the gun into the back of his jeans.

'You make sure she knows the lengths we're going to, to keep our family safe,' Dale said, stopping at a set of traffic lights.

He wanted to make things right with Ashley, and the whole family. But right now, it seemed he wasn't in control of that. This madman was, and Dale would make sure he found him.

Away from the lights, Dale drove for a further ten minutes before they arrived at the house. Conor climbed out of the car and headed for his own. Dale hoped that Ashley would listen to her brother.

—

A short while later, Dale pulled into Bryson Constructions and headed for the Portakabin office. Seeing Angie's car wasn't enough to settle his mind. He needed to see her in front of him. And Jack. He needed to know they were safe and in one piece.

Opening the door, he saw Angie sitting at the desk, staring out of the window in a daydream. She turned, and when he looked, he saw she'd been crying.

'I'm sorry, I was in a meeting,' he lied. He didn't want to tell her that he'd had a moment where he'd felt like an utter failure to the family and couldn't face her. 'Where's Jack?'

'He's playing on the diggers with Paul and a few of the boys,' Angie said, getting to her feet. 'He's fine. But we're taking him out of school, Dale. Until we find this bastard and I know he's dead in the ground, Jack doesn't leave our sights.'

Dale nodded. 'Fine. Whatever is best for Jack. Have you spoken to the school?'

'I saw the head today, but that was before I got that message.'

She handed her phone to Dale and he looked at the words on the screen. 'Anyone on the payroll able to get an ID on where that came from?'

Dale shrugged. 'Maybe. I don't know if I want to get the polis further involved in this right now. I think we can get this sorted ourselves.'

Angie's expression soured. 'Are you *fucking* kidding? Our child is being threatened and you don't want to use the resources we pay for on a monthly basis?'

Dale exhaled slowly. 'Angie, we pay them to turn a blind eye to what goes on in the casino. I don't pay them to look into personal matters. We murdered the wrong guy for this. You don't think that'll come back to haunt us? I don't have the whole of Police Scotland on the books, just a handful of officers.'

Snatching the phone from Dale, she pushed past him and out of the office. Dale closed his eyes and took a few steadying breaths before following her out.

'Look, this isn't just about you, or me, or Jack. This is about all of us. I have to do this properly. We've got security. I'll make sure that you're both safe at all times. Just…' he paused, 'just let us handle this, okay?'

Chapter Forty-Seven

Still out in the delivery van, Ashley was glad to be away from Craigton Heights. Jamie hadn't mentioned anything about going back there with her, and she was glad of that. Her dad's words had echoed in her ears ever since. Craigton Heights was a dangerous place, especially for someone like Ashley. Her dad was one of the city's biggest gang bosses. Everyone linked to the crime world in Glasgow knew who he was. And everyone knew his family. That was why she'd decided to leave. Even though she was away from the family home, Ashley still didn't feel safe. Not really. What would Jamie be able to do if someone came after her? He'd end up hurt because of her.

'You seem far away over there,' Jamie said. 'Something on your mind, apart from the obvious?'

Ashley gave a smile but it was forced. 'I'm just thinking about everything that's happened. It's hard not to when I've got nothing else to focus on.'

Jamie reached his hand over and gave her knee a squeeze. 'You want to talk about it?'

'Not now,' she sighed. 'But when we get back to the flat it might be nice to vent.'

'Well, in that case, you'll be glad to know that I've just done my last drop of the day. Why don't we go back, I'll get us a drink and you can rant until you have nothing left to say?'

Ashley smiled at Jamie, and her heart felt full for the first time. He was lovely, letting her stay with him when her family was in such a mess. And taking her out with him when he was working just so she wasn't cooped up all day. It was a wonder she hadn't spoken about everything before now. But she hadn't wanted to, not really, and Jamie hadn't put pressure on her to speak about things. That was decent of him.

They weren't far from Jamie's flat at all, and within a few short minutes, they were sitting in the living room and Jamie had put the kettle on already.

'So, what's going on in that head of yours?' Jamie asked.

She nodded. 'My mum called me the other day to tell me that they'd found the man who'd killed my Uncle Bob. Turns out they were wrong.'

She watched as Jamie's forehead crinkled under his frown. 'What do you mean?'

Ashley wanted to tell him about it, but how could she? He'd be horrified at what her dad had done, and to the wrong person too. Just as she was about to move the subject on by dodging the question, the buzzer sounded from the hallway.

Jamie got up to answer it, and when he lifted the receiver, Ashley recognised the voice on the other end of the line immediately.

'I'm here to see Ashley. I'm Conor Bryson, her brother.'

She stood up quickly from the sofa and moved out to see Jamie's reaction. He was staring at her, receiver in hand by his ear. It was clear neither of them knew what to say or do.

'Hello?' Conor said, and Jamie waved his other hand at her, gesturing for her to give him an indication on how to respond.

'Just let him in. He obviously knows I'm here so he's not going to leave until he sees me.'

Jamie suddenly looked furious, but pressed the button on the buzzer before hanging up.

'How did he find you? Did you tell him where you were?'

'No, of course I didn't.'

'Then how does he know you're here, Ashley?'

She couldn't understand why he was so annoyed, but then it clicked in her head. He'd be anxious about getting dragged into her family's deadly shit.

'Jamie, I'm sorry. Look, I don't want you being involved in this. I should never have come to you about this. I just didn't know where else to go.'

Jamie's expression softened. 'Och, no, it's not that, Ashley. You know I'd do anything to help you. It's just that, well...' he swallowed, 'your family aren't exactly the Waltons, are they?'

She gave a little laugh. 'Conor's fine. He won't be here to knock your head off. He's probably just come to see if I'm okay. I am his wee sister.'

The tap at the door halted the conversation, and Ashley opened up. Conor stood tall in the doorway, dressed in all black, just like their dad.

'Never thought I'd be so glad to see your face,' Conor said.

Ashley stood back and allowed Conor to enter the flat. Once inside, he took one look at Jamie and nodded, but didn't say anything.

'Conor, this is Jamie. Jamie, this is my brother, Conor.'

Conor held his hand out, and Jamie hesitated.

'I don't bite,' Conor said, eyeing Jamie's hand which was still by his side.

Jamie shook Conor's hand and then looked at Ashley. 'I'll make those teas, then?'

'I'll have a coffee, please. Black, no sugar,' Conor replied, expecting Jamie to react to the direct instruction.

Jamie smiled and disappeared into the kitchen and closed the door, while Ashley led Conor into the living room. They sat down on the sofa and Ashley couldn't help but hug her brother.

'How did you find me?' she asked.

'I was in the area and saw you,' he said. 'What are you doing, Ashley? Just come back, eh? It's better if we're all together.'

She shook her head. 'No. I can't.'

'Do you know about Jack?' Conor asked. 'Did Mum tell you that some weirdo bastard turned up at his school and was talking to him through the fence? He was talking to him about what happened at the wedding. And then today, Mum got a text when she was at his football game. They knew Jack had missed a save. They were there, watching her and Jack.'

Ashley stared at Conor, unable to blink. 'How do they know which school Jack goes to?'

'It's obvious. Whoever this person is, they've been watching us. All of us. That means they'll know where you are, Ashley. I mean, I found you just by seeing you on the street. And they'll know you're on your own.'

'I'm not on my own, I'm with Jamie.'

She watched Conor stifle a laugh. 'No offence to your man through there, Ashley. But he doesn't look like he could punch his way through a wet paper bag.'

'Oi,' she remarked, slapping his upper arm.

'We all want you home. Please, just come back. Dad's organised extra security, and there's men guarding the house twenty-four/seven. Mum's even taking Jack out of school. Just until we find the fucker.'

Slumping back on the sofa, Ashley thought about it. She wanted to see her little brother, give him a hug. But she was still angry with her parents. They'd lived a life that put the rest of them in danger. Conor seemed to be made of the same stuff as their dad and it was clear to Ashley that he was handling things a lot better than she ever could. But Ashley wasn't like that. It wasn't in her to live in the underworld. She hated the idea of it. It should only exist in crime fiction via books or Netflix. She *was* living it, had lived it her entire life and was still suffering from the effects of what she saw all those years ago. And now it seemed Jack had been sucked into things too. That was what these people were capable of, using the most vulnerable to get what they wanted.

'No, I'm fine here.'

Conor rolled his eyes. 'Are you, though?' He lowered his voice and leaned closer. 'I mean, what do you really know about Jamie? How long have you even been seeing him?'

'Long enough to know that when I needed him, he was there, no questions asked.'

Conor raised a brow. 'Then maybe I should get to know him a bit. I mean, if you're going to stay here with him, then I would like to know who you're living with.'

Ashley shook her head. 'No chance.'

'Like you've got a choice, Ashley. Who would you rather took him out for a drink? Me, or Dad and Uncle Paul? Let's face it, he could be God reincarnated but if he went out with them he'd still come back with at least a threat on his head.'

Ashley wanted to laugh, but it wasn't actually funny. Conor was right, it would be like feeding a puppy to a pack of lions. But with Conor, at least they'd be equals in age. And it would be less intimidating for Jamie.

'You want to go for that drink, then?' Jamie's voice filtered in from the doorway. Ashley looked up and saw Jamie standing there with a mug in each hand.

'Aye, just to get to know you a bit better. Would be nice to know who my sister is living with.'

Jamie nodded, 'Aye, alright, then. How's now suit you?'

Ashley was surprised that Jamie had agreed to it, having over-heard the entire conversation. But if Conor ended up giving his approval – not that she needed it – then her dad was more likely to back off a bit from trying to get her to go home.

'Sounds good to me.'

Ashley mouthed a thank you and smiled at Jamie. This meant a lot to her.

'I promise not to keep him too long,' Conor said as he moved out of the living room towards the front door.

'Just don't send him back hammered, please. I know what you're like at the pub, Conor.'

Jamie gave Ashley a kiss and she thanked him again.

'Anything for you, babe. Family's important. And you're mine.'

For a moment, the comment stunned her. She hadn't expected that from him. They'd only been together a short time. But the truth was, she was really falling for him. And now she knew he felt the same way.

Chapter Forty-Eight

Glancing down at the text from Conor, Dale nodded and showed it to Angie.

'He's taking Jamie out for a drink, to get to know him a bit. I suppose it means that at least one of us will know what he's like.'

'Why aren't you going with him?' Angie asked. 'Why aren't you going along and meeting the lad that our seventeen-year-old is living with, when there is a deranged enemy of ours on the loose?'

Dale sighed. 'Because I don't want him thinking that we're ganging up on him. And he'll be able to relate to Conor more because they're younger. If there was anything to worry about with this lad, my being there would only make him shut down. He wouldn't show his true self.'

Angie shook her head. 'Maybe I'll go, then, but not tell Conor. I'll just slip into the back and watch from a distance.'

Dale reflected. It wasn't a bad idea, when he thought about it. But that would mean Angie going out on her own.

'I'll send one of the lads with you, so you're not alone.'

She nodded. 'Great. I'll get ready. Find out where they're going.'

Angie disappeared into the bedroom and Dale sent Conor a reply, asking where he was taking this Jamie lad. He got a quick response and Dale had to wonder why he hadn't thought of it himself. Conor was taking Jamie to the casino. Of course. Perfect place. Surrounded by Bryson employees and security.

'You're a Bryson right enough, boy,' Dale said under his breath.

Angie was barely upstairs five minutes before she was standing at the front door. She looked stunning, all in black.

'So, where's he taking this guy?'

Dale smiled. 'Our casino.'

Angie raised a brow. 'Did you tell Conor to do that?'

'No,' Dale shook his head, 'but it's a good idea. Why not take him to a place where he'll have eyes on him from every corner of the room. Cameras everywhere. If it turns out he is dodgy, then we'll get to see it with our own eyes.'

Angie smiled. 'I'll sit in the office, watch from the cameras. You're staying here with Jack. I don't want him out of your sight, Dale. I mean it.'

Smiling, he said, 'Loud and clear, boss.'

The 'boss' part made her laugh a little, and it was the first time Dale had seen any form of humour in Angie's expression since this had all started.

'I'll see you later,' she said, opening the door and heading out to the car. Dale gave a nod to the security lad standing outside and he followed Angie, climbing into his own car parked behind hers. He would follow her to the casino, allow her personal space. But he'd only be feet from her, the entire night. That made Dale feel better.

Dale closed the door behind her and sighed. How had his family come to this? Sneaking around, watching people involved in their lives from a distance, just in case they were a danger to them. Back in the day, the Brysons gave no shits about anyone. Having someone fire at them on their wedding day when the kids were around had really changed the way Dale looked at things. And Angie. All of them, for that matter. Especially Ashley. He wondered how she felt about her brother taking her boyfriend out for a drink. She'd have been nervous, in normal circumstances.

'Dad?' Jack called out from the games room. 'Come and play *Sonic* with me.'

Jack's little voice drew Dale out of his thoughts and he locked the front door. He opened the security app on his phone and checked all of the cameras surrounding the house, as well as the ones inside. His men were at their posts. There was no way anyone would get past them.

'Dad?' Jack called, a little more forceful this time. 'Come on, I want to play *Sonic*.'

Dale smiled and moved across the hallway, past the spiralling staircase and into the games room. Upon seeing his son sitting on the huge corner sofa, his legs crossed and the controller in his hand, Dale couldn't help but think about how vulnerable he was. For some reason, the person who'd approached him at the fence at school hadn't done anything to harm him. If they'd really wanted to harm the Brysons, they could have taken Jack, but they hadn't.

Smiler's face snuck into his mind's eye. It really had seemed that he'd been the one to approach Jack, give him the sweets. But Dale had got it so wrong, and Conor had known.

He couldn't get it wrong the next time. He had to be one hundred per cent sure of who their attacker was. And before Dale ended his life, he would make sure to find out why he'd targeted them. Even if he had to torture him to get to the truth.

Chapter Forty-Nine

Counting the cash that Sean had handed her, Cara Fraser couldn't help but be impressed. Her sons were beginning to make enough money to sustain themselves, just like their dad had done before he'd been brutally murdered.

'And this is what – this week's takings?' she asked as Sean busied himself wrapping up orders.

'Aye. Mostly from Craigton Heights, but we branched out a bit too. Headed further north to the schemes in Maryhill. You know what it's like, word of mouth is better than any kind of paid advertising.'

Cara smiled. 'You sound like your old man. He used to say things like that.'

Sean looked up at her with a sadness in his eyes she hadn't seen since he was little and it reminded her of how she'd sat them down to tell them what had truly happened to their dad. She'd waited a few months until they were settled in their new home and school. Telling them that their dad and uncle had been shot and killed was something that would always haunt her. They'd both cried, but mostly, she remembered how angry they'd got. As young boys, it worried her how much they'd voiced their desire to kill the person who'd been responsible. Especially Sean. Being the youngest, she thought he might have understood things less than Ryan. And still to this day, Sean seemed to be the one who – as much as he said he was fine – suffered from anger issues relating to what happened.

As if hearing her thoughts, he said, 'I'm so angry, Mum. I can't think about him without thinking about the Brysons.

And that prick, MacTavish. He put them in the line of fire, you know that, don't you? It's his fault Dad and Uncle Ian were murdered.'

Cara nodded. She did know that. But it wasn't MacTavish who'd shot them both in the head and left their bodies to rot.

'You have to stop thinking like that, Sean. It will mess with your vision, with what we're trying to achieve here.'

He dropped his eyes back to the packages in front of him and started labelling them from the order list on the wall.

As Cara watched him, she couldn't help but worry that history might repeat itself if the boys weren't careful. This was how things had started for Kyle and Ian. They hadn't wanted to work for the man, they wanted to *be* the man. The Brysons had no competition. The city of Glasgow got their drugs from one main supplier only, and there was no budge in the amount anyone could make for themselves. Cara thought back to when she'd expressed her concerns to Kyle, how she worried what would happen if they got caught. He'd assured her they wouldn't, that the Bryson brothers underestimated how clever Kyle and Ian actually were.

She shook her head at how that had turned out. She'd never planned for Ryan and Sean to know what their dad did for a living, but after she'd explained to them how he'd died, she'd decided to tell them the whole truth. To some extent, Ryan already knew, having discovered the cannabis farm for himself, with Kyle basking in the glory of it. She'd had to explain to Sean first, though, what a gangster was and second, what that meant for his dad. Cara knew that telling them the truth was what had led to their choice to come back to Glasgow and carry on their dad's work.

Chapter Fifty

Sitting in the office, Angie watched the screens without blinking. There were no black spots anywhere in the casino. Even the alley at the back had been fitted with a security camera. She zoomed in on the bar, and watched as Conor ordered two drinks. It was at that point that she wished she'd had the idea to get him wired before she'd arrived, so she could hear the entire conversation. Although she knew what Conor would have said to that. He'd have said no. It was just a drink with his sister's boyfriend. And if there was anything to be suspicious of or worried about, then Conor would tell the family.

Conor turned to his right and nodded across to someone. Zooming out and panning the camera to the right, Angie noticed a lad close to Conor's age, sitting at a table on his own. He nodded back, and Angie realised that this must be Jamie, Ashley's new boyfriend, the one she'd left home to live with after what had happened at the wedding.

Conor was soon at the table, sliding a glass across to Jamie. As her son sat down, he raised his glass, as did Jamie and they both took a drink. It annoyed her that she had no audio. She thought about going out and introducing herself, but she knew that wasn't a good idea. The boy would feel bombarded and Ashley wouldn't like that.

They chatted for a while. They even laughed, smiled and it came across as if they'd known each other a while. She thought about the kind of person Jamie might be. Did he work? What did he do? Where did he live? More importantly, was he taking care of her daughter?

After around ten minutes, Jamie got up from the table, moved through the bar towards the bathrooms. Angie followed him through the bar on the screens. Of course there were no cameras in the toilets themselves, so she kept her eye on the door for Jamie to appear. While he was in there, she quickly picked up her phone and called Conor. She went between screens, and watched as Conor picked up his phone.

'Mum?'

'How's it going? How is he?'

She saw him frown, then he glanced up at the camera she was watching him from.

'You're here, aren't you? Jesus, Mum.'

'I just had to know what he was like.'

'And you'll achieve that by hiding in the office, watching him on security footage, will you?'

Angie shook her head. 'My daughter, your sister, is living with this guy. I've never met him; know nothing about him. You really thought that when your dad told me this was happening that one of us wasn't going to come down here?'

Conor shook his head and turned away from the camera. 'I'm hanging up now, before he gets back. Just be patient. I'll tell you everything you need to know when I know myself. Okay?'

Before Angie had the chance to respond, Conor hung up and she watched him slide his phone into his pocket. Turning her attention back to the camera on the bathroom door, she waited for Jamie to reappear.

'Guys don't take this long to piss. What's he up to in there?' she whispered. Then, as if he'd heard her, he appeared. Stepping out of the bathroom, he let the door close behind him. But he stopped. Stood still. He was on his phone, tapping away on the screen. Sending a message, perhaps? Probably to Ashley, telling her how things were going.

Dropping his arm to his side, phone in hand, he walked back through the bar to the table where Conor was sitting. Angie shifted in her seat, finding it a struggle that she couldn't hear a thing. But she trusted that if Conor had any concerns, he'd tell her.

She considered sending Ashley a message, to let her know that she was happy Conor and Jamie had had a chance to meet, but thought better of it. Ashley wasn't stupid, if she knew they were at the casino – a Bryson casino – then she would put two and two together with the message and know that Angie was watching what was going on.

So instead, Angie sat back, and with all the strength she could muster not to go out to the bar and introduce herself, she watched them on the screen for the rest of the night.

Chapter Fifty-One

Ashley Bryson wasn't one for drinking alone, but tonight was different. She was nervous about Jamie being out with her older brother, and couldn't help but worry about how things were going. She'd opened a bottle of gin and was on her third as she sat alone in Jamie's flat.

The television was talking to itself in the corner as she sipped from her glass and stared out of the window. Jamie and Conor had been gone for two hours now, and if she knew her brother like she thought she did, then it would be several more before Jamie was back.

Sighing, Ashley got up and stood at the window.

The street in which Jamie lived was semi quiet, with a large patch of grass bisecting his block from the flats opposite. She took in the sights as she sipped on her gin. A few dog walkers, a couple of teenagers sitting on top of an electricity box, chatting and smoking. An older woman sat by her window in the bottom flat opposite. Ashley watched her as she opened the window and lit up a cigarette. She looked lonely. Ashley knew the feeling in that very moment. She didn't want to end up that way, but if her family didn't get their act together and sort this person out, she might never feel safe enough to go back. They needed to take a stand, to show the city and even further beyond that they weren't going to take this lying down.

As the sun turned the sky a deep orange colour, Ashley thought about her past, and how it had shaped her as a person. What had happened – what she'd witnessed – had changed her. She was the shell of who she was supposed to be. Her childhood therapist hadn't had much of an impact, as she still saw his face. Every single day. She thought about what she'd done that day, to save her dad. It was utterly horrific, and no matter what she'd done over the last eight years, the memory plagued her.

'Fucking hell,' she muttered to herself as she gulped back the last of the gin and moved away from the window. She went into the kitchen and poured her fourth, a slightly larger measure than the last. The effects of the alcohol were starting to loosen her up a little, but also making her think more about everything. If she drank enough, maybe she'd pass out and then she wouldn't have to think at all.

She wandered around the flat aimlessly for a few minutes, wondering what to do with herself. It was too quiet, the television wasn't making enough noise to drown out the thoughts in her head. So, she switched on the Alexa speaker and asked for a rock classics playlist. It was the kind of music she'd grown up listening to because her mum and dad had loved it. It comforted her a little and as it came on, she turned the speaker up as loud as it would go and stood in the middle of the hallway in the flat, stock still, for several minutes. She gripped her glass in her right hand, and her left hand gripped the hair on the top of her head at the root. 'Paranoid' by Black Sabbath screamed out of the speaker and a smile spread slowly across Ashley's face. Fitting, she thought.

Letting go of her hair, she began wandering around the flat again, and realised that she didn't know anything about the place she'd been living in for two weeks now. She knew where the bathroom was, where her own clothes were, which drawer the cutlery lived in and where to find towels. But the contents of the various cupboards and drawers around the rest of the place were alien to her.

Bobbing her head along as Ozzy sang, she went into the kitchen and opened the doors, peering inside at the mismatch of plates, pots and various tinned goods. She smiled: every house had a messy drawer, filled with takeaway menus, old receipts, dead batteries and manuals for the white goods. She rummaged through it, unsure as to what she was actually looking for. She pulled out various Chinese, Indian and Italian takeaway menus, taxi company cards, a few old receipts on which the ink had rubbed off. She knocked the drawer with her hip and it slammed shut but quickly bounced back open again. Something inside was preventing it from closing properly.

Ashley squatted, looking into the back of the drawer and sure enough, there was a collection of bunched-up papers at the very back. Sliding her hand in, she managed to wiggle them free and dumped them onto the worktop. In among the pile of miscellaneous leaflets and more menus, a white card poked out from inside one of them.

Ashley tugged it free and read the words on the card to herself. *Shona Henry, registered BACP counsellor. Glasgow.*

Ashley wondered why Jamie would have this in his flat, stuffed into the back of a drawer. Flipping the card over, she saw the list of various ways to contact this woman. Phone number and email.

Should she ask Jamie about it? Maybe he didn't want her to know about his past, and why he may have needed therapy. It was none of her business, she supposed. If he'd wanted to tell her, he would have. Then she thought, maybe this Shona person could help Ashley with her own issues. Maybe, she was *meant* to find the card.

She shoved the card into the back pocket of her jeans, placed the leaflets back into the drawer, switched off the kitchen light and went back into the living room. As she sank back into the sofa, Liam Gallagher was screaming about cigarettes and alcohol. Ashley closed her eyes, and sang along with him.

–

She watched his mouth agape, his eyes wide with terror. His hands were free, and he pushed down on the bonnet of the car as though he was strong enough to free himself. He wasn't, of course. No one would be able to do that.

'Ashley...' his voice called in a hoarse whisper. She wanted to look away from him but she couldn't. And the longer she ignored him, the louder and more persistent he became. He wanted her to set him free. But she couldn't do that, could she? It was too much of a risk.

'Ashley... Ashley... Ashley...'

Suddenly, he was free, crawling along the bonnet of the car towards her, his arms outstretched, trying to reach her.

'No!' she screamed, launching herself up and off the chair. Her eyes adjusted to her surroundings. Jamie was stood in front of her, concern etched on his face.

'Jesus, it's me.' He jumped back. 'Are you okay?'

She exhaled slowly, allowing herself to adjust to reality. It was a dream. It was just a dream. Blinking away the images, she glanced down at her phone and saw that it was almost midnight.

'Sorry,' she said, looking up at Jamie and relaxing her shoulders. 'I must've dozed off waiting for you.'

'You nearly gave me a bloody heart attack,' Jamie laughed.

With her mouth as dry as a bag of sand, Ashley got to her feet and headed for the kitchen to get a bottle of water from the fridge. She'd had enough glasses of gin to become dehydrated and send her dreams wild.

'Bad dream?' he asked, following her into the kitchen.

'Yeah. I can't remember what it was about, though,' she lied. 'So, how was it?'

Jamie nodded. 'Your brother's alright, you know. And he thinks a lot of you.'

'So you both got on okay, then?'

Jamie frowned. 'Why wouldn't we?'

'Well, you're a stranger to the family. And he's my big brother, so he's going to be suspicious of any guy I'm interested in, isn't he?'

'I suppose so. But yeah, it went fine. He just asked me the usual stuff; what I do for a living, where I'm from. That sort of stuff. He didn't say much about your family, though.'

Ashley couldn't say she was surprised by that. The Brysons didn't speak much about themselves to new people. And Conor wasn't about to do that given the circumstances the family now faced.

'Yeah, we're kind of private like that,' she replied.

Jamie narrowed his eyes as she turned to face him, a bottle of water in her hand, wondering whether or not to tell him about the dream; about everything.

'Are you okay? You seem… I don't know… off.'

Gulping back a few mouthfuls of water, she swallowed hard and placed the lid back on. There was so much darkness inside her, so much that had happened in the past that was hard to let out.

'I'm just trying to work through some shit. That's all.'

'Want to tell me about it?' he asked.

She shook her head. 'Not really. I don't want to talk about it. Well, I know I should, because talking is better than keeping it all stored away inside. I had a childhood counsellor for a few years. But I don't think it worked. I'm still fucked-up in the head.'

'Aren't we all?' Jamie said in a solemn tone. 'Did I ever tell you about my dad?'

Ashley shook her head. 'No.'

'He died when I was little. I hardly remember him, to be honest.'

'What happened to him?'

'He was…' Jamie trailed off. 'He was sick. Well, we didn't know he was sick. Aneurysm. It was really sudden.'

Ashley looked down at the floor and then back up into his eyes. 'I'm sorry.'

'I didn't deal with it very well at first. Couldn't work out why he was suddenly gone. It fucked up my childhood, if I'm honest. I didn't do well in school, couldn't concentrate. Wasn't good at forming relationships because I was scared of losing people suddenly. But then I found a therapist not so long ago. Figured I had to deal with it at some point.'

'Shona Henry?' Ashley said, thankful that the conversation about therapy came from Jamie first. She didn't want him to know that she'd been snooping around.

'Yeah, how did you know that?'

'I erm… I found her card while looking for a takeaway menu in the drawer.'

Jamie rolled his head back a little and then said, 'Ah, didn't think that was still in there.'

'Did she help you?'

'She really did. I mean, sometimes I don't talk about Dad at all. It's all the other crap that comes with losing someone. The inability to live life normally. I'm not fixed, by any means. But I'm getting there.'

Ashley nodded. She'd already made up her mind about giving this woman a call. But it was something she wanted to keep to herself. She didn't want to tell anyone about it. Even Jamie. This was something she had to do alone.

'Did you get some food delivered?' Jamie asked. 'Did you find a takeaway menu?'

'No, I fell asleep instead. In fact, I ended up tanking almost half a bottle of gin on my own. Not good for the old head. In fact, I think I'm going to call it a night. We can talk more tomorrow?'

Jamie moved closer to her and slid his arms around her waist. 'Conor wanted me to tell you that your family want you home.'

'Yeah, I thought he might say that.' She sighed. 'I'll go and see them, but I'm not moving back. So long as it's okay with you that I stay?'

He kissed her gently on the mouth and rested his forehead against hers. 'You can stay forever.'

'Thank you. Maybe you could come with me when I go to visit? You could meet my mum and dad, and maybe even my wee brother Jack?'

Jamie didn't say anything. It was as though he were hesitant. Just as she was about to ask him what was wrong, he said, 'Do you feel comfortable with that?'

'I wouldn't have asked you if I wasn't. I mean, you'd be meeting the entire family, including my uncle. That's definitely more pressure for you than it is for me.'

Jamie laughed. 'Yeah, you're not wrong there. Okay, so long as you're sure. I'd like to meet the rest of your family. But... be honest, should I wear a bullet-proof vest?'

'That's not funny,' she responded, before playfully punching him. She knew he didn't mean it in malice.

'Sorry, that was in bad taste.'

'It's fine. Look, I'm going to bed. I'll contact them in the morning and we can arrange something then. Right now, I just need to get my head down.'

Jamie smiled, kissed her again and she let herself fall into him. He held her the way she needed to be held. Comforted. As much as they hadn't been together long at all, she was glad she had Jamie. She couldn't imagine how else she would have dealt with everything without him by her side.

Chapter Fifty-Two

Cara Fraser sat on the bench overlooking the reservoir as she stared out at the city ahead of it. It was early morning, early enough that the summer sunshine had already risen, but no one else had ventured out for their morning run or dog walk. It was the most peaceful, yet most sinister place in the world to Cara. Knowing that her husband's body had been dumped in the water in front of her was still horrifying, yet she always felt at peace when she sat there; somehow she felt closer to him.

'It's a shame your brother didn't come,' Cara said to Ryan, as he sat next to her on the bench. They'd been silent for a while, ever since they'd arrived. It was a place for reflection; at least it was for Cara.

'I'm sure he has his reasons,' Ryan replied, taking Cara's hand in his.

The water was still, not a single ripple on the surface. The geese were at the other side of the reservoir. Cara couldn't see them, but she could hear them in the distance. She'd often wondered if those geese had always inhabited that particular spot. Maybe they'd been around when the car had gone into the water. If they had been, they would be the only witnesses to what truly happened to Kyle and Ian that fateful night.

Cara thought about how callous the press had been when it had all come out. It was an image she'd rather not have seen, but the papers had printed a picture of the car being pulled from the water. Unfortunately, Ryan and Sean had eventually come across it. Ryan was older than his years and had understood exactly what had happened to his dad and uncle. She'd managed to keep the truth from Sean, somehow, until recently.

That image still haunted Cara, but the only reassuring thought to come from it was the fact that Cara knew Kyle and Ian were already dead when the car went into the water. They wouldn't have known about their watery grave. They may not have even known about the shooting. It would have been too quick, with the bullets penetrating the skull and then the brain. She'd tried to explain that to the boys as gently as she could when they were young, although she knew there was no truly gentle way of doing that.

'I can't believe your dad would have been forty-two today,' Cara said, pushing the images out of her head. 'We should be celebrating, as a foursome. He'd always joked with me that reaching forty would send him into a fit of depression. He said he'd live his life hard and fast before reaching that milestone.'

Ryan gave a humourless laugh. 'Yeah, I remember him saying that too. It always stayed with me. I never actually thought he'd be dead before that point. Or at all, really. You don't ever imagine your dad not being by your side.'

Cara watched as Ryan pulled a pack of Mayfair cigarettes out of his pocket and lit one. The smell hit her and she was flooded with memories – of how Kyle's clothes smelled, how he tasted when he kissed her. Most people would have hated that, but it was the one thing she held on to after he'd died.

'That smell reminds me of your dad so much,' she said.

'Me too. It's why I smoke them. I know I shouldn't, but it's my way of feeling close to him.'

Cara nodded, understanding completely.

'I have something to tell you,' Ryan said, moving the subject on. 'I'm going to meet the Bryson parents tonight with Ashley.'

Cara shot him a look and a feeling of fear gripped her chest. 'Where?'

'At their house.'

Shifting on the bench so she was facing him, Cara took a breath. 'Ryan, I don't know if that's such a good idea. What if it's a trap? What if the Brysons know who you are?'

Ryan shook his head. 'They've no clue, Mum. They killed Smiler, thinking he was the one responsible for Bob's death. And Conor didn't seem to click either. Don't worry about me, everything is going according to plan.'

Cara wished she felt as calm as Ryan appeared but she couldn't. The idea of Ryan being in the Brysons' home scared her more than she could have imagined.

'Are you sure?'

'Mum, if I didn't think I was going to get away with playing the part of Jamie, I wouldn't have done it. They're going to do whatever they can to get back into Ashley's good books. And that means making an effort with Jamie. I have to go along with this if we're going to get justice for Dad and Ian.'

When Ryan had first told Cara about his plan to seduce Ashley as a way of getting closer to the Brysons in order to take them down, she'd been against the idea. But the more he'd talked to her about it, and the more she'd considered it, the more it made perfect sense. She couldn't afford to think about this in any other way except justice for her husband. If they were going to take them down, it was all or nothing.

Cara nodded, but her heart thumped in her chest. As much as she believed her son knew what he was doing, she couldn't help but worry about what Dale Bryson would do if he worked things out.

'If those bastards hurt any of my family, I don't know what I'll do,' she said.

'That's not going to happen, Mum. I promise.'

—

Ryan watched as Sean unpacked the holdall. Envelopes filled with cash piled one on top of another should have made Ryan smile, but they didn't. All he could think about was his dad, and the fact that it was his birthday and Sean had failed to notice.

'Not bad for a week's takings, eh?' Sean said, rubbing his hands together after placing the last envelope on top. He glanced up at Ryan when he hadn't answered and frowned. 'What's up with your mush?'

'Do you know what day it is?'

'Aye, fucking pay day,' Sean laughed. But his laughter soon faded when he noticed the look on Ryan's face.

'It's Dad's birthday today.'

A shadow fell across Sean's face and he glanced down at the envelopes. He didn't say a word, simply started tearing into the envelopes and pulling money out.

'Did you forget, or something?' Ryan pressed.

'No, I didn't fucking forget, Ryan.'

Ryan pursed his lips. 'So, what then? It just wasn't worth mentioning, is that it?'

Sean dropped the money down on the table and glared at Ryan. 'What do you take me for?'

'I don't know, Sean. But you knew me and Mum were going out to the reservoir this morning and you just didn't show up. Why?'

Sean sighed and continued the task of counting the cash. Ryan frowned before snatching the money from his hands. 'Fucking answer me.'

'It's sick, Ryan. That's why. It's sick that we go to the place they were dumped. I don't like it. I don't have to remember him that way, Ryan, for fuck sake.'

Ryan relaxed his shoulders and sighed. He hadn't thought of it that way. 'Sorry, bud.'

'I mean, it's alright for you, you were his favourite. So, of course, you're going to honour his memory in some weird ritual. But that's not me.'

Ryan took a step back. 'What do you mean, I was his favourite?'

'Och, come on. It was so fucking obvious when we were growing up. You were his golden boy. You couldn't do or say a thing wrong. Me, on the other hand, I was always told to be more like you.'

'That's not true,' Ryan replied.

'Aye, it is. Mind the day he died? I was on the PlayStation in the living room, and you both thought I wasn't listening. But I was. He told you that you would be the man of the family and that I would follow your lead. Like Uncle Ian followed his. It might have sounded like nothing to you, but that made me feel like I was just in the fucking way. Then I'm the last to find out MacTavish didn't kill them, and here I am, following your lead. Just like he said.'

'Jesus, you make it sound like a fucking job you were forced into, Sean. What the hell is wrong with you?'

Sean turned his back on Ryan and moved through to the kitchen. Ryan followed and leaned against the door frame.

'Nothing, I just didn't want to go to the reservoir. Look, forget I said anything,' Sean replied, standing with his back to Ryan as he stared out of the window.

'I wasn't Dad's favourite. I'm just the oldest. It's what happens, Sean. And this isn't something that he'd want us to be arguing about. He'd want us to get on with things.'

Sean nodded, sighed and turned to face Ryan. 'Yeah, you're right. So, what happened with Jamie?'

Ryan narrowed his eyes. Sean wasn't one for just moving on from a moment like that, but Ryan had to be honest with himself: he didn't have the time or the energy to argue with his brother about this.

'It went well. Just as it should have. Jamie will continue to infiltrate the Brysons via Ashley and we will keep up the job in hand.'

Sean nodded, but Ryan could tell he wasn't really listening. He had other things on his mind, and unless he told Ryan what the problem was, Ryan was going to go on as if nothing was wrong. He couldn't let Sean's hissy fits get in the way of their plan.

'Right,' Sean said. 'Don't you think things have slowed down a bit on that front?'

'What do you mean?'

'Well, it's been two weeks since the wedding, and nothing else has actually happened.'

Ryan shrugged. 'Nothing else has happened? Sean, you approached their kid at school and indirectly threatened him. As much as I didn't like what you did, it put the shitters up them. They know that they're not off the hook and they don't even know who's doing this to them. There's a lot happening.'

Sean shook his head and moved past Ryan back into the living room. He knelt in front of the holdall and started to count the cash, sorting it into bundles.

'All I'm saying is, I think that we should do something else. You know, really get into their heads.'

'That's what's happening with Jamie and Ashley. Sean, there's this concept I don't think you're familiar with. It's called patience.'

Sean shot Ryan a look. 'Watch your mouth.'

Taking a few steadying breaths, Ryan decided that the best thing he could do atin that moment was leave Sean to deal with whatever was going on in his head. It was like Sean wanted to pick a fight, or give Ryan a reason to start one.

'Look, I've got to go. I'll catch up with you when you're in a better mood.'

Chapter Fifty-Three

Angie had set Jack up with some lunch and was busying herself around the house with tasks that didn't actually need doing. After Conor had gone to meet Jamie the previous night, she couldn't help but worry about her daughter living with a stranger. As much as Conor had assured her that Jamie seemed to come across well, and Conor had no real concerns, something in the back of Angie's mind still niggled at her.

'Mum?' Jack said through a mouthful of food. 'What's wrong with you today? It's Saturday, the best day of the week.'

Angie stopped midway through emptying the dishwasher and frowned. 'What do you mean?'

'You're all wriggly. Like you've got ants in your pants.' Jack laughed but kept his eyes on her. For a seven-year-old, he was very switched on. Too switched on, sometimes.

'No, I don't have ants in my pants, cheeky.' She smiled at him. 'I'm just missing your sister, that's all.'

Jack nodded, as though he understood. But how could he? He was just a little boy, caught up in some gang war that even Angie didn't fully understand.

'You should phone her,' he replied, before shovelling a forkful of pasta into his mouth. 'She probably misses you too.'

Angie felt her shoulders relax a little. Jack's attitude always softened her mood. Maybe he was right, though. Now that Conor had met Jamie, then perhaps Ashley should feel more relaxed about everything.

Bending down to pull a pot from the dishwasher, she said, 'Yeah, maybe.' Then her mobile rang. It was sitting on the charging pad on the other side of the kitchen and when she reached it, she saw Ashley's name flash up on the screen.

'Hi,' she answered. 'I wasn't expecting to hear from you today. At all, actually.'

'I take it you know what happened last night?' Ashley started.

'Well, yeah. Conor told me.' Angie chose to leave out the part where she'd sat in the office and watched the meeting from the security cameras. It did sound intrusive and would send Ashley on one of her rants if she found out.

'I'm phoning because I think you and Dad should meet Jamie. Well, Conor thinks you and Dad should meet Jamie. And I suppose I don't disagree with him.'

Angie closed her eyes in a long blink, relieved that her brother had managed to get through to her on some level.

'We'd like that a lot, Ashley.'

'We'll come to you. This afternoon. And Mum, please don't make a fuss. And don't ask me to come home. I'm happy where I am.'

Angie shook her head. Her daughter had such a guard up. Not that she could blame her.

'Fine,' Angie replied.

'We'll be there for two o'clock. See you later. Tell Jack I'm excited to see him.'

Angie smiled across at Jack, who was staring at her as he finished off his lunch. He returned the smile, and gave a cheeky thumbs up.

'Mum, I can't believe it. I was just telling you to phone Ashley and she phoned you. It's like we're telpatic,' he said with a wide smile.

Angie laughed. 'You mean telepathic?'

He nodded as he climbed down from the table and placed his empty bowl on the counter next to the dishwasher, before disappearing through the hall and up to his bedroom.

'How can you be so calm? Aren't you nervous about meeting this boy our daughter is living with?' Angie asked as she paced the hallway while Dale stood next to her.

'No, because believe it or not, *I'm* the dad. Not him. If anyone should be nervous it should be this Jamie,' Dale replied.

'Mum, just calm it,' Jack said. Dale laughed loudly at their son's remark and winked at him.

'You're right, Jack. Mum needs to calm it down. I don't know why you're so nervous. He's just a lad who's dating our daughter. Do you think your mother was this nervous meeting me?'

Angie raised a brow, remembering that very day. 'No, because my mother was desperate to get me out of the house. She would have sold me to a cattle market, given half the chance.'

Dale shook his head and gripped Angie's shoulders, holding her still. 'Stop it. You're being ridiculous. Ashley isn't going to appreciate you acting like a neurotic mother when meeting this guy. Please, just breathe, eh?'

Before Angie could reply in defence, the sound of a key in the door made her turn in time to see it open. Ashley came into view, with a sheepish looking Jamie behind her.

'Hi,' she said as she stepped into the house.

'It's good to see you, pal,' Dale said, moving forward and hugging her. This was the longest either of them had gone without seeing Ashley, and although three weeks wasn't that long, to Angie it felt like a lifetime had passed since the wedding. So much had happened since then.

Dale let go of Ashley and peered around her to Jamie. He held out his hand and said, 'Jamie? I'm Dale, Ashley's dad. Nice to meet you.'

Jamie nodded, gave a slight smile and shook Dale's hand. 'Thanks for having me, Mr Bryson.'

'This is my mum, Angie,' Ashley said as she closed the door.

Jamie nodded again, and offered out his hand first. Polite, smartly dressed; not bad so far, Angie thought.

'Come in, come in,' Angie said. But before she could lead them through to the lounge, Jack had already wrapped himself around his sister's legs and was squeezing her tight.

'Wee man, you've grown since I last saw you,' Ashley said. Angie heard a crack in her voice, and it almost set her off too.

'Are you my sister's new boyfriend?' Jack asked, pulling away and staring up at Jamie. 'My mum was so nervous about you, I had to tell her to calm down.'

Ashley glanced up at Angie and Dale started to laugh before ruffling Jack's hair.

'I erm… Yeah, I am,' Jamie said. 'And you must be Jack? Ashley is always talking about you.'

'Do you like PlayStation?' Jack asked, placing his hands on his hips as though the correct answer would grant him access to the rest of the house.

Angie smiled and shook her head as Ashley moved in for an awkward hug. It was a hug, all the same.

'FIFA champion standing right here,' Jamie smiled. Jack seemed overjoyed by this, and turned to wink at Angie in approval.

'Why don't I get us all a drink?' Dale suggested, before placing his hands on Jack's shoulders as if to calm him down. 'Jamie, what's your tipple?'

'Oh, erm, well, I'm driving. So, I'll have anything non-alcoholic, thanks.'

Dale nodded. 'Okay, well why don't you help me in the kitchen and the women can take a seat in the lounge?'

Jamie looked more nervous than Angie felt; like it should be, she thought. She was so glad of Dale taking charge of the situation. She watched as Dale led Jamie away, and Jack followed them. Ashley shrugged off her jacket and hung it on the coat stand beside the door before heading for the lounge. Angie followed her and soon they were sitting on opposite ends of the sofa. The way they used to when Ashley still lived there. They would chat at the end of every day, about everything and nothing.

'I'm so glad you came here today, I've missed you,' Angie said.

'Yeah, it's been weird not being at home. I just…' Ashley trailed off. 'I've just got some stuff to sort out, you know, in my head.'

Angie nodded. She wanted to understand as much as she could. She wanted to be there to help. 'We'll catch the guy who did it, you know. We will.'

'It's not just that, Mum. It's everything. This family, it's like we're cursed or something. First that psycho Reilly, now this.'

Angie sighed. 'Sweetheart, Reilly was a *long* time ago.'

'Yeah, but it's the same shit, isn't it? Hostile ex-employees attacking us because they didn't get their own way. Or scorned clients and associates—'

'Ah,' Angie held her hand up, 'we don't know who attacked us or why, Ashley.'

'Yeah, exactly, Mum. That's the thing that scares me. I mean, they turned up at Jack's school.'

'We've decided to take Jack out of school and have him home schooled until this blows over.'

Ashley shook her head, and a shadow of fury crossed her face. 'But how is that fair on Jack? He's only a little boy, Mum, and he's been taken away from his friends, his school, his normal everyday life because of the kind of business this family is involved in. This isn't just about you and Dad, or Conor, or Uncle Paul. They murdered Bob. And they'll try to kill again. That's why I moved away.'

Angie sat up and took Ashley's hand, giving it a gentle squeeze. 'And you think that by moving away you're safer? Sorry, sweetheart, but what makes you think we aren't being watched right now? I don't mean to scare you, but if they knew where we were getting married, and they knew where Jack's school was, then what makes you think they don't know where Jamie lives? And that you're living with him?'

Ashley's face paled, and Angie felt guilty for putting it so bluntly.

'I know, Mum. But distancing myself seemed like my only option.'

Angie didn't know how to respond. Would she have done the same in Ashley's situation? Probably, she thought.

At that moment, all Angie wanted was the head on a plate of the person who'd split up her family in front of her.

Dale entered the lounge, breaking the silence between Angie and Ashley. Jamie and Jack followed close behind him, carrying trays of snacks. 'Right then, who's for wine?'

Chapter Fifty-Four

Smiling up at her dad, thankful for the distraction, Ashley got up from the sofa and took the bottle from his left hand and placed it on the coffee table in the centre of the room. Jack and Jamie put the tray of snacks down too, and Jack threw himself onto the sofa between Ashley and their mum. He was hugging her again and she couldn't resist giving him a squeeze herself.

'Jamie, sit down,' Ashley said, looking up at him and wondering why he was standing almost in the centre of the room, looking like a stunned animal.

'Yeah, make yourself comfortable,' Dale said. 'So, tell us what you do for a living, Jamie.'

Ashley noticed how Angie's eyes were on Jamie. She was watching him with intense scrutiny. Almost as if she wanted him to fuck up by saying something stupid.

'I'm a courier driver,' Jamie replied, taking a seat on the couch opposite Ashley.

Dale was nodding as he poured three glasses of wine. He glanced at Jack and said, 'Wee man, go and grab us some water bottles from the fridge, eh?'

Jack bounced up off the sofa and ran out of the room to the kitchen, before quickly returning and throwing one of the bottles to Jamie. He caught it quickly and smiled at Jack.

'What kind of couriering do you do?' Angie asked.

'I work for a small company that gives me the packages on a daily basis. So, I don't actually know what people are ordering. I just deliver them.'

There was an awkward silence which was saved by Jack. 'We should play FIFA. I bet I'm better at it than you are.'

Dale laughed as he passed a glass of wine to Ashley and then one to Angie. 'In a while, Jack. We're talking right now. Why don't you go and get some practice in, and Jamie can join you later?'

Sighing, Jack skulked out of the room and into the games room.

'He's just really excited to have someone else to beat, don't take it personally,' Ashley said to Jamie, who smiled at her.

'So, Jamie. Tell me about yourself?'

'Not much to tell, really. I have my own flat, don't have much contact with my mum, and my dad died when I was little.'

'I'm sorry to hear that,' Angie said, her tone softening a little. 'So, where did you grow up?'

Jamie hesitated for a second, enough for Ashley to notice. She felt sorry for him, being grilled by her parents. She wanted to tell her mum to shut up but refrained from doing so.

'All over, really. Was born in Glasgow. Have lived in various parts of the country before settling back here.'

Ashley watched as her mum narrowed her eyes, as though she suspected Jamie was lying.

'Any siblings?'

Ashley rolled her eyes, but no one seemed to notice.

'Nope, just me,' Jamie smiled.

'So, you two are pretty serious then, to be living together so soon, I mean?' Dale broke the awkwardness of the situation, and Ashley was glad of it.

'Well, when you know, you know,' Jamie replied and Ashley felt her tummy flutter. Smiling at her parents, she saw her mum's expression. She wasn't happy with that answer, for whatever reason. 'But Ashley has said that she wants her own place. So, I'll respect that and let her do her own thing.'

Dale glanced at Ashley with surprise. 'Ah, so it's not a permanent thing then, you two living together?'

'No. I want to be independent, live by myself, rely on myself.'

Ashley still wasn't sure how she was going to do that. She'd lived off her family her entire life. She was only seventeen, so of course she had.

'And how do you propose to be independent, Ashley?' Angie asked. Ashley glared at her mother, wishing that she would just come out and say whatever it was that she wanted to say.

'I want a job, my own money. I want to save for my own flat, my own car.'

Angie was nodding along with every word, but Ashley could tell she wasn't being taken seriously.

'What, Mum? What is it?'

Holding up her wine glass free hand in defence, she said, 'Nothing.'

'No, come on. What is it? You think I can't do this, don't you?'

Angie smiled, but it wasn't genuine. She was patronising her in front of her dad and her boyfriend.

'All I'm saying is, in this day and age, with the climate how it is and you having no real-life job experience, what kind of job do you expect you will get that will allow you to save up for all the things you want? I mean, I assume you're paying Jamie rent?'

Jamie leaned forward on the sofa and opened up his water bottle. 'Actually, no she isn't. I said she could live with me rent free until she sorts something out for herself.'

Ashley wanted to leave. She wanted to slam her wine glass down on the table and get the hell away from her mother. How could she think it was okay to speak to her like this in front of anyone, let alone Jamie?

'Angie, come on,' Dale said. 'Haven't we always told Ashley she can do whatever it is she wants to do?'

Angie didn't answer, and a build-up of fury from the pit of Ashley's stomach was threatening to explode.

'Yes, but with circumstances the way they are, I think we'd all agree that living on her own away from home isn't a good option right now,' Angie replied.

Ashley got to her feet and Dale stood with her. 'Ashley, please. Sit down.'

'No. I knew she was going to do this. She's just annoyed that she can't control me.'

Jamie stood and placed his bottle on the table. 'I think I'll give you three a minute or two to talk in private.' He slipped out of the room and closed the lounge door.

'See, now look what you've done. You've made him uncomfortable and he's only been here five fucking minutes,' she spat at Angie. 'This is all just about you not wanting me to have control of my life.'

Angie shook her head, and Ashley saw a sadness in her eyes. 'That's not the case and you know it, Ashley. I'm trying to protect my family, my kids.'

'And what about Conor? Would you do this to him if he moved out? No, of course you wouldn't. Because he's male and works alongside Dad and Uncle Paul every single day. So you don't worry about him as much.'

Angie ran a hand through her hair and placed her glass on the table. 'Exactly, I *worry* about you. It has nothing to do with control. Look, I'm sorry if it comes across like that. It's a defence barrier I have. I just want you to be safe and I really do believe that the safest place you can be is here with us.'

Ashley shook her head as Angie spoke. 'No.'

Dale stepped between them and faced Ashley. His eyes were dark with concern. 'You're having counselling again?'

Sighing, Ashley replied, 'Well, not yet. But I have the number of someone who can help me process what happened far better than any childhood therapist could. But you know what? If I wasn't a Bryson, none of this would have happened to me.'

Dale lowered his eyes and Ashley's heart sank. She didn't mean that. She didn't want to hurt any of her family. But what she said was true. Being a Bryson was dangerous.

'You should never have had to do what you did, Ashley. You should never have been there that day. You'll never know how sorry I am that you were.'

Ashley closed her eyes and took a few, steadying breaths.

'I know you are, Dad. But I need to sort my head out. And with what happened to Bob at the wedding, I just can't do that here. I love you both, and Conor and Jack. But I have to go down my own path with this. Can you both understand that?'

Ashley waited for their response. She wanted them to support her on this. She hated the fact that she wasn't on great terms with her mum. It wasn't Angie's fault that this had happened. But it wasn't Ashley's either.

'Of course we can,' Dale replied. 'We didn't know you were still struggling with what happened with Reilly.'

'I didn't either, not really. Not until I was triggered by what happened at the wedding,' she sighed. 'Okay, look. Let's not ruin this today. Let's put everything to the side. I want you both to get to know Jamie and I want to spend some time with Jack.'

Ashley saw her mum's shoulders relax, as if she was relieved that the conversation was turning. If she was honest with herself, she was too.

'Is Conor joining us?' Ashley asked.

'He will at some point, I imagine.' Angie smiled. 'He's out with Paul at the construction site today.'

Dale pulled Ashley into him and held her close. She hugged her dad back, thankful that even though things were hard between them at the moment, they were all alive.

'Why don't I go and get Jamie, bring him back in and we can start this meeting from the beginning? No more attitude or the third degree, I promise,' Angie said.

Ashley nodded, smiled and pulled away from her dad. She allowed her mum to hug her tight, but wondered if things would ever be the same in their family again. Until the person who attacked them was caught, the tension was always going to be there.

Angie let go and moved out of the lounge, leaving Ashley and her dad alone. They sat down and Ashley picked up her wine glass before taking a larger than normal mouthful. It would calm the nerves, she thought.

'Ashley, now that it's just us here, I want to ask you something,' Dale said.

'Okay.' Ashley set her glass on the table and turned so she was facing him.

'Are you doing, okay? Like, *really* okay?'

Ashley didn't know how to answer that without hurting her dad's feelings. But she'd already been honest during their heated discussion, so what would be the point in lying now?

'Honestly? No, I'm not doing okay. But I think seeing this therapist will make a huge difference. Jamie had some really good things to say about her.'

Dale nodded. 'Jamie's had sessions with her?'

'He has. And don't ask me what for, because I won't tell you. That's private.'

'I wasn't going to ask what for. But I'm glad that he's taken your feelings seriously and helped you like that. That's all I want for my girl.'

Ashley sighed, and felt a lump form in her throat. She swallowed it down. She didn't want to cry.

'Right,' Angie said as she appeared back in the lounge with Jamie at her back. 'Let's start again, shall we?'

Ashley smiled up at Jamie. But when she looked at her mum, the smile seemed forced. 'You okay?' she asked Angie.

'Yeah,' Angie replied, her tone a little higher than normal. 'Just glad we're together. Why don't I pour us another drink?'

Jamie sat down next to Ashley and took her hand in his, giving it a gentle squeeze. 'Thanks for having me, today,' he said to Dale and Angie. 'It means a lot, and I know it means a lot to Ashley. Families should never be kept apart from each other, no matter the circumstances.'

Dale nodded and raised his glass. 'I'll drink to that, Jamie.'

Ashley reached for hers and did the same, but she was still looking at her mother. A shadow crossed over Angie Bryson's face, and Ashley didn't like the look of it one bit.

–

Angie waved her daughter and Jamie off as Jamie pulled out of the driveway, and closed the door. She turned towards Dale who looked expectant, as if waiting for her to start her rant.

'Go on, then, tell me everything you don't like about him,' Dale said. She knew he was joking, but she wasn't.

'There is something about him I don't trust, Dale. He was being really cagey when answering my questions. And then when I went out to get him to come back into the lounge, he was pretty much inspecting the house. I found him in the main lounge, looking at plug sockets. I mean, who does that?'

Dale frowned and then smiled. 'Maybe he wants to be an electrician?'

Angie didn't laugh. 'This isn't funny, Dale. I'm being serious. I think we should keep an eye on him.'

Shaking his head, Dale sighed. 'Fine. I'll get Conor on the case. But you know, Angie, this kind of behaviour isn't going to help Ashley to come back. It's only going to push her further away.'

Dale turned and headed upstairs, and Angie watched him go. A mother's instinct was rarely wrong. She would keep an eye on things herself.

263

Chapter Fifty-Five

A few days had passed since Ashley and Jamie had gone to meet her parents. A lot had happened in those few days. Ashley had been having more sleepless nights. Jamie had been out at work a lot, leaving her alone with her thoughts. Thoughts that were pickling her brain. Her murdered uncle and the idea that the person who did it was still wandering free, ready to strike again; the fact that she wasn't on great terms with her family because of that. It was all so much to process. She'd decided to call Shona Henry and make an appointment. And now, she stood outside Shona's home, from where she worked, and her heart hammered so hard inside her that she thought she was going to be sick. Going to a child therapist was entirely different to seeing an adult therapist. She understood the severity of what happened much more clearly than she had back then, and the thought of talking about it made her stomach roll. But she had to do this. She had to get these thoughts out of her head and move on with her life.

Reaching the front door, Ashley rang the bell and waited just a few short seconds before a woman answered. As she opened the door, Ashley was ready and waiting with a fake, wide smile. It was something she always did when she was nervous.

'Ashley?' the woman asked. Ashley nodded as she opened the door further. 'I'm Shona. Nice to meet you. Come on through.'

Ashley stepped over the threshold and glanced at her surroundings. It looked different to what she'd thought, having expected a clinical feel to the place. Instead, she was surrounded by warm colours and accents of personality. A vase with white flowers, a frame with a picture of a baby beneath the glass. Almost immediately she noticed the frames on the wall proudly displaying Shona's certificates.

'It must be nice to work from home?' Ashley said, removing her jacket and hanging it over her arm.

Shona smiled. 'It is. Gives me much more time to do other things, with the commute being so short from the bedroom to the office.'

Ashley returned the smile and followed Shona through the hallway towards a closed door. Shona welcomed Ashley into a room at the back of the property, which looked a lot more like an office. The room was plain white. A leather couch sat against the wall to her left, facing a window that was framed by white curtains pulled into perfectly measured plaits on the pole they hung from. A small desk with a computer sat in the far corner, the screen facing away from the room.

'Take a seat,' Shona said, gesturing for Ashley to sit down. Shona sat on the opposite end of the sofa, and smiled. 'I know, it's a bit bare in here. But as a therapist, I like my client's surroundings to be minimalistic. I believe it helps stop any distractions.'

Ashley nodded, and felt her nerves ease a little, although they didn't completely leave her.

'So, let's begin. Why did you want to have these sessions with me?' Shona asked.

'No small talk in here, then,' Ashley joked. Shona didn't respond, instead she stared, unblinking, before giving a gentle smile.

'What brings you here, Ashley?'

'A childhood trauma that I never got over,' Ashley replied solemnly. There was no getting away from it, she had to speak, otherwise what was the point in being there?

Ashley waited for questions. What happened? When? Why? But they didn't come. Shona simply sat there, in silence, and waited patiently for Ashley to continue.

And she did. She told Shona about Reilly; about how as a child, she killed him on purpose to save her dad.

Chapter Fifty-Six

The house was empty. Dale and Conor had taken themselves off to the office, Paul was at the construction site and Jack was in the garden playing football with one of the security guards. The house was still surrounded by them so Angie felt a little more at ease allowing Jack to go outside by himself.

It was nice to have some time to herself, and as she sank back into the bath, the lavender-scented bath salts soothing the aches and pains caused by the stress of the last few weeks, Angie reached for the wine glass on the bamboo bath caddy and took a sip. *Friends* played out in front of her from the iPad, something she'd seen a million times and didn't have to concentrate on, and for the first time in weeks, she actually felt relaxed.

Her phone lay on the unit next to the bath. As much as she'd have rather left it in another room so it wouldn't disturb her, she needed to have it close by in case there were any developments with finding out who'd attacked them – and who was still at large.

Angie was staring at the screen, laughing as Ross screamed about his fajitas, when her phone rang. Sighing loudly, she picked it up and glanced at the screen. It was a withheld number, and she refused to answer it. If it was important, they'd leave a message. Ending the call, she placed the phone back down and sank deeper into the warm, lavender water, and closed her eyes.

For a moment, things felt semi-normal. She'd managed to smooth things over with Ashley, even if she wasn't hugely keen on her new boyfriend, Jamie. Her suspicions of him still lingered in the back of her mind, but unless she could come up with proof that he wasn't good for her, she'd have to back off.

Jack wasn't at school now, but he was safe at home. She wouldn't send him back until the person who was trying to kill them was caught.

Angie felt herself relaxing more and more as the warm water lapped around her body. As she began to drift off, her phone rang again, the shrill sound startling her.

She sat up and glanced at the phone. Withheld number again. She took a breath and answered it.

'Hello?' she said sharply.

'Angie Bryson?' a male voice asked.

'Who wants to know?' Angie said, leaning forward and pausing the episode on the iPad.

'I have a message for your family, about Kyle and Ian Fraser.'

Angie froze. Her heart felt like it was going to stop. Pulling the phone from her ear, she stared at the screen, as though it would reveal the identity of the caller.

'Who are you?' she said, trying to sound unaffected by the reference to those names.

'Just call me an old acquaintance,' he said.

Angie opened her mouth to speak, but no words came out; the shock paralysing her voice.

'It won't be long until your family are exposed for what you did to them. They might be dead, but there are people who want justice for them. And I don't mean the legal kind. So, you all better keep an ear to the ground and eyes in the back of your head. Because none of you are safe. None of you. Not you, not Dale, nor any of your kids. Do you hear me, Angie?'

Angie jabbed her finger at the screen, ending the call abruptly. Her breath caught in her throat and she started to panic. Standing up quickly, she got out of the bath and wrapped a huge cotton bath sheet around her body before rushing downstairs to the back door that led to the garden.

She saw Jack kicking the ball back and forth between him and one of the security men. The man looked up, startled by her sudden presence and the fact that she was dripping wet and wrapped in a towel.

'Jack, come inside right now,' she said.

He turned and frowned. 'But we're playing football.'

She raised her voice. 'I said *now*.'

'Is everything okay, Mrs Bryson?' the security man asked. The security man who, at this moment, she realised she didn't know well at all. Only that he was employed by Bryson Security and that Dale had dealt with arranging him to stand outside the house, along with the rest of them.

'No. I need to phone my husband. You stay there. Keep an eye on... well, everything.'

Jack passed the ball to the man and skulked into the house, his face like thunder. 'It's not fair, Mum. I'm fed up of staying in.'

'I know. Sorry, Jack. But I'm your mum and you need to do what I say. Now, go and find something to do, I need to phone your dad.'

Jack moved through the kitchen and Angie listened as he thundered up the stairs to his bedroom and slammed the door. Angie pulled up Dale's number, and as she was about to hit call, she stopped. Dale wasn't the person she needed to get in contact with.

She waited with trembling hands as the number rang. And then he answered.

'Angie?'

'Paul,' her voice shook as much as her hands did, 'something's happened.' Silence fell at the other end, and it rang in her ears.

'What is it?' he replied, sounding just as nervous as she did.

Angie felt her legs buckle beneath her and she gripped onto the kitchen counter for support. 'Just get here. Now.'

–

It hadn't taken Paul long to arrive at the house. While Angie waited on him, she had tried to calm herself. The house was secure, Jack was inside, the security outside were doing their jobs. So far, it was just an anonymous phone call; someone was trying to fuck with them.

'Hey,' Paul said as she welcomed him in. 'Are you okay?'

Angie shook her head. Her skin prickled with a coldness that she told herself was because her hair was still damp from her bath. Only she knew that wasn't the case.

'I got an anonymous call earlier. It was a man; he didn't say his name. But he said he was an old acquaintance of the Frasers. He said they wanted justice; that none of us are safe. He knew our names. All of us, even the kids. It was him, the man who approached Jack at school. I just know it.'

Paul's expression didn't change. He seemed calm. 'And you didn't recognise the voice?'

Angie shook her head.

'Do you have your suspicions as to who it could be?'

'No, I haven't a clue. Paul, I think they're getting desperate. I think they'll come here, no hesitation. Whoever it is, they want revenge.'

'But MacTavish's in prison. Surely they must know that?'

Angie shrugged. 'Unless they don't think it was MacTavish who did it?'

Paul nodded and began pacing the floor. 'Right. I'll have to speak to Dale about this.'

'You can't,' Angie replied sharply.

'Angie, I have to. I can't deal with this on my own. We're all in this together as a family. Don't worry, I won't say a word about Conor. That lie doesn't just affect you, it affects me too, remember? I've been lying to my brother for *years*. How would that help? Dale finding out that Conor is Kyle Fraser's by blood isn't something I want getting out any more than you do.'

Angie felt her chest constrict. The very idea made her nauseous and hearing the words out loud just brought on a feeling of shame, the same way it had when she told the lie for the first time.

'I should have come clean back then. I just didn't want to hurt him,' Angie said.

'Aye, you should have. But it's too far down the line now. And I don't want him knowing that I've covered for you when I shouldn't have. Just let me deal with this, eh?'

'Okay. Just, I don't know… Just be careful.'

Paul nodded and raised a hand and placed it on her shoulder. 'Always am, Angie.'

Chapter Fifty-Seven

Ryan and Sean sat opposite each other and smiled as they listened to the voices on the device. Angie and Paul Bryson had no idea they were being listened to, and no idea that their entire conversation would be used against them.

'This has to be the best idea you've ever come up with, Sean,' Ryan said.

'It's simple, we get the information we need from the horses' mouths. We find out which one of them was responsible for killing Dad and Ian, how they did it and then we fucking end them.'

Ryan took in Sean's expression. He was smiling, but his eyes weren't shining the way they normally did when a plan came together. Something was bothering him.

'Are you still annoyed about the other day?' Ryan asked.

'What? That you were Dad's favourite and I'm just a follower? That's not your fault. I'm not angry at you, Ryan. I'm angry that Dad never had any faith in me.'

Ryan sat back in shock. He hadn't thought Sean would keep this so close to his chest. 'Sean, don't be angry at him. It was in the past. And he's not here to have it out with him. Also, you were just a kid, he'd never have let you in on what he was really doing. It's not that he didn't have faith in you, you were just too young. You can't let it turn you into someone bitter and twisted. It could ruin what we're trying to achieve.'

But Sean wasn't listening, he was leaning in closer to the listening device that Ryan had planted in the Bryson house, and his expression was focused. He shooshed Ryan, putting a hand up in gesture.

Ryan fell silent and listened too.

'*Angie, I have to. I can't deal with this on my own. We're all in this together as a family. Don't worry, I won't say a word about Conor. That lie doesn't just affect you, it affects me too, remember? I've been lying to my brother for years. How would that help? Dale finding out that Conor is Kyle Fraser's by blood isn't something I want getting out any more than you do.*'

Sean raised his eyes slowly and stared at Ryan, open mouthed. Ryan let the words sink in. Had he heard that correctly?

'Surely not,' Ryan said. 'Is there a rewind option on this thing?'

Sean shook his head. 'No, it's a transmitter via the internet.'

'You heard that the way I heard it, didn't you? He just said that Conor Bryson *isn't* actually a Bryson. He's a Fraser by blood. Kyle Fraser. As in…' Ryan trailed off.

'As in,' Sean replied slowly, 'Conor is our half-brother.'

Ryan shook his head and laughed. 'No chance. No fucking way. Why would they say that?'

'Why would they lie? They're in the house by themselves. You heard Paul Bryson. He said he needed to get in contact with Dale. It's just them. No one else in the family knows about it. Fucking hell!' Sean said. 'This is crazy.'

Ryan stood up from the sofa and began pacing the floor slowly as he tried to think. 'Hang on. What age is Conor?'

Sean shrugged. 'I don't know. Twenty?'

Ryan nodded. 'Aye, he's twenty. And I'm twenty-one. Which means Dad had it off with Angie Bryson when he was with Mum.'

Sean lowered his gaze to the floor and placed his head in his hands. 'Fuck. This is going to kill her. Unless she already knows?'

Ryan gritted his teeth and shook his head. 'Nah,' he said. 'She'd never have let him get away with something like that if she'd known.'

Sean nodded, but his eyes stared into the distance. How could this be happening? This was the last thing either of them had expected.

'Do you think Dad knew?' Sean finally asked.

'Not a clue. But it would explain a lot. Maybe *that's* the reason he's dead. Maybe they killed him to keep him silent.'

'Doesn't explain why Ian's dead, though? Why did he have to die because of it?'

Ryan didn't answer, and both brothers fell silent.

Chapter Fifty-Eight

Ashley Bryson felt surprisingly better after her first session with Shona, and as she walked home, she wondered if she'd finally be able to move past what had happened all those years ago. In doing so, she might even be able to move on from what happened at the wedding; provided that the person responsible was caught.

She sent a text to Jamie, telling him that the first session went well and that she was on her way back to the flat. He replied, telling her that he was on his way out to work and that he would see her later that evening.

Smiling, Ashley felt the sun on her skin and for the first time in weeks, she allowed herself to feel happy. Just as she was about to slide her phone into her pocket, a message appeared. The notification came through without a name or number and when she read the content, she stopped walking.

> Your family are dead.

There was no option to reply, no way to detect who the message had come from. Her chest constricted, as Ashley reread the message. Over and over again, she let her eyes move across those four words. *Your family are dead.* Her fingers began to tremble, and the tremors quickly travelled up her arm, and soon her entire body was quaking.

She tried to call Jamie, but he didn't answer. Then she tried her dad, but he didn't answer either.

'For fuck's sake, does no one keep their phone on them these days?' Ashley said out loud. A man walking past with his dog gave her an odd look as he moved around her.

Reluctantly, Ashley decided to call her mum, knowing full well that it would cause nothing but sheer panic and she would insist that Ashley returned to the family home. But what else could she do?

'Mum?' Ashley said as Angie answered.

'What's up?'

Ashley frowned, hearing the quiver in her mum's voice.

'I got a message today.'

Silence hung on the other end of the line and then Angie quietly replied, 'What did it say? Are you safe, Ashley? Where are you?'

That response sparked further concern in Ashley.

'Ashley, are you safe? Are you alone?'

'I'm on my way back from my therapy session with Shona. I'm walking back to Jamie's flat. But—'

Angie cut her off. 'What did the message say, Ashley?'

Ashley hesitated. Her mum was already on high alert. Something had already happened; she could feel it.

'Your family are dead.'

The words hung between them, and Ashley heard her mum gasp.

'Mum, has something happened?'

'You're coming home. Right now. Where are you?'

Ashley rolled her head back and closed her eyes. This was exactly what she knew would happen. She could hear the hysteria in her mum's voice.

'No, I'm going back to the flat.'

'No, you're not, Ashley. Someone has threatened us, and you're alone. Tell me where you are and I'll get Conor to come and collect you.'

Ashley puffed out her cheeks and sighed loudly in protest, but she knew there was no getting round this.

'Fine. But Conor can get me from Jamie's. I'm almost there anyway.'

'Okay. Good,' Angie said. 'Keep your eyes open, Ashley. And if anyone suspicious approaches you, you fucking run. You scream and you run. Understood?'

Those words kickstarted something deep inside her. A deep-rooted fear that she hadn't felt even when she'd watched Bob die. *That* attack was unexpected. But *this*? There was an inevitability that someone could leap out from any corner, right then, and take Ashley out.

'Okay, Mum. Calm down,' Ashley said, trying to make sure that at least one of them stayed on an even keel. 'I'll wait for Conor at the flat.' She started walking again, this time picking up the pace.

'And tell no one what you're doing. That includes Jamie.'

Frowning, Ashley shook her head. 'Mum, that's a bit excessive, is it not?'

'No. We can only trust each other. Anyone outside the family is a threat.'

Ashley almost had to laugh. 'And you know all the security at the house personally, do you?'

'Ashley, don't joke with me on this. It's serious. I'm not asking you, I'm telling you. Keep your mouth shut. You tell Jamie nothing. Understood?'

Ashley normally argued every little detail with her mum, but for some reason, she had an inkling that now wasn't the time.

'I'll see you when Conor brings me to the house.'

Angie thanked her and hung up. Ashley tucked her phone away and speeded up, keeping her eyes focused on the road ahead. She was only ten minutes away from the flat. It was broad daylight. But all she could think about was that someone was watching her and she had no idea who, or where they were. Ashley wanted to turn and look over her shoulder, but the fear inside her was real, and it wouldn't let her do anything other than look ahead.

An hour had passed since her mum had said Conor was going to pick her up, and as Ashley stood at the window, with her packed bag at her feet, she waited impatiently for her brother to arrive.

'Fuck's sake, Conor. Trust you to be on a go-slow in an emergency,' Ashley said as she moved away from the window. She paced the floor, wondering whether or not to go against Angie's instructions to keep things quiet and not tell Jamie about what was happening. But how could she do that? He'd been so good to her, allowing her to stay in his flat rent free, supporting her, encouraging her about seeing a therapist. It seemed so unfair.

'It won't do any harm to warn him that I'm not going to be here when he gets home. I can't just disappear with no word,' she said aloud, taking her phone in her hand and sending him a text.

> Jamie. Something has happened and I need to go home. Please, don't try to follow me. I just need to be with them right now. As soon as I know what's going on, I'll be in touch. I love you. Ashley. X

She watched the message go, and the delivered ticks appear underneath. Then, she heard a beeping sound, coming from the bedroom. Frowning, she glanced down at her phone again, and decided to call him. As it rang in her ear, a ringing sounded from the bedroom.

'I swear no one takes their phones anywhere these days,' she sighed, moving through the hall to the bedroom. The door was slightly ajar, just as she'd left it when she was collecting her things. Pushing it open, she looked around for Jamie's phone but couldn't see it. Calling it again, she followed the sound over to the chest of drawers under the window, and pulled open the top drawer. Rummaging through his T-shirts, she felt something solid at the back left corner. She wrapped her fingers around it, drew it out and saw that it was Jamie's phone.

'Why the hell would it be in there?' Ashley frowned, staring at the three missed calls and text from her. Hers weren't the only missed calls, or messages. There were others. One from someone called Sean. And a missed call from someone called Cara.

'Who the hell is Cara?' she wondered aloud.

Ashley bent down and looked into the back of the drawer. She slid her hand in and moved some of the T-shirts around, before discovering something else that wasn't made of material. It felt like a small notebook. Ashley pulled the passport out, and as she opened it to the back page, more confusion washed over her.

Staring up at her, was Jamie's face. But when she read the details, she froze.

> **Surname/Nom(1)**
> **FRASER**
>
> **Given names/Prenoms(2)**
> **RYAN KYLE**
>
> **Nationality/Nationalite (3)**
> **BRITISH CITIZEN**

'What the hell is this?' Ashley said, pulling it closer to her and staring at the image. 'Who the fuck is Ryan Kyle Fraser?'

The doorbell rang loudly and it startled her to the point where she almost dropped the passport. Gripping it in her hand, she moved out of the bedroom and across the hallway to the front door. When she opened it, she was relieved to see Conor standing there. But when he saw the expression on her face, his own fell.

'What's up? Apart from the obvious?'

She didn't say anything, simply handed him the passport and let him look at it. She watched as his eyes scanned the information and a look of confusion much like her own washed over his face.

'Yeah,' she said. 'My question is, who the hell is Ryan Kyle Fraser, and why is Jamie's picture next to that name?'

Conor looked behind her and said, 'Are you alone?'

Ashley nodded.

'Right, get your stuff. We're going home. I don't know what's going on here, but it doesn't feel good. Come on.'

Ashley moved through to the living room and grabbed the bag she'd left by the window. When she got back to Conor at the door, she held the phone up. 'What should I do with this?'

'What is it?'

'Jamie's phone. Ryan's… Whoever the hell he is.'

'Leave it here, and let's go.'

Ashley quickly moved through to the bedroom and Conor followed her. She shoved the phone back into the drawer and as she went to put the passport in, Conor's hand fell over her arm and he said, 'No, bring that with you. I have a feeling this has something to do with the trouble we've been having. Dad will want to see that.'

He took it from her as she shut the top drawer, and she followed him out of Jamie's flat, closing the door behind her.

Chapter Fifty-Nine

The sound of her kids entering the house brought a sense of relief she hadn't known existed until that moment. She rushed out of the kitchen to the front door – seeing their faces made her shoulders relax.

'What the hell took you so long?' Angie asked as her eyes darted between them.

'I had to get back from the casino to pick Ashley up. The city was rammed with traffic,' Conor said. 'Calm down, we're here now.'

Angie saw a look pass between her son and daughter, and then Conor reached into his pocket.

'Is Dad here yet?'

'No, he's on his way with Paul. Should be any minute now.' She glanced down at his hand. Seeing the passport, she frowned. 'You thinking of leaving the country?'

Conor shook his head. 'We found this in Jamie's flat. Seems as though Ashley's boyfriend has been lying about his identity since day one.'

He held the passport out to her and stole a glance at Ashley. She looked angry, confused. Heartbroken. Angie took the passport from Conor and opened it at the photograph page. Staring down at Jamie's face, and then reading the details, her stomach clenched. The name made her blood run cold.

Ryan Kyle Fraser.

Shit, she thought. Don't react. Stay calm.

'Recognise the name?' Conor asked.

Angie cleared her throat. 'No.'

That was a lie and Angie worried that both Conor and Ashley would see right through it. Just as she was beginning to think about how to deal with this, Dale and Paul came through the door. She knew there was something suspicious about Jamie, she just never thought that he'd be linked to the Fraser family.

'Ashley,' Dale said, pulling his daughter in for a hug, 'I'm so glad you agreed to come home. Your mum's right. We all need to be together right now. Have you had any more messages?'

Ashley shook her head. 'No, but we did find something that you might want to see.'

Angie took a breath and reluctantly handed the passport over to Dale. She watched his face, how it changed when he read the page. She saw the anger, the rage build in his eyes, before he handed it to Paul. He read over it and shot Angie a look.

'Fucking hell,' he said a little louder than he'd probably intended. 'Back from the fucking dead, eh?'

'Not quite,' Dale said. 'I can't believe I never thought of this as a possibility.'

Angie watched as Conor glanced from his uncle to his dad. 'What is it?'

Dale sighed. 'I think we should sit down.'

Angie manoeuvred around them and locked the front door, but not before she considered opening it, climbing into the car and driving away from this nightmare. But she couldn't do that. She couldn't leave Jack. He was too young, too innocent in all of this. It was her mess; all her fault.

'Dad?' Ashley's voice cracked. 'Do you think this is the person who killed Bob, and who tried to kill us?'

'Aye, but I don't think he's working alone. He can't be.'

Ashley started to cry. 'Oh my God. And I had him here, in this house. Fucking hell.'

'Hey,' Paul said, as Angie turned and leaned against the door. 'This is *not* your fault.'

At that moment, Angie felt her stomach begin to roll and she knew she was going to be sick. She excused herself, ran up the stairs and into the en suite in the bedroom and slammed the door closed behind her. Emptying her stomach into the toilet bowl, she flushed it away and stared at the white porcelain, wishing in that moment it was the light at the end of life that came to take you away from Earth. It was the only way she was going to be able to escape this. But that was cowardly, wasn't it? If this was how things were going, then she would have to face it.

Conor would never forgive her. Dale would never forgive her. If she'd just come clean at the beginning, they wouldn't be faced with this completely insane situation now.

'Angie?' There was a gentle knock on the bathroom door. It was Paul's voice.

She got to her feet and with quivering legs, crossed the cold, tiled floor and opened the door. As Paul stood there, his face was etched with concern.

'Are you okay?'

She shook her head, and hot tears sprang to her eyes.

'We'll sort it.'

'How?' she whispered. 'How will we sort it?'

Paul closed his eyes and exhaled slowly. 'By keeping quiet, like we always have.'

'He knows about Conor. He must do. That'll be why this is all happening. He'll have been aiming at me, or Dale, and got Bob instead.'

'Well, if he does know, I'll silence him,' Paul said, and Angie felt her blood boil. It was too late for that. One of their family was already dead. The Frasers weren't going to stop.

Angie felt herself begin to panic, but forced herself to breathe. In and out, slowly. 'You have to silence him. You have to.'

They headed back downstairs and Angie went through to the kitchen where the rest of the family had congregated, quietly seated around the table. Dale and Conor were looking at something on a phone and Ashley had her head in her hands.

Angie sat down at the table, as did Paul. Dale glanced at his brother and took a breath, before settling his eyes on his son and daughter.

'Okay, you're not going to like this. But now that Ashley has been taken in by this fucker, you both need to know what happened.'

'What do you mean?' Ashley asked.

Angie couldn't bear to look at any of them. As she sat there, her stomach constricted, but she kept her expression straight.

'Paul?' Dale said.

'Aye, right.' Paul cleared his throat and began. 'Eight years ago, I shot and killed two men. Kyle and Ian Fraser.'

Conor sat up in his seat and leaned forward, as if the position would help him take in the words better.

'Why?' Ashley asked. 'Why did you do that?'

Paul's eyes moved to Dale, and then back to Ashley.

'They were screwing us over and when I confronted them about it, they got really arsey, and basically told me to go fuck myself. The anger just got the better of me and I shot them.'

Dale shifted in his seat and cracked his knuckles and Paul continued. 'We – as in me, Bob and your dad – got rid of the bodies, and that was that. Don't feel bad for them. They were scum. Utter fucking scum. They deserved everything that was coming to them. Didn't they?' Paul said, turning to Dale.

Dale nodded, his expression dark. 'Aye. They did, unfortunately.'

Ashley took a few breaths and Angie worried that she was going to start panicking again. Her lie was on the surface of all this, and it was as if it was hovering over the family.

'You say this happened eight years ago?' Ashley asked. 'Around the same time that Reilly attacked you, Dad?'

'That's right. The incidents are completely unrelated, Ashley. I promise.'

'They're not, though, are they? Not really?' Ashley's voice got louder. 'They might not have anything to do with each other directly, but again, this is all to do with the kind of business you're involved in. Money, drugs… all of it.'

Angie placed a hand on Ashley's shoulder. 'Ashley, come on.'

'No, Mum.' Ashley shrugged her off before glaring at Dale. 'You're telling me that the guy I've been seeing only got involved with me to get closer to the family because he wanted to kill us? Because you all had a part to play in his dad's death? That story he told me about his dad dying from an aneurysm was all bullshit. Oh my God, this family really has no boundaries at all, has it?'

'He seemed so fucking normal when I took him out for that drink,' Conor said, slamming a hand on the table.

'Well, he would. He was trying to reel us in and used Ashley as the rod,' Dale said, looking down at his daughter with a slight sadness in his eyes. Angie could tell he felt sorry for her, and guilty that he'd caused it.

Ashley jumped and got up from the table quickly. 'I'm going to go and check on Jack.'

This Fraser lad was trying to destroy them, and it was working. The family were unravelling right in front of her. She followed Ashley through the house, and up the stairs to Jack's bedroom.

'Are you okay?'

'No, I'm not fucking okay. How could I be? Did you know about this?'

What was Angie meant to say to that? She couldn't lie. She had known about what had happened. Of course she had.

Angie sighed. 'I did, sweetheart. I'm sorry.'

'I just feel like a bit of an idiot. How did I not see this coming? I should have expected this from you lot.'

Angie shook her head. 'Ashley, come on. What did you want them to do, allow the Frasers to go ahead with their plan?'

Ignoring her, Ashley opened Jack's bedroom door and peered inside, before moving out and closing the door quietly. 'He's asleep. I need to get out of here.'

Angie shook her head. 'Absolutely not.'

'Mum, don't. I need to speak with my therapist. This is not negotiable. I'll be back later.'

Ashley pushed by her and ran down the stairs, before grabbing her coat and bag and heading out the door. Conor was at her back and out in the driveway.

'I'll come with you,' she heard Conor say as she reached the front door herself. 'You can't go on your own. Not now.'

'Ashley, Conor's right. But I think your dad or your uncle should go with you.'

Ashley wasn't responding. She was already in Conor's car. She closed the door, started the engine and took off down the driveway so quickly that if Angie had blinked, she'd have missed it.

'Shit,' Angie hissed as Conor stood with his back to her. Dale and Paul appeared next to her, and Dale instructed Paul to go after her.

'Follow her. Just make sure you keep eyes on her. Don't try to force her into coming back, that didn't turn out well for us the last time. Just make sure she's safe. Conor and I will stay here and try to work out how the hell we're going to put an end to this fucking mess.'

Conor turned, his shoulders high up at his ears. Angie had never seen her son look so angry. Dale kissed Angie on the cheek before heading back into the house with Paul and Conor.

As she stood there, facing out to the driveway, Paul unlocked his own car. He turned and nodded at Angie. 'Don't worry, Ange, I'll make sure she's safe. Half the Frasers are already in the ground. We'll make sure the rest of them end up there too.'

Once Paul had reversed down the drive, Angie entered the house and took a few steadying breaths. Suddenly, her eyes fell on the plug socket by the skirting board at the bottom of the stairs. It was one of the least-used sockets in the house but it bore a plug and the switch was on. It resembled a phone charging plug but without the USB wire attached. She bent down and inspected it, pulling it out, turning it upwards and inspecting the bottom: a small slot with what looked like a sim card inside.

'Conor? Is this yours?' she shouted, getting to her feet and moving through to the kitchen. Conor looked up at her as she presented him with the plug.

'No, my charger is in my room.'

'This was plugged in at the bottom of the stairs. It's got a sim card in it.'

Dale glared at it, and snatched it from her.

'Is this the only one?' he asked, frantically.

'I don't know. I just saw it there when I was coming back in from outside. What is it?'

'Shit,' Dale hissed, pushing his chair back. He darted around the kitchen, checking all the sockets. Then, as he moved through to the lounge, he checked the sockets in there too. Angie and Conor were at his back, and something in Angie's gut told her that something was terribly wrong.

'Dale, what is it?' Angie asked.

'This is a plug-in listening device,' Dale replied, handing it to Angie.

'What the hell?' Angie said, looking down at it in her hand.

'You plug it in and you put in a sim card linked to your phone. It sends a signal to your phone and you can listen to what people are saying. They have a range of about seven metres. There has to be at least another plugged in somewhere.'

Angie's stomach flipped and she thought back to when she found Jamie – Ryan, wandering around the house that day. He'd been looking at plug sockets, and she'd found it strange.

'That little bastard, Fraser. It has to be him. It makes sense.' Dale gritted his teeth. 'Angie, you said you saw him inspecting the sockets.'

At the top of the stairs, Dale bent down and pulled another from the socket next to the bathroom door. Angie's mind was going at a million miles an hour, as Dale turned and held a finger over his mouth, indicating for everyone to be silent.

Angie rushed along the hallway towards her bedroom and opened the door. She crouched to the floor by the bedside table and peered in behind it. There, staring back at her, was another device. She pulled it from the socket and got up. Turning, Dale was at her back and she handed it to him.

'That must've been what he was doing when he and Ashley came to visit. He must have planted them when I went to find him,' Angie said.

Dale's eyes were dark, and there was a fury in them that Angie knew would result in someone's death. And soon.

'You know what this means, don't you? It means that they know. They know what happened that night,' Dale said. 'Doesn't matter if we're quiet now. It's too late. We have to face this.'

Conor sniggered. 'What? Face one guy? What does he think he's going to do?'

Angie felt sick again. She didn't care that they knew what had happened to Kyle and Ian, that MacTavish was innocent. All she cared about was making sure that Conor didn't find out he wasn't a Bryson by blood.

Chapter Sixty

'Thanks for seeing me at such short notice,' Ashley said as she sat down on the leather sofa. 'I really appreciate it.'

'It's not a problem, Ashley. You sounded very upset on the phone, I couldn't very well tell you no.' Shona sat opposite Ashley, her expression soft. 'How are you today?'

Ashley shrugged. 'I'm okay, I suppose.'

'You suppose?' Shona remarked. 'If you were okay, you wouldn't have come here without an appointment. So, what's happened?'

Ashley thought about the question. It could be answered in a number of ways. What had happened? That day? That year? Throughout her life? So much. And so much of it wasn't anything to do with her, yet she was the one suffering because of it.

'My family happened,' she sighed. Rolling her head back, she rested it against the back of the sofa and stared up at the ceiling.

'What do you mean?'

Ashley thought about how to word her response. She couldn't just sit there in silence and waste Shona's time. The memory of Reilly's death had always been at the forefront of her mind. The memory of how she'd rammed the car into him, crushing his torso and watching the knife fall from his hand – watching the life drain from him as she sat behind the wheel. Ashley had tortured herself ever since, always wondering if there was something wrong with her because she hadn't thought about what she was doing. All she'd wanted was to stop him. Was killing in her blood? Was it part of her genetic makeup?

Blinking away the images, she said, 'I've just found something out that I wasn't meant to. God,' she sighed, sitting up and eyeing Shona, 'my family killed two men when I was a kid. Turns out that the guy I was seeing is the son of one of them, and he's been using me to get close to my family so he can take revenge.'

Shona uncrossed her legs before leaning forward and lifting the glass of water from the table between them. 'Sounds like something from a film.'

'Yeah, well, it's not. It's my life. Or at least it was a life I was dragged into.'

Shona's eyes flickered as she sat back on the sofa, glass still in hand. She didn't say anything.

'Who killed these men?' Shona asked after a few seconds of silence.

Ashley shook her head. 'It's too awful to say out loud.'

'Anything you say in this room will be treated with the strictest of confidence,' Shona replied softly. 'You can trust me.'

It seemed Ashley couldn't trust anyone these days. But she wouldn't have come to see Shona if she didn't have trust in her on some level. She was impartial.

'I know,' Ashley whispered. Exhaling loudly, she readjusted her sitting position. Wiping her clammy hands on her jeans, she said, 'Okay. Here's goes.'

She watched as Shona fixed her eyes on hers and waited for her to start. What would be the first thing she would say? Should she start with the end?

'My uncle killed them. Apparently, they were going to screw our family over, and Paul put a stop to it. And then my dad and other uncle helped get rid of the bodies.'

Shona's eyes flickered, and Ashley noticed it more this time. Perhaps she wasn't expecting that.

'Fuck, I was supposed to be seeing you about something I did. Now, I'm here talking to you about something else.'

Shona smiled a little, but it didn't reach her eyes.

'Who were the men that your uncle killed, Ashley?'

Ashley watched Shona's face for a change from impartial to interested.

'I don't actually know. All I know is they were called Kyle and Ian Fraser.'

Shona rose from the sofa and began pacing the floor very slowly. Her brow furrowed and she took a mouthful of water, emptying the glass of its contents.

'And you're sure? You're sure that your uncle killed Kyle and Ian Fraser?'

Now it was Ashley's turn to frown. 'Yeah, that's what he told me. He said he shot...' She stopped, and something inside her went cold. 'Why does it matter what their names are, Shona?'

Shona stopped pacing and turned to face Ashley. She noticed that Shona's knuckles had turned white, and the glass was trembling in her hand.

'He what? He shot them?' Shona pressed, and now, Ashley could no longer see the impartial expression, or the interested. Shona looked angry, fury creeping across her face.

Ashley got up and shook her head. There was a change in Shona, her reaction was off and it made Ashley nervous. 'I shouldn't have bothered wasting your time, Shona. I'll make an appointment to see you again.'

Reaching for the door, Ashley pulled on the handle and as she opened it, she started at the face staring back at her.

'Jamie!'

He took a step forward and tilted his head to the left, a smile raising the corner of his mouth. A second lad stood behind him, and he had the same expression etched on his face as Shona did.

'Go on, then, tell my mum how your uncle killed my dad.'

Ashley felt her blood run cold as she turned to face Shona. She opened her mouth to speak, but before she could say anything, Jamie continued.

'Meet my mother, Cara Fraser.'

Before she could duck out of the way, Ashley saw the empty water glass encased in Cara's hand coming towards her face. It cracked loudly against her skull, before everything went dark.

Chapter Sixty-One

Ryan and Sean carried Ashley to the sofa, and laid her flat before binding her wrists and ankles together. The blood was seeping from her head onto the leather, but at this point in time, Cara didn't care. She was too delighted by the fact that she'd managed to finally get some answers. The truth.

'You did good, boys. Your dad would've been proud of you,' she said, staring down at Ashley, who wasn't quite conscious but also not completely out. She was at that in-between stage, which Cara was fine with. She wanted her to be awake, to witness everything when it happened.

'Erm, Mum,' Ryan said. 'We haven't had a chance to tell you yet. But it looks like the Brysons have found the listening devices. So, they know it's us... well, me. They know who I am. And my passport is missing. Ashley must've found it.'

Cara nodded and smiled. 'Good.'

Ryan and Sean seemed off. There was something about them; they could barely meet her eye. This was never good, it usually meant one of them had done something stupid, like when Sean approached Jack Bryson at school and Cara had had to get rid of the CCTV footage.

'Right, spill. What's got your faces looking like that?'

They exchanged a glance, and then Sean looked away. Ryan stepped closer to his mum and took her hands in his.

'We found something out about the Brysons. Something that you're really not going to like, Mum. But you need to know.'

Cara frowned. 'What is it?'

Ryan took a breath and turned his gaze to Ashley for a brief second before resting his eyes on Cara. 'Well, as you know, I planted the listening devices at the house. And we've been screening their conversations. We heard one between Angie and Paul Bryson. And it turns out...' his voice trailed off and he cleared his throat. 'It turns out that Dale Bryson isn't Conor Bryson's dad.'

Cara narrowed her eyes and Ryan continued. 'From what we could gather, it looks as if Conor is our half-brother.'

Silence filled the room then. The words that had just come out of her son's mouth were jumbled in her head. Blinking, Cara tilted her head a little and said, 'Half-brother?'

Ryan only nodded, and Sean remained silent.

'You're saying... what? That your dad fathered a child with Angie Bryson, twenty-odd years ago? You must have picked them up wrong, Ryan. That's not possible.'

Cara pulled her hands away from Ryan's grip and took a step back, trying to get away from the horror of what that information meant. That her entire life with Kyle had been a lie.

'We didn't pick it up wrong, Mum,' Sean interjected. 'We both heard it. Conor isn't a Bryson. He's a Fraser.'

Cara dropped her chin to her chest and closed her eyes. 'No. You're wrong.'

'We're not wrong. I wish we were. Look, we're fucking livid with Dad. If he was here right now, I'd cave his fucking head in for doing this to you. But he's not. The Brysons *are* here, though. And we can get our revenge on them, Mum. We can. Especially now,' Ryan said.

Lifting her head and meeting her son's gaze, Cara bit the inside of her lip.

'Get Angie Bryson here. Now.'

Ryan turned, then he and Sean moved into the living room, leaving Cara standing on her own to process things. The sound of Ashley shifting on the sofa made her look round, and when she met Ashley's eye, it was abundantly obvious that she'd heard the conversation.

'Well, well, well. That was a turn-up for the books, wasn't it? Your slut of a mother has been lying to you and your family for a very long time – and she's made me out to be an absolute fool.'

Ashley's eyes were wide with terror and confusion. She was breathing heavily under the tape that was over her mouth and shaking her head.

'Let's see what she's got to say for herself when she gets here, shall we?'

Cara closed the door, leaving Ashley in the room on her own, but not before checking the windows were locked. Not that she'd attempt to get out that way, unless she wanted to kill herself.

Locking the door behind her, Cara called into the lounge and told Ryan and Sean to keep an eye and ear on Ashley, as she was going outside for some fresh air.

Once outside, the sun shining on her skin, she lit a cigarette. She hadn't smoked since the boys were young. She gave up once she'd got sober, long after Kyle and Ian had died. She didn't know why the urge took her, and she knew that the first puff would make her feel awful, but she still did it. It tasted the same as it did all those years ago. Disgusting and delicious in equal measures.

Cara sat down on the wall outside the front door and felt more relaxed than she'd ever felt, which was strange considering she'd just found out that Kyle had fathered a child before Ryan was born, with a woman she despised.

Maybe this was how psychopaths felt when they knew that their plan for revenge was about to unfold. Satisfaction in the most brutal form would make things better, surely?

Chapter Sixty-Two

Angie paced the kitchen floor, while Dale, Conor and Paul discussed how they were going to deal with Ryan Fraser. She wasn't listening, she was too busy fretting about how she was going to break the news to Dale and Conor that they weren't father and son by blood. There was no way around it. She would have to come clean. She'd rather they heard it from her than from a Fraser. They'd twist things, make it sound seedier than it was. When it came down to it, there was no way she could explain her way out of it. Angie had stupidly slept with her ex when she was with Dale. It had only happened once. But once was enough to set alight years of lies and deceit on her part.

'Angie, would you sit down. Your pacing is driving me nuts,' Dale said.

Angie stopped and leaned against the worktop. Dale's phone rang, and he grabbed it quickly.

'Paul?'

Angie felt a breath catch in her throat, and then she saw the look on Dale's face. The blood drained from his face.

'You're fucking kidding!'

'What? What's wrong?' Angie pressed. Dale ignored her, instead grabbing the notepad and pen sitting next to the fruit bowl and scribbling something down. 'Right, we're on our way.'

Dale hung up and pushed his chair back, causing it to scrape loudly on the floor. 'We're going. Now!'

Angie pushed herself off the counter and followed Dale out to the hallway. Conor was at her back, and she reached out and grabbed Dale's hand. He turned and she saw that his jaw was set in a grimace.

'Paul followed Ashley. He saw her go in, and she hasn't come back out. But someone else did. It was Cara *fucking* Fraser. It's them, they're the ones behind all of this.'

'Someone needs to stay with Jack,' she blurted out. Which was true. They couldn't all go and leave him behind. He was just a kid. 'Conor, you stay. I'll go with your dad to meet Paul.'

It was the perfect solution to keep Conor from finding out that he'd been lied to his entire life.

Dale shook his head. 'No. I don't want you near the place. It's bad enough Ashley's caught up in all of this.'

'Oh, but it's okay for Conor to get involved? No way. I'm not sending any more of my kids into the web we've woven, Dale.' She turned to Conor. 'You're staying here, and watching Jack. I don't want an argument.'

Conor's eyes darted between her and Dale, but Angie was already leading him up the stairs towards his younger brother's room.

'Angie, now is not the fucking time for games,' Dale bellowed.

She turned sharply on her heel and said, 'You think this is a fucking game? Cara Fraser has my daughter. She's not having my son too. We might be a gangster family, but I refuse to drag my kids into any more of our messes. I'll see you out at the car.'

Conor shook his head. 'I'm not staying behind. You should stay here where there's security and—'

Angie held her hand up. 'Conor, I'm not some weak little woman. I'm your mum. And you will do what I say. This won't take long. Now, don't let Jack out of your sight. Understood?'

Before Conor could say anything else, Angie had already turned and was halfway down the stairs. Dale and Paul were still standing at the bottom, and she glared at them both. 'You're still here? Am I doing this on my own?'

Pulling the door open, she stepped out into the drive and eyed the security guard in front of her. 'Don't let Conor or Jack out of this house, even if it's to go to the garden. I mean it.'

He nodded, and said, 'Loud and clear, Mrs Bryson.'

She climbed into Dale's Range Rover and fastened her seatbelt. Dale got in and she could feel the tension. She was prepared for how much worse it was going to get. By the end of this, her marriage would be over. One of them might even die. But the one thing she *was* sure about was that the rest of the Frasers would end up the same as Kyle and Ian.

Chapter Sixty-Three

Ryan stood by the window and looked down at his mum as she smoked the cigarette. If he was honest with himself, he was surprised that she wasn't sinking a bottle of vodka out there. Hearing about his dad's betrayal from her own sons must have hit her hard; hard enough that it might send her hurtling back to the booze.

'She's a greetin'-faced cow in there,' Sean said, coming through from checking on Ashley.

'Aye, I suppose being smashed over the head with a glass and being tied up will do that to you,' Ryan said, his eyes still on Cara. 'Anyway, we've got a phone call to make. So, who's doing the honours? You or me?'

Sean was shoulder to shoulder with Ryan and looking down at the entrance where Cara was now extinguishing a cigarette.

'I'll do it,' Sean replied. 'I want to hear what that bitch has got to say for herself. And the rest of them.'

He turned and picked up his mobile from the coffee table, but just as he was about to make the call, Cara was back in the flat. Sean lifted the phone to his ear and he listened for the call to be connected. But it didn't ring. It went straight to voicemail.

'Sean, I don't think we need to phone them. They're already here,' Ryan said.

'That was quick,' Cara said, entering the lounge and looking out at the street.

'How did they know where to find us?' Sean asked.

'Fuck knows, probably followed Ashley here,' Ryan replied. 'But we're ready for the bastards.'

Ryan watched as a Range Rover pulled up outside, and Angie and Dale got out. From another vehicle parked up the street, he saw Paul Bryson get out of the car.

A rush of footsteps on the stairs in the communal area alerted him to the door. He moved through to the hallway with urgency, knowing that the door could be kicked in. He didn't want his mum standing in the way if that happened.

He reached the hallway, and as Ryan approached the door, he turned to face Cara and stopped.

Sean disappeared into the kitchen and returned with a knife in his hand.

'You're going to plug all three of them, are you? Yourself?' Ryan hissed.

There was a gentle tap on the door. And then a voice. It was Angie Bryson.

'Cara? I know you're in there. I think we need to talk.'

Cara's shoulders arched. 'You're fucking right we need to talk, Angie.'

'Let me in, and we can air everything right now. No one needs to get hurt.'

Cara glanced at Ryan and Sean, and motioned for them to get behind the front door. She peered through the spy hole, and then mouthed, 'She's on her own.'

Ryan headed through to the lounge quickly and looked out of the window. The Bryson brothers had gone back to their cars. He frowned and moved back through to the hall.

'The rest of them are outside,' he whispered.

'I know Ashley's with you. I'm alone,' Angie said, as if hearing him. 'I'm unarmed too. I just want to talk, that's all.'

Cara moved back from the door and looked at Ryan and Sean. 'Go into the office and shut the door. Keep her quiet in there. She and I have a lot of old ground to cover.'

'Can you trust that she's telling the truth?' Sean asked.

'As much as she trusts me.'

Ryan and Sean retreated from the door and headed into the office. Closing and locking the door behind him, Ryan stood by it and listened.

Chapter Sixty-Four

Angie stood back as Cara opened the door to her. They hadn't seen each other in eight years; since just before Kyle and Ian were murdered. She'd aged quite a considerable amount; her hair had greyed at the roots and crow's feet crinkled the corners of her eyes.

'Cara,' Angie said.

'Tell me – why are the rest of your family all sitting in the car outside?' Cara asked, eyeing Angie with caution.

'The rest of my family aren't in the car. Bob's dead, but I guess you know that already. And my kids are safe, somewhere away from here, except Ashley that is.' Angie took a breath. 'I told them that I should do this alone. You know, mother to mother.'

Cara sniggered and rolled her eyes. 'Woman to woman? Seriously?'

'Seriously. You clearly have an issue with us, or perhaps me? And let's face it, if I turned up at your door with an army at my back, that wouldn't guarantee my daughter's safety, would it?'

Cara didn't respond. She simply stood to the side and allowed Angie to enter. She stepped into the flat with caution, and looked around.

'Where *is* Ashley?'

Cara closed the door and locked it behind her. 'She's fine. She's being taken care of. And no, before you ask, I haven't killed her.'

'Why would I think that?' Angie asked, noticing how Cara's hand was twitching.

'You're probably worried I'd do it out of rage, considering what I know about you.'

Angie felt her heart leap in her chest. 'And what do you know about me?'

'That your precious son is actually half-brother to my two boys? Ring any bells?'

Angie froze, even though she'd known this was coming.

'So, why don't you tell me, from the beginning, why my husband and brother-in-law were murdered. And don't bother trying to lie your way out of this, Angie. Because I know fucking everything.'

Angie stood in the middle of the hallway and her skin prickled. She was glad she'd come in here on her own, even though it put her in more danger. Standing here with Dale listening would have already raised questions. It had taken a lot of persuasion, but she'd managed to convince them that if she wasn't out in fifteen minutes, they could go in after her.

'And what's everything, Cara?'

'Don't do that.' Cara pointed at her. 'Don't stand there and pretend you haven't got a fucking clue. There's no way on this planet that you had nothing to do with Kyle dying.'

'I didn't,' Angie answered.

'Liar. You better tell me the exact truth. The truth that my sons heard over their listening bugs. I know you slept with Kyle. I know Conor is his son. I know it was you, Angie. I *know* you killed Kyle and Ian.'

Angie sighed. 'Okay. You really want to know what happened?'

'You wouldn't still be breathing if I didn't.'

'I'll tell you everything. But first, you need to let Ashley out of here.'

Cara shook her head and began pacing the floor. 'No way. Not going to happen.'

'Then you won't get the answers you want. And then what? You kill me and you're left without knowing the truth? Come on, Cara, we both know that's not what you want.'

Cara narrowed her eyes and then moved past Angie. She knocked on one of the doors in the hallway and it opened. Angie turned and looked in to see Ryan Fraser standing there. Behind him, Ashley was tied up on the sofa and she was bleeding from the head.

Rushing forward, Angie grabbed Cara by the hair and pulled her back. There was a scuffle and Angie was toppled to the ground with a punch to the gut. The air was knocked from her as she fell to the floor and the sounds of Ashley's muffled cries gripped her.

'Get up,' one of the boys said. Then she was being pulled to her feet. 'I said, get up.'

Then she noticed the blade in his other hand. Glancing up at him, Angie saw that there was another young lad, the one carrying the knife.

'Sean, this is Angie Fraser. The mother of your half-brother,' Cara said, adjusting her clothes and hair from when Angie had tackled her.

Sean glared at her and she saw Kyle in his eyes.

Angie looked down at Ashley, who seemed horrified. Her eyes were wide as she stared back.

'Now, you're going to tell us exactly what happened that night. And then I'll decide if Ashley gets out. Got it?' Cara said, as Ryan and Sean pushed her onto the sofa next to Ashley.

'You heard her,' Sean said, holding the blade to her throat. 'Start fucking talking.'

Part Three

Then/2013

Chapter Sixty-Five

Sitting in the car, Angie's heart thrummed in her chest. The voicemail had been followed by a text message just a couple of hours later. She'd been instructed by Kyle where to meet him. Under no circumstances was she to ignore his instructions, or he would spill her lie to everyone who needed to hear it.

Staring up at the building, Angie knew what she needed to do. It was the only way that she was going to be able to protect herself and her family. Knowing that the flat was unoccupied, she had a small window of time to get in and get out before she was seen.

Angie took a breath and slid her hands into her leather gloves, pulled her hood up and got out of the car before heading along the street towards the building. She'd taken the address from Dale's employee information book, so she knew where to find it.

Once inside, she climbed the stairs to the third floor until she reached the front door she was looking for. The place was empty, and the only sounds that could be heard were thumping music in the distance from other flats and the odd shouting voice.

Reaching into her pocket, Angie pulled out two kirby grips, already prepared for picking the lock. When she was a teenager, she used to lock herself out of the house all the time after losing her keys. So she always kept kirby grips in her pockets and was forever picking the lock of her front door to let herself in. Now, she was a pro, and that skill was about to come in very handy.

She slid the first grip into the bottom of the lock, and used the second to pick. It took a few attempts but she heard a click and the door opened. She made her way inside and closed the door quietly behind her.

'Right,' she whispered. 'Bathroom or kitchen. That's where you were told to hide it, MacTavish, so that's where it should be.'

Angie opened the second door to her left and it led into the kitchen. The sink was under the window opposite the door. She went to it, crouched down and opened the cupboard doors. Leaning in, she felt her gloved hand along the underside of the sink and checked every corner she could physically see. Satisfied it wasn't there, Angie closed the cupboard, stood up and left the kitchen, closing the door and leaving it exactly as she found it. She checked the other doors, looking for the bathroom. When she found it, she crouched down and pulled the bath panel away. There was no gun taped to the back of it.

'Come on, MacTavish, where did you put it?' Angie whispered. She crouched even further, and lay flat on her stomach to peer under the bath, hoping that he'd stashed it further behind.

'Bingo,' she said, spying the gun which lay against the back wall under the bath. She reached in, fingers outstretched, and pulled it into her grasp. Getting to her feet, she tucked it into the belt of her jeans at the back and dusted down her clothes, before replacing the bath panel. Closing the bathroom door, Angie peeked out of the door's spyhole, making sure that there was no one in the communal area before leaving. Satisfied that she would get away unseen, Angie stepped out and into the close, shut the door behind her and checked that it had locked itself, before putting a jog on down the stairs and out to the street.

Back at the car, Angie took a few steadying breaths and started the engine.

She left the car in the park and ride near the Bellpark train station, then walked the short distance to the disused railway station where Kyle Fraser had instructed her to meet him. This was it, the moment he confronted her about Conor. She couldn't back down. She *wouldn't* back down. Ian had told him what he'd heard at the casino, and there was no way she was going to be able to talk her way out of it. Kyle would do whatever it took to prove that what Ian had heard was the truth. He'd blackmail her in every way he could, no matter what that meant for him and his family. He wouldn't care that Cara would find out. It was before they were together, but after Angie had started to see Dale.

Why had she done it? Why had she fallen for his charms back then? And why did she have to fall pregnant? As much as she loved Conor, it would have been a lot easier if it hadn't happened. She wouldn't be in this position now.

The streets were deserted; either everyone in the small estate of Bellpark would be in the pub or in their homes. Bellpark train station was just a few minutes away, and with every step she took, Angie could hear the sound of her blood rushing in her ears.

She kept her eyes on the ground as she walked, and the station came into view. Climbing through a gap in the fence, Angie felt for the gun at her back. She didn't know if she intended on using it but knowing it was there as a threat was good enough. Angie wasn't like Dale and the rest of the Bryson brothers. She hadn't killed anyone before; although she'd wanted to kill that bastard Reilly when she'd found out what had happened to Dale and Ashley. But he was already dead.

Crossing the railway line, Angie climbed up onto the disused platform and sat on the bench inside the shelter. All she had to do now was wait for Kyle to show up.

Chapter Sixty-Six

Trembling, Angie couldn't work out if it was genuinely cold, or if she was terrified. Could she go through with this? If she did, it would change her future forever. She'd have to live a lie for the rest of her life, and put up an act, not just to Dale, but to the rest of her family. Kyle being Conor's biological father was one of the worst things she could have ever allowed to happen. What was she thinking that night, when she'd fallen back into his charm trap? She'd done everything she could to make him see that she wasn't interested, and then, just as easy as breathing, she was back in his bed. And all the while, Dale and Cara were clueless.

She shook her head and pushed the thoughts out of her mind. Angie had to focus on making sure that she kept Kyle and Ian quiet. Keeping one of them silent would have been hard enough.

The sound of stones being displaced on the railway track alerted her to a presence. Peeking out of the shelter, she saw them. Both Kyle and Ian had turned up. Of course, Kyle would want to make sure he had a witness to their meeting. He was always the same.

Angie stepped out of the shelter and into the blanket of darkness that hovered over them, and stood on the platform as Kyle and Ian stood on the old track, staring up at her.

'You had to bring your security with you?' she asked, glaring down at her ex.

'Had to see if you were going to blatantly deny the conversation my brother, here, overheard at the casino. Although, I think by now we both know that I'd never fall for that. I trust Ian far more than I could ever trust you,' Kyle replied. His right hand was stuffed into his jacket pocket, and his left hung by his side. Taking in his expression, she could tell he'd been drinking and more. His eyes were wide, and his words came at a speed which was only induced by cocaine.

'Go on, then,' Ian said, the speed of his voice matching Kyle's. 'Deny it.'

'Deny what?' Angie asked.

Ian sniggered and rolled his eyes. 'There she goes – even though she knows full well she's backed into a fucking corner, she's going to stand there and deny all knowledge of what we're really here for.'

Angie forced a smile and tried to remind herself of who she was. She was a Bryson, married to the most powerful businessman and drug lord the city had seen in decades. She didn't need to be scared of the Frasers. Yet they'd brought her here, to this disused railway station that was covered in a blanket of darkness – they'd obviously planned something hideous for her.

'I'm not here to deny anything,' she replied.

'Is that right? Go on, then,' Kyle said. 'Tell me the truth. Tell me about my boy. The one you've been keeping from me for… how long? He must be twelve years now, give or take?'

Angie's stomach churned at the sound of Kyle calling Conor 'his boy'. He wasn't Kyle's boy. He was Dale's son and always would be.

'Being a sperm donor doesn't make you a dad.'

Kyle scoffed. 'I'm only a sperm donor because you made it that way, Angie. You had no fucking right to keep him from me. He's got brothers, an uncle. He has the right to know where he comes from.'

Angie frowned and shook her head. 'He comes from scum, Kyle. You're scum. You and your family amount to nothing but street dealers. You really think that we don't know what you're trying to do? We know everything, Kyle. MacTavish is working for us. Watching your every move. He's told us everything about your plans to try to take us down, to steal our patches. It's not going to work.'

Kyle glanced at Ian and his eyes widened, and even in the darkness, Angie saw a shadow pass across his face.

'MacTavish's working with you lot? He'd never go against us. We're his meal ticket,' Ian spat.

'No, *we're* his meal ticket. You've been scamming us and him. We've got evidence that you've been fucking us over. And you're not going to get away with it.'

Kyle went to move and Angie pulled the gun out from her waistband and pointed it in his direction. He stopped, the stones crunching underfoot.

Ian let out a low, vile snigger. 'Jesus, you really are desperate to keep us quiet, aren't you, Angie? You don't want your precious family to know that you opened your legs for Kyle and birthed a Fraser sprog, do you?'

Angie swung her arms and now the gun was pointing at Ian. 'Shut up, you utter piece of shit. Both of you, shut up.'

The sound of stones crunching made Angie turn and Kyle was on the move, attempting to jump up on the platform. Pulling the trigger, the power from the bullet leaving the gun shunted her back, and then she heard Kyle grunt as he fell down onto the stones.

Her heart hammered in her chest and she watched as Ian rushed to Kyle, who was on his back and groaning in pain. She'd shot him in the left shoulder, and even under the darkness, she could see the blood seeping out into his clothes.

Ian was quick, he got to his feet and – as quickly as blinking – he too had a gun in his hand. Fight or flight, Angie thought, as she pointed the gun at him and pulled the trigger a second time. She aimed right for the head, and hit him just above the right eye. He fell back, hitting the back of his head on the track. Her shoulder and arm ached from the power the gun blasted through her.

'Fucking Jesus, Angie,' Kyle hissed.

She stepped closer to the edge of the platform and took a few steadying breaths. She felt like she was out of her body, as though someone else had taken control of her limbs.

'Sorry, Kyle. But you're not going to ruin my life because you think you have some claim on my son. You can fuck right off.'

And for a third time, Angie aimed at Kyle and fired.

–

Sitting down on the bench in the shelter, with the gun still in her hand, Angie stared out at the dark night and could still hear the echoes of the gunshots in her ears. It was as though she'd left her body again, and this time, she wasn't sure how long it had been since she'd killed the Frasers.

'Angie?' a voice whispered in the dark. She glanced up, feeling like she was floating. It was Paul. 'Angie, what the fuck?'

He crossed the track, keeping a wide space between himself and the bodies that lay sprawled. Climbing up onto the platform, his frame appeared in the shelter doorway.

Angie glanced up at him. 'I had to. He was going to tell Dale. He wanted to see Conor. He kept calling him *his boy*. I couldn't let that happen, Paul. It would ruin all of us.'

Paul exhaled loudly and moved towards her. He stared down at the gun still in her gloved hand. 'You came prepared. It's not the night for leather gloves, Angie.'

'Like I said, I couldn't let him ruin my family.'

Paul turned and looked back at Kyle and Ian as they lay dead on the ground. 'Is there any chance someone saw you come here?'

Angie shook her head slowly. 'I don't know. Possibly. But I parked the car further away and walked here. I had my hood up.'

Paul nodded as he gestured for her to get up. 'Okay. I need you to do something. I need you to tell me where you got that gun from.'

She glanced down at it and then back at Paul. 'It's the one that we gave to MacTavish when we told him to watch them for us. I went to his flat and got it.'

Paul frowned.

'It's got MacTavish's prints on it.'

'And it doesn't have yours? Or Dale's?'

Angie pursed her lips. 'Do you think we're that stupid?'

Paul breathed loudly through his nostrils. 'Okay, Angie, I need you to focus here. I need you to go to MacTavish's flat, put the gun back exactly where you found it. Then I need you to bring an item of his clothing, like a shirt or a jacket. Once you've done that, I want you to go home, burn your clothes and wait for me to get in touch. You don't speak to anyone about what's happened here tonight. Understood?'

Angie nodded. 'Why are you doing this for me, Paul? I've betrayed your brother and dragged you into my lies.'

'I don't want to see him hurt. And if he finds out it was you who killed Kyle and Ian, he'll start to ask questions. Under pressure, I don't think you could keep the truth from him even if you wanted to. And I don't want to see what it would do to Dale if he found out that he wasn't Conor's dad.'

Angie felt hot tears spring to her eyes and she stifled a sob. She was the world's biggest, most deceitful bitch. She would have to live with this for the rest of her life.

'Right, hood up. Gun away. Go, now. I'll stay here and make sure…' he trailed off.

'I don't think they're going anywhere, Paul,' Angie sniffed.

'No. But I don't think that we should travel anywhere together. If we're seen, this could go tits up. Just go and do what I said and meet me back here in half an hour.'

Angie hesitated, glanced down at the dead bodies on the track and then back at her brother-in-law. 'What will we do with them?'

'*We* won't do anything. Just go, Angie. The quicker this is done, the better.'

Angie moved along the platform towards the dip and crossed the stones before climbing through the gap in the fence and heading back to the car.

—

Standing in MacTavish's flat, having put the gun back where she'd found it and lifting a T-shirt from his bedroom floor, Angie Bryson took in the enormity of what she'd just done. She'd committed murder. The murder of Kyle Fraser wouldn't go unnoticed. He had a wife and kids, minus Conor, of course. They'd question his disappearance, start looking for him. And Ian. Then what? What if the plan Paul was putting into place didn't work and she was caught? Being found to be a killer was the least of Angie's worries, but like Paul had said, it would lead to many, many questions. Not from the police, but from Dale. He'd want to know why. She could lie, could make something up about Kyle luring her to the train station, threatening her. But she'd already told so many lies already; it was inevitable that she would trip herself up. Framing MacTavish for the killings was her only hope of surviving the mess she'd created.

Rolling the shirt carefully and stuffing it into a carrier bag, Angie left the flat for the second time that night and made her way back to the station, where Paul was waiting. She did it in the half hour time frame Paul had asked her to, and when she got there, he was sitting in the shelter where she'd left him. But he had something in his hand. A key. A car key.

'What's that?' she asked, handing him the carrier bag with the shirt inside it.

'It's Ian's car key. I thought it could be used to get rid of them.'

Angie nodded, but tried not to picture the scene. They sat in silence for a few moments, and she couldn't help but stare down at them, lying there, wounded, covered in their own blood.

'Are you okay?' Paul asked.

'I will be once this is done. Just keep me in the loop.'

Angie left the station, and as she did, she could hear Paul speaking with Dale on the phone. His words echoed in her ears as she moved further and further away.

'Dale, it's me. It's done. The Frasers, they're dead. I need you and Bob to get here now. We need to get rid of them.'

Chapter Sixty-Seven

Angie stood in the back garden and watched as the fire pit charred and seared through her clothes and the gloves that she'd been wearing earlier that night. The smell of smoke was a welcome one. It was the smell of evidence swirling up into the air and leaving behind no trace – she hoped.

Folding her arms around herself, Angie fought to keep Kyle and Ian's faces out of her head. As much as she hated them and was glad that they were gone, she'd still taken a dad from his sons. A pang of guilt hit her in the gut, over and over, the more she thought about it.

It had been two hours since it had happened. Two hours since her secret had been claimed by the dead. The only other living person who knew about it now was Paul.

The crackling of the flames filled the silence of the night, and as she thought about Conor and Ashley, asleep upstairs in their beds, she was thankful that her kids were safe from the Frasers.

Her phone pinged in her dressing gown pocket and when she pulled it out and read the text from Paul, she knew it was time to get the game face back on. Dale, Paul and Bob were on their way back to the house.

All the text said was, *Done. Go with it.*

She watched as the materials of her clothes disintegrated into ash, before putting the fire out and heading back inside. She thought to shower quickly, get the smell of smoke off her. Once out of the shower, Angie sat in the lounge, television on low and glass of wine in hand. The sound of Dale and the rest of them coming into the house set her heart racing and her skin prickling with fear.

Getting up, she met them in the hallway and gave them a smile, before kissing Dale on the cheek.

'You three look like you've seen a ghost,' she said, hoping that she sounded convincing. She didn't make eye contact with Paul.

'Angie, it's done,' Dale said. 'The Frasers. They're dead.'

She feigned her most convincing shocked expression and took a step back. 'How did it happen?'

'That doesn't matter,' Dale replied quickly. 'All you need to know is it's done. We've covered all bases and it won't come back to any of us. Okay?'

Angie frowned, took in each of their faces. Paul looked normal, as if the last few hours hadn't happened. As if he didn't have another version in his head.

'I think I should know, Dale.'

Paul and Bob both shook their heads. 'It's better if you don't. We've got our boys on the clean-up job and an alibi,' Bob said. She could tell he was disappointed not to have been the one to do it himself, but of course she wasn't going to acknowledge that – because that would be admitting that she knew what had happened.

'Okay,' Angie replied, 'you three look like you could use a drink.'

She turned and headed to the kitchen to get the whisky bottle. She exhaled slowly, and as she poured the whisky, she failed to control the tremor in her hand. They didn't notice, content with their own thoughts about their version of what had happened.

Handing the whisky glasses to them as they sat around the kitchen table, Angie watched as they knocked them back.

'Good fucking riddance to them,' Dale said, placing his glass back on the table.

Angie leaned back against the worktop and considered necking a whisky herself. It might numb the reality of what was going on. A thought entered her mind.

'And this won't come back on any of you?'

Dale didn't turn to meet her eye; he simply nodded and ran the tip of his finger around the rim of the glass. 'Certain.'

'Aye,' Bob said, getting up and retrieving the whisky bottle from its place behind Angie on the worktop. He returned to the table and refilled his own glass, before offering more to his brothers. 'Everything's taken care of. Those fuckers won't be coming back to haunt any of us anytime soon.'

Angie felt Paul's eyes on her, and she cautiously looked up at him. He was nodding, confirming that Bob and Dale were right. Things were sorted, at their end at least. She just had to pray that nothing came back to her.

She'd been careful. Had learned from the best over the years. Her husband and his brothers had dealt in this business a long time, and they were still free men.

Yeah, she thought to herself. I'm going to be fine. My family are going to be fine.

She nodded in thanks at Paul, who returned the gesture. Neither Dale nor Bob noticed.

Part Four

Now/2021

Chapter Sixty-Eight

Ashley Bryson sat up, and even though her mouth was taped shut, she felt her jaw had dropped in shock at the huge confession her mother had just made to a room filled with the people who wanted the Brysons dead. Ironically, the thing that concerned Ashley the most, more than Sean Fraser sitting by her side with a knife at her throat, was the fact that all her life, she'd grown up with a liar for a mother. Conor wasn't her full brother? They didn't share the same biological dad? And she'd killed two men to cover it up. How could she have done this, and kept it a secret for so long?

Ashley met her mum's eye and glared at her. Her gut feeling to leave the family home after the shooting had been right, but she hadn't had the chance to do it properly, because Ryan Fraser had tricked her into thinking he was a genuine guy. And she'd had no reason to think of him in any other way. She'd been fooled into thinking that Cara Fraser was a kind, sensitive and professional therapist, when in fact, she was using Ashley as a way of taking revenge on the family.

'You're lucky you're still breathing,' Cara said through gritted teeth as she stood opposite Angie. 'What the hell is wrong with you? How could you do that to my boys? Take their dad and uncle away from them just so your dirty little secret wouldn't get out? You're an evil fucking bitch, Angie. You'll never get away with this?'

Ashley's eyes darted between her mum and Cara, and then Sean increased the pressure of the blade against her skin. She felt the heat from his body as though it was a fiery rage coursing through him, and it set off a fear deep inside her that she wasn't going to make it out of this flat alive. Why the fuck had her mum encouraged her dad to sit outside?

'I'm not expecting to get away with it. Not anymore. But this isn't Ashley's fault. This is my fault. If you want to hurt anyone, let me take her place, Cara.'

Cara stepped forward and then raised her hand, slapping Angie so hard across the face that Ashley wondered if she'd have cracked a cheekbone.

'No one's going fucking anywhere,' Sean hissed. His voice roared in Ashley's ear, but she didn't move. Staying still was the best option for her. Any sudden movement could render her dead.

Sean laughed as Angie stood back upright, but Ashley quickly saw the humour fall from his expression.

'Of course. I should've checked you before I let you in,' Cara said. Ashley's eyes fell on the gun in her mum's hands and knew that this was it. At least one of them was going to die in this room.

'Tell your son to take that blade away from my daughter's throat and I won't shoot him in the head like I did his dad,' Angie said. Ashley heard the venom in her tone and realised that she didn't know her at all anymore. This wasn't the mother she'd grown up with. The mother she'd known wouldn't know how to use a gun. Her dad and uncle, yes. But Angie?

Cara didn't say anything, and Angie raised her arm and pointed it at Sean's head, which in turn was just inches from Ashley's too.

'You won't shoot him,' Ryan said. His tone was unconvincing. Ashley was frozen with fear.

And then her ears rang out from the sound of a single gunshot. Ryan was on the ground, and everything around Ashley seemed to dull before she passed out.

Chapter Sixty-Nine

Ryan Fraser clutched his right knee as he backed himself up against the wall. Ashley had passed out, but had immediately woken up again. She was still being held tightly by Sean, and the knife was still against her throat, although Angie could see that he'd loosened his grip slightly. He was staring down at his brother, eyes wide with fear and fury. The ringing in her ear was a loud, shrill pitch, but she ignored it as she turned to face Cara again.

Angie pointed the gun at his head once more, and eyed Cara. 'I'll say it one more time, Cara. Tell your boy to let my daughter go. She is not a part of this.'

Cara stared down at Ryan, and Angie could see her motherly instincts kicking in. She wanted to go to him, to help him. But no one moved a muscle as Ryan cried out in pain and blood gushed from his knee. He sounded just like Kyle had when she'd first wounded him.

'Come on, Cara. You're a mother yourself. You'd do anything to save your boys, wouldn't you? He's only wounded. If you let Ashley go, let her walk away unharmed, you will be able to get Ryan treated and he'll be fine. You'll all walk out of here alive. We can call it even.'

Cara glared at her through dark, narrowed eyes and shook her head. 'You're un-fucking-believable. Do you really think this makes us even, Angie? You murdered my husband and his brother eight fucking years ago, and your family covered it up – put an innocent man away for it, for Christ's sake. How the hell can we call this even?'

Angie kept the gun aimed at Sean and stole a glance at Ashley. She was awake, stiff in Sean's grip. Sean was staring back at her, his knuckles white from the solid hold on the handle of the knife.

'Because if you don't call this even, I *will* kill all of you. We got away with it the last time. What makes you think we won't this time?'

Cara's eyes glistened under the light filtering through the blinds on the window. She shook her head rapidly. 'You're a fucking nutter. I should have killed you all at that wedding.'

Angie's eyes widened upon hearing the words.

'Yeah, it was me who tried to take you all out at the wedding. I'd just found out MacTavish was innocent. And he was telling the truth, wasn't he?'

Angie nodded. 'Fair enough, Cara. I would have done the same. But trust me, I will kill your boy if he doesn't take that knife away from Ashley's throat in the next ten seconds.'

She watched as Cara's breathing laboured. She turned to Sean and said, 'Lower the knife.'

Sean shook his head. 'No chance.'

'Sean, do what you're fucking told. Lower the knife. Put it on the fucking floor and shut the hell up.'

Angie didn't allow herself the relief that was teetering on the surface. She wouldn't feel true relief until Ashley was untied, and in the car with her dad.

Sean's jaw clenched and he lowered the knife.

'Don't put it down. I want you to cut the ties, let her free,' Angie said. Then she caught her daughter's eye. 'Ashley. When Sean removes the tape from your mouth, you're going to be silent. When your hands and ankles are free, you're going to get up, walk to me and stand at my back. Understood?'

Ashley blinked, but didn't move.

'Do what she says, Sean,' Cara said, sounding defeated. Sean gritted his teeth so hard Angie thought he would crunch through them. He cut Ashley free and ripped the tape from her mouth. Tears streamed down her cheeks as she got to her feet and staggered across the room. She took her place behind Angie; the whole time Angie kept the gun pointed at Sean.

'Drop the knife and kick it away,' Angie instructed.

He reluctantly pushed it away with his foot and it skittered across the wooden floor, hitting off the skirting on the opposite wall.

'Mum, let's just go,' Ashley whispered.

'Angie, wait,' Cara said. 'Before you leave, I just need to ask you one thing. You said you talked Dale and the other two into staying in the car. What about Conor? Is he back at the house with your other boy? Jack, is it?'

Angie felt a rage inside her ignite.

'That's a good school he goes to – or went to, should I say.'

'Mum,' Ryan said. 'Leave it. It's done.'

Angie didn't take her eyes off Cara, but could tell from Ryan's tone that he was getting weaker as his knee bled out. He grunted, the pain from a shattered kneecap clearly becoming too much to bear.

'It was one of your boys who approached him at school, wasn't it? You really tried to cover all bases with targeting my kids,' Angie said, backing into Ashley and trying to guide her to the door. 'Well, looks like you failed there.'

'Actually, I don't think we did,' Cara replied. 'You see, your daughter here has told me everything. She unknowingly told us that your family were responsible for the murder of Kyle and Ian. But she told us something else too. And we've used it as our last option. You see, we know all about what little Ashley did to Reilly. The scorned security guard that Dale sacked all those years ago? When he attacked him in the alley behind your casino with a knife? We know that Ashley crushed him with the car.'

Angie shrugged. 'And?'

Cara rolled her head, as if to loosen the neck muscles. 'Well, someone we know who was close to Reilly – I say close, he was Reilly's brother – I got in contact with him. Told him everything. And you know what he did?'

Angie couldn't breathe, let alone respond.

'He got a job, just like his brother before him; as a security guard. A personal security guard for the Bryson home. And he knows all about Ashley and what she did. Reilly's body was never found, was it? Now he's at the house, with Conor and Jack, and he's waiting for my signal to take your boys out. Well, not boys. Just boy. Conor, actually. I wouldn't have him murder a small child. I'm not evil.'

Angie felt sick to her stomach. Behind her, Ashley was already weeping.

'So, how we going to play this?' Cara asked.

'I'll tell you how we're going to play this, Cara. As far as I can tell, I'm the one standing here with a gun. Ryan is bleeding out, and any sudden movements from Sean and I'll blow his fucking eyes out. So, you're going to call this guy and tell him to back off.'

'Mum,' Sean said. 'Do it. She's not kidding. She's already killed Dad and blown Ryan's knee off. She wants to end us. Just do what she says.'

Cara turned to face her boy, but she moved suddenly, catching Angie by surprise. Cara grabbed hold of the gun, but she wasn't quite quick enough.

Ashley's scream was muted by the sound of the gun going off. A bullet left the barrel and Cara fell to the floor. Blood spattered across the back wall and Angie caught a glimpse of Sean going for the knife. She spun her body and aimed; another bullet left the gun and caught Sean's hand. He too fell to the ground, and as Angie turned, Ashley was already gone.

'You fucking bitch,' Sean hissed.

Cara wasn't moving as Sean crawled to her, his own blood pissing from his hand.

She hadn't wanted to do this. Angie hadn't wanted to kill anyone else. But she had to protect her family. The Frasers would rip the Brysons apart if they got out of here alive.

'Sorry, Sean, but I have no other choice.'

As she aimed at Sean for the second time and pulled the trigger, Angie promised herself it would be the last bullet she ever fired.

-

'Ashley,' Angie said, catching up with her on the stairs. 'You stay silent. You don't tell your dad, or your uncles anything. Do you hear me? Not a word. You let me do the talking.'

Angie's hands were on Ashley's trembling shoulders, but she didn't answer. The sound of footsteps on the stairs silenced them both.

'Angie, what the fuck happened?' Dale said, reaching them both and taking Ashley in his arms as she sobbed.

'Let's just go. Now, before the police turn up.'

Angie flew down the stairs, with Dale and Ashley at her back. She felt sick. But knowing that the Frasers were dead didn't ease the nausea. They had one more man to deal with. And it sounded like he was the most dangerous of them all.

They got outside. Dale bundled Ashley into the car. As Paul started the engine, Angie eyed her husband and said, 'A man has infiltrated the security at the house. It's Reilly's brother. He has Conor and Jack. We need to get home. Now.'

Dale's brow creased as he climbed into the driver's seat. 'What the hell are you on about?'

'Cara, she was posing as Ashley's therapist and Ashley told her about Reilly. She knew his brother, told him everything. He's at the house with Conor and Jack. He's waiting for Cara's signal to kill Conor.'

Dale had already pulled away, the engine screaming as they left the street.

'I fucking told you not to go up there by yourself,' Dale shouted.

'I got her out, didn't I?'

'And what about them? Up there? Are they—'

'Dead? Yes. We can get someone to deal with it. Right now, I just need to get to my sons.'

Chapter Seventy

Dale pulled up outside the house, and the lad who would usually be standing at the front door wasn't there. In his place was a pool of blood.

Dale rushed past it, with Paul at his back, having given Angie and Ashley strict instructions to stay in the car. He wasn't taking any chances this time. Angie going in alone wasn't an option.

As they entered the house, there was an eerie silence, and Dale glanced across at the games room. The sound of FIFA blared out from the speaker, and through the gap in the door, Jack could be seen by Dale. He was perched on the edge of the sofa, with his innocent little smile wide as he played his game.

Dale moved across the hallway and opened the door. Jack was alone. He looked up at his dad and smiled. 'Hi, Dad. I beat Conor at FIFA. *Again*,' he laughed.

Dale forced a smile back at his son and said, 'Where is your big brother?'

Jack shrugged. 'I don't know.'

'I'm in here,' Conor's voice called from the kitchen. Dale turned, left the room and closed the door behind him.

Paul crossed the hallway first, and when Dale reached the kitchen door, Conor was standing in the centre of the kitchen on his own. His hands were bloodied, as was his T-shirt and trousers.

'What happened?' Dale asked, rushing to Conor.

Conor turned and moved to the back door, with Dale following closely. The back door was already opened, and when they went out to the garden, three of the security men were standing around a man laid out on the grass.

'He came into the house and tried to attack me. Luckily, Jack saw nothing. Too busy wrapped up in his game.'

'We took care of him, boss. We heard the commotion and came in to help,' one of the lads said.

Dale took a breath and shook his head.

'Who is he, Dad?' Conor asked.

'He's the brother of the guy your sister crushed with the car,' Dale replied. He turned to Paul. 'Can you check on Jack and Ashley? Tell Angie to come in here.'

Paul disappeared back into the house and Dale moved to Conor, lifting his hands in his to inspect his wounds.

'I'm fine. The bastard wasn't quick or young enough to take me down. I'm just glad I had my wits about me, otherwise I dread to think what would have happened to my little brother.'

Dale exhaled loudly and hugged Conor tightly.

'What a fucking mess, eh?' Dale said. 'I swear this family is cursed.'

Chapter Seventy-One

Angie sat in the back with Ashley, who was still trembling, but had stopped crying. Her face was ablaze, eyes puffy.

'Are you okay?' Angie asked.

'What the hell do you think?' Ashely snapped. 'I don't even know where to fucking start, Mum. I mean, Jesus...'

'I know, it's a lot to take in.'

'*A lot to take in?* I've just found out that you killed two men to keep the identity of Conor's real dad a secret from the rest of us. Are you fucking sick in the head?'

'Oi,' Angie raised her voice, 'I know how much of a mess of things I've made. But you need to remember who you're talking to.'

Ashley shook her head and a look of disgust washed over her. 'You make me fucking sick. All of you. You do realise that all of this is your fault, don't you? Your lies, your deceit, it's all led to this.'

Ashley pulled on the handle and got out of the car. Angie got out and moved around the car to her just as Paul came out of the house.

'Don't go in there,' he said, stopping Ashley from moving any further. 'You don't need any more trauma today. Reilly's brother attacked Conor. Don't worry, he's fine. The rest of the security lads dealt with it. I'm taking you away from here. Both of you.'

Ashley shook her head. 'I'm not going anywhere with her. She's a fucking con artist. I'm going in there and I'm telling Dad everything. And don't you dare try and stop me. Did you know that Conor isn't one of us? Did you? His real dad was Kyle Fraser.'

Paul gripped Ashley by the shoulders and held her still. 'Ashley, if you do that, it'll break him. Do you really want that?'

Ashley shrugged him off. 'And you! You're supposed to be his brother, and you've been lying to him for years. What the hell is wrong with you two? In fact, what the hell is wrong with this family?'

Conor appeared at the front door, and Angie held her breath. His expression was solemn, and his complexion grey. He stared out at them with confusion.

'This family, Ashley, is fucking cursed,' he said, stepping out of the house and onto the driveway. He pulled his sister in for a hug and Ashley fell silent. 'Are you okay?'

With her face pressed into his chest, she nodded. Angie stole a glance at Paul, but he wouldn't meet her eye.

Ashley pulled away from Conor and glared at Angie. Her mouth pulled into a tight line, she closed her eyes, and something inside Angie knew that Ashley was going to keep her secret. For now, at least.

Chapter Seventy-Two

Ryan Fraser opened his eyes and stared up at the white ceiling above him. The pain from his knee intensified in seconds, but he still attempted to sit up.

'Hey!' he shouted. A nurse was by his side immediately and she pressed a hand on his shoulder. 'You need to rest.'

'How long have I been here? Where's my mum and brother?'

In the back of his mind, he already knew where they were. In the same place as his dad and uncle. Dead. But he still asked the question, in the hope that he was wrong.

The way the nurse looked at him told him everything he needed to know.

'I'm so sorry for your loss, Ryan. I can't imagine what you're going through.'

Ryan shook his head and swallowed the lump in his throat. He didn't want to cry. He wanted to scream with rage.

'I know you might not be up for this right now, but the police want to speak to you about what happened at your mum's flat?' the nurse said. 'I can tell them you're not well enough, that they should come back later?'

Ryan's head swirled with the thought that his entire family were dead because that bitch, Angie Bryson, murdered them. He was totally alone in the world now. He always said he'd get his own justice for what happened to his dad and Uncle Ian. That was a long-gone dream. Now, there was a different way he could take them down, just like his dad had always wanted.

'No, it's fine. Send them in. I need to make sure the people who did this are caught.'

The nurse nodded, smiled and left the room. A few moments later, two officers in suits entered the room and sat down next to Ryan's bed.

He hadn't told his mum or Sean, but Ryan had launched the voice record app on his phone when Angie had turned up at the flat that day. Setting the bugs up in the Bryson house had been a good plan, but it was always one that could go wrong. And they never recorded conversations, only transmitted them. This way, Ryan could get dirt about the Brysons direct from a Bryson. Not only had he recorded Angie's confession to killing his dad and Ian, he'd recorded the entire incident in the flat too. Everything from shooting Ryan to killing his mum and Sean and then fleeing the scene. Yes, it would implicate Sean and his mum due to holding Ashley against her will, but they weren't here anymore to have to suffer the consequences. One way or another, he would get his final revenge on the Brysons.

Chapter Seventy-Three

Angie Bryson nursed the cup of hot coffee between her hands as she sat at the table with her eyes closed. Ashley had disappeared up to her bedroom, Conor was sitting with Jack and keeping him away from everything that was being discussed. The security lads had taken Reilly's brother away to be disposed of, leaving her, Dale and Paul in the kitchen.

'I won't get away with this,' Angie said. 'Cara lived in a flat, surrounded by other flats. Someone would have heard the gunshots. They'll have phoned the police by now.'

'Angie, shut up,' Dale said. 'We'll be fine.'

She shook her head. 'There's no "we" in this. I was the one in the flat. I was the one with the gun. Someone will have seen me. I'm done. We all are.'

'No, we're not,' Paul said. 'We've got plenty of boys who can do a clean-up job. We'll sort it.'

Angie was about to protest when the sound of sirens came screeching up the drive. She got to her feet and looked out of the window.

They all glanced at one another, and Angie moved out to the hallway. Ashley was standing in the middle of the staircase, and Conor appeared at the games room door, Jack peering out behind him.

'It's fine,' Angie said. 'I can't do this anymore. I've lied for too long.'

She opened the door and stepped out, her hands above her head. Officers rushed into the house behind her, and she listened as her husband and brother-in-law were arrested. She didn't fight the officers who cuffed her. There was no point.

After all these years, their past had finally caught up with them.

Chapter Seventy-Four

Three Months Later

'I can't believe I'm out,' James said, sitting on the bench next to Ryan. 'I genuinely didn't think I'd ever see the light of day on the other side of those prison walls.'

Ryan blew out the smoke from his joint and leaned forward, resting his elbows on his knees as he stared at the water. 'Aye. Don't think any of us involved would have imagined being here now.'

MacTavish turned to Ryan and saw a sadness behind his hardened expression. 'The Brysons fucked us both over. The difference being they put me in prison; you got me out. I'll forever be in your debt, wee man.'

Ryan shook his head and offered the joint to MacTavish. He refused it.

'No more debt. No more owing people favours. No more lies. My whole life has been based around the life my old man lived, and his one-night stand with Angie Bryson leading to his death. My entire family is dead because of her. And they killed Smiler too.'

'Aye,' MacTavish said. He thought back to when he found out that Dale Bryson had thrown his nephew off one of the flats at Craigton Heights. He used the term 'nephew' loosely, but it was still a life; another life the Brysons had taken. All in the name of power and drugs. The Frasers weren't much better, MacTavish knew that. But like he'd said, Ryan was the one who got him out.

'So, what are you going to do now?' Ryan asked.

'I don't know. Probably just go to the council and get a flat again. I don't have anything else – no money, no family. I don't even class this as starting again, because I didn't have anything to lose in the first place, other than my freedom. At least in prison I didn't have to find money for food or rent.'

Ryan sat back on the bench and took another draw from the joint. Exhaling loudly, he nodded. 'Yeah, the way things work is all kinds of fucked up.'

'What will you do?'

'Me? I don't know. Might move away, try to start my life over again. Or I might stay here, continue on with my plans to grow the farm, make some money out of it like my dad would've done. Fancy a job?'

MacTavish smiled and shook his head. 'No offence, Ryan. But I wouldn't accept a million quid to work for a Bryson or a Fraser ever again.'

They both laughed, but not with humour. MacTavish looked across the water and remembered the last time he'd been at the reservoir. The night he'd found the Frasers' car, their dead bodies inside and immersed in the water.

'I might request a visit to the prison, go and see how Angie Bryson and the rest of the bastards are suffering in there. As for Ashley and Conor...' he trailed off. 'Technically, they did nothing wrong. They were born into this mess as much as me.'

'You're still planning on fucking them over?' MacTavish asked. He would be surprised if the answer to that was yes. Although the Brysons were behind bars now, they still had strong connections outside. One wrong move from Ryan and he'd join the rest of his family.

'Nah,' Ryan replied, taking the last draw of his joint and dropping it to the ground before stubbing it out with his foot. 'But that isn't to say I can't wind Angie Bryson up, make her think that now more than ever, her precious kids are in danger because she 'fessed up without checking if her words were being recorded. You'd think after they found the listening devices in the house that she wouldn't be that stupid.'

MacTavish looked at Ryan, taking in his expression. It was clear that he was still angry, and that the Bryson family being banged up hadn't given him the closure he thought it might.

'You shouldn't come here as often as you do, Ryan. It's not good for you, being reminded of your dad's last…' he trailed off. What was this place? It wasn't a resting place. He'd been dumped here, not laid to rest. 'Well, you know what I mean. It's not good for your head, going over everything. You should move away, get some space from all this shit.'

'Aye, maybe.'

MacTavish rubbed his hands on his jeans, stood up and glanced down at Ryan. He felt sorry for him, but he felt even sorrier for himself. He'd been the innocent one in all of what had occurred.

'See you around, Ryan.'

'Aye, see you MacTavish.'

MacTavish walked along the edge of the water and around the reservoir, before going through the gate and heading back to his homeless shelter in Craigton Heights. Back to the life he had before prison, but a little bit worse.

Chapter Seventy-Five

GLASGOW GANGLAND FAMILY SENTENCED

Glasgow's biggest criminal family were sentenced at the High Court today for their part in the killings of rival gang family members.

Kyle and Ian Fraser were shot dead at a disused railway track in the Bellpark area back in 2013 by Angie Bryson. Their bodies were then placed in Ian Fraser's car and dumped in the Bellpark reservoir by Dale, Paul and Bob Bryson later that evening. James MacTavish was later convicted of the murders and was sentenced to life in prison. Forensics found evidence strongly linking him to the crime.

Just three months ago, Cara and Sean Fraser were murdered in cold blood by Angie Bryson, which led to the family's arrest. All of this followed the death of Bob Bryson, for which no one has yet been convicted.

All of the Bryson family members involved were sentenced to twenty-five years in prison. However, it has come to light that the construction company owned by the Brysons is being investigated by Police Scotland and SOC officers. During an excavation operation, human remains were uncovered. The remains are suspected to be that of missing men David and Gordon Reilly.

David Reilly went missing in early 2013. He once worked as a security officer for the Bryson family. Gordon Reilly has been missing for three months. The Reilly family have been informed and are awaiting confirmation.

Kyle Fraser's only surviving son, Ryan Fraser, wasn't present for the sentencing, neither were Dale and Angie Bryson's son and daughter, Conor and Ashley Bryson.

Chapter Seventy-Six

Opening the familiar envelope from the prison service, Ashley knew it was another visitation order from her mother. She'd sent three in the last few weeks, with the request to take Jack with her. Ashley hadn't responded to any of them. As much as Jack was missing his parents, and as much as he asked when they were coming back, Ashley knew it was in her little brother's best interests to keep him away from the prison, and his mother. If she could do that, Jack might grow up without lasting trauma from the life his parents had chosen to bring them into.

'You won't even go by yourself?' Conor asked, sitting behind the desk in what had once been Dale's seat. He'd taken over the running of the casino, and in turn, Ashley had taken over the care of Jack. Social workers were working closely with her, but it was likely that he wouldn't be removed from her care. She wasn't a threat to him or his safety. Neither was Conor.

She glanced at Conor and wondered if he'd be asking the same thing if he knew the truth. Ashley had considered telling him the truth about their mother's infidelity. But it wasn't her truth to tell. It had to come from Angie. And it wouldn't. She'd never tell him because she claimed it would kill Conor and their dad. But the truth was Angie didn't want to face up to what she'd done. Of course, there was always the chance that Ryan Fraser would turn up and tell Conor, but that was unlikely. He'd not come near them since everything had happened at Cara Fraser's flat.

'No, I don't want anything to do with her. She's a murderer, Conor. I don't want Jack surrounded by that. He's the only one

344

of us who has a chance at a normal future. And if I take him to the prison to see her, the social workers might not be happy about it.'

Conor frowned. 'She's his mother, she won't do anything to hurt him.'

'Not directly, Conor. She didn't do anything to directly hurt either of us, but look at us now. We've been left with her mess. They were supposed to be the adults. She claimed what she did was protecting her family, but has that turned out to be the case?'

Conor sighed, and she knew he wouldn't argue with her. That was the one good thing she'd inherited from Angie: her willpower not to back down.

'You could write her a letter?'

'No. Pen can't be erased and I'd tell her exactly what I think of her. I don't want that letter falling into Jack's hands at any point in the future. Just leave it, Conor. I've made my decision. They'll all be in the jail for a very long time, Jack will be an adult by the time they get out and hopefully he'll have forgotten all about them by then.'

Conor got to his feet and moved across to the drinks trolley. He poured a whisky and returned to the desk. Ashley watched him drink it back, and even though she knew that Bryson blood didn't flow in his veins, she knew that he would turn out just like Dale, Paul and Bob. Now that he was running the casino, he'd be sucked into the life of crime that the Brysons knew only too well. By that time, Ashley and Jack would be long gone. She planned on taking a lump sum from the bank account when Jack was no longer under the watch of his social worker, and she was going to take him away from Glasgow. Maybe abroad. She hadn't quite got that far yet.

'At least we're still standing, eh?' Conor said, raising his glass.

Ashley forced a smile. He was still her brother at the end of everything, even though she was planning on leaving everything behind and never contacting any of them ever again.

'Yeah,' she said. 'We're still standing.'

Chapter Seventy-Seven

Sitting alone in her cell, Angie Bryson had come to the conclusion that she was never going to see her daughter or sons ever again. Ashley had consistently ignored her visitation orders, and had gone radio silent on her. Conor hadn't been to visit for a few weeks, and even he'd gone quiet. Likely, Ashley had told him to stay away. Or he'd found out about Kyle. It killed her not knowing.

The darkness swallowed her in the tiny space where she was now going to be living for at least twenty-five years. She lay on the springy mattress and thought about her home. The master bedroom with the en suite bathroom, the pool, the gym, the huge kitchen with wine fridge. Her life as she knew it was gone. It was her own fault. All because she'd made one mistake, and tried to cover it up. She'd dragged everyone down with her and now they were all split, the family torn apart.

The light above her clicked on and she squinted at the sudden brightness. Soon, it would be time to go down to the canteen for breakfast. This would be her routine until she was in her late sixties at the earliest.

Had it been worth it? Killing and wiping out almost an entire family to keep one secret from everyone? If Conor was still happy, and had never been hurt by her actions, then she had to say yes. It was worth it. Every single shot fired, every ounce of blood spilt.

Deciding not to run from the police that day wasn't the only thing that had changed her life. She'd decided to write to Dale and tell him about Conor. And she hadn't hesitated to tell him that Paul covered it up. What would be the point in leaving out any details now, after everything? He'd written back, a very short letter.

> Angie,
>
> I'll never forgive you for lying to me about Conor. My firstborn son, or at least that's what I thought he was. It's not Conor's fault that you couldn't keep your legs shut. So, I'm not going to punish him for your fuck up. And I'm not going to tell him that I'm not his real dad. That's up to you. He's the only man on the outside now, looking after Ashley and Jack. I won't mess that up.
>
> It's a good thing that we've been separated by prison, otherwise I don't know what I'd have done. And as for Paul, well, he and I are separated by block, but I'll see him one day. I've been betrayed by both of you, and I promise, you'll pay for your lies.
>
> I hope you rot in your cell, Angie. You deserve every shred of guilt and terror that faces you.
> Dale.

She'd only read the letter once, and couldn't bring herself to read it again.

Angie had tried so hard to be a good mother. All she'd ever wanted to do was protect her kids. In the end, she'd sacrificed herself in the process and had lost everything. She'd caused them nothing but pain and she would have to live with that for the rest of her life. She'd have a twenty-five-plus-year prison sentence to think things over.

Angie sighed, got up from her bed, pulled on her clothes and stood at the door, waiting for the prison officer to let her out.

347

A Letter from Alex

Well, my eighth book. Where has the time gone? Since signing with Hera in 2018, and *No Looking Back* releasing in early 2019, the time has just gone by so fast. I am absolutely amazed and thankful for you, the readers of my books. If it wasn't for you, I wouldn't be where I am now. Writing full time has always been an absolute dream of mine, ever since I started my writing journey in 2010, and now I can say that's what I do.

I started writing this book at some point in August of 2021, found out I was expecting my first baby at the end of September 2021 and then wrote most of it between January and March 2022 due to severe sickness. It was a good distraction, and I loved how it took me away from reality for a while.

It's quite something that I became a mother myself as I was preparing this book for release ☺. I truly hope that you enjoy this book, and that you'll come back for book nine.

You can follow me on social media, Facebook, Twitter and Instagram.

Just search Alex Kane writer, or you can email me at alexkaneauthor@gmail.com.

Acknowledgments

Firstly, I want to thank Keshini Naidoo for her phenomenal support over the time it took me to write *The Mother*. About to become one myself during the process, I struggled with deadlines due to sickness and she was incredibly understanding the entire time. Working with you, Keshini, has been an absolute Godsend and pleasure.

My next thank you goes to my agent, Jo Bell at Bell Lomax Moreton. Again, you've been so supportive and kind over the time I took to write *The Mother* and without you or Keshini, I'm not sure I'd have managed it.

Thank you to everyone involved in the publishing process at Hera and Canelo. It still amazes me that I get to work with such an amazing team.

I want to thank you, the reader, the blogger and supporter of my work. It's amazing that you all come back for more after this many books. And if you're new to my writing, thank you for choosing me.

Again, last but by no means least, I want to thank my husband for his continued support of my work. I've had a really tough time writing the last two books over the course of the last year, and he made sure I kept going when I needed to, as well as making me take time for myself. I couldn't have done this without him. Thank you so much for everything you do for me and our beautiful baby girl.